Praise for David Lee Jones's previous fantasy

UNICORN HIGHWAY

"MAGNIFICENT . . . A QUIET TRIUMPH . . .
Earthy, wise, sad, humorous . . . A rather
marvelous and unexpected flight of fancy."
Anne McCaffrey, author of All the Weyrs of Pern

"WARM AND SATISFYING . . .
A memorable and heartwarming debut
with a great deal of charm"
Locus

"DELIGHTFUL . . . REFRESHING . . .
A different kind of unicorn story"
A. C. Crispin, author of The Starbridge Chronicles

"A combination of
Cold Sassy Tree and *Field of Dreams*,
with the best parts of both stories."
Kliatt

"STRANGELY POWERFUL AND BEGUILING.
David Lee Jones promises to become a bright,
strong voice in contemporary fantasy."
Katharine Kerr, author of Polar City Blues

"INTERESTING, WARM
AND UNDERSTANDING . . .
This is surely the way to tame a unicorn."
Piers Anthony

ZEUS AND CO.

DAVID LEE JONES

AVON BOOKS • NEW YORK

ZEUS & CO. is an original publication of Avon Books. This work has never before appeared in book form. This work is a novel. Any similarity to actual persons or events is purely coincidental.

AVON BOOKS
A division of
The Hearst Corporation
1350 Avenue of the Americas
New York, New York 10019

Copyright © 1993 by David Lee Jones
Cover illustration by Stephen Youll
Published by arrangement with the author
Library of Congress Catalog Card Number: 92-97434
ISBN: 0-380-76963-8

First AvoNova Printing: June 1993

AVONOVA TRADEMARK REG. U.S. PAT. OFF. AND IN OTHER COUNTRIES, MARCA REGISTRADA, HECHO EN U.S.A.

Printed in the U.S.A.

RA 10 9 8 7 6 5 4 3 2 1

For my brother, Jeff, the fallen warrior. For Debbie, Linda, and Gladys, who loved and helped him. And for all of his friends at the Veteran's Administration hospital in West Los Angeles for keeping up the fight against Post Traumatic Stress Disorder.

Acknowledgments

A second novel can be easier than the first if a story shows up on your doorstep begging to be told, more difficult if the doorbell doesn't ring and the story doesn't show. This book was both. Easier because the story showed up. More difficult because it was bigger than I was. These words are to acknowledge those who helped and waited patiently for me to wrestle it to the page.

First and foremost to my wife, Paula. Without her knowledge of computer systems, this book would never have been attempted. And for giving me the time and privacy to write.

To Michael Larsen and Elizabeth Pomada, for advice both economic and editorial.

To Chris Miller at Avon Books, for reading it in the rough and buying it prior to rewrites and revisions, for coming up with the title, and for eloquence in both editorial and human matters.

To Sara Schwager, for doing a fine job of copyediting, and Stephen Youll for his terrific cover.

And finally, thanks to all of the muses—especially Erato and Euterpe—for showing up at my computer and whispering this story in my ear.

Once in a golden hour
I cast to earth a seed.
Up there came a flower,
The people said, a weed.

—TENNYSON

Contents

CONTENTS

Greek Mythology Cast of Characters

Before I started writing this novel, I didn't know a heck of a lot about Greek mythology. Just in case you haven't been studying it lately, here's a brief rundown on the characters who are in this story.

Zeus:	Supreme ruler of the heavens, often pictured throwing a thunderbolt, reported to be one of his favorite pastimes. Father of the muses, who are spirits that inspire and watch over poets, musicians, and artists.
Mnemosyne:	(knee´moss-si-knee) The goddess of memory. Mother of the muses.
Calliope:	The muse of eloquence and epic poetry.
Clio:	The muse of history.
Erato:	The muse of love poetry.
Euterpe:	The muse of lyric poetry and music.
Melpomene:	The muse of tragedy.
Polyhymnia:	The muse of sacred poetry and hymns.
Terpsichore:	The muse of dancing.
Thalia:	The muse of comedy.
Urania:	The muse of astronomy.
Poseidon:	Ruler of the seas, brother of Zeus.

1

The Secret File

I never used to believe in myth and magic, sword and sorcery, and all of the stuff from which fairy tales are made. There was sure no reason to believe in muses. But that was before meeting Erato and Vincent Van Gogh, and before the incident with the secret file. Perhaps I never should have logged on to the computer that night. Maybe I should have quit before all of the strange things started to happen. But then I wouldn't have met the muse, and been entranced by her magic spell.

It may not seem like it to the uninitiated, but even in the software world there is artistic expression. Programs are judged by their eloquence, their subtlety of expression and ease of execution. It takes an artist, sometimes, to squeeze between the lines of code and find the back door into the locked memory banks, someone who can listen to the soft sounds of the system like a safecracker spinning a dial and then, "tap," the door swings open and you're in, behind the electronic screen that's guarded only by a secret password. Once inside, you're free to indulge in the riches of that most precious of gems, information, or perhaps to hide secrets. Some secrets are too valuable not to hide, and some, if only a few, can change heaven and earth, and everything in between.

A lot of break-ins occur at night, when the terminals are at rest. The hackers come out at dark like cat burglars. That's what happened around midnight one July, about a year into my job as programmer and night shift computer security officer. Funny job description for an ex-hacker, part-time surfer, and full-time loner, but having cleared myself of a prank computer break-in at college had gone a long way toward getting me the job.

I never would have thought that such a strange and eerie message would turn up on my terminal. It looked like the beginning of a poem, but seemed more like a cry for help, rather than someone just composing at the terminal. Besides, no one at Sigma Systems had ever been accused of writing serious poetry on the company computer. This was something new and very different.

The message had splashed across my screen for a brief beautiful moment when I was initiating a maintenance program. Suddenly my whole monitor glowed with the glory of phosphorescent green, like an ocean sparkling on a summer's day. Since I worked with only a desk lamp on, my screen was so overflowing with green light that it filled the entire cubicle. I was transfixed by its powerful, luminous presence. Then, slowly, it began to fade. Soon it was gone, leaving only the single strange message:

> *This is the shipwrecked daughter of Zeus*
> *Calling from inside the banks*
> *Save me from the terrible ocean*
> *Save me from . . .*

I couldn't decide if it was a cry for help or some prankster leaving a nonsensical puzzle, but it didn't matter. It was gone, and there was no telling where. My screen returned to normal.

I quickly checked the system to see how many terminals were on line. There were only two, mine and one in the classified computer lab. Someone had signed on from that one using the account *Iberlin*. That user name didn't look familiar. When I checked further, he had created a one-hundred-megabyte file, and given it the name Euterpe. There was something else; Iberlin was accessing the Top Secret disk.

I wasn't cleared for it, but could check to see if other users were authorized. A special screen listed the account names and clearance levels. Out of two hundred fifty employees, there were fifteen cleared for Top Secret access. A few more keystrokes revealed that Iberlin wasn't one of them.

Now I had a real problem. Either he had been accidentally left off the list, or he was a hacker. If I shut the system down, I might ruin someone's experiment. And if I let him keep working, then maybe I was admitting an illegal user. I sent a mail message to Iberlin asking him to identify himself, but there was no response. I was getting nervous.

Calling the systems manager at home didn't get me an answer. No one picked up the phone, even after fifteen rings. Then I phoned the company president, the only other one with complete system privileges, but got an answering machine. I left a message saying I was going to try to find out as much as possible and then turn off access to the system at midnight as usual. That left me pretty well stuck.

I got ready to trot off to the location of the active terminal, but remembered to call security instead.

Grabbing the phone, I was about to call the front desk. Just as I picked up the receiver, there was another sudden brilliant flash of green, but this time it left no word message, just an image that looked like the outline of a musical note.

By the time the voice on the other end said, "plant security," the active terminal was suddenly off-line.

I informed the guard and he went over to the classified lab. He called me five minutes later, saying the user had met him at the lab door and shown proper clearance. He could not divulge the user's name. There was nothing more to discuss. I still didn't like it.

Too tired to pursue it further, I hung up the phone, deciding the matter could wait until daylight. I sent a mail message to the systems manager detailing what had happened, and left the building.

I walked out to my faded red Mustang convertible with torn seats and a ratty, white top. It was the only car in the lot, except for the security guard's.

Opening the door to my car, I noticed a young woman sitting alone at the bus stop, not a hundred feet from me. This was not the big city. It was a sleepy tourist town on the central coast of a laid-back state. The buses had stopped running hours ago. It was one o'clock in the morning.

2

Erato

I got in my car and started the engine. Driving down the entrance road, I turned right, moving slowly past the young woman on the bus bench. It was positioned directly under a streetlight so that she was in its aura like an actress under a stage lamp. The soft yellow light surrounding her seemed to make her glow all over, as if she were vibrating with some magical inner energy, a star in the shape of a woman. She looked to be in her early twenties, with shoulder length, sandy blond hair, mussed up in the latest style. Her slender face had a regal bearing, with a few well-placed freckles and a slim, straight nose. Her lips were full and light pink. Her eyes sparkled like green emeralds. She looked about five feet seven, wearing high-tech tennis shoes, Levi's, and a black leather jacket, open in front. A small matching leather purse was strung over her shoulder. Underneath the jacket she wore a black Harley-Davidson T-shirt with the words *God Rides a Harley* emblazoned in red just below the trademark symbol. Seeing someone of such striking beauty hypnotized me, and I stopped the car.

"You may not know this," I offered, wrinkling my forehead, "but buses don't run this time of night. You've got a good five hours until the next one comes by."

"Oh, darn," she said, frowning innocently. "It didn't say that in my brief." She shook her head. "Boy, you just can't get good research help anymore. Not like the monks were, anyway. They were the best."

"Look," I said, raising an eyebrow, "it's dangerous to be out this time of night, even in this town. There's an all-night gas station just up the road. I'll call you a cab from there." When she didn't say anything, I added, "If you haven't got the fare, I'll call you a cop, if it's all right with you."

She shrugged her shoulders. "Well," she finally said, batting long, wispy eyelashes, "you *could* give me a lift, I suppose. You have a nice face. You sort of remind me of Poseidon in his younger days—tall and tan, wavy blond hair, short beard, straight nose and teeth, muscular body. Very Greek, you know, except for the Levi's, Hawaiian shirt, and blue eyes. Got those eyes from your mother, I'll bet."

"Boy, you must *really* be from a small town," I said in disbelief, rubbing a sun-bleached eyebrow. "Look, you shouldn't get into cars with strangers. Your parents taught you that much, didn't they?"

"Then I'll introduce myself," she answered, undaunted. She stood up and walked over to the car, sticking out her slender hand. It was perfectly manicured, but with long, unpainted fingernails. "Erato," she said, and before I could answer she added, "and you're Cyrus, Cyrus Lance Major."

"*Air*-uh-tow? What kind of a name is that?" My forehead

began to wrinkle. "And how did you know *my* name? I don't even *use* my middle name anymore; haven't since grade school."

"Like I said," she told me, smiling and showing rows of straight, white teeth. "I've been briefed. They were wrong about the bus schedule, but nobody's perfect. I'll set them straight on that when I return."

"Look," I said, still confused, glancing down at my frayed tennis shoes. "You may know who *I* am, but I don't know *you* . . . Are you sure you don't want a cab?"

"What I want," she said, opening the door and climbing into the passenger's seat, "is a ride." She sat upright and looked ahead at the road. Her posture reminded me of a finishing school debutante balancing a book on her head. "Now, what are you waiting for?" she added in a proper tone.

I shook my head, too speechless to say anything, but didn't want to leave her alone at the bus stop. Crime never sleeps, and I sure didn't want to read in the morning paper about her being attacked. I pulled out into the lane and headed down the boulevard. When the car reached the corner she said, "Turn right. Let's cut through the university. It's a beautiful night for a slow drive under the stars, wouldn't you agree?"

I didn't answer, just turned right and looked up, holding the wheel with both hands. It was as clear as a night on the ocean. Millions of stars sparkled overhead. Then one of them suddenly shot across the sky.

"Look, a shooting star," she said excitedly, pointing with her hand. "The sky's entertainment."

"I hate to be nosy," I apologized, rubbing my neck and looking down the road, "but what do you want from me? This hasn't got anything to do with what happened at work tonight, does it?"

"How did you guess?"

"Uh-oh," I said involuntarily, staring at the asphalt on the road. "Somebody sent you to shut me up, didn't they? Look, all I want to know is why this . . . this file was created . . . Can you tell me?" I asked seriously, looking over at her. "Or have you got a gun in your purse to do me in with?"

She reached into her purse, so I grabbed her hand so that it couldn't come out, not sure of what to expect. Even in my haste, I noticed the soft smoothness of her delicate hand.

"Being a little paranoid, aren't you?" she asked, suddenly trapping my hand in her purse with both of hers. They were unusually warm, and seemed to vibrate with energy.

"I was getting some lipstick," she explained, a little perturbed. "But I can see you're nervous about what happened at Sigma tonight. Don't worry. We'll work something out. There's no need to get upset. It's only a matter of opening the file. That should be easy for someone with your ... experience."

She was right. I *was* nervous about what had happened, especially since she seemed to know all about it. I was also nervous about her commanding good looks—the way everyone gets nervous in a beautiful person's presence.

"Look," I said, reluctantly pulling my hand away and pointing to my head. "I'd like to help you out, but the memory bank in here didn't store data on the contents of that file, and doesn't want to. Whatever was in here, which wasn't much, has already been erased." I glanced over at her. "Besides, I'm not cleared to look at it. I can't access Top ... certain files. So I can't help you."

"You've been watching too many spy mysteries," she laughed. "I'm not with the KGB or anything like that."

"Then who sent you? And why do you want my help?"

She just smiled. "The beauty of the human memory is that it doesn't erase," she finally said, looking up at the stars and ignoring my questions. "Everything stored is retrievable."

She removed her leather jacket and tossed it in the backseat, then leaned toward me, turning a little in her seat. She had no trouble filling out the T-shirt or the jeans. In modern terminology, she was a hard body, with a decidedly feminine edge. She carefully placed her left arm over the back of my bucket seat. I felt her warm breath on my neck, and could smell expensive perfume, judging by the subtlety of its delicate fragrance. It was starting to get to me.

We left the university and swung down the hill toward the beach. The ocean shimmered in the soft starlight. It was warm out, and even with the top down I was heating up, fanning my shirt with my hand to cool off.

"Okay," I said at last, "since you won't tell me what's going on, and my knowledge of the file can't be permanently erased, then it looks like you'll have to terminate me. And if *you* don't get me, they'll probably just send someone else. That's how these things work, isn't it?"

"You've *got* to stop watching espionage films," she said, rolling her eyes and messing up the back of my hair.

She had me there. I was a sucker for mystery and spy stuff—Agatha Christie, Sherlock Holmes, "Murder She Wrote," and my favorite rumpled detective, Columbo. I was beginning to feel a little silly. Either she *was* as innocent as she sounded, or a very good actress. I sure couldn't tell which, but running her hand through my hair was awfully friendly for a stranger.

She looked me straight in the eyes. "I'm here," she said, touching me lightly on the back of my neck, "because I need your help."

Giving up on her identity for the time being, I decided to gain what information I could about her.

"To do what?" I asked nervously.

"Get my sister back," she said softly, almost in my ear.

"Your sister? What's she got to do with the file?" When she didn't answer, I added, "Oh, I get it. Next you're going to tell me she's been kidnapped or something, and you need me to get her back."

"You might say that," she said coyly, tracing my beard with her index finger.

"Then why don't you go to the police? Or your parents? That's it, isn't it?" I asked, jumping to conclusions. "Your dad makes a lot of money and it's a ransom job. The Harley T-shirt is just a disguise. It's out of character for someone who looks as upper-class as you. What does he do? Bank president? Corporate raider? Brain surgeon?"

"He's a ruler."

"Ruler?" I pulled over and stopped the car, sliding the wheels on the passenger's side into the sand by the entrance to the beach parking lot.

"I knew it," I said, pulling away from her and slapping the steering wheel. "What country?"

"All of them."

"Nobody rules *all* of them," I protested. "That's impossible. What's his name?"

"Zeus," she answered matter-of-factly.

"Zeus who?"

"That's it."

"That's it? Just Zeus?" I listened to the waves crashing in the distance. "Was he named after the Greek god or some-thing?" I glanced at her, not happy with the way things were going.

"The god of heaven and earth, and everything in between."

Looking at her elegant beauty, a thought suddenly flashed through my head. "Hey, wait just a minute. You're telling me your dad is *the* Zeus. The one and only. That's impossible. You're crazy."

I looked up at the stars. "Look," I apologized, "I'd like to help you, but I can't get in any more trouble. I've had this job less than a year, and I can't afford to lose it. If you want what's on the file, you'll have to go to the systems manager, or better yet, the company president. For all I know, *you* hacked-in tonight. Besides, even if I wanted to, I can't help you until I know what's going on.

"I'm sorry." I shrugged. "But I gotta go. I'm too tired to play spies. The sun will be up in a few hours and this body needs some sleep. I'm starting to lose it already. Where do you want to be dropped off?"

"Then you don't believe me," she sighed.

"All I know is that it's late, I'm tired, and there are no such things as . . . as Greek gods. Those are myths. Wait a minute— did you get let out of . . ." I looked at her. "You know . . ."

"The nuthouse? That's what you call it, isn't it?" she asked, shaking her head in disbelief. "I can see I'm wasting my time with you," she added. "I thought you were different, and then you go and make a typical remark about me being nuts just because you don't understand what's going on." She threw up her hands. "You nonbelievers are all alike. You classify everything you don't understand as crazy."

"Well . . ."

She thought for a moment, and regained her composure.

"Cyrus, I'm sorry for the outburst," she began, folding her hands in her lap. "And for coming on to you. I'm upset about my sister's being . . . I guess kidnapped is the right word. But . . . it could still have been an accident, I suppose," she added.

She looked over at me apologetically. "It's my fault, really," she admitted. "I come here out of the blue sky and expect you to believe my wild story. You see, my brief says you believe in unicorns. I thought that would be enough, but I can see I've got some more work to do if I'm going to convince you." She sighed and leaned forward, placing her head in her hands.

"Wait," I said, startled by her announcement. "How did you know that? I mean, about unicorns? Nobody knows that. I said that on a date two years ago." I leaned over and put my arm on the back of her seat. "All I meant was that I believed in the *idea* of unicorns. What they stood for and all that. Mainly, that they were a mythical symbol for freedom and were connected to nature."

She lifted her head from her hands and turned toward me. There was just a hint of mist in her eyes. "So you don't think they ever actually existed?"

"How do *I* know?" I answered like an apology. "But if they did, I'm not surprised they're extinct. I'm not an ecology nut, but look at all the other animals we've pushed off the planet. In another hundred years, there probably won't even be cats and dogs."

"You like dogs, don't you?"

"Where else can you get such loyalty, such happiness when you come home, such . . ."

"Marriage?" she asked, almost hopefully.

"What century did you say you were from?" I asked in jest, leaning back against the door and folding my arms. "Have you seen the divorce rate lately?"

"It's pretty high," she admitted, sitting up and putting her feet on the dash. "But that doesn't mean all marriages are doomed. My parents have been together for a long time."

"If you say so," I conceded, looking up at the stars. "But the truth is, I can't really talk about what it's like. I'm . . ."

"Single. I know," she said, smiling.

"What else do you know about me?"

"That's classified."

"Oh, great," I said sarcastically. "I'm locked out of everything tonight. Well, put this down for the record. When Ms. Right comes along, then I'll try marriage. Until then—"

"Yeah, me too," she said wistfully, looking straight into me. "Look, I gotta go. I've got homework to do. Obviously, I didn't come very well prepared." She looked around, but there wasn't much except the road and the beach parking lot. "I'll walk from here," she said, reaching for the door handle.

"Walk? There aren't any houses within a couple of miles of here. We're at the pier, remember? Or do you live on campus?"

"No, not exactly," she answered, shrugging her shoulders. "But it's a lovely night for a walk on the beach. I want to see what it feels like to touch the sand and the water. See what it's like to be . . ."

"To be what?" I asked, leaning over and putting my hand on the gearshift. Before I could say any more she was pulling her jacket out of the back. Then she opened the door, stepped out of the car, and walked toward the water. As she moved into the darkness she pointed to the southern sky.

"You were named Cyrus," she said over her shoulder, "after the brightest star in the sky: Sirius, in the constellation Canis Major. The big dog, as you call it. Lance is short for Lancelot, the legendary medieval knight."

I wasn't sure what it meant, but she seemed to have a pretty good file on me, and a tight grip on my eyes. I couldn't stop staring at her as she walked away. Her sandy blond hair swished back and forth down her back, pouring over her black leather motorcycle jacket with the Harley wings on the back. In the moonlight, they almost looked like angel's wings. Her slender hips swung gently back and forth. She stopped and pulled off her tennis shoes and socks, then disappeared into the night, her feet silent on the sand.

"Cy!" I yelled to the beach. "My friends call me Cy—Wait. Will I see you again?"

"Maybe."

"Maybe? When?"

"When you believe, of course." She might have said something else, but her voice was drowned out by the waves smashing onto the shore. Then, as sometimes happens in a room full of conversation, there was a break in the sound waves, and all was still for a second. In that second a soft wind carried a message loud and clear to my ears. It was the excited giggle of a young woman—the kind someone makes when her feet touch the ocean for the first time.

As I pulled away I noticed in the rearview mirror a single bright headlight following discreetly behind the car at a safe distance. It stayed with me all the way home. When I pulled over to park, a motorcycle stopped behind me, about a hundred feet back.

It turned and drove away. Under the streetlight in the middle of the block, I could see that it was someone wearing a black leather jacket with the Harley-Davidson emblem on the back. Whoever it was had on a jacket several sizes bigger than the one Erato wore, and filled out the shoulders completely.

Great, I thought, going up to bed. Just what I need: some woman's jealous boyfriend taking a gear chain to my face. But she didn't look like a biker, or act like any motorcycle mama I'd ever met in twenty-three years. Maybe she had a renegade brother or, more likely, her sister was a runaway and Erato had come to get her back. But that still didn't explain the file. I should have asked more questions.

I lay in bed and dozed off, thinking about what a strange night it had been, and wondering whether Erato was really Iberlin, and hoping that she wasn't. But if she was, maybe I could clear up the whole secret file mess in the morning. If no one would tell me the facts for security reasons, then I'd ask Erato outright if she was the new user. It was worth a shot—if I ever saw her again.

3

The Poetry of Motion

At ten o'clock the next morning I called the systems manager. He wasn't available to come to the phone. His secretary said he was tied up in a meeting. She wouldn't say with whom. I dialed the company president, but she wasn't taking any calls.

Deciding to drop it for the time being, I drove down to the beach around noon to go surfing. Pulling up in my Mustang convertible, I got my board out of the backseat. The waves were breaking pretty good, and soon my arms were paddling me out to catch a few.

The spot I liked to surf was pretty secluded, so usually nobody was around. That particular hot summer day, it was just me and the seals.

The sight of the waves cresting in perfect rows of blue and green always gave me a lift, and that day was no exception. I lost myself in wave after wave, riding the curl the way a cowboy rides a wild stallion.

In rodeo, eight seconds is a long ride, and in surfing, that wouldn't be a bad ride either on a lot of days. But there were times when you caught just the right wave. You shot across its face, cutting the edge of your board into the wall of water. You could reach out and touch the wave with a playful flick of your fingertips, and if you worked it just right, the ride could take you all the way to the shore.

It was times like those that brought you back. You lived for that feeling of effortless grace, bought by hours of practice, pull-outs, and falls. You longed to be lost in a world made only of water and sky. When that happened, it was the closest I ever came to the poetry of motion.

I'd been surfing for a couple of hours when such a wave came along. It picked me up and shot me forth like a bullet from a gun barrel. I reached out and touched the cool, clean saltwater, creeping slowly up to the front of the board until all my toes were on the edge, riding a tube of water toward the sand.

The wave rushed and roared behind me. I retreated deep inside the hollow tube of water that was breaking over me like a waterfall. I was lost in time, lost to everything but the feeling of riding the wild stallion, his white mane flowing powerful and free behind me. And then my board shot out of the front of the wave and it was suddenly over. I had reached the beach.

Picking up my board, I headed for the car, knowing that to go out again would spoil the day. There might not be another ride like that for a month, and catching another one might ruin the feeling. The part of me that was still heavily connected to the sea wanted to soak it up, remembering it as my last ride of the day.

I turned and gave the ocean a nod. A wave crashed on the shore, and I made a bow for my performance, giving thanks to the moving mountain of water before me. My eyes were still looking out to sea when something caught them in the distance. A girl in a pink bikini with flowing, sandy blond hair and a striking figure was running down the beach away from me. It almost looked like Erato, but she was a good quarter mile away by the time my feet hit the parking lot.

A note was stuck under my windshield wiper, so I pulled it out, surfboard still in hand, and read:

> *That was a beautiful ride. But time is running out, and right now you have homework to do. Muses are in the mythology section of the library.*
>
> *E*

I looked down the beach, but she was gone. Getting in the car, I drove two miles to a public phone and made another call to the systems manager.

Maxwell Cooper was one of those people you never really get to know. For the most part I didn't try as hard as I could have. My few attempts to learn anything about him were thwarted by those none-of-your-business kinds of looks. He was in his forties, very clean and neat, five feet seven, and had skin the color of a vampire's victim. Since he considered casualness against some unwritten law of work behavior, he didn't make many friends, especially in California where Hawaiian shirts and shorts meet the sea.

Obviously, he was intelligent and well-educated, though not bursting with creativity. He had excellent organizational skills and a work ethic that almost put the Amish to shame.

There was supposed to be some deep, hidden family secret that had led to his current rigidity, but either no one knew or no one was telling. I spent a lot of time trying to lighten him up, which was usually just the opposite of what he wanted.

As systems manager, Mr. Cooper was always very business-like, and would have preferred that I wear a three-piece suit like he did instead of my Hawaiian shirts, jeans, and high-tech tennis shoes. He disliked my just-off-the-beach tan, occasional wet hair, and dried salt forearms from catching late waves.

Since there was no official dress code, he had nowhere to go with his unwritten style requirements, especially since I worked second shift when hardly anyone was around. He put up with me because I did all my assigned jobs and reported all security violations. Since Sigma was a research and development firm, employees were always trying to sneak a peek at new plans and products without proper authorization. That way they could forecast their budgets and manpower needs ahead of schedule, and get the jump on other departments. Occasionally a theft was attempted, and was promptly thwarted either by me or Mr. Cooper.

I showed him some tricks and shortcuts I had devised to detect break-ins, but he never liked to vary from set procedures. Anything done out of order or out of the ordinary seemed to frighten him.

"Mr. Cooper," I said into the pay phone, still dripping ocean water, "somebody created a new file last night. It's a hundred megabytes, and has the filename . . ."

"I know," came the icy reply. "The name is classified. So is the file. You are not to mention it again. Where are you calling from?"

"A pay phone."

"See me before you start your shift."

"But . . ."

The dial tone blared in my ear. He had hung up. Obviously this was a serious matter that could not be discussed over phone lines. Of course we had company secrets, but this seemed a little too serious for my taste. After all, who was I going to tell? The president? Surely Janet Stewart knew by now, especially after my phone message.

Hanging up the pay phone, I drove to the public library, drying off further by convertible wind. Once in the mythology section, I began scanning the titles, looking for something on Greek myths that wasn't too thick. I was thumbing through a book too big to be of any real use when there was a thunk on my head.

I bent over and picked up a thin book on Greek gods. It must have fallen off the top shelf. Stuck in the middle was a bookmark that had a picture of Zeus throwing a thunderbolt, apparently his favorite pastime. The page was open to the nine muses, or daughters of Zeus and Mnemosyne (knee moss-si-knee). Zeus was indeed the god of heaven and earth, and Mnemosyne the goddess of memory. The muses were spirits that were supposed to inspire artists, poets and such, and had strange names like: Calliope, Clio, Erato, Euterpe, Melpomene, Polyhymnia, Terpsichore, Thalia, and Urania. Euterpe was the muse of lyric poetry. Erato was the muse of love poetry. That was about all it said.

It didn't prove anything, but at least it provided an answer to where she got her name. But how did she know a file had been created using the name of a Greek muse?—unless she had created it. It struck me as very strange. I needed to know why she was using the name Erato, what kind of trouble her sister was in, and what she really knew about the secret file. I had many questions and no answers.

Then there was Cooper. Unless he could convince me the file was a routine matter, I would have to go over his head to get to the bottom of things, whether I wanted to or not. But I was getting ahead of myself. For the moment I would hear him out, and see if he mentioned anything about the strange Ms. Erato. And I was anxious to see just what he was planning to say to keep me quiet about the file.

4

Canis Major

When I got to work, another guard was on duty. I asked her where the regular guard was, and was told that he had been temporarily reassigned. I then asked if she knew anything about who had used the computer lab in E4 the night before, but she said she couldn't discuss classified lab use. Knowing her superiors would give me the same story, I dropped it and went to work, first stopping by one of the engineering labs to discuss some software with a circuit designer. I went back to the front building about an hour later. Cooper was waiting for me—horn-rims, bald head, beak nose, and gray pin-striped suit.

I didn't report to him directly. The arrangement was somewhat unusual. He was my superior when it came to system security files, but I still retained my freedom when it came to the engineering software I developed. Technically, I reported to Mr. Henkins, the head of operations, but he was out on medical leave for the month of July. His job had been assumed by the president until his return.

I didn't dislike Cooper himself as much as what he stood for: hyperconformity. My prejudice against the stuffed shirt approach to work came fully alive in his presence, and I just couldn't help it.

I walked past him into my cubicle and sat down, Hawaiian shirt, stone-washed jeans, high-tech tennies and all. Before I could launch into any kind of attack about the new file, he tried to get me on the defensive.

"Cyrus," he began, staring sternly at me through his horn-rims, "I want to inform you . . ."

"Cy," I answered in jest, looking up from my chair. "All my friends call me Cy."

"Mr. Major," he replied with forced patience, straightening his lapels. "Let's move into the vault. This has to be a . . ." He looked around nervously, and seeing no one else in my cubicle or down the hall, added, "classified conversation. You're not carrying, are you?" He frowned and pushed his glasses back on his nose.

Checking my shirt pockets and coming up empty, I said just for laughs, "No, I don't believe so." I leaned over and scratched my sun-bleached beard. Looking around, I whispered, "Carrying what, drugs? You want a blood sample or something? Be my guest, but it's all saltwater in my veins, remember?"

"A recording device," he said slowly through his clenched teeth. "This has to be strictly . . ." He motioned toward the tape vault. "Come with me."

He was being a little extravagant with the spy impersonation, especially since it was twenty after four and almost everyone had already raced for the exits. Out of two hundred fifty employees, there probably weren't ten left in all six buildings. In the computer center where we worked, there were only the two of us. I followed him to the vault anyway, not wanting to ruin his dramatic moment. We both went inside the air-conditioned room, almost meat locker cold, and he closed the thick metal door behind us.

He spun the locking mechanism that looked like a ship's helm. Then he turned toward me, pushed his glasses back on his nose, and crossed his arms. We were alone with shelves of computer tapes, except for a single metal desk that sat lifelessly in the middle of the windowless vault.

"That file," he whispered gravely, running a hand over his shiny bald head, "is a Top Secret project. You are to ignore its existence, say nothing about it . . . and do nothing with it. Is that . . ."

"But—"

"The usual rules apply." He stopped for a moment to emphasize his point, and his eyes got big behind the already magnified lenses. "You are not allowed access to Top Secret files," he reminded me. "Legally or otherwise. They are not to be condensed, reformatted, or relocated to any other disk or file. You *do* remember that, don't you?"

"Look," I answered, cooling off for the moment, and thrusting out my upturned palms. "All I really want to know is whether Iberlin is cleared for access."

"We're processing the paperwork on that now," he said matter-of-factly, backing away a little. "She will be on the computer account list by tomorrow. Janet Stewart cleared her yesterday."

"Now, was that so tough?" I smirked, noting his reference to the company president. "Look, I was just trying to protect the security system." I crossed my arms to emphasize my point. "You can imagine how it looked."

"Janet wanted the new user to have an account right away," he explained. "She's someone new in product development." He leaned back against a shelf of tapes, tucking his arms behind him. "That's all I can tell you."

I moved over and sat on the bare metal desk in the middle of the vault, then looked up at the acoustic ceiling. "All right," I replied coolly, "but why the witching hour tactics? You know, when an unknown user logs in on my shift, I'm going to be concerned about it. Did it have to be created when no one else was on-line? Is it really of such earth-shattering importance that even I wasn't supposed to know of its existence?"

"I told you," he said flatly, trying to remain expressionless. "The user's authorized. So let's drop it."

I got up and walked around the vault, my breath almost freezing, goose bumps growing on my arms. But I wasn't ready to let it go.

"I'll tell you why I got upset," I began, attempting intimacy. "It looked like somebody thought she could sneak in the last fifteen minutes, just long enough to transfer or create a one-hundred-megabyte file, and I would never know it. It would be on the classified disk when you came in, and she could leave me completely out of the loop. But I scan the system right up until the clock strikes twelve and the ghosts come out."

He didn't say anything at first, but he had the look of someone who had just been caught playing a computer game on company time.

"All I can tell you is that there are secrets in the microchip industry that must remain under lock and key," he said. "Even the mention of the filename could destroy this company."

"Destroy?"

"Des . . . Yes, I . . . I mean economically, of course."

I stopped pacing and stared at him. "Does Janet really know about this?" I asked, wrinkling my forehead, and giving him a doubtful glance, still not sure if she had ever got my messages. "Or is she out of town?" I sat back on the desk, crossing my arms to warm up.

"Ms. Stewart," he said crisply, looking down at me from six feet away, "is the only other user who *does* know about this file, except for the creator."

"Iberlin?"

"Only a code name, so don't try to look it up in personnel records. You won't find it listed anywhere. And while we're on the subject, I would advise you never to mention that name again, nor the filename.

"Is that clear?" he added with a raised eyebrow.

"Euterpe?"

He just glared at me, his bald head reflecting the overhead fluorescent tube lights.

"All right," I finally said, perturbed by his renewed arrogance and pushing my mustache off my upper lip. "Have it your way. But any more suspicious midnight computer hack jobs, and I'm going to have a long talk with Janet Stewart myself. Top Secret or not."

He turned and walked briskly to the door, then spun the dial. "I'm sure that won't be necessary," he said, looking over his shoulder. "Files come. Files go. This one won't be there forever. In less than two years technology will have caught up. But for now, it's a killer invention, or so I'm told."

He suddenly turned around and cracked a sly grin. "And if Ms. Stewart finds out I said even this much, she could have us both fired. You wouldn't want that, would you? We'd both be out looking for work. Why, you might even have to give up your . . . your precious ocean and move inland. Maybe even to another state. There's no surf in the Midwest, you know, and Silicon Valley's played out right now." He straightened his suit and glasses. "Well, enough small talk. Better get started on the files. And remember . . ."

"Remember what?" I said in jest, getting to my feet. "I don't even remember this conversation."

"Good boy."

I went to work, not feeling a whole lot better about things. Cooper still couldn't be trusted. He was being a little too heavy on the subject, even for his melodramatic style. Calling Ms. Stewart's private line about six o'clock didn't do any good. No one answered. It was worth a try, at least, since she often worked late, but this time no dice.

For security reasons no one but her was allowed to pick up the red phone in her office, or its twin in her lab, and no recorded message could be left. Hanging up after fourteen rings, I logged on to the computer, noticing that Janet was signed on, so I sent her a mail message to call me.

She must not have been at her terminal because she didn't

respond to the message. I went back to work, lining up programs to run while the plant slept. I couldn't resist scanning the Top Secret disk just before midnight, but there was no new activity. Euterpe was still intact, and there wasn't any indication that it had been altered since its creation. So I logged off, shut down system access, and left the building. When I got to my car a note was stuck under the wiper blade.

> Tonight is a very special night.
> Sirius is sleeping low in the southern sky
> But will awaken when the
> Chimes ring a dozen times
> Look up when the hour is near
> And behold the Canis Major
> Sirius is the brightest star
> In the heavens
> But that is not the only magic
> In this night
> For tonight
> On the road to your destiny
> You shall meet
> Vincent Van Gogh

E

It was ten minutes after midnight.

5

Starry Night

Stuffing the note in my shirt pocket, I got in, started the car, and drove out of the parking lot. It was a warm, clear night, so the top was down. I slowed when passing the bus stop, hoping to see Erato, but there was only an empty bench under the streetlight.

Pulling out onto the boulevard, I cut through the university
and swung by the beach where she had disappeared the night
before.

I parked there, pulled out the note, and read it. Astronomy
wasn't my strong suit, but I did know which way was south,
and had seen my star before. I looked for it, but there weren't
any lights that looked extra bright. I was about to give up when
suddenly the screeching of tires and the high-pitched yelp of
a dog pierced the quiet night. Standing up on the car seat,
I looked toward the freeway that led away from the beach
and university. All that could be seen was a pair of taillights
disappearing in the distance, heading toward town.

Then something caught the corner of my eye. I turned and
looked back toward the ocean. There, along the southern horizon, where the night met the sea, sat a boldly shining light,
surrounded by the pattern of stars that gave off a familiar
brilliant glow. Sirius blasted its presence back to earth from
its vantage point in the heart of Canis Major. It *was* there, and
it was bright, the brightest star in the sky.

I watched it for a few seconds and then, sitting back down,
started the car and sped toward the freeway, slowing where
fresh skid marks appeared on the roadway. I pulled over and
stopped, shining the headlights on the spot where the tire marks
ended and the accident began.

There was a red-stained hubcap lying in a small pool of
blood, with fresh drops leading off to the side of the road.
I followed the trail along the ground, but it disappeared into
thick bushes. Turning away, I walked back to the car, intending
to call 911 as soon as possible.

My car, desperately in need of a tune-up, suddenly died
when my foot stomped on the gas. I cut the headlights and
reached for the ignition key.

In the split second before the starter engaged I heard a faint
whimper. It was the low moan of an injured animal, and it was
coming from the bushes.

I got the engine started, pulled up close to the bushes, and
turned on the high beams. I left the engine running so it would
stay warm since it always ran better hot, then got out of the car
and headed into the bushes. I followed the line of red drops,
but lost it again in the thick underbrush.

Then came another whimper, this time from the roadway
ahead on the other side of the bushes. I made my way through
the brush to the edge of the pavement. There, standing in

the center of the right-hand lane, was a fully grown black Labrador retriever, bleeding from a wound on the left side of his head. He turned and looked at me, fear and pain in his eyes.

I took a step toward him and then stopped, remembering that it wasn't too smart to approach a wounded animal. But if I could get him to come to me, it might be safe. Slowly crouching, I called, "Here, boy. Come on. Come here, boy."

He whimpered, but didn't move. He began to shake all over with fear, blood still dripping from the side of his head.

I called again several more times, but he wouldn't budge. It was a stalemate. Then a set of headlights came barreling down the freeway from the university. The car was only a quarter mile away, and closing fast.

If the dog was going to be helped, I would have to go get him, and try not to frighten him into the center lane where the approaching car would be in just a few short seconds.

I had to think, but nothing came to mind. Thrusting my hands into my pants pockets in frustration, I hit something at the bottom of one. I pulled out a forgotten pack of peppermint gum. All but the last piece was gone. Quickly unwrapping it, I began to move onto the roadway on all fours. I had to be careful, but he had to see the gum, or maybe just smell it.

The headlights were almost upon us. The dog glanced quickly at them and back at me. Then, scaring me half to death, he took a step towards the center lane.

"No!" I yelled. "Come here!"

He stopped and stared at me. We were both crouched on all fours. I lifted my left hand and held out the gum in nervous desperation.

"Here, boy," I pleaded, sweat beginning to bead on my forehead. "Let's eat."

He turned away from the center lane just as the car sped past. It slowed, but didn't stop. Cautiously, he walked over to me, still shaking with fear. It seemed like an hour, but must have been only a minute. He sniffed the gum and opened his mouth, but didn't go for it. He began to lick my hand, and then came in close, putting his head on my shoulder, smearing me with blood.

I reached over his body and held him. We stood together for a long moment, until the shaking stopped.

"Come on, boy," I said, noticing that he had no collar. "Let's get you to a vet."

Guiding him to the side of the road, I took off my Hawaiian shirt, carefully wrapping it around his head several times to stop the bleeding. With so much blood, it was hard to see how badly he was hurt. But one thing was certain; he had lost an ear flap. He whimpered a little when the bandage touched him, but seemed to understand, and just let me do it. I tied the ends of my shirt under his chin and we walked over to the car.

He jumped right over the passenger's door and onto the seat, barking loudly in the process. He was anxious to get the heck out of there, and didn't seem to be hurt anywhere else.

I put it in gear and pulled away. Just as the wheels hit the roadway, he leaned over and licked me on the side of the face.

"Don't worry," I assured him. "We're going to get you patched up, and get you home, wherever that is. . . . No wonder you can't be seen at night. Your fur's as black as asphalt—except for the blood, anyway."

I got off the freeway and turned onto Ocean Avenue, which ran all the way through town and paralleled the shoreline. Stopping at a pay phone, I flipped through the yellow pages, picking the nearest animal hospital. I dialed the doctor's home phone, rousted him out of bed, and agreed to meet him at his office. It was only a few blocks away.

Doc Sutapu was a burly Hawaiian with exceptionally delicate hands for a guy six feet four and two hundred fifty pounds. He had tight, curly gray hair and a matching beard. His intense brown eyes were softened by compassion. It was obvious he liked his job, and he liked animals. His size came in handy when he easily lifted the seventy-five-pound dog up on the examination table.

After a limited exchange of thank-you's by me, and that's-what-I'm-here-for by him, we settled down to the business of fixing the dog.

He carefully unwrapped the bandage and looked the animal over. "Judging by the looks of this, he's going to be all right," he assured me, rubbing sleep from his eyes. "Labs are pretty tough. He's lost some blood and an ear, but he doesn't look all that bad considering the circumstances. We won't need to put him out unless he gets unruly. I'll give him a local, get the wound cleaned up, and survey the extent of the damage."

I agreed with a nod and a wave of my hand.

He gave him a shot of anesthetic, and then quickly and skillfully got the wound cleaned out before sewing forty or so stitches along the place where the ear flap had been. Then he gave the black Lab a good going over.

Washing up in the rest room, I stood around and waited for the diagnosis. Doc Sutapu came out carrying the dog, who was all but asleep, hanging over Doc's strong forearms like a fur coat.

"He's lucky," Doc finally said in a tone that spoke of a lot of patch-up jobs. "That car just clipped his ear off. No broken bones, skull fractures, or internal injuries as far as I can tell."

Doc set him on his old wooden desk. The dog moaned, and dozed off. "He's lost some blood," Doc repeated, "but he'll do just fine. Keep an eye on him for a day or so. Bring him back in a week and I'll take out the stitches. I'll give you some pain-killer and something to fight off infection.

"You can leave him here for a couple of days if you like, or you can take him home. He might like that better. Most dogs do. It's up to you."

"If I only knew where his home *was*," I said. "I don't even know his name. . . . Oh, well, what do I owe you for patching him up?"

"Well, sir," he said in a friendly manner, grabbing a clipboard hanging on the wall. "All we need right now is a name to put down. We'll worry about finances later." He began filling out the boxes on the form.

"Any ideas?"

"How about Skidmark?" he said right off, stopping to look up from the form. "Or Midnight."

"Skidmark," I repeated. "Say, that isn't half-bad. Kind of crude, but it sure fits." I sat in an oak chair by the desk. "Guess you've just about heard them all."

"Just about," he smiled. "You have to have a sense of humor in this business. Besides, I don't have anybody on the books right now using that name."

I nodded.

"Then Skidmark it is," he said, and got ready to write it down.

"Well . . . wait a minute. Doc," I said, walking over to the window and looking up at the stars. "A name is a pretty important thing." I glanced at him over my shoulder.

"Take your time," he said with a wave of his hand, then stood up and went back into the operating room. "I'll be back in a minute."

I walked over to the south-facing window. There was a gap between the buildings and, oddly enough, there was my star, just above the horizon.

"You want this?" Doc asked, coming out of the back room and holding up my blood-soaked shirt.

Turning around I answered, "Naw, toss it."

He went to throw it in the trash can by his desk when the note, now stained with red, fell out on the floor. Walking over slowly, I reached down and picked it up. Without opening it, I looked up at Doc.

"*Vinnie*," I said with a smile. "His name's Vinnie. And I'll take him home . . . tonight. Got a spot on the porch for him until I find his owner. I'll pay his bill now."

He reached over and patted the Lab's back. "Then Vinnie it is," he agreed, making a point not to question my choice. He knew it was a personal thing, and no one had the right to intervene in the choosing of a name, even if it was only temporary.

We left after paying the bill. Vinnie came to and got into the car under his own power, but he was starting to move a little more slowly. Doc had given him some pain-killer, and he was starting to nod off again. Driving home, I watched him sleep on the seat next to me.

"Don't worry," I said a couple of times. "We'll get you home. I promise." I stroked his sleek, black fur, remembering how much I missed not having a dog since high school.

He had to be draped over my shoulders to get him upstairs to my over-the-garage apartment. I didn't have the heart to leave him outside on the balcony. Besides, he might run off when he woke up, so laying him down on the foot of the bed seemed to be the safest thing to do.

Despite the water shortage, I took a long, hot shower. On my way to bed I stopped to look at my print of *The Starry Night* hanging in the hallway. It was a beautiful, emotional painting, bleeding purple onto the canvas in thick, bold strokes, and sprinkled with bursts of bright yellow. Van Gogh was my favorite painter.

I placed the bloodstained note on the nightstand, wanting to know just how much more Erato knew about me. Had she set the whole dog incident up? Or could she see the future? I didn't know. One thing was certain, though: a one-eared Lab had come into my life on a starry night, and he could only have one name.

I wondered if the great painter had ever had a friend who called him Vinnie. Had anyone ever got close enough to use a nickname, or had he always been called Vincent? But there were more immediate things to worry about. The dog's owner had to be found, and Erato, if I ever saw her again, had some explaining to do.

6

Ghosts

Friday morning came early, but we both slept well. The living pile of black fur at the foot of the bed made a few deep groans during the night, but otherwise, Vinnie slept soundly.

Changing his bandage, I got the pills Doc had given me down him—one for the pain and one to ward off infection. Then I let him go back to sleep. Doc had said he would probably sleep a lot for the next couple of days because of the medication, so I let him drift off uninterrupted.

I notified my landlady, Mrs. Okana, of my guest and was relieved when she said it would be okay. She was a small, silver-haired widow with a mellow disposition and a peaceful air about her. She had a round flat face and was slim and straight as a yardstick. I admired her well-adjusted attitude and her foresight in building an apartment over the garage after her husband's death. It provided her with steady income and a warm body knocking around upstairs, which she said was reassuring. She didn't follow my life too closely, but she wished me well and wanted to see me "meet a nice girl," as she put it.

"Companionship is a wonderful thing," she had told me once with a knowing smile and a twinkle in her eye. "It wards off all kinds of ills of the mind, body, and spirit. My husband is gone now, but we'll always be together. Whenever I want to visit him, he's there in my thoughts."

When I gave her a *yeah, maybe* kind of look, she almost scolded me, saying, "You'll see someday yourself. When people go on to the next world, if they still love you, they come back once in a while to see how you're doing. Thinking of them brings them back. I can feel him in the room sometimes. It's not scary or strange; it's warm and wonderful. I know when he's been here."

I can't say her story was true, but then I can't say there aren't ghosts either. Somehow it seemed different from believing in myths and magic. Ghosts were people who actually existed and had just moved on to a higher place.

I never gave it much thought as a child until one night at the age of ten. I woke up from a nightmare, and a ghostlike angel was sitting on my bed, holding me down, of all things.

At least that's what I thought was there. Maybe it was just a dream image that hadn't yet erased when I awoke. There was no way to be sure. None of the features of my angel ghost were distinct to me, but she was wearing a flowing gown, and when I snapped awake, she lifted off and floated through the ceiling.

I asked my mom about it and she said guardian angels sometimes stop by to keep little boys from walking in their sleep, or having their souls leave their bodies and fly off somewhere to get into trouble. But I never forgot that incident. Even though it may have seemed unscientific, I still believed it was a spirit come to keep me from getting into trouble. Being a mischievous child, I wasn't surprised.

Mrs. Okana made me think back on that childhood encounter the Friday morning in July that Vinnie came to stay. If Erato could somehow convince me she was a personified spirit, I just might believe it. It showed me how much I wanted her to be for real—and that I didn't want to have to turn her in for spying.

"Might be nice to have a dog around to ward off intruders while you're at work," Mrs. Okana had said about Vinnie, brushing silver hair from her smooth, flat forehead. "There was a time when a quiet cul-de-sac was safe from crime," she sighed. "But not anymore. Not a single street is safe after dark these days, and sometimes, not even during the day."

Naturally she wasn't going to get an argument out of me, especially since two houses on the next block had been broken into the month before. I also wanted to keep Vinnie until his owner was located, knowing what likely fate would await him if he was turned over to the animal shelter.

I left a message with the shelter about finding a lost and injured dog, placed an ad that would run the following Monday in the local newspaper, and picked up some dog food at the store, along with a chain collar and leash.

Vinnie was still asleep when I got back around noon, but bolted awake when he heard me pour Dog Chow into a bowl usually reserved for spaghetti. Buying a dog dish seemed like it would be a waste of time since he would be staying only a couple of days—a week at the most.

He made short work of the food, and when he finished, I put his collar on him and we went downstairs to lie out in the backyard. Vinnie sat in the sun to warm up while I sat in the shade and read the paper.

I had just finished the funnies and started on the sports page when the phone rang. Running upstairs to the kitchen, I grabbed the receiver. It was the company president.

7

The Call

Janet Stewart was black, beautiful, and a hard-driving fast tracker out of Stanford. She was an excellent engineer, and had invented a computer processing chip while still in graduate school. After getting her masters in electrical and computer engineering, she started the company to do microchip research. She had her own personal lab installed adjacent to her office. That way she could work on pet projects whenever she got the urge. Unfortunately, running the company didn't leave her nearly as much time as she wanted, so she often worked late, coming and going by a back door to her lab.

She was a remarkable woman. Besides being a knock-'em-dead engineer, she had an executive smile, the kind that never gives anything away. She could lay off the whole plant and move to Mexico after giving a rosy sales forecast an hour before and you'd never see it coming. There was just no telling with her when she called you into her office. You just had to hope for the best.

Her father had been a physics professor at Stanford, and her mother an economics professor at Berkeley. Janet had several scholarships waiting for her, but chose Stanford. She liked the research labs and the curriculum, and her dad had clout.

Not only had she been an outstanding engineering student, patenting her microchip prior to graduation, but she was president of her class. In short, she was a classic too-good-to-be-true overachiever. After graduation, naturally, she was recruited by several major companies including IBM, Apple, and Hewlett-Packard, but instead chose to start her own company at the ripe old age of twenty-four.

That was five years before I came to work for her. To say the least, I admired her greatly, but at the same time, it was intimidating to be around such an accomplished person.

"Cyrus," she said energetically into the phone, "I got your message. What's up?"

There was a long silence. Suddenly I wasn't so anxious to tell her. Not until more was known about the strange Ms. Erato. But I had to say something.

"Oh . . . nothing," I stammered. "I just thought I saw something on the system the other night. But it . . . well, I'm sure it was just a ghost."

"What was it, exactly?" Her tone had become more serious.

"Cooper said it was some new invention," I offered, "and that it was none of my business."

"He's right," she admitted. "It *is* a new invention. Something I've been working on for a long time. No one was supposed to know. I even used a new account name to keep it completely under wraps."

I was relieved that it was her file. But I was still curious as to why it had been created so late at night.

"Is that why you created it at a quarter to twelve?" I asked. "Thinking I wouldn't be checking the system?"

"I'm sorry, Cy," she apologized. "I should have told you, but there wasn't time. Just when I got it working I realized it was too big to store on a PC. I had to use the mainframe disk so I wouldn't lose it. The timing was crucial to the experiment."

When I didn't say anything she added, "Look, it was supposed to be a surprise. We're going to knock the microchip industry on its wallet, but it's not quite ready. I haven't got the bugs out yet . . . See me when you come in, and I'll give you a sneak preview. I just can't chance talking about it over the phone."

"Thanks," I said. "That answers a lot of questions. To tell you the truth, I was worried about it. All sorts of things crossed my mind—piracy, espionage, hackers. My imagination was getting the best of me."

"I'm glad you reported this. But everything's fine with the file. You can forget about it now. My new account will appear on the list today. I've told Cooper to set it up . . . And Cy?"

"Yes?"

"You won't tell anyone about this, will you? It could ruin our jump on the competition."

"Not a word. I swear it."

"Not a word to anyone, especially strangers. There may be spies lurking about. These things are hard to keep under wraps. If anyone approaches you about the file, anyone at all, call me immediately. Promise?"

"Promise."

I hung up the phone feeling better, but not much. I was almost on the brink of telling her about Erato, but something stopped me. It seemed to me that Janet was overplaying her hand just a little with that last remark, as if she knew Erato was out there or something. Before she would be informed of my strange visitor, I wanted to hear more from her about the file. Then a decision would be made whether to report Erato. Or if I couldn't decide, a call could be made to the FBI, CIA, or one of those secret agencies.

A feeling inside me said I would be seeing Erato again soon, though she had said it wouldn't be until I believed. She had to be pretty clever to set up the car and dog scene and make it look like an accident, just to get me to believe. It seemed a little cruel to make a poor dog pay with his ear just to get my attention. It was painful to admit, but I was obviously wrong about her. She was no innocent girl from the Midwest coming out to touch the surf for the first time. She was slick, and judging from Vinnie's condition, she was quite capable of playing hardball.

Maybe the clipped ear bit was supposed to scare me. If so,

it was starting to work. It was plain to see I was in way over my head. I wasn't some gumshoe out of a detective novel, just an average guy trying to make ends meet and get in a little surfing.

The problem was how to get out of this with all *my* body parts intact. Oh well, one thing at a time. I would see Janet first thing when I got to work, and take it from there.

8

Cooper's Town

When I got to work, Janet was busy, so I went over to engineering and followed up on some circuit design software, then went back toward my cubicle. Before I got there, Cooper was waiting for me. When I passed his office, he was sporting a sly grin. The battle of wits was about to begin, so I braced myself with the usual flip attitude reserved for such unhappy occasions.

"So you found out," he said dryly, fingering his lapels. "Good—now if this leaks to the outside world, they'll know whose fault it was."

"Yeah," I frowned, reaching down to retie my tennis shoes. "It'll be mine . . . or yours," I couldn't resist saying. I stood up and walked away before he could say anything.

"It won't be mine," he said to my back. "I can *keep* secrets."

"Ah, shoot," I said in a smart-aleck tone, stomping my foot and turning to look back at him. "I'm sorry. I told Janet *you* were the one who . . ." I looked around. There were still a few people who hadn't left. I zipped my lip with my finger and went into my cubicle.

"You what?" he yelled down the aisle, and got some stares from people glaring over their partitions. We lived in the quiet world of software, and outright yelling was rare, especially for Cooper. Looking around, he motioned for everybody to keep all their body parts inside their cubicles.

"All right, back to work," he ordered, and then saw the clock on the wall. "Or go home. It's after four."

I was in my cubicle, but hadn't sat down, knowing there would soon be a visitor in my humble abode. When he hastily appeared in the doorway, I offered him a seat in my guest chair.

"Mr. Major," he said impatiently, rolling his eyes, "my office . . . *now*, please."

I followed so closely behind him that everyone laughed, seeing my poor attempt at vaudeville. Once inside his office I said, "*Mr*. Cooper. Please. You've got to calm down. Heart attacks don't respect age anymore. You think I want to take a day off from riding waves just to go to your funeral? With my luck, it'll probably be breakin' in ten footers."

My sarcasm was getting out of hand, even for me, but I couldn't stop myself just then.

"You told Janet," he glared, ignoring my speech and forcing himself to control his nerves, "that *I* informed you about the file?"

"Relax, Coop," I said, looking him over. "You're too stiff. You're pressing your suit just by standing in it. Don't you ever give it a chance to get just one wrinkle . . . There," I added, pointing to the back of his knee, "right there. A crease is starting to form behind your back."

"What in the—"

"The point is, Coop," I explained, trying to control myself. "That things happen. Suits *get* wrinkles. Fighting it only makes it worse. Let things happen for once, will you? And hear me out. I left Janet a mail message after I discovered the file. After all, it's her company. She's got a right to know when some unknown user is penetrating her secret files. If I don't tell her, then I'm not doing my job. How was I supposed to know it was her account? The records sure didn't say so."

"I've already told you more than you needed to know," he said, unaffected by my explanation. He didn't say anything else, so I finished. Leaning on his desk, I attempted a half-apology.

"All I said was that you claimed it was some new invention and that it was none of my business. I would've guessed *that* much. Now she's going to brief me or something. Give me a sneak preview, she says. Coop, she was going to tell me anyway. She just didn't have time. It was a last minute thing. Apparently the file was too big for a PC."

"I know."

"Okay, you *know*," I said, waving my hands. "And in a minute we'll both know. Don't worry." I turned to leave. "She told me not to tell a soul. And I won't. Scout's honor."

"You can't be trusted."

"What?"

"Anybody that hacks into the university's computer . . ."

"Coop. That's in the past. Besides, I cleared that up, remember? Things are different now. You'll see."

His phone rang. He reached over and picked it up. "Cooper," he answered, then nodded and said, "Yes, he's here. I'll send him right over." He hung up the phone and looked at me. "It's time," he grinned, "for your briefing."

On the way out he added, "If this . . . this invention leaks out, you're gone. Might say you've caught your last wave around here. Then it will be my town."

That seemed like an odd remark. Did he think I was in competition for his job or something? If I was, it was news to me. Since he seemed to be pitching fast and hard, I razzed him a little, though my anger was spent.

"The hardball hall of fame," I smirked, "is definitely in Cooperstown." Since he didn't know anything about sports, he just gave me a funny look. "Trust me," I said with an exaggerated smile. "Hey, gotta go."

"Cy," he said as I walked away, and the informality caught me funny. "Look, no hard feelings. I'm . . . things are tough in the industry right now. I can't afford to lose . . ."

"Hey," I retorted. "Forget it. I'm just trying to protect myself. Maybe we both are. Anyway, wish me luck with Janet."

"You'll be fine," he assured me. "You've got nothing to hide."

That comment struck me almost as odd as his sudden admission of insecurity about his job, but I shrugged it off and headed down the hall.

Janet's office was sparse, almost Spartan. A few microchip blow-ups hung on one wall. Some leather chairs and a matching couch were scattered about. A purposely understated oak desk sat comfortably in the middle of the room, sporting a simple desk set and one of those dolls that usually has several smaller ones stacked inside each other. She was an engineer at heart, not an interior decorator. Her one extravagance was a CD jukebox in the corner, filled with her favorite pop sounds.

When her secretary sent me in, Janet greeted me at the door with a firm handshake and that smile. Her skin was a rich shade of dark brown. She was tall, slim, and had her hair pulled back in a ponytail. She was not model beautiful, but pretty close, and when she smiled, she showed movie star teeth, though not quite as glaring and white. She wore an elegant, purple velvet, warm-up suit and matching high heels, not unusual for her unless she was having a board meeting or traveling. She gave you the feeling that she only slipped into the shoes when somebody walked in, and rumors of her shoeless style had earned her a nickname—the barefoot genius.

"Sit down," she said casually, "or stand if you like. I'll give you the scoop."

She closed the door behind us and kicked off her heels, tossing them almost carelessly under her desk.

"These things kill my feet," she frowned good-naturedly. "Tennis shoes take too long to lace, and I refuse to wear those Velcro jobs. . . . Would you like a beer?" she asked to my surprise, "or maybe a soda?"

"To tell you the truth," I quipped, "I'd just like some answers." I hadn't sat down.

"Would you be more comfortable if we went to my lab?"

"Naw," I answered, purposely trying not to act scared, and not wanting to get distracted by the oscilloscopes, signal analyzers, and power supplies I knew were in the next room. "This is fine. I'll sit here." I plopped down in a comfortable leather chair and sat back. "Well, what have you got that's so secret?" I blurted.

Standing by the desk, she reached over and pushed a button on her phone. "Hold all my calls," she commanded. She sat on her desk facing me, and before I had time to get too nervous, she began explaining how the the computer world had evolved by a series of quantum leaps, beginning with the transistor, then the microchip, hard disks, RAM, ROM, and all that.

She reminded me that Random Access Memory storage capabilities were currently running sixteen megabits per chip, or sixteen million Ones and Zeros. There are usually eight bits to a byte, a byte representing a single character, such as a letter, number, or punctuation mark.

If you wanted more RAM you just strung a bunch of chips together to expand your working memory. For typical computer applications, this was done by assembling them onto a SIMM, or Single Inline Memory Module. The more bytes you could squeeze into a small space, the more working memory you had. And in memory, more was better.

Obviously people were always working on improvements. A prototype sixty-four meg memory chip was in the works, and a two fifty-six in the concept stage.

She slid off her desk, walked to the window, and closed the drapes, then turned and looked intensely at me. "What would you pay if you needed a lot of RAM in a tight space, and today I could give you two hundred fifty-six megabits on a single chip? A quarter of a gigabyte on one SIMM?"

My eyes widened. I was impressed. "The new file," I said, thinking out loud, "is one hundred megabytes, much too big for the sixteen meg SIMM, even too big for the proto sixty-four."

"Transferred," she added, "to the hard disk from my new RAM module."

"What's in the Euterpe file?" I asked, almost without thinking.

"What's in it," she stated, walking over and sitting in her desk chair, "is not important. What's important is maintaining the data's integrity until I put it back in RAM. By checking the contents of memory I can verify that I have bidirectional storage and retrieval capability. That's why nobody is allowed into that file until I put the data back in RAM."

"When are you going to do that?" I asked excitedly. "I'd like to be there."

"Do you remember I told you on the phone that it has some bugs?" She spun the chair so that she was facing a picture window on the side of the room, though it was behind closed drapes. "Well, so far I can only get it going one way," she admitted. "But I'm working on it."

She didn't seemed too worried about it, but after all, she was a woman of ability and accomplishment, so I wasn't surprised by her confidence.

"If it's like every other advance," I said, sitting back in the chair and crossing my legs, "everybody will want it. The possibilities are almost endless. Can you tell me how it works, or is that classified?"

"Microminiaturization," she grinned, "as usual. Only instead of shrinking the circuitry size, it stores information in a new way." She turned toward the doll on her desk, leaned forward, and picked it up. "Ever see one of these?"

"Sure. It's got a bunch of dolls nested inside of each other."

"Simple, really, when you think about it," she said, smiling.

"The chip works like this doll set." She pulled it apart and began to place each doll in a row on her desk, until all of them were lined up. "It stores data in a way that's similar to these dolls."

"But they have that now, with files and folders."

"This is beyond that. The data actually comes apart, and then reassembles, exactly as before. What we're talking about here is molecular level storage, almost down to single molecules."

"Is that possible? Information stored in molecules?"

"Ever heard of DNA?"

"But how does it code and reassemble the data?"

She sat back in her chair. "That, Cy, *is* classified information. I should have the data back in my RAM in a couple of days. So you won't have to worry about the file much longer."

"Why the name Euterpe?"

She smiled slightly and got up, walking over to the jukebox. "You'll never believe this," she began, turning to glance at me over her shoulder. "But I always wanted to be a songwriter. I could do the notes pretty well; never could get the lyrics right. And I wouldn't use someone else's words—too much of a glory hog, I guess . . .

"It's a tribute," she said finally, punching in a Phil Collins tune, "to the muse of lyric poetry—the one thing I wanted to do most, but never could." She turned to face me, leaning back on the jukebox. "Engineering was my second choice, you know, after music, and I like my music with lyrics." Phil Collins began singing softly in the background. "What was *your* first choice?"

"Surfing," I said with a self-conscious laugh, "but they didn't offer it as a major." Something else was bothering me. So I stood up and asked why she needed the Euterpe file. Why couldn't she use just any one hundred megs of data to check out the chip's performance, since ones and zeros all look alike to the computer.

She informed me that the Euterpe file contained specially coded test data that checked the breakdown and reassembly process of the new chip, the key to the molecular nesting she'd been working on since grad school. That was why all the secrecy. She walked over and parted the drapes, looking out into the parking lot.

"I'm trusting you not to say a word of this to anyone," she went on. "Not even to Cooper. The future of this company depends on that chip. And no one . . ." She looked at me. "Absolutely *no one* can be allowed to jeopardize the future of this company. I'm not trying to be heavy, Cy. But you now know more than anyone, and I'm asking you to erase your memory on this subject."

I thought about what Erato had said about human memory. "I may not be able to do that," I said, pointing to my head. "But I can seal off access to these memory banks."

"Thanks, Cy. I knew you'd understand."

As I turned to leave, she said, "I'm putting you in for a raise."

"That won't be necessary," I answered. "I don't need hush money."

"It's not for that," she grinned. "It's for doing your job too well. I owe it to you."

"All right," I agreed, reaching for the doorknob. "Maybe you do. But this could burn Cooper up."

"He could use a little burning once in a while." Her grin broadened as she slowly walked toward her desk. "He gets a little uptight sometimes. Maybe this'll shake him up a little."

"Thanks," I said on the way out the door. "I needed that."

"We need each other, Cy," she added seriously, reassembling the dolls on her desk.

"Yeah, guess we do. Well, gotta get back to work."

"That makes two of us. If anything else suspicious happens, let me know . . . But I can only the afford one raise right now," she teased. "So don't *invent* something just to get my attention."

"You're the inventor," I said over my shoulder. "I'm only support."

"Good. That's what I need most right now."

I was pretty well convinced she was telling me everything— almost. I still had some unanswered questions, and needed someone to fill in the rest of the puzzle. The piece of blue sky where Erato fit in would do nicely—if I could just find it lying around somewhere.

9
Foggy Night

As I left Janet's office, my head began to fill with the possibilities her new RAM chip could open in the computer world. But it didn't last long. More questions started to surface.

If Janet had been working for so long on the chip, why was a test-data file just now being created? Maybe in the heat of the experiment she decided to open a new file on the spot, or maybe she kept moving it around and renaming it to foil hackers. Perhaps Euterpe was just her latest pet name for it, though it seemed like too much of a coincidence to me, especially with the sudden appearance of Erato.

Despite the fact that I had only met her briefly, Erato was having a profound effect on me. She had me thinking that the line between myth and reality might be finer than I thought, and that maybe it could, under special circumstances, be crossed. All of that kind of thinking would have to wait, though. It was time to get back to work.

Cooper was waiting for me when I passed his office, but I waved him off, telling him that Janet had explained everything except how the chip worked, and hadn't mentioned his name once. After that, it was a routine night except for a few minor bugs I spotted in a task authorization program, bugs which were easily corrected by writing a few lines of code.

Checking the system just before closing, I found Iberlin logged-on and accessing Euterpe, this time from Janet's lab. If Janet was Iberlin, I wondered why she had logged on the other night from the computer lab instead of her office, which was also a classified work area, but dismissed it, figuring she had probably needed some special equipment to hook up to her chip, equipment she didn't have in her lab that night. By now she had probably moved the equipment into her lab so she could work on her experiment in private, and had accessed the file again.

A few minutes later Iberlin logged off. I shut down access

and went home, noticing on the way to my car that the top was up. Funny, I didn't remember putting it up, but my mind had been elsewhere the last few days.

The fog was rolling in fast and thick by the time my hands were on the steering wheel, so I couldn't see the bus stop very well. I cranked the starter for quite a while before finally firing up the engine and rolling off down the drive, reminding myself to tune the engine the next day.

I couldn't keep myself from looking for Erato, and was sorely disappointed when she wasn't there. I was cursing under my breath by the time the car got to the university turnoff.

Turning right, I drove towards Cal U., planning to swing down by the beach where Erato had been dropped off two nights before. I drove slowly through the thick fog, making sure the car stayed in my lane. Up ahead a figure suddenly appeared from out of the mist, walking along the side of the road. I passed someone wearing a leather jacket with a familiar symbol on the back.

Stopping the car, I let Erato come up alongside. Much to my surprise, she didn't stop walking. She didn't even turn to acknowledge my existence. When she got past my front bumper I yelled, "Hey! I thought you wanted a ride?"

She didn't stop, and wouldn't answer. What was she up to? I put the car back in gear and pulled up even with her. Reaching over, I rolled down the passenger's window.

"Erato, what are you doing? It's me, Cy. You know, the Dog Star and all that." She didn't look at me. She just kept walking. "Look, you should have waited at the bus stop," I continued. "It's dangerous walking alone at night."

"I thought buses didn't run this late?" she reminded me, not looking my way. "And *you* were the one who said not to take rides from strangers."

"Strangers? Erato, please," I begged, leaning over and looking out the window. "This may be your last chance. Someone accessed the file tonight."

She stopped abruptly. When the car got next to her she opened the door and got in.

"Who?" she asked seriously, looking out the windshield.

"Janet, using a new account."

"Janet Stewart," she said coolly. "How do you know it was her?"

"It was from her terminal," I replied, sitting back in my seat. "She said the new account was hers."

"Figures," she said, still looking straight ahead. "She's about the only one smart enough to pull it off."

I had something to say, so I didn't waste time with incidentals. "Look," I said, putting the car in gear and pulling back onto the road, "you've got some explaining to do. First, Janet wants me to report any strangers lurking about. She thinks there are product spies around. Second, if you want the contents of that file, you'd better show me some ID. FBI, CIA, I don't care which, just show me some official authorization. And third, I don't like what you did to that poor dog. That wasn't clever and it wasn't funny. It was cruelty to animals. You should have known I wouldn't go for that. I cried when my last dog died, and she was fifteen and toothless. Playing on my sympathy was mean, as far as I'm concerned. I ought to turn you over to the SPCA for engineering that little demonstration."

"I had to get your attention," she replied seriously.

"Well, you could've chosen something a little more . . . humane."

"Cyrus," she said, turning to face me for the first time. "You may not believe this, but he was destined to lose that ear. I just borrowed him to get your attention. At least now he has a home."

"He was homeless?" I asked, gripping the steering wheel harder.

"Well, not *exactly*," she confessed. "But his owner neglected him. I knew he was going to get hurt. I can't change destiny, but I can influence it a little. This way two things were accomplished: he got a good home and I got your attention."

"Okay, I'll give you that much," I shrugged, trying to keep my eyes on the road. "So, now that you've got it, what do you really want?"

She touched my arm lightly and whispered, "The contents of that file."

"I can't help you," I replied stiffly. "Janet says it's some new . . . wait." I glanced over at her. "Let's see some ID."

"I don't have any," she confessed, pulling her hand back and running it through her bushy hair.

"Oh, great," I said. "Like I really believe that. Look, everyone's got ID. Show me a driver's license, a major credit card, or a birth certificate. I'm not picky."

"I don't have any of those," she shrugged. "I just arrived Wednesday night, and where I come from you don't need ID."

Clenching my teeth, I slapped the steering wheel. "Well, then how do you pay for stuff in *this* world?" I asked, looking at her expensive leather jacket.

"With these," she answered, nonchalantly opening the leather purse on her lap. It was filled to overflowing with hundred-dollar bills. We had already gone through the university and swung down by the beach. The fog was clearing a little. I pulled over and stopped, but left the engine running.

"Great!" I shouted, reaching over and closing her purse. "You fix me up with an injured dog. You want what's in a secret company file. You have no ID, and now you show me a purse full of money. Is this some kind of sting operation? Because if it is, you've got the wrong guy."

"I know it looks bad." She thrust her hands into her jacket pockets. "But . . ."

"Looks bad? This is starting to make the *Falcon and the Snowman* look like shareware." I motioned toward the roadway. "I think you'd better get out of the car. I'm sorry, but I want out of . . . of whatever it is I'm into up to my eyeballs."

"But you're the only one who can help."

"I'm not helping you or anyone else until I know what's really in that file," I began, then continued, "Wait, what am I saying? That's what you want, isn't it? You want me to hack-in so you can gain access to the file through me. Well, nothing doing. My hacking days are over.

"Besides," I added, "if I remember correctly, you said I wouldn't see you again until I believed. Well, I *don't* believe. So good-bye."

I hated saying it, but the water was clearly getting too deep, and I thought I'd better get out before I drowned, despite my attraction to her.

"You mean Vinnie didn't convince you?" She was disappointed; her emerald eyes had lost their sparkle.

"Scared me, yes. Convince, no."

She got out of the car without saying a word. I didn't know what else to do. I put it in gear. Before the car got ten feet away she yelled, "Wait! I've got it."

I stopped the car, and she got back in. She looked me straight in the eye and said, "I'll prove who I am."

"Okay," I agreed, scratching my beard and looking at the road. "Where's your magic wand?"

"Look, just take me to a nightclub," she ordered, dropping

her hand casually on the back of my seat. "One that has live music."

"Either you're kidding," I smirked, "or you're stalling."

She took off her jacket and tossed it into the backseat, showing a stunning figure beneath her tight T-shirt. "Let me put it to you this way. If I'm for real, I'm a muse and my dad's a god. If you think regular fathers get upset when their daughters come home past twelve, what do you think my dad will be like when he finds me missing? Especially when I tell him I was with a . . ." She brushed her hair back with her hand, showing the lovely profile of her face. "a mortal."

"Missing?" I said, forcing my eyes back on the road. "Doesn't he know you're gone? And hey, I resent being referred to as a mere mortal." I looked at her glowing complexion. "Being human isn't so bad, you know. We're running the world now, or hadn't you noticed?" I was getting perturbed, and a little distracted.

"One chance," she pleaded, reaching over and holding the steering wheel. "That's all I ask. Take me dancing. And if I can't prove it, I'll . . . I'll go back to my world and never bother you again."

"All right," I said, putting it in gear. "But this had better be good. What kind of music do you like?"

"Something we can dance to," she quipped, and began beating out a rhythm on the dashboard. "Something with a beat— something you'll be able to recognize."

"And it's got to be a live band?"

"Unless you want prerecorded, like disco." She rolled her eyes. "Boy, did I hate that era. Besides, muses don't usually do their best work on disc jockeys."

"Funny," I said, pulling back on the road. "Somehow, I could have guessed that . . . One chance," I added. "No more, no less. Prove it tonight or I go to the FBI."

"That," she frowned, "is not an inspiring thought."

"One more thing," I said. "You didn't answer my question. I thought you'd only appear when I believed. Well, I don't."

"I couldn't wait," she confessed. "You're too thickheaded. Besides, we may be running out of time to save Euterpe."

"The muse of lyric poetry."

"Very good," she said excitedly, looking at me. "You did your homework."

"Did you drop that book on me?"

"No, Sir Isaac Newton did."

"Maybe." I studied the clean lines of her face. "But that's not important right now. I want to know why your dad doesn't know you're here. Didn't you talk to him about this?"

"One thing at a time," she answered. "And watch the road—the fog hasn't completely cleared yet, and you never know what you're going to run into on the road at night."

I laughed, slapping the steering wheel. "You're really someone to tell me that. I can hardly wait to see what booby trap you'll set next."

"I'll give you the whole scoop, but not until we go dancing. Then we discuss accessing the file."

"*If* you can convince me who you really are," I answered.

"You watch the road. I'll worry about the rest."

There was a long silence, after which I turned to her and asked, "Hey, did you put the top up?"

"Yes. I didn't want to sit on a damp seat."

Heading down the road, I was filled with the hope that she could somehow prove her otherworldly identity, though it seemed impossible. Then again, the transistor had seemed impossible fifty years ago. But first the nightclub. The rest was in the sure hands of destiny.

10

Every Breath You Take

"I've got it," I said, turning north onto Ocean Avenue. "I've got just the place. Let's see . . ." I looked at my watch. "It's twelve-thirty now. You've got an hour and a half to prove yourself."

I tried to sound as serious as possible, but I wasn't sure just how convincing I was until she responded to my threat.

"Boy," she said with raised eyebrows, "for a California surfer, you're not what you call laid-back. If I didn't know, I'd say you were from the East Coast."

"Let's just say I don't want to be laid six feet under."

Ocean Avenue ran between the 101 freeway, California's main coastal artery, and the Pacific. At about its midpoint, i became Main Street. To the north of this transformation line lay the community of Channel Islands. Santa Isabella lay to the south.

The towns were like two sisters sitting on the beach with their heads resting on the mountains and their feet in the water. Santa Isabella was the rich sister, deriving her income mostly from tourism. People came from all over the world to bask in her mild climate, to tour the Spanish mission, the Moorish courthouse, the wooden wharf, and the quaint shops downtown.

Channel Islands was the working-class sister, and spent her days in the factories and the fields. It was where most of the electronics companies were located, along with the airport and Cal U., although they officially belonged to the city of Santa Isabella.

Turning north onto Ocean Avenue took me toward the old downtown area of Channel Islands, which had the look and feel of a small southwestern desert town transplanted to the coast, except for the surf shops.

I pulled into Alondro's and parked, finding a rare vacant space when a truckload of students pulled out. A local band, the Haymakers, played a pretty good mix of oldies, country, and current pop. I was nuts about the electric violin, especially when it really got ripping.

The place was still crowded, though starting to thin out, but I knew the band was good for another hour or so. We snagged a small table in the back and sat down. I ordered a mixed drink. My date had a plain Coke.

"All right," I said, after paying the waitress, "it's show time. Do your stuff." I was still playing tough, though I didn't know how long I could keep it up.

"What's that you're drinking?" she asked over the music, hanging her jacket over her chair.

"R and C."

When she gave me a puzzled look I explained. "Rum and Coke. Sorry, I'm not too sophisticated when it comes to liquor."

"I've never had hard liquor before," she said matter-of-factly. "Tried some wine at the junior goddess ball once, but I didn't like the taste."

"So?"

"So let me try it. See if I like hard stuff any better."

"How old are you?"

"Five, maybe six thousand years," she joked. "I've lost track. But I've only been human for a couple of days. So, even if you average it out, I'm still over twenty-five hundred."

"Why did I even ask?" I said, shaking my head, knowing I deserved that one.

She switched drinks and downed the whole thing in one gulp, as if it were only a Coke. Then she clutched her throat.

"Holy cow!" she gasped, her eyes getting big. "That stuff's got quite a kick to it." She grabbed the plain Coke and drank about half of it before setting it back on the table. "But it's not bad with a chaser."

I didn't know what to say. I had seen people want to get drunk quickly, but this was something else. I ordered another one, saying, "Better make it a double this time."

When it arrived, I was determined not to let her chugalug my drink, and guarded this one with my cupped hands. The waitress set down the chrome tip-tray on the table next to my drink and left the change.

"Come on," Erato said, and grabbed my hand. "Let's dance."

She pulled me up on the dance floor and we boogied to a Bruce Hornsby tune. She was wild and very creative with her dancing, like she was doing a sequel to *Flashdance* or something. Everyone soon got out of the way and just watched, clapping and carrying on like it was a dance competition final. When the song finished she beat me to the table and downed most of my drink before I could get to it.

"Hey, this stuff is supposed to work for artists," she explained, catching her breath. "Or so they believe. I just want to see what all the fuss is about. *I'm getting in the mood* as they call it. . . . Now, what do you want to hear? Go ahead; pick a tune."

"Where on earth did you learn to dance like that?" I asked, fanning my shirt to cool off.

"The Mount Olympus Ballroom," she smirked. "And who said it was on earth, anyway? People think everything was invented right here on this small planet. Boy, have you got a lot to learn. Besides, I have eight sisters, remember? One of them is a helluva dancer." She was starting to blink, and the booze was affecting her speech.

"Go on, pick a tune," she ordered.

"What are you, some kind of jukebox?"

"Look, you want proof, don't you? Pick something, anything except 'Happy Birthday.' I don't do birthday parties."

" 'Surf City,' " I said sarcastically, "by Jan and Dean."

She started to get up.

"Hey," I said, grabbing her arm. "Nothing doing. Anybody can whisper in some guy's ear. Do it from here."

"Don't trust me, huh? Well, all right." She thought for a second, staring intently at the band as they finished up an instrumental I didn't recognize. Then she frowned. "It won't do. They don't know it. Pick something else."

I almost believed her. After all, the guys in the band were in their early twenties. They probably didn't know too many surf oldies. But I had heard plenty of that stuff from some of the guys at Cal U. A lot of them said their dads still had old surf records at home, and brought some of them to the dorms for party nostalgia, trivia, and laughs.

" 'Every Breath You Take,' " I said at last, wiping beads of sweat from my forehead, "by the Police. Everyone knows that one. It sold seventeen million copies or something."

"Yeah." She nodded, almost sentimentally. "Euterpe had a hand in that one. She has a way of being in the right place at the right time when it comes to lyrics."

"Except lately," I said, sipping my R and C and trying to be clever.

The band stopped. The tall, skinny lead guitarist brushed his long platinum hair off his face and gulped down something in a glass, spilling half of it on his tank top and jeans. Then he announced, "Request time! Anybody want to hear something special?"

"Well, I'll be," I remarked sarcastically. "Here's your chance." But Erato had her eyes closed. She was concentrating. People were yelling so many song titles that it sounded like the floor of the stock exchange. The guitarist waved them off and stepped back.

"Wait," he said, tossing his hair back dramatically. "Changed my mind. Too much input. Here's one you haven't heard tonight. It's dedicated to Big Brother. And . . ." He turned toward our table. "To that dynamite dancer over there with her eyes closed."

As soon as the first familiar notes peeled off his guitar I was stunned. Erato had somehow picked it. She opened her eyes and looked at me. "Not good enough for you?" she asked, reading my face and smiling. She was starting to glow from the liquor.

"It could still be a trick," I argued, raising my eyebrows. "Or a coincidence. It's a popular song, you know."

"Then pick something else," she answered, unshaken. "Something that *will* convince you. Something so obscure I couldn't guess it. But remember, they have to know it." She finished off her plain Coke, but the booze was catching up fast. She looked at my glass like she wanted another drink. I put my hand over it.

"Look, you've had enough to drink," I said, beginning to worry about her. "And I can see you're not used to it."

"Whoa," she said, rolling her eyes, and looking a little dizzy. Then she recovered and commanded, "Pick something." She was getting loud, and losing control.

"All right," I agreed, trying to level out the situation. "But then I take you home. This time, though, I won't tell you what it is. I'm going to write it down on this napkin and put it in my pocket."

I pulled an old golf pencil out of my back pocket and scribbled something on my napkin. Then I stuffed it in my shirt pocket. She did her work again, but she was getting more dizzy with her eyes closed.

"Geez," she said. "Sorry, some other time for the parlor tricks." She got up and grabbed her jacket. "I gotta go out-side—now."

She looked green around the gills, but before I could say anything, she ran for the door with me in hot pursuit. She raced across the parking lot and heaved into a hedge. When she finished, she wiped her mouth with her jacket sleeve and fell backward into me. I caught her just before she hit the asphalt and carried her to the car. She was only half-conscious by then.

I fired up the Mustang and drove slowly out of the parking lot. The band had stopped, and was changing tunes. I heard the lead guitarist start playing as I pulled up to the stop sign at the corner. The notes rang crystal clear through the night. It was the beginning of a song I knew well. Erato suddenly bolted awake and looked at me. She reached over, grabbed the napkin out of my shirt pocket, and opened it up.

"What is this supposed to be?" she asked, still groggy with booze.

"That"—I flushed, pointing to a circle on the paper—"is the moon. And the wavy lines underneath it are supposed to represent a river. I don't know how you did it, or if I even believe it yet, but you called it. Now, what's on the file?"

"My sister," she said with deeply felt concern, and fell asleep with her head on my shoulder.

I shook her when we pulled up to my apartment on Walnut Place, but couldn't get her awake. Carrying her upstairs, I laid her on my bed. Vinnie lay conked out next to her, so I left him there and went to the couch. I'm sure Erato would have caught Zs until morning if Vinnie hadn't licked her awake about three o'clock. Hearing her groan, I got up and went to the bedroom doorway.

She sat up and held her head. "You got any of those modern pain relievers?" she asked at last, petting Vinnie in the process. "I've got a world-class headache."

I quickly got her some Advil and a glass of water. She took the pills and gulped down the water.

"Well," she said, trying to shake off the headache. "I've done enough damage for one night. I'd best be going before your landlady finds out you've got a second guest." All the while she spoke she was petting Vinnie. "How's he doing?" she finally asked.

"He sleeps a lot from the medicine," I answered, standing over her, still in my street clothes. "But other than that he's fine. Now, tell me. What's really on the file?"

In an odd way she had been right. She did return when I was ready to believe, at least on the same night anyway. For the moment my mind was convinced, and was in agreement with my heart. I was ready to hear her out.

"It's late," she said, holding off my curiosity, and rubbing her forehead. "Let's talk about it in the morning. How far's the beach from here?"

"A mile, if you take the bike path," I replied. "One and a half on the freeway."

"Just point me in the right direction," she said, trying to stand up. "The walk will do me good."

"Where are you staying?" I asked, looking through the venetian blinds at nothing in particular.

"The sand and surf."

"That some kind of motel?"

"Hey, it's great. It's got sand, waves, sea gulls, even a dead seal or two. Course, you have to watch for high tides." She got up and headed for the front door. I followed her into the living room.

"My god," I answered, shocked. "You're sleeping on the beach."

"It's not that cold in the summer," she explained, grabbing the doorknob. "Besides, there are lots of stars at night. Especially in the southern sky."

"Erato, that's dangerous," I said, sounding like a parent. "Let me take you to a motel."

"I don't go to motels with men," she informed me, half-serious. "Besides, what isn't dangerous these days?"

"Stay here," I offered. "Sleep on the couch. Better yet, sleep in my bed."

"Cyrus! I'm surprised at you," and this time she *was* serious.

"No, I mean *you* sleep in the bed," I defended, hiding my face in my hands. "I'll sleep on the couch." I was turning red. "Besides . . ."

"Besides what?"

I looked out between my hands. "There's only room for one person and Vinnie on the bed."

"Good boy, Vinnie," she said, giving him a wink. "A girl needs protection from late night sleepwalkers."

"I *beg* your pardon."

I talked her into sleeping over, though she insisted on taking the couch. As we got ready for bed, she agreed to tell me everything in the morning. I gave her a pillow and blanket and soon she was out. Sometime in the early morning she wandered into my bed and fell asleep like a child wanting to curl up with her parents. Vinnie moved to the foot of the bed, curling up with a happy groan.

Erato was only wearing her T-shirt and panties, and thinking about her lying there got the best of me. I wanted to lie there forever with my arms around her, stroking her hair, and almost could have, but it was just too much to take, even with Vinnie nudging my feet.

Since I didn't want to wake her, I decided to leave. I got up and went to the couch, knowing it was my only chance to get some sleep. Ten minutes later a set of feet was on the hardwood floor heading my way. They were followed closely by another set of feet. Soon, all four of Vinnie's paws were at the foot of the couch, along with his good-sized body.

Wrapping my legs around his warm, furry body made him groan happily. I thought about Erato and wondered what tomorrow would bring. If she *was* a spy or working with some secret agency, she was so good at it that I couldn't fight her. She had overpowered me with her femininity and her magic.

The few moments I lay in bed with her a feeling of free-falling into her had come over me. I was as helpless as a sky diver without a chute, just hoping something soft was waiting for me below. For the first time in my life I was, god help me, starting to fall in love. Even in my wildest dreams I never thought it would be under such unbelievable circumstances. But she had everything I had been waiting for in a woman and more: beauty, brains, wit, and a strong personality.

In short, the opposite of my mother. I had always hated the way she let Dad push her around. I preferred women who stood up for themselves without knocking everyone else down in the process. I just hoped my feelings for Erato would last.

But love is beyond time and space. It comes into your life wherever and whenever it wants, does with your heart whatever it fancies, and stays as long as it likes. For in all of heaven and earth, there is no magic more powerful than love.

I fell asleep feeling the warmth of Vinnie at my feet, a floating sensation in my head, and wonder pulsating in my chest. I drifted off dreaming about holding Erato. We were dancing slowly, and she was laughing. There was a huge, silver moon overhead and a paddle wheel churning beneath us, beating out a steady rhythm as we spun together on the deck of a riverboat. Andy Williams sang softly in the background about crossing the river in style someday.

A fog drifted over the river and everything disappeared. As he sang the last lyrics we turned endlessly in space, and didn't touch down until the moon sank forever into the time-less river.

I awoke later and looked at the clock. It was five in the morning. Something had been bothering me. I got up and stood in the bedroom doorway, watching her sleep like an angel in repose. She turned over and opened her eyes.

"What is it?" she asked, half-awake. "You sleepwalking?"

"No, I have to ask you a question."

"Hmmm?"

"Do you have a boyfriend with a Harley?"

"Nope," she yawned. "Come back to bed. I'm getting cold."

I wasn't satisfied. "Do you have a boyfriend at all?" I asked.

"Not yet," she smiled. "But I'm accepting applications. Do you want to fill one out?"

"Just curious," I answered, protecting my heart. "Some guy on a Harley followed me home the other night. I thought . . ."

"Free as a bird," she said, stretching. "And tired as a dog. Look, if you're not going to warm up the bed, leave your application on the nightstand. I'm going back to sleep. Good night."

"You want another blanket?" I asked, almost serious.

"Don't be silly," she scolded, and pulled the covers over her head.

"Pleasant dreams," I said with a half-smile, then turned and walked back to the living room.

Once on the couch, I gave Vinnie an extra-hard squeeze with my feet. I had never been in a more difficult situation in all my life, and had never been happier.

For the first time something had made me feel the timeless harmony I felt aboard a wave, and the world beneath me wasn't even moving, except for spinning slowly on its axis. My head was spinning in harmony with it, or so it seemed. It didn't make me dizzy as I thought it would; it rocked me to sleep like a baby in a cradle. Soon, I was gone, dissolving into sweet eternity.

11

Energy

The next day was sunny, hot, and Saturday. Sometime in the morning my feet weren't quite as warm, and I awoke knowing that Vinnie was probably on the bed again. I got up and went to the bedroom, pausing in the open doorway. Erato had her arms wrapped around a seventy-five-pound sleeping fur pillow. Vinnie heard me come in and sprang awake, then began to lick Erato on the face. Needless to say, that woke her up pretty fast.

"Morning," I said, noticing she still looked a little pale from the night before. "How are you feeling?"

"Oh," she said, rubbing her neck. "Not too bad, I guess. How did I get in here?"

"You were sleepwalking. So I moved to the couch."

"Oh, yeah, now I remember. . . . Before, or after?" she joked, raising an eyebrow.

"Before or after what?—Hey, wait a minute. I didn't . . . Besides, if you've only been human for a couple of days, you should still be . . . Unless there's someone else you haven't told me about."

"Someone else?" she said, stretching. "There hasn't been *anyone* yet. But my stomach sure does hurt."

"You probably have a hangover," I informed her. "And when was the last time you ate?"

"Hey, that must be it." She lit up. "Food. Say, what's for breakfast? I'm starved. I haven't eaten in . . ."

I shook my head. "Yeah, I know. Thousands of years."

"Well," she winked. "Not that long, really. I had some ambrosia last century."

"What's it like?"

"Better than artichokes and avocados," she chuckled. "As you Californians might say."

"So, how do pancakes sound?"

"Great," she said, looking out the window. "Mind if I pick some oranges off your landlady's tree? Fresh-squeezed orange juice would be outrageous."

"I see the headache's gone."

"It never really was an ache," she said, getting out of bed. "More like a boat ride. Mind if I take a shower?"

"Go ahead, just don't make it too long. There's a water shortage. Better yet, let me in there first, so *I* can go out and pick some oranges while you're in the shower. I haven't explained my extra guest to Mrs. Okana. With *two* strangers staying here, she'll probably kick me out. Then we'll all be homeless."

I was making an effort to hide my pleasure at being in her company, but probably wasn't doing very well.

Taking a two-song shower, I got dressed and headed downstairs to the orange tree. Mrs. Okana always let me pick whatever I wanted, so I got a dozen or so. When I turned to go back inside, there she was, wearing a simple blue housedress and oversized work boots. She was sweeping her back patio, and when she saw me, looked up and grinned. Her forehead was almost wrinkle-free, despite her sixty or so years, and her wide smile was softened by compassionate eyes.

She asked how Vinnie was doing and I said "Fine, and thanks for taking care of him while I was at work."

I corralled the oranges in my arms and headed for the stairs.

When I got to the third step, Mrs. Okana spoke to me again, wiping perspiration from her forehead. "Don't forget to introduce me to your . . . friend."

"Oh, sorry. She didn't have any place to stay and . . ."

"It's all right," Mrs. Okana said with a wave and a smile. "She can stay as long as she likes."

"Thanks," I said, turning back towards the stairs. "But I'm sure it'll only be a few days. . . . We just met, you know," I added, not able to conceal my excitement.

"Ah," she said, leaning on the broom. "Love at first sight. My favorite kind."

When I got upstairs Erato was dressed and offered to squeeze the oranges while I made some pancakes on the griddle. She ate like a famished beast. Vinnie managed to steal a couple of mine, so I had to make quite a few trips back to the stove. I stared at Erato quite often, purposely not asking any questions that might spoil the breakfast. She didn't seem to mind me watching her, and looked back a lot and smiled.

Once finished, we decided to take a walk on the beach. All three of us piled into the Mustang and drove the mile and a half to the Channel Islands pier. I took a Frisbee in case Vinnie got the urge to play catch.

The pier is about a quarter mile from Cal U., which sits boldly on the cliffs over the Pacific. The parking lot allows you to get right up to where the cliffs begin. I parked at the end closest to the campus and soon our feet were sinking into the sand.

The tide was just touching the rocks, so we had to wait a few seconds and make a run for it to get around the point. We almost didn't get wet. I was worried about Vinnie's getting saltwater in his ear, but Erato said it wouldn't hurt him. The salt might actually be good for the wound, she informed me, as long as we cleaned and dried him afterward.

I accepted her explanation about Vinnie's condition and just let him run wild, not yet asking for a complete rundown on her sister and the hard disk. I just didn't want to spoil the moment.

Vinnie was definitely a real Labrador, because he could hardly wait to go swimming and running in the surf. When he took off down the beach after some sea gulls, it was time to talk.

"I should warn you," I began at last, tossing a rock into the waves, "that Janet told me all about the file. How it's data for a new invention and must not be accessed until she finds a way to retrieve it."

"She's right," Erato answered to my surprise. "Only she doesn't know that the data on the disk is my sister."

"All right," I went along, wrinkling my forehead. "Go ahead and explain. But this better be good."

"I'm not sure how Janet did it," she began, shading her eyes from the sun with her hand. "It might even have been an accident. But it looks to me as if my sister has been transformed from the spirit world into a bunch of bytes and bits, as you say. I'm not an engineer, so I don't know the details. All I know is that Euterpe was somehow able to send out a cry for help just as it happened—that poem you saw on your screen. It was really quite brilliant of her. She purposely didn't finish it, knowing that it would be picked up by me."

"Picked up how?" I asked, going along for the moment. "There are probably thousands of poems written every day. Assuming your story is true, how could you spot *her* message? How would you even know where to look?"

"You'd be surprised," she said, smiling. "Almost nobody writes serious poetry anymore, especially love poetry. It's not like it used to be, when all of the great poets were working at it night and day. I've got a lot of time on my hands. So I sometimes help my sister out with lyrics, stuff like the poem she sent you."

She watched the surf rush to shore while explaining that each poem vibrates with the signature of the author. The vibrations create sound waves. Muses were tuned to certain very high frequencies. That way they could weed out poems and lyrics that didn't vibrate with the kinds of feelings that only come from the heart.

Her sensors had picked up on Euterpe's vibrations. There was no mistaking them. They were very high on the vibe scale.

"Okay, just for the heck of it," I said, kicking some shells on the sand, "let's say I believe you for now. But that still doesn't explain how she got trapped, somehow digitized, and stuck on a hard disk. Let's face it. That sounds impossible."

She stopped walking and stood in front of me, then grabbed me by the arms and looked into my eyes. "Wait, listen to what I'm saying," she said, almost upset. "When she sends a message she vibrates at certain frequencies. If someone were able to replicate those frequencies and digitize them, who knows?"

"Dr. Juanita Vaya," I said, thinking out loud. "She's done some work with superhigh-frequency signal analyzers. . . . You realize," I went on, pulling free of her grip, "that this whole idea sounds crazy."

She gave me a desperate look, so I added, "But if it's at all possible, Dr. Vaya's the one person who could explain how it could happen—besides Janet."

"Now you're getting the idea," she said excitedly. "Besides, it's Dr. Vaya's invention, according to my notes."

She suddenly grabbed my hands and held them in hers. They were alive with excitement. She was like a human power station, putting out a lot of energy, and it was pouring into me. It was like holding onto two high-voltage lines, only without the searing, painful shock, just the surge of enormous electricity. It climbed up my arms and filled my whole body. I began to vibrate all over. Then suddenly it overcame me and I passed out. When I came to, she was holding my head in her hands, but the power surge was over. Her hands felt normal again.

"My god," I said, shaking off the unconsciousness. "What was that?"

"I'm sorry," she said, running her fingers through my hair. "I just got excited, that's all."

"I'll say. How did you do that?"

"It happens sometimes when I get too worked up. Usually I can control it, but I wasn't thinking."

"But where does this . . . this power come from?"

"From inside me," she answered, holding her hands to her chest. "I'm afraid I inherited it from my dad. He handles lightning bolts a lot, and . . ."

"Yeah," I said, rolling my eyes. "I saw his picture in the mythology book."

"Are you all right?"

"Yeah, I guess so," I answered, sitting up at last. "We'd better go."

"We can't," she said, looking down the beach. "I'm afraid Vinnie's disappeared."

"Wait a minute." I grabbed her arm. "What's this about Dr. Vaya's invention?"

"Look, we've got to find Vinnie, then I'll tell you what I know about her."

She took off running down the beach, with me chasing her.

12

Wet Seal

We ran up and down the beach calling, "Here, boy, Vinnie," and anything else we could think of, but still no dog. After fifteen minutes of wasted effort I grabbed Erato by the arm.

"You don't suppose he's gone home, do you?" I asked, catching my breath.

"I don't know," she said, dropping to her knees on the sand. "Sometimes neglected animals don't know where else to go."

"Where does he live?" I asked, sitting down across from her. "Maybe we can cut him off before he gets there." She just gave me a look. "Oh," I said, tossing a handful of sand at some nearby seaweed. "I get it—classified information." I threw up my hands. "Well, what *can* you tell me? This is starting to get on my nerves." I grabbed her T-shirt by the neckband, as if she were a spy and I was interrogating her. "I want some answers. . . . Please," I added, softening my expression.

"The chip," she answered, reading the desperate look on my face. "Dr. Vaya invented it. Or at least the concept. My sister Urania was there when she came up with the idea for nesting data at the molecular level. All Janet did was to fabricate the hardware—the chip. The idea belonged to Dr. Vaya."

"What?" I let go of her neckband and fell back on the sand. "If you knew all this, why didn't you just go to Dr. Vaya yourself, leave out the middleman?"

"She's a scientist," Erato answered, leaning over me on her knees. "Seeing is believing for her. In order to convince her I was on the level, I needed someone Dr. Vaya would recognize . . . and trust."

"Oh, then I suppose as far as believing in wild New Age stories goes, I'm an easy target."

She laughed good-naturedly. "That'll be the day. Here you make me drag out that old song, 'Moon River,' and you say you're easy?" She lay down on her stomach next to me, propping herself up on her elbows. I had an irresistible urge to pull her on top of me, but she wasn't finished talking. "Besides," she went on, "she doesn't have experience with . . ."

"With what?"

"Hacking."

"Hacking?" I turned over on my belly and looked out to sea, watching seals play in the waves. "Forget it," I said automatically. "I'm not in that business anymore."

"But we may need your skill to access the file," she said, sifting sand through her fingers. "Even if we convince Dr. Vaya about what's . . . *who's* on the disk, she's not cleared for the Euterpe file. Janet sealed off all access to it."

I watched a wave crash on the shore and rush up just short of us, then turned and looked at Erato. I told her I still didn't see how her sister could have been digitized and then stored on a hard disk. That wasn't science; it was black magic. There had to be some other connection besides just frequencies and signals. Euterpe was supposed to be a spirit, not a radio signal. Besides, if she was just a bunch of ones and zeros, she couldn't still be alive, in the spirit or any other world. I was sure digitizing would have done her in.

"Maybe she's just inactive," Erato defended. She picked up a sand dollar and tossed it at a retreating wave. "Look, it's all the hope I've got. Accessing the file could bring her back to life. Or at least give us a clue to where she is if she's not on the disk."

I got up and walked toward the ocean, looking down the beach both ways for Vinnie. Out in the water, the seals were beyond the waves, diving for fish. Erato came up behind me. "Did you talk to your sister about this?" I asked, still looking out to sea. "If she was there when the chip was invented, she might know if it's possible to digitize a spirit."

"Well, it just so happens I did," she replied, her head resting on my shoulder. "And she said what Dad's always saying: 'Anything's possible, if you only know how.' She said a spirit could possibly be digitized if the frequencies matched."

I turned around, getting an idea. "Look, why don't you give Urania a call or whatever you do?" I suggested. "We might need some technical expertise. Exactly what is she in charge of?"

"Astronomy," she said, playing with the buttons on my Hawaiian shirt. "I talked with her just before my arrival. That's where I got the scoop on your star. But she understands all sciences. And for your information, I can't just call her. She only picks up science vibes. I'd have to wait for a family reunion, and that's only every hundred years or so."

I gently placed my hands on her shoulders, feeling the bikini straps through her Harley T-shirt. "Why not just leave her a message to show up in the flesh?" I asked.

"Mom would only let one of us come," she answered, looking up at me and slowly unbuttoning my shirt. "We tossed a coin."

"And you lost?"

"No, I won," she said coyly. "That's why I'm here. And I'm getting hot . . . black T-shirts absorb too much sun," she explained, and pulled it off over her head.

"Look," I began, trying not to stare at her pink bikini top. "We've got to go to Dr. Vaya with more than just some wild story. Haven't you got something else we can show her? I don't think the song trick will work with her. If she's like many people, she probably doesn't believe in spirits at all, let alone muses."

"But you believe in the spirit world, don't you." She said it more like a statement than a question, and went back to working on my last shirt button.

"You don't miss much," I said, rolling my eyes. "Yes, for *your* information, I do believe in spirits. But at least they were real people once. Not fairy tales."

"True, and I'm real for now too," she said, popping the last button and opening my shirt. "Look, just because you don't believe something doesn't mean it's not true. It only has to be proved."

"Great," I nodded approvingly. "Now we're getting somewhere. But how are we going to convince Dr. Vaya that a bunch of bits and bytes are really an immobilized spirit? Listen to how it sounds. She'll laugh us out of her lab. That is, if we're lucky."

"Let's just tell her," she answered, unshaken, as she ran her hands over my chest. "The truth is always worth trying first. Besides, I can't think of anything else right now."

She looked up at me and pulled herself close, pushing her body against my chest, then wrapped her arms around me as her bikini top touched me. She arched her head back and pushed herself into me. This time the electricity was the human kind, the man and woman kind. I leaned down to meet her parting lips. The water had slowly moved in, caressing our feet as it rushed past, but I was lost in the moment.

Suddenly, a good-sized wave hit me from behind and we went flying. By the time we sat up in the water, we were turned around, facing the next wave. There was something coming towards us in the center of it—all furry and black, and it wasn't a seal.

"Vinnie!" I yelled as he rode the wave over the top of me, dog-paddling as if there were no tomorrow. He knocked me flat and we rolled over and over in the surf. I finally got my bearings and managed to sit up. The three of us just sat there, splashing around in the surf, Vinnie trying to lick us to death. He had lost his bandage, and out in the water he had looked like one of the seals. No wonder I couldn't find him. And he sure wasn't used to being called by his new name.

"Where'd *he* come from?" Erato finally managed to ask, spitting saltwater.

"Out there," I said, pointing to the herd of seals beyond the waves. "I guess he thought he was a seal or something."

"And I thought this being human was going to be fun," Erato said, getting up at last, dripping wet. She shook her head. "Great memories I'm going to have. Boy, just when it gets interesting, I get knocked flat."

"Welcome to the human race," I said, staggering to my feet. "Wait, what did you say?"

"I said, I thought being human was going to be fun."

"No, not that part. You said something about great memories. Look, didn't I read that your mother is the goddess of memory?"

"Yeah. So?"

"That's it!" I shouted, suddenly hugging her and trying to keep Vinnie down at the same time. "That's the connection I'm looking for."

"I don't get it," she said, returning my hug.

I explained that memory used to be available only in the mind, but that now, with RAM, machines can have memory too, as long as they're plugged in and turned on. Since Euterpe was half memory from her mother's side, maybe she could be stored in memory—RAM. There was only one problem.

Erato looked at me, and then at an oncoming wave. She ran ashore to get out of its path, with me in hot pursuit.

"I still think putting her on the hard disk may have done her in," I said, catching my breath.

"Why?" she asked, squeezing saltwater out of her hair.

"The hard disk isn't memory," I explained, taking off my wet shirt. "It's long-term storage. Maybe, though, there's still a chance. If we can excite the data somehow, maybe she'll come alive again."

Vinnie had been following us, and now that we were starting to dry off in the hot sun, decided it was time to shake off.

"How is all of this going to convince Dr. Vaya?" Erato said, running away from Vinnie toward our towels.

"It's not. It was to convince me."

"But I thought you believed already." She was disappointed. We were at our little pile of stuff on the dry sand. She grabbed a towel and tossed me one.

"I'm sorry," I said, wiping most of the water off myself. "My heart does believe. But I still have a doubting mind. I can't help it. I'm a computer scientist, not a poet. The heart is willing, but the mind is stubborn. It needs explanations to stay happy."

"I think there's too much mind these days," she said, looking me over. "And not enough heart."

"Yeah, I know," I agreed. "It's a twentieth century disease."

We sat on the sand, soaking up the sun. I kept one eye on Vinnie, so he wouldn't get lost again. He lay down and rested next to us.

"Hey," I said, changing the subject a little. "I wonder why she only occupies one hundred megabytes. You'd think there'd be more."

"She's only a spirit, you know," Erato reminded me. "She doesn't need much space, at least not physically. If you ask me, a hundred megabytes is a lot for someone without an earthly body. But then, she's inspired many poets." She picked up a stick and tossed it for Vinnie. "Say, if we get out of this, and there's time, will you teach me to surf?" she asked to my surprise.

"Sure," I laughed, "but let's just take this one wave length at a time. First we go to Dr. Vaya's." Vinnie had come back with the stick, so I wrestled him for it.

"Whew!" Erato said, holding her nose. "What's that smell?"

"Vinnie," I said, still thinking about our predicament, "has rolled in a dead seal or something."

"First," she decided, holding her nose, "we give Vinnie a bath."

Before we left the beach, I washed Vinnie in the waves as best I could. It helped a lot, but the stink was deep down, and wouldn't be coming off soon, not without some soap and water. Giving up on his smell for the time being, I decided to let him run around in the hot summer sun. I tossed the Frisbee for him a couple of times, and he really got into it. At first he shied away, but it was obvious that he wanted to play, so I let him sniff the plastic disk and he was okay.

He ran full-out after it and made some incredible leaps, catching most of my tosses in his mouth. It didn't occur to me until we got ready to leave that he was probably shy because of the red Frisbee. It looked an awful lot like the bloodstained hubcap I'd found on the freeway the night he lost his ear.

Afterward I cleaned the sand out of his ear with some drinking fountain water, and wrapped a towel from the trunk around his head to keep the dirt out. He didn't complain, though I'm sure it was still stinging from saltwater. Labs can take a lot of pain, and a little sting was nothing for a full-grown retriever.

We all piled in the car and headed for home, anticipating a visit soon with Juanita. If she thought we were crazy, then fine, as long as she helped us. Erato had certainly piqued my interest about the file. Hopefully, Juanita could satisfy my curiosity. I was about to find out.

13

Juanita Vaya

Juanita Vaya was pure inventor, more concerned with the subtlety and beauty of a discovery than its marketability. She was handsomely paid for her efforts, though, and would share in the profits generated by her inventions with stock issues, bonuses, and the usual company perks. So by turning her inventions over to Janet, she could get back to pure research, her real love.

With a bachelor's degree in computer engineering from Cal Tech and a doctorate in physics from MIT, she was a formidable brain trust who dwelt in the upper atmosphere when it came to high-tech applied physics. She could have taken a professorship just about anywhere and continued her work unaccosted by the real world, but she liked to see her electronic toys put into action.

Juanita had been teaching a microchip symposium at Cal U. when she met Janet, and the rest was history. Janet stole her away from teaching physics by offering her a forty percent salary increase, a high-tech private lab, and the satisfaction of seeing her inventions put into production. It was not only a major coup for Sigma, but the start of a good working relationship.

I wasn't completely surprised to hear of the invention, given Juanita's abilities, and should have figured right away that she had a hand in it. But Janet was so competent in her own right that it just didn't occur to me to look further. It took Erato to lead me to Juanita. Now, if we could only convince her that we needed her help without looking like we had gone mad.

Deciding not to wait any longer, I called her at home to set up a meeting, preferably immediately. Much to my surprise, she was home and bored and would like to discuss my problem. Yes, I could bring my friend, and Juanita understood that some things could not be discussed over the phone, though neither of us figured our lines were bugged.

After a dog bath that got everyone wet and soapy, we all dried off and got dressed. Vinnie sported a fresh bandage, along with his chain collar, while I put on another Hawaiian shirt, some khaki walking shorts, and Mexican sandals. Erato insisted I wear the shorts, saying it was too hot for pants and legs shaped like mine should get out more often. I gave her a pair of walking shorts I had outgrown and a T-shirt with dolphins on it. Both were too roomy, but she gathered the waist with a belt and we were off.

We piled into the car and headed to Juanita's, with a short stop at Taco Bell for lunch. Vinnie, who had remarkable speed when it came to scooping up food off the seat and floor of the car, vacuumed up all of the leftovers, even though I had gotten him his own burrito. I wondered if his owner had ever fed him real dog food, or just table scraps, and whether I would be getting a call to claim him. Erato made the mistake of trying some of my jalapeños, and did something that looked like a rain dance for a couple of minutes. No one complained, since we needed the water.

Juanita lived on the ocean side of the mountains that practically push Santa Isabella into the Pacific. Her house sat on a hill that the locals referred to as the Riviera, named after the famous one in France. She had purchased an old style Spanish mansion overlooking the city, but had high-teched it as one might expect. Electronic gates, computerized heating, lighting and security systems said old world charm meets modern electronic wizardry.

She greeted us at the front door in a traditional Spanish dress, even though the annual Fiesta celebration was still three weeks away. But I was not surprised, since she seemed to be a collection of tradition and futurism anyway. She was fifty-seven, petite, had just a few wrinkles, and a narrow, straight nose. Her short, black hair went with her dark brown eyes. She was originally from Mexico, and went back there yearly to bring gifts to her family in the little village where she had been born. She had recently talked her parents into moving in with her, and they occupied one wing of the mansion. All of this defined a woman of brilliant intellect, worldly accomplishment, and humble beginnings. If anyone could help us, it was she.

She offered us iced tea and we sat on her patio among the cacti, succulents, and red floor tiles. She insisted on bringing in our hurt dog, inquired about his condition, and let him lie on the patio.

Erato and I had agreed on the way over to avoid the truth for the time being, not giving away the file's contents unless we had to, and not wanting to be turned away as lunatics. With that in mind, I decided to take it slowly at first, starting out with generalized technical questions.

I asked how easy it would be to receive high-frequency signals, digitize them, and store them long-term on a hard disk. She immediately launched into an explanation, saying that it was really quite common for astronomers to receive signals from the atmosphere or even deep space and save them on some medium. Recent advances had made it possible to record directly in a digital format onto tape or hard disk.

"What about RAM?" I asked, already knowing the answer.

"Obviously, having a lot of RAM allows manipulation of massive amounts of data," she confirmed, then set down her iced tea on a glass table next to her chair. "Now, what's the problem you're concerned with?"

"We think there's been a mix-up," Erato replied, leaning forward in her lawn chair. "There seems to be a file on your company computer that belongs to me."

"Shouldn't you be talking to Mr. Cooper?" Juanita asked, slightly annoyed. "Instead of me?"

"We weren't sure about the possibility of storing highly sensitive signals on the hard disk," I answered. "That's why we came to you."

"You'll have to explain," she said, reaching over and taking a sip of her iced tea. "What signals?"

I got up and looked at the mountains behind her estate, trying to think of a way to explain what was going on.

"We're not sure," Erato said behind me. "But we know that someone was doing some work in one of the computer labs the other night, and created a certain file. We have reason to believe that the file contains . . . atmospheric energy signals."

I turned around. "The signals," I began, phrasing my words carefully, "belong to her sister. At least that's what we think. Evidently, she was working with someone at Sigma on a Top Secret project and now she's disappeared, along with her experiment."

"This sounds strange." Juanita frowned, her eyes narrowing. "Have you talked to security? or Janet Stewart?" She looked at Erato. "There's probably a simple explanation for the whole thing."

"That's just it," I explained, thrusting my hands in my pockets. "Janet claims that she was the one working in the lab that night, and that the new file is hers. She didn't say anything about Erato's sister."

"Which file is it?" she asked, then got up and walked over to a tall, potted spiny cactus.

"I'm not allowed to talk about it," I said flatly.

"Then I don't see what I can do," Juanita said, running a finger along one of the three-inch thorns. "I suggest you go to the authorities if you suspect foul play."

Erato got up and began to pace the courtyard. "We believe the file is the key to my sister's whereabouts," she said impatiently, turning to face Juanita. "She sent Cyrus a screen message just before she disappeared. We don't want to go to the authorities until we access that file.

"If we go to them now," she went on, "Janet, or whoever is responsible for my sister's disappearance, could erase the file. Then we might never find my sister alive. The file is on the

Top Secret disk, so Cy's not able to access it."

Juanita was intrigued, but cautious. She stopped stroking the cactus thorn. "You think Janet is covering something up?" she asked, moving toward a Spanish-style fountain in the middle of the courtyard; it was overflowing with succulents instead of water.

"We can't say for sure." I moved toward the fountain. Glancing at Erato, I said, "Maybe the file only contains Janet's new invention, as she claims. But it might contain a clue to the whereabouts of Erato's sister."

"There are no other clues?" Juanita asked, sitting on the fountain ledge.

"All we have is this," I replied, pulling a scrap of paper out of my shirt pocket and handing it to her. It contained the screen message I had written down in case we needed it.

She opened it carefully and read. A look of concern came over her face. "This is either a bad practical joke"—she frowned—"or your sister's in serious trouble. What project was she working on at the time of her disappearance?"

"We're not sure," I answered, sitting down next to her on the ledge. "But we know it has something to do with atmospheric signals, possibly voice pattern signals."

Erato moved in and stood over us, only a foot away. "Well, can you at least tell me her name?" Juanita asked, looking impatiently at Erato. "*That's* not classified, is it?"

"Yes, it is," I told her, holding Erato back. "Janet and Cooper said so."

"Wait a minute," Juanita said, her eyes growing intense. She raised her hand and pointed at Erato. "I thought Janet didn't know about your sister's involvement with the file? So how can her name be classified?"

"The name of the file is my sister's name," Erato explained. "That's why we think it's stolen and she's been, shall we say"—she brushed a strand of hair from her face—"Immobilized."

Juanita was surprised. "You don't mean to say that Janet wasn't smart enough to change the filename, do you? It seems unlikely that she would think no one would come looking for your sister and the file."

Erato knelt on the tiles opposite Juanita and looked her straight in the eye. "Janet doesn't know about me," she explained. "It probably never occurred to her that someone would come here looking for my sister."

"Why not?" Juanita asked, undaunted. "Didn't she know your sister had friends or relatives?"

"My sister has no living friends or relatives, except for me, and I'm sure Janet didn't even know I existed. I'm supposed to be . . ." She stood up and smoothed her shorts. "Well, let's just say I've come out of hiding after a long time."

Juanita got up and walked over to the small table next to her chair, picked up her glass, and took a sip of iced tea. She held out the glass and pointed it at Erato. "Why now?" she persisted. "Why did you come back? And how did you know your sister was in trouble?"

Erato sat on the fountain ledge next to me and explained that she kept in contact with her sister by shortwave, and had received a distress signal last Wednesday night. She got the same message as I did, only Euterpe left her locational coordinates. Erato was able to determine that the signal was coming from somewhere inside Sigma.

"Does your sister always leave such strange messages?" Juanita asked, waving the note in her other hand. "Is this some kind of code?"

"In a way," Erato nodded, crossing her legs at the ankles. "She's a poet of sorts. The message was very much like her." Suddenly losing all patience, she marched over and got nose to nose with Juanita.

"Look," she said, throwing up her hands. "Cyrus can't tell you, but *I* can. Her name's Euterpe."

Juanita looked puzzled. "I can't say I've heard of her." She sat down again in her lawn chair.

"All right," I cut in. "The cat's out of the bag." I got up and walked over to them. "It's Janet's name for the new two-hundred-fifty-six-meg RAM chip you developed. Or at least she said so."

"That's odd," Juanita replied, setting her iced tea on the glass table. "I named it DATANEST, after the theory behind it. I guess she figured that name might give too much away, or be too easily recognizable to product spies."

I explained that Janet said the file contained test data to check the RAM chip's parameters. She couldn't release the data until she got it operational. And maybe not even then.

"Look," Erato added, a little frustrated. "All I want is to get my sister back. Can't we find a way to swap what's in the Euterpe file with some other file? If the data really belonged to my sister, and Janet erases it or something, we may never know what happened to her."

"I'm sorry," Juanita said, handing me the paper. "I'm afraid I can't help you."

"But . . ." Erato was speechless.

"Come on," I said to Erato, taking the paper and grabbing her arm. "This is a lost cause. Obviously, the doctor can't help us."

"Or won't," Erato said sharply.

I pulled her away and we headed for the door. Vinnie got up from his spot in the sun and ran after us. "Don't show us out," I said over my shoulder. "We'll find the door by ourselves."

"Wait a minute," Erato said angrily, just before we left the patio. "I didn't finish my tea."

"What has that got to do with anything?" I asked, frustrated and confused. But Erato went over and picked up her full glass of iced tea and drank it all, clinking a half dozen ice cubes against the glass before she set it down. I accidently dropped the note when Vinnie licked my hand, and when I picked it up, something caught my eye. The ice cubes had melted instantaneously in Erato's glass, now half-full of water.

I didn't say anything, we just left and rode home in silence. When we got upstairs, the light on the answering machine was blinking. It was Juanita. She wanted to talk.

14

Legs

I dialed Juanita, who didn't waste any time. "Look, I've got an idea that might solve everyone's problem," she suggested over the phone. "I'll be at your place in fifteen minutes. How do I get there?"

Before Juanita arrived, I noticed Erato surveying my apartment, with a quizzical look in her eyes. "What do you call this . . . this eclectic style of decorating?" she asked with a wry smile.

"Eclectic means the best of various styles combined," I told her. "This"—I pointed around the place from my bedroom doorway—"is California bachelor. Or in other words, one step up from early orange crate and dormitory style." I looked around at my stuff. To an outsider it might have appeared strange, but to me it was home.

I had my latest surfboard in the corner of the kitchen, complete with a small puddle of sand. A green Formica dining table from the early sixties sat in the middle, surrounded by matching period chairs. The living room sported embarrassingly drab drapes, a brown sofa with a weave that looked like a neurotic TV test pattern, a torn Naugahyde recliner, some vaselike lamps with ancient shades, and my simulated oak entertainment center that covered one wall. Add to that an aging double bed in the other room, some rickety rattan nightstands, a mismatched dresser, and there you had it. What more could a guy want?

"Okay, interior decorator I'm not," I said, scooting across the living room. "But I call it home."

"It's you," she said, making an okay sign with her hand, and I wasn't sure if it was a compliment or not. "Besides, I've seen some poets' places that make this look like the Biltmore."

"Poets have an excuse," I replied, sitting down in my recliner. "They don't give one whit about materialism. Whereas I, dear lady, am just tasteless and cheap. Look, you've got a purse full of hundreds, why don't I take you to a good hotel. You don't have to stay in this dump."

"I don't know the first thing about hotels," she said, plopping down on my dusty couch. "Besides, somebody has to sleep with Vinnie."

"Sorry," I laughed, "I thought he was with me."

"What I'm trying to say," she offered, "is that the couch is fine with me. We could use the money to get you some decent furniture."

"What? And ruin my image?" I leaned back in the recliner and made a grand gesture. "Nothing doing. But you're welcome to crash here if you want. Mrs. Okana cleared you for landing on the couch."

Juanita showed up a quarter of an hour later, a glass half-full of water in her hand. She set it on the kitchen counter, knowing she owed us a favor before we got into the physics of Erato's human microwave ability. She didn't sit down, preferring to stand in the corner of my microscopic living room instead.

"Let's duplicate the file," Juanita suggested after a long,

slow glance at Erato. "Then we'll take the copy and see what's on it. That way, Janet will still have her data, and you'll have what *you* want."

I got up and began to pace. We were getting in too deep to keep Juanita out of the loop much longer. I looked out the window at the ocean; sunlight reflected brilliantly off the water. The islands in the channel sat calmly off the coast, looking much closer than twenty or so miles. I wondered how much longer Erato and I could remain islands, or whether we'd have to make contact with the mainland at any moment.

"Well . . ." I began, still looking out to sea. "The only way to duplicate the file is to have Janet let us in. She insists that only she and Cooper have complete access to all Top Secret files."

"Let's try Cooper, then," Erato suggested, leaning forward on the couch.

"Nothing doing," I said, turning around. "This might be just what he needs to get me fired."

Juanita cut in. "You want me to talk to Janet, don't you?" We both nodded. "She can be pretty stubborn," Juanita continued, straightening her white Fiesta dress. "I'll have to tell her I want to run some experiments and see if she tells me about her RAM problems. That's all I can do." She walked over and leaned against my kitchen counter.

"But I must warn you," she said ominously, "if Janet looks on the level to me, I'll be forced to report this visit. And even if I'm granted access to the data, I can't just let you thumb through it like the Sunday *Times*. It would have to be a very controlled experiment." She looked at the glass she had brought as it sat on the counter not a foot away from her.

"Doctor," I said gravely, running my hands through my hair, "we believe what we're looking for is some kind of audio signal Euterpe would have stored in the file. All we want you to do is play it back. If she left a message, we'll hear it. If it turns out to be computer test codes, we'll know. It'll probably sound like a modem transfer or something unintelligible." I put out my hands. "That's all we ask. We don't want to see any data. Only hear it."

She looked at me with a very serious expression. "I want you to promise you won't try to find a back door into that file until I talk to Janet," she ordered. "Otherwise . . ."

"You've got our word on it," I said, looking quickly at Erato. "I promised myself no more hacking. Getting caught once was enough. We're counting on you to get Janet's permission. Convince her to duplicate the data. She should at least allow you that much, Doctor, unless she's hiding something."

"If Janet was having trouble with the chip," Juanita said, "she should have called me by now."

"Yes, she should have," Erato agreed. "That's why we're counting on you to get her to budge. After all, it is your invention."

Juanita was sympathetic, but practical. She stopped tracing the rim of the glass and explained that it was not her data. Once it made it to the hard disk her chip was out of the picture. She stared at us and shook her head, but finally agreed to test our hypothesis about the file—in the name of scientific discovery. She would present our case as if it were her idea. If Janet vetoed it, we were on our own. She picked up the glass, swirling the water inside.

"Then you'll help us?" Erato asked, starting to get excited.

"As soon as you explain this," Juanita said, drinking the water. "I tested it in my lab at home before I left the message. You did melt the ice, didn't you?" It was more of an accusation than a question.

Erato was up to the task.

"First, the data," she said. "Then the secrets of my . . . shall we say, electric touch? Now, are you sure you can't contact her today? It could be a matter of life and death."

"All right," Juanita agreed after a pause, holding up the empty glass. "Let's just say you've piqued my curiosity . . . I'll contact her," she advised us, setting the glass firmly on the counter. "Then I'll call you." She looked around my woefully decorated apartment. "Are you staying . . . here?"

"Uh, yes," I replied. "Yes, she is. If we're not here, leave a message on the machine."

After Juanita left, Erato asked from the couch, "Do you really think Dr. Vaya's going to help us?"

"Can't say for sure." I shrugged and closed the front door. "But if your sister's on the disk, playing it back should give us her voice as it was last heard. Then, we'll take it from there."

"I agree it's a start," Erato said, planting her feet on the coffee table. "But what good is her voice without *her*?"

I turned around, walked into the kitchen and grabbed a Diet 7UP out of the refrigerator. Popping the top, I reminded her that if a voice pattern was on the disk, then we'd at least have something to go on. I didn't know if it was possible to replicate a spirit. That would be tantamount to audio cloning. But if anyone could bring her back to life, it was Juanita.

"Besides my father," Erato said cautiously, lying back on the couch.

"Cy," she added, changing the subject. "Thanks for believing in me."

"I'll try anything once," I laughed, leaning against the kitchen counter. "Except maybe wearing a suit and tie to work or bungee cord jumping. But if this lands me in jail, I'm going to be very disappointed."

"I'm sorry," she said, putting her hands behind her head and fluffing one of my mismatched couch pillows. "I didn't want to involve you. But it seemed as if I had no choice."

"Except for calling in your dad, of course," I said sarcastically.

"Yeah, I know. Answering to him can be . . ."

"No, it's not that." I wandered over and sat down on the coffee table. "I'm not scared of him," I joked. "He's supposed to be a great guy, right? After all, he did make the oceans. It's just that you can't surf from a jail cell, that's all."

"I'm glad to see you're taking a worldview," she quipped, turning on her side toward me. "It's great to see someone who's not selfish. Someone who sees the big picture."

"Hey," I said, "everyone's not trying for the Nobel peace prize, you know."

"Yeah," she agreed. "And everyone's not in your sandals, either."

"Thanks," I answered, taking a sip of soda. "For reminding me of my responsibilities. It helps to take the pressure out of the situation."

She sat up and put her hands on my knees. "I was just trying to add some perspective to your life, that's all. To help round out the package."

"What package?"

"Nothing," she said, getting embarrassed for the first time. She pulled her hands back and folded them in her lap. "Other than the fact that a woman could, and I did say *could*, find you attractive."

"Well, at least that's a start." I smirked, setting my can of soda down on the coffee table. "Because in case you hadn't noticed, you're not half-bad yourself."

"Which half do you like?" she teased.

"The outside . . . so far. But I'm working on liking the rest."

"When you get it worked out, let me know." She lay down on the couch and put her shapely legs in the air. "But keep in mind that I've only got until next Saturday." She winked.

That was the part I didn't like, I thought, studying the line of her legs, though I was beginning to think it didn't matter. After all, she was the one who said nobody knows how long they have. With some luck, this thing with her sister could be over by that night.

"There's no point starting something we can't even begin to finish," I finally said.

"Good idea," she sighed, putting her legs back down and pulling her shorts over her thighs. "I was starting to think about that motel offer you made the other night."

"What I meant," I said, defending myself, "was that I would have dropped you off by yourself."

"I know," she smiled. "But that's not what I meant just now. I was seeing us . . ." She looked at the ceiling. "You know . . . between the—"

"Don't say any more," I said, getting up. "I'm getting excited just thinking about it."

"Yeah," she agreed, rolling over on her stomach. "We'd better drop it for now. We've got work to do."

Maybe she wasn't falling for me; perhaps it was all just an act to get to the secret file. But there was always hope, and that was good enough just then.

15

Father Figure

The bigger one of us decided he was still starved, so I made a mad dash to Colonel Sanders', leaving Erato to field any calls. After I returned we were sunning on the back patio, eating Kentucky Fried chicken and mapping out our next move, when the phone finally rang. I had to dash upstairs to catch it before the answering machine did, barely making it in time.

Janet had said no, Juanita informed me, saying she didn't

want another copy of the test data floating around until the bugs were out. She did say Juanita could use her backup, but wanted to be there before any experiments were run with the data. She didn't make it sound like anyone without Top Secret clearance would be welcome. "I'm sorry, Cy," Juanita concluded, "but I'm afraid that leaves you out of the picture."

Expecting as much, I launched into a planned offensive, asking if Janet had been using some kind of signal processor the other night. Juanita admitted discussing the nature of the data, but Janet had said it was strictly RAM chip commands.

"Look, it's your invention," I said, finally getting upset. "Why don't you muscle her out? Tell her you want to run an experiment by yourself."

"I tried that," she sighed. "She wasn't buying. But I can't say that I blame her. She just wants to be there when I work with her data. She thinks maybe we could solve the transfer problem if we worked on it together."

"Don't you think she's being a little too cautious with the data?" I protested. "After all, you said she has a backup."

Juanita was nonplussed, saying that Janet just didn't want to be left out when a solution was found to the transfer problem.

"Frankly, I'm not surprised," she said. "It will be a momentous occasion. I'm sure she wants to share in the glory. It seems only natural."

I agreed with a sigh, then asked Juanita if she had mentioned me or Erato. No, she hadn't, though she had thought about it. Apparently she wanted to give us a chance to clear things up. She gave us until Monday to talk to Janet. Then Juanita would tell her everything.

"I'm sorry, Cyrus," she apologized. "But I can't afford to get involved in matters of missing persons. You may go to security, the authorities, or Janet as you see fit. But I've done all I can. It seems to me, however, that Janet deserves a chance to clear herself of any accusations by outsiders. But that's up to you."

I sighed. "Thanks for doing what you could. I don't suppose you'd play the data on a recorder just to see if there's any audio message on it?"

"I'm sure Janet wouldn't go for that. . . . Well, good-bye Cyrus, and good luck . . . oh, before I forget. You don't suppose Erato would explain her magic trick, do you? I'm a fan of

David Copperfield, you know. I like to figure out how illusions work."

"No kidding," I said, almost laughing, "I didn't know. But that will have to wait, I'm afraid." Erato must have found something in Juanita's file about it—before zapping the ice in the glass.

I hung up the phone and turned to Erato, who had come upstairs and been pacing the floor, taking it all in. Vinnie had joined her, following her back and forth on my gold shag carpet.

"I guess you heard all that."

She stopped pacing and gave me a cold stare. "Sure did. Now what? Mr. Reformed Hacker."

"Look," I began, staring at her. "How do I know your sister—the missing 'spirit'—is on the file anyway? How do either of us know whether a spirit occupies exactly one hundred megs of disk space? Maybe it's not really her. Maybe she just . . . broke up. Maybe she's . . ."

"I've thought about all that," she replied impatiently. "But it's all we've got to go on right now. Where else are we going to look? She's not on the . . . other side, as you call it. She's missing in action. Look, why can't we just . . . sort of *borrow* the hardware."

"You mean steal the disk? Well, besides getting fired and arrested, we'll probably get caught trying to get it out of the building.

"Wait a minute," I added, "that's pretty immoral for the daughter of a god to be suggesting. And so are your hints about hacking. What kind of spirit are you, anyway? You don't sound like one from the heavens, talking like that."

She thought for a moment and flushed red. Then she went to the couch and sat down, head in her hands.

"You're right," she confessed. "Listen to me. I'm starting to sound like a common thief. I've never had thoughts like that before. Being human must be doing this to me. The truth is, I'm worried. Because if Euterpe is on the disk, she's a prisoner—and she's only ever known freedom. Except for the house calls we make, we can go anywhere we like, do what we want."

"But . . . your dad's a god," I protested, standing my ground. "He'll take care of her soul. She does have one, right?"

"Of course." She looked up at last. "But if *he* steps in . . ." She shook her head. "Never mind. We'll think of something."

"Why don't you just ask your dad where she is?" I was getting perturbed and gesturing wildly. "He should know everything. Tell him *you'll* get her back. That way *he* doesn't have to get personally involved."

"I can't," she said, frustrated, and lay down on the couch. Vinnie crawled up and put his head on her stomach. She looked me straight in the eye while she petted Vinnie. "Dad still doesn't know I'm here. I was hoping *someone* would be able to access the file and I could get her back before he found out. But since it's apparently password-protected, only you can help."

"Password-protected? Muses don't talk like that." I rubbed my forehead. It was my turn to pace the floor. "Look," I said finally, "*I* believe you, or at least I want to, but . . . we may need more proof if we're going to convince anyone else."

"Starting with the doubts again, huh?" she said to the ceiling. "Well, Mr. Skepticism, for your information, I did some reading about computers at the local library. Besides, muses talk whatever language is in vogue. We have to keep up on these things, you know. When in Rome, and all that.

"Look," she added, "couldn't we just think of it as freeing a prisoner who's been unjustly jailed?"

Stopping to lean against the kitchen counter, I said, "I don't do break-ins. And that's that."

She went on as though I hadn't even spoken, sitting up to make her point. "Cy, listen. This could be very serious. Someone may have wanted her locked up and the password thrown away."

"Who would do such a thing?" I shrugged. "It doesn't make sense."

"Someone who doesn't like poetry, maybe. Or the opposite—an unpublished poet. There could be a revenge motive. We know from our files that Janet was a frustrated lyricist."

"Wait a minute," I argued, marching over and sitting on the other end of the couch. "Just because Janet's unfulfilled doesn't mean—"

"What I'm telling you is that I think somebody may have wanted my sister out of action," she interrupted. "Either that, or it was some incredible accident. It doesn't make much difference. Either way, I've only got another week to free her. Then I'm gone."

"But I was just starting to—"

"When I transformed myself to human," she broke in, "my mother made me promise I'd come back no later than a week from today. Then, I'm a spirit again, whether Euterpe is free or not. And . . . she tells Dad. If he doesn't know already." I gave her a look, so she explained that her mom thought being human was too dangerous. Too many temptations. "Frankly . . ." She looked at me intensely. "I'm beginning to think she's right."

"What will Zeus do?" I asked sarcastically. "Throw a thunderbolt? And by the way, we could use a little help, you know."

"He normally doesn't interfere with mortals," she said, putting her feet on my lap. "The earth is human beings' work. . . . Unless . . ."

"Unless what?"

"Unless he finds out both Euterpe and I are missing."

"Then what?"

She lay back with her hands behind her head. "Remember the great flood?" she asked half-seriously.

"He did that? What a lousy deal that was."

"Poseidon liked it. . . . Hey," she winked, trying to cheer herself up, "I thought you *liked* water?"

"Yeah, but even surfers have limits. We like a little dry land once in a while."

I got up, went over to the window, and looked out. From my upstairs apartment you could see the mountains on one side and the ocean on the other. It was beautiful, but sometimes it seemed like you were in an elaborately set trap. Paradise has its price. And that price is freedom. I didn't feel that way very often, but on that Saturday afternoon, I felt as trapped as a beautiful village squeezed between the mountains and the ocean—with nowhere to go when the earthquake hit.

"Didn't he say," I asked, looking out to sea, "that he wouldn't use water again?"

"There's always other stuff," she said matter-of-factly. "Thunderbolts start fires too, you know."

"Would he really do that just to get his daughters back?"

She sat up and began petting Vinnie again. "Wars have been fought for less."

"Why doesn't he just come and get her?" I asked with a gesture, as if I had a magic wand. "Wave his hand or something?"

"Not his style. He's got an image to protect. Father figure and all that."

"That's kind of old-fashioned, isn't it?" I smirked.

"Not really," she said right off. "Even today everyone wants their leaders to be men and women of action. People still need strong leadership. Otherwise they run amuck."

"You don't suppose," I said facetiously, "we could get in a little shopping before the world ends, do you? You need your own toothbrush."

"Cyrus, be serious," she replied with a frown. "We've got to think of a way out of this without Dad's influence."

"I am being serious," I defended. "Shopping will take our minds off it for a while. Help us relax. Besides, we can't do anything now, unless Janet's at home."

"Try her," she ordered.

I dialed her number, but only got an answering machine. Leaving a message for her to phone, I then called Sigma: no answer. Hanging up, I turned to Erato, suggesting again that we get out of the apartment for a few hours. I could check my messages by remote from any phone. I pointed to the stuff around my apartment and said, "As you can see, shopping's not one of my great skills; you could give me some lessons."

She laughed nervously. "All right. But I'd say we're both in trouble. I haven't bought anything, ever . . . except those motorcycle duds in the other room."

Looking at the faded dolphin T-shirt I had given her to wear, and then down at her baggy shorts, even I thought it was time for some new clothes.

"Look," I said. "We've got all that's required: need, desire, and what's in your purse. Taste isn't a prerequisite."

She looked around my apartment. "I see what you mean. Okay, I'll tell you what. It's my money—I'll make the choices in what we buy."

"I wouldn't have it any other way."

"You don't think we're being frivolous?"

I walked over the the couch. "Frivolous? Somebody's got to stimulate the economy. Besides, life's too short and full of pressing problems. You've got to have *some* fun. Otherwise, it's not much of a thrill to be human."

"Yeah," she said, grabbing my hands. "That's part of the reason I'm here anyway—to experience life firsthand. But . . ." She pulled herself up and into my arms. "Promise me you'll try to think of a way to . . ."

"Of course." I lifted her over the coffee table and set her down on her feet. Looking at her profile I added, "I can hardly think of anything else."

"Me too," she said, giving me the once-over.

I had her convinced to go to the mall. Maybe getting out of my too small apartment for awhile would help an idea to bubble up to the top of one of our minds. And with some luck, we could catch it before it flew away, or popped.

16

Seamen's Wharf

Just as we were about to head downstairs and pile into the car, Erato said, "Hey, let's take Vinnie."

"Naw, I don't want to leave him cooped up in the car while we're having fun."

"Can't we take him in the stores?" she asked, grabbing her purse.

"Not unless he's a seeing-eye dog," I answered, combing my hair.

She gave me a look that I didn't like. "Forget it," I said on the way out the door. "We are not buying a red-tipped cane just because you want to have a little fun. Besides, it's against the law to impersonate a visually impaired person."

"Yeah," she agreed, standing on the porch. "But it'll get us a better parking space."

When I didn't say anything, she added, "Okay, I was just kidding. Some of the greatest artists of all time have been blind: Stevie Wonder, Ray Charles, José Feliciano. They see better with their music than most people with eyes."

"You're right," I agreed, closing the front door behind us. "But we're still not taking Vinnie. We can take him for a walk when we get back. Besides, if someone I know sees me with a white cane, dark glasses, and a bandaged dog, I'm off their Christmas card list forever."

"*You*," she said, surprised, "get Christmas cards? You're so lucky. I'm never gotten one single card."

"Well, where would they send it?" I asked, starting down the stairs. "Mount Olympus? Or would they address it to the Spirit World? Sounds like a new attraction at Disneyland."

She caught up when we got to the car and gave me a stare. "Don't give me any ideas," she said, climbing over the door to my convertible. "Besides, Anaheim is one-hundred twenty miles south of here, and we're going shopping, remember? Now, which way to Nordstrom?"

"Nordstrom? You've got expensive taste for someone who just crawled over a car door."

She opened her purse, reminding me of the stacks of hundred-dollar bills. "*I* can shop anywhere I want," she said in a fake snooty voice, "because I have what *they* want."

"Well," I said, opening my door and getting behind the wheel. "We'd better get going. We have to stop by my bank and change those bills into something smaller. Fortunately, they're open Saturdays."

Once at the bank, you can only imagine the looks we got when she popped open her purse. I had to make up some wild story about how her identification was stolen and luckily her money was locked in the trunk.

The clerk stared at us, and didn't quite believe it. When the manager came over, he was happy to see all of that cash, but quietly and remorsefully explained that some form of ID was needed to open an account for Erato. She said her dad was a ruler, and she was from Greece. The manager certainly didn't want to create an international incident, but still needed proof of identity.

"You can't call him up," Erato said straight-faced. "He doesn't speak to just *anyone*. It would take an act of God to get him on the phone."

She further explained that she goes by the single name Erato, like other jet-setters: Madonna, Cher, Sting, and such. She even pointed to a bright red Ferrari we had parked next to. Okay, so she forgot to mention ours was the beat-up Mustang; at least she pointed in the right direction. Despite all of our efforts, the manager just said that rules were rules and had to be strictly obeyed.

Erato finally lost all patience and stormed out of the bank, bulging purse in hand. I ran after her, saying we could always deposit it in my account for the time being. She was too upset to listen, telling me that she wasn't going into a bank again. She obviously didn't like being hassled, cooling off only when I dropped the subject and whisked her away in my badly tuned car to the downtown shopping paradise called El Centro Nuevo. It translates to "the new center" in English, but the real interpretation was big bucks.

She bought all kinds of wonderful clothes: a genuine safari outfit, some classy jeans, and an evening dress that looked like something she could wear to the Academy Awards, complete with pearls, diamond watch, and high heels. She turned to me at that point and said, "All I get to wear in the spirit world is one of those flowing Greek gown things. Dumb. They never keep up with fashion up there. The clothes are ancient."

"I thought they didn't have bodies up there?" I asked, ignoring the odd stare of the salesclerk.

"Our spirits are in the shape of human bodies," she informed me. "Unfortunately, my family still dresses as if Greece ruled the world."

"What do you use for material, clouds?" I smirked, standing between racks of dresses.

"Something like that," she replied, not really intending to answer my question. So I dropped it.

Before it was over she also got perfume, a negligee, makeup, and what she had come for—a toothbrush. Then she turned on me, forcing me to buy a CD player, a Rolex diver's watch, some expensive casual wear, designer sweaters, and even a suit and serious shoes. She cared nothing about price tags. The suit cost a grand, and the tie was a hundred bucks. A hundred bucks! My dad paid fifty dollars for his first car, and I'm walking out of the store with two old cars worth of tie. I tried to protest, but not too hard, especially with store clerks going crazy, as if we were celebrities or something. I called home once but there were no messages. Just as we were pulling away, leaving the place restocking its merchandise, I had a serious thought.

"Erato," I said, looking over at her. "Something's bothering me. In the New Testament it says God only had a son."

"Let me put it this way," she replied, arranging some packages in the backseat. "Before you ask any classified questions—*and*, for your information, questions about the beyond *are* Top Secret—I must inform you that I am forbidden to address matters about heaven, hell, and such. It would spoil the great plan." She squeezed my neck with her hand. "And don't you dare ask about that."

"I . . . I wasn't going to. Sorry."

"I can only tell you this much," she answered, turning back around. "Or else I'm in serious trouble. There may be only one God, but he has lots of names and many helpers." She looked at her makeup in the rearview mirror. "You do the best you can to follow your own particular beliefs," she added, "and he'll do the best he can to point you in the right direction."

"So is Zeus God?" I asked, grabbing the mirror back at a stoplight. "Or just a helper?"

"You don't seriously think I am going to answer that, do you?"

"Well, it was worth a try. And by the way, you're fine with or without makeup."

She smiled at that, and batted her eyes at me for fun. No, we hadn't thought of any solutions to her sister's dilemma, but the day wasn't over yet.

When we got home Vinnie was waiting anxiously for us. He even went over and grabbed his leash off the hook by the door. That was enough of a clue. We put away the things we had bought, stashed the cash in my beat-up suitcase in the closet, and piled into the car, deciding to take a walk on the main pier, and to think some more—since no messages had yet been left on the answering machine.

We discussed a few ideas on the way, but none that bear repeating. Some were as bad as my idea to hack-in to the class schedule files my last year at Cal U. All I was really trying to do was impress some of my dorm buddies with my computer skills, and arrange a few classes to accommodate my schedule, but it backfired.

Yeah, I got kicked out, but on my way off campus, security stopped me at the gate. There was another hacker. This one was after grade files. It took a week, but I got her, and was allowed to graduate with my degree in computer science. Then I managed to get hired by Sigma, over Cooper's objection, but with Janet's blessing. That incident was the reason I promised to swear off hacking, and dropped it as a possible solution to getting into the file.

Seamen's Wharf was an old wooden pier that had survived many storms and two major fires. It stuck out into the Pacific about a quarter of a mile, and had room on the side for shops and a couple of restaurants. From out on the wharf you could see the city lodged between the four-thousand-foot mountains and the sea, homes terraced up as far as they could before the raw terrain took over. Since the California coast took a detour west, the city faced south toward Los Angeles, as if looking down from its lofty perch a safe distance away. Next to the pier was the man-made harbor, lots of hotels, and tourists by the busload.

Cars, roller skaters, and even dogs on leashes were allowed on the pier. We watched a couple of crabs crawl around in a saltwater tank at the end of the wharf and a few fishermen catching little more than bait, took a long walk on the boardwalk, and stayed for the sunset. It was a magnificent array of reds, pinks, oranges, and yellows. But it wasn't long before the sun pulled the bright colors and warmth with it as it disappeared for the day, leaving deep blues, purples, and stars to take its place. We took one last walk on the pier, counting stars and almost forgetting our predicament, though I called home twice: no messages.

It was after nine when Erato finally turned to me and said, "That was really something, especially watching the sunset. Not that I haven't seen it before, but it feels different watching it with someone besides your sisters."

"Hey," I said, jabbing her lightly in the ribs. "Your old man makes a heck of a day. Let's eat—aren't you famished?"

"Yeah, now that you mention it. Maybe that's why my stomach is growling."

We walked along the noisy wooden planks on the pier to the Breakwater Restaurant and ate fresh fish. She had lobster and I had shark. We drank some wine. This time she went much more slowly on the down-the-hatch trick. Then we left, giving Vinnie a rare fish fillet treat that Erato ordered "to go." A local band was playing a slow song upstairs, and I turned to her as Vinnie finished his fish outside the restaurant overlooking the harbor.

"You ever do any slow dancing?" I asked, glowing from the wine.

"Yeah," she shrugged, "but only with my . . ."

"You're not going to . . . you know . . . turn on the high voltage lines are you?"

"No." She smiled. "I'm in control now."

"Oh, really?" I grinned. "I like that in a woman. I find it exciting."

"Okay," she apologized, "so I blew it once. It won't happen again."

"And the ice cubes?" I asked, frowning good-naturedly.

"Nothing any microwave couldn't do," she defended. "But as long as I don't lose . . ."

I raised my finger to her lips and made her stop midsentence. I put one arm around her waist and held her in the classic dance embrace. The softness of her delicate hand in mine sent a warm tingle down my arm that filled my whole body. She was wearing just a hint of perfume, and it blended with her natural scent into a sweetness like jasmine in bloom. She smiled, arched her back, and looked into my eyes. Slowly we began to circle, swirling beneath the stars, lost in the lyrics to "Slow Dancing."

She gently placed her head on my shoulder while we moved as one, gliding effortlessly until, at last, the final note echoed into the night.

We stopped and looked at each other. I was drawn into her and leaned forward. Just before our lips met Vinnie let out a loud howl, and we both jumped back. Then we burst out laughing.

"Thanks a lot, Vinnie," I said, rolling my eyes at him. "I suppose you want the next dance?"

He howled again, and tried to jump up on us.

"Poor dog," Erato said. "He feels left out." She looked up at the stars. "Well, I suppose it *is* getting late."

"Yeah," I agreed, a little perturbed. "We'd better get going." I bowed from the waist. "Thank you for the dance."

"My pleasure," she beamed, not a bit of sarcasm in her voice.

"Come on, Vinnie." I reached down to pet his head. "Let's go."

Erato fell asleep on my shoulder on the way home, exhausted by the day's events. Vinnie had his head on my other shoulder as he leaned over the car seat.

When we got home I carried Erato upstairs and put her in bed with her clothes still on. I changed Vinnie's bandage, grabbed a blanket and pillow, and dozed off on the couch. Vinnie took my place in the bed. Sometime around midnight Erato came out of her room, this time wearing her new red negligee. With the night-light on in the background I couldn't make out her expression, but the words were clear enough.

"Cyrus," she said with concern. "I can't sleep."

17

The Whisper of the Muse

"Can't sleep?" I asked, sitting up on the couch. "Why not? Still worried about your sister?"

"It's just that nothing like this has ever happened before," she said, hands on her temples. "I guess I need to know that she's all right."

"But you said she's immortal, right? What could happen to her?"

"I know," she answered, leaning on the doorjamb. "But there are things worse than death. This could be some weird method of torture or something. Who knows what it feels like to be digitized? How would you feel, being broken up into a hundred million bytes?"

"I've got to admit, it would be disorienting."

"Disorienting," she repeated. "Or worse."

I put my feet on the carpet, but didn't get up, then explained that we didn't know how Euterpe felt or where she really was. I didn't even think she was on the hard disk—that she only left a message on it to guide us to her.

"You really think so?" she asked hopefully.

"Sure. You can't digitize a spirit, even in this day and age. It would take black magic or something."

"Yeah," she frowned. "That's what I'm afraid of."

"There's something else you're not telling me," I asked, staring intently at her. "Isn't there?"

She didn't answer, just turned and went back to the bedroom. I got up and followed her, sitting on the end of the bed as she got under the covers.

"Okay," I said at last. "I know a lot of stuff about the other world is still classified, but answer one thing if you can. I just want to know what it's like being a muse. I mean, you're the only one I've ever met. I'd like to know more about you—to even things up a little."

She fluffed her pillow and lay back on it. "It's okay, I

guess," she answered, as though she got this kind of question every day. "There are drawbacks, like any job. We can only go where we're called. The human heart sends out signals and we come. That's how the life of a muse is. Sort of like being a fireman, always on call."

"What if two people call at the same time?" I asked, touching her feet through the covers.

"We toss a çoin, as you say. Or go with the stronger signal. A lot of poetry doesn't get written because the signal-to-noise ratio is too low."

"Are you sure you're not an electrical engineer?"

"I'm just trying to explain it in your terms," she answered, pulling up her legs. She told me that sometimes there's too much outside disturbance for potential poets—work, wars, family responsibilities mainly. And lots of crying-in-your-beer stuff. She was tired of answering the woe-is-me calls . . .

I assure you," she added, shaking her head, "it gets tedious. Right now, though, you may have noticed that I'm on special assignment."

"So I noticed." I chuckled. "Does your dad really *not* know where you are?"

"He usually doesn't interfere with my life. Endless as it is."

"So it's like being a vampire," I surmised. "I mean, you never die and all that."

"Yeah," she agreed, baring her teeth like an angry dog. "Except the artists suck *your* blood for their creative juices."

"Get many calls?" I asked, pretending to look for teeth marks.

"Not like my sister. Euterpe is so busy that she can't screen all of her calls. That's probably how she got fooled on this one. She didn't have time to check the circuit for sincerity."

"What about love songs?" I asked, looking out the window at the moon. "Aren't they just poetry set to music?"

She shook her head and looked out the window. "Some of them," she said. "But many so-called 'love' songs don't have much to do with love."

"Sounds like you're getting bitter," I remarked with a raised eyebrow.

"No, not really," she said with a sigh. "Just a little tired after five thousand years, I guess. And maybe a little disappointed— especially after the fall of Greece and Rome. I'd hate to see that happen here."

"No hope for the human race, then, I suppose?"

"Sure, there's always hope. Besides, there's still some good stuff out there. You just have to look harder to find it."

"One more question, and then I'll leave you alone."

"Shoot," she said, fluffing her pillow.

"How do you inspire artists?"

"You want our trade secrets, huh?" She lay back on the pillow and looked at me. "Well, you're in luck. Just so happens I've been dying to tell someone this for centuries. Besides, if *you* go around telling people, you'll probably get locked up in the loony bin. So here goes."

She put her hands behind her head and began, telling me that muses speak softly in the ears of artists, sometimes even giving them the words they want to write. Other times, just ideas. Muses are speaking from another dimension, so the words are not audible. They just convey the thoughts they want to transmit. The ear can't make out the words, but the message gets through to the brain as thought patterns.

"People who hear voices," I interrupted.

"Yeah," she smirked, "except everyone who hears voices isn't a poet, in case you hadn't noticed. Some guy was taking orders from his dog down here, as I recall."

"Touché, Vinnie," I said to him at the foot of the bed, and looked back at Erato. "Go on, I'm listening."

"When artists stop to think, they are listening for the muse. We only talk when the person stops to listen. More people should try it. It does wonders for communication."

"Could you cut the editorials?" I requested, grabbing her legs through the covers, "and just get to the story?"

"After the artist listens, she writes down the message. Poets call this the whisper of the muse."

I lay there absorbing what she had said, not saying anything for a long while. The next thing I knew she was fast asleep. Yawning, I got up and went back to the couch, leaving her on the bed with Vinnie, and me on the couch with blankets.

Calling Janet again didn't get me an answer. So I left another message to emphasize the urgency of our talking and dozed on the couch, still not sure what to make of Erato. Either I was a blind fool, or there was much more magic in the world than it looked like. Until meeting her, it was enough to see the magic in a sunset or beautiful wave. I hadn't thought much lately about the beauty of poetry, and how it didn't exist much anymore except in songs.

Sometime later she got up again and stood in the doorway. With the night-light behind her, she almost looked like a ghost. I was both startled and captivated by her image.

"Frankly," she began with a sigh, "I'm still worried. If we don't get to the file before Monday, it may be too late for us to do anything. Dad probably knows we're missing by now."

I was getting frustrated. "She's *his* daughter," I snapped. "I think he should be the one to do something about it. Look, he's supposed to be full of love, right?"

She gave me a serious look. "So's the parent who tells her son not to play on the freeway. But the child may not think so. Don't forget as humans you . . . *we* have a limited understanding of the universe. What may be in our best interest may look like punishment to us."

"Do you really think," I asked in an exaggerated tone, "that he's going to pull another stunt like the great flood?"

"Well," she shrugged. "There has been an awful lot of volcanic activity lately. Not to mention seismic movements."

I could see she was serious. "That's what I was afraid of." I held out my hands and looked up, as if speaking to the heavens. "Look, don't get me wrong, I just was just checking."

I looked down at Erato and added, "I left Janet another message while you were sleeping. If we don't hear from her by eight o'clock, I'll call Dr. Vaya and see if she'll at least listen to the tape backup. Then if she won't help, I might— *might*, I said—even try to enter the file without permission if I have to."

"You mean . . . you'll hack-in?" She beamed.

"No, I didn't say that," I answered, waving her off. "I mean try to enter the file merely to check its security. Just to make sure nobody else can access it—make sure it's fully protected. If it's really secure, no one should be able to enter without authorization, not even me."

"Exactly." She grinned, playing along. "Now, wouldn't Janet want you to check every possible hole to make sure the file is secure?"

"Right," I agreed. "I'd just be doing my job. Of course, I'll probably get fired. But what the heck, California has a thousand miles of coastline—maybe there's a job somewhere near the beach with my name on it. I'm past the point of no return as it is. I'll most likely get fired when we tell Janet about our scheme anyway. So I might as well go out with my keyboard blazing." I winked to emphasize my satire.

"Something in your eye?"

"There must be. All I keep seeing is this tempting junior goddess in a negligee standing in my doorway."

"The file," she said. "Then, maybe, if there's time, we can discuss other things." She looked at me. "I said discuss, and *if* there's time, which I doubt."

"Hey, I'm sorry. Forget I said anything. Forget I brought it up. I just thought the way you've been acting that—"

"Cyrus," she scolded, "don't ruin it. A woman likes to feel wanted too, you know—same as a man."

She went off to bed and soon we were both asleep. This time I found *myself* "sleepwalking" to the bedroom. I got in and lay on my side of the bed, thinking about my vow never to hack again. But somehow this seemed different.

It would be wrong to say I was thinking about saving the world, but helping Erato was definitely on my mind.

Just before I dozed off Erato scooted over next to me and put her head on my shoulder. I put my arm around her and she groaned pleasurably. As the moon shone in the window, I looked at her face. She was becoming more beautiful every day. I was asleep when something big, warm, and furry came between us.

18

Day-Glo

I woke up Sunday morning hugging Vinnie, only his head was not the end in my face. Erato was still sleeping soundly on her side of the bed, looking as if she were lost in dreamland. So I got up, made coffee, and took a shower.

After breakfast, reality and caffeine were starting to settle into my head, reminding me that I had work to do.

Not hearing from Janet, and realizing that leaving another message was probably futile, I called Juanita, but her mother said she was out. I left a message for her to call and got ready to go to Sigma to check the file's security. Just to make sure the coast would be clear, I called the office. No one answered, so Cooper wasn't there. I dialed Janet's private line and she picked it up on the fourth ring. She had received all my messages, but flatly refused to discuss anything about the file. Then she hung up.

I informed Erato that I could go to Sigma and try to hack-in, but it would be pretty risky with Janet in her office, probably working on the Euterpe file.

In the meantime, I talked Erato into letting me take her to the beach to teach her surfing. She would have preferred accessing the file, but considering the circumstances, reluctantly agreed to wait a few hours to see if Janet went home. Of course, we could have staked out the parking lot at Sigma and tried to get in right after Janet left, but that might have taken all day. Besides, I had this weird feeling that the clue to Euterpe's disappearance was somehow at the beach.

I was too embarrassed to explain to Erato, but did tell her I was getting strong vibes pulling me toward the ocean. Naturally, she wasn't surprised by that, figuring I was just trying to be cute.

I'd actually had some premonitions in the last few years, but always wrote them off as some kind of weird déjà vu. One was about a car wreck that happened near my apartment. It seemed like I had seen the whole thing in a dream beforehand, but I wasn't exactly sure. Another time I had a dream the night before the Super Bowl that actually showed the scoreboard at the end of the game, and sure enough, it appeared as advertised. I should have bet on that one, but gambling didn't interest me.

I purposely didn't tell anyone, anticipating a questioning response at best. But once every couple of years since the age of sixteen I dreamed something weird. I must have dreamed something about the beach the night before Erato's surf lesson and couldn't remember it, because going to the beach that Sunday felt like I was chasing a premonition that was about to manifest itself. Erato did give me one of those I-did-see-something-in-your-file kind of looks, but we didn't discuss it.

"Surfing *is* something I've wanted to do for centuries," she confessed over coffee. "But Poseidon was always too busy to give me lessons."

We decided to leave Vinnie at home, away from seals both dead and alive, and took off for the beach with the top down and my surfboard in the backseat, knowing full well that we wouldn't be able to stop thinking about our predicament, but needing some fresh air and sunshine all the same.

When we got to the beach I had her watch me first, and then took her out on the waves. After awhile we had to move down the beach, since there were a lot of surfers out for the weekend. Seemed like many of them felt the need to offer lessons in case I got wiped out. It might have had something to do with the way Erato almost fit into her pink bikini.

We went down the beach to a less crowded spot and struggled together on the board, trying to catch waves. It was like trying to wrestle on a floating log—fun, but we kept falling off. She almost got to where she could stand a couple of times, but ended up with a few knee and belly rides. We clowned around, splashed, and played Jaws until we laughed so hard we both began swallowing too much water.

We were so lost in the excitement that we completely forgot ourselves and my premonition. I thought about it once, but dismissed it as a false alarm, or perhaps subconscious wishful thinking about saving Euterpe.

When we grew tired of water sports, we went tide pooling and shell gathering for hours. One time she put a crab on my leg and I yelled and ran after her. She disappeared around the point by the university, and I caught her in a private cove nearby. Just when I grabbed her we fell on the sand. I landed on top and began to tickling her ribs. She screamed, laughed, and buried her head in my neck.

I was about to kiss her when she pushed me off and began running down the beach toward the car. At first I thought she was still playing, but there was no playfulness in her stride. She was running for her life.

I looked behind me. In the distance, at the spot where we had been, stood a silver-haired old man in a Day-Glo wet suit, holding a surfboard. He was smiling, and then began to laugh as he ran for the water and started paddling out.

Suddenly the dream feeling was back, but I suppressed it, not wanting to alarm Erato. I finally caught up and grabbed her.

"Hey, you're not afraid of some old goat watching us, are you?" I asked, almost out of breath. "He's probably just trying to remember what it was like." Even as I said it, I still couldn't shake the feeling there was something strange about him.

"Get your stuff," she ordered. "We have to go *now*."

"Okay, so you're not used to dirty old men," I argued, making a nasty face. "This is earth, you know, not 'Fantasy Island.' What did you expect? Ricardo Montalban?"

"Don't be a smart-aleck," she snapped. "Please just get your stuff."

I didn't say another word until we got into the car. At first it wouldn't start, and that made her more upset.

"Why don't you get a decent car?" she complained, looking furtively in the rearview mirror, "instead of this old bathtub?"

"Well, I'm sorry, your highness," I said with an exaggerated wave of my hand. "But first year programmers who still owe college loans are not, I repeat, not, usually profiled on 'Lifestyles of the Rich and Famous.' Some people may come into the world with a purse full of hundred-dollar bills, but most of us have to work for a living."

"Wait!" she said as I pulled out of the parking lot. "Isn't there some kind of crafts show at the wharf on Sundays?"

"Yeah, so?"

"So, we'll hide in the crowd until we figure out what to do," she answered, reaching up to adjust the rearview mirror to her liking, then slinking down in her seat.

"You know," I said, getting perturbed, "I'd take you home if you had one, but I'm not taking you anywhere until you explain what's going on."

"I can't."

"You can't? Who the heck was that guy? Poseidon or something?"

"Worse."

"Yeah? What could be worse, the CIA?"

For the first time she stopped looking in the rearview mirror to see if we were being followed. She turned to me and said straight off:

"It was *him*."

I hit the brakes, pulled over, and stopped the car. I had something to say.

19

Antarctica

"Well," I said, exhaling. "I think that explains my weird feeling of being drawn to the beach. You mean that senior citizen back there was . . . Oh no. I thought you said he didn't interfere with your career."

"He must have found out that we're missing. Now I'm in big trouble."

"*You're* in big trouble?" I remarked, resting my hand over her bucket seat. "I just called God a dirty old man, and you think *you're* in trouble? There goes everything for me. I had dreams of going to heaven someday. Perfect weather, perfect waves . . ."

"Cyrus," she answered, staring at the floor. "Just drive, will you? Head for the wharf. We've got to plan our strategy."

"Strategy?" I shook my head. "Now I won't even get purgatory. I probably won't even get hell. Is there something worse than hell?"

"Antarctica," she said flatly, not looking up, then proceeded to explain that Antarctica was worse than hell. Hell was hot, but down at the bottom of the earth, you never got warm. God could put you down there for ten thousand years without any clothes and you'd freeze your rear off. You'd shiver until all of your teeth fell out, and your eyelids froze shut. Then you'd just lie there in a frozen mass. Not dead, not alive. They say the coldest cold is worse than the hottest hot. It burns like fire.

"But hey," she hit my arm with a friendly slug and suddenly sported a sly grin. "You might get off in seven thousand years with a good lawyer."

"That's not funny. There's nothing worse for a southern Californian than freezing your rear end off."

"I'm only trying to point out," she said with a look behind us, "that humans have a one-track mind. Do something wrong, and some guy up in the clouds is going to punish you. People do so much harm to each other that I don't think anybody needs to add to it."

I threw up my arms. "Well, you were the one who said lightning bolts could be thrown. So why are we running away if he's such a nice guy?"

"He *is*," she answered, pulling my arms back down. "But he's still a father. He gets worried when he doesn't know where his children are, and what they're doing."

"Then let's go back," I suggested, motioning behind us with my head. "Talk to him. Tell him what you're up to if he doesn't know already."

"I can't," she frowned, sliding back down in the seat.

"Why not?"

"I feel partly responsible for Euterpe's predicament," she mumbled.

"What do you mean?" I asked, banging on the steering wheel. "What did *you* have to do with it?"

"She was filling in for me the other night." Erato replied, biting her lip. "There was a poetry reading I wanted to attend and she covered for me. She took one of my calls, and I feel like it's my fault. I can't face Dad until I get her free. I have to make things right first."

"Okay. I can understand that. Listen, what call did she take? Maybe that will give us a clue to her captor."

"Irving Berlin."

"Irving Berlin? He's dead."

"Yeah, I know. That's what's weird about it."

"That, and a lot of things. But it does confirm one thing, the account name Iberlin. Obviously, somebody set a trap for your sister. She must have forgotten that the real Irving Berlin was dead. Well, I'm not surprised. He lived to be a hundred or something before he died a few years ago. I wonder what Janet is up to."

"That's why we need to get going on that file," she reminded me, reaching over and placing my hands on the steering wheel. "We need to know why she would set a trap for one of us. Not to mention, if we get Euterpe out, then Dad goes home a happy camper. Otherwise, who knows?"

"Thanks for the reassurance. . . . Look," I said, turning onto the pavement and heading for home, "I think we'd better forget the arts and crafts for today. If that guy on the beach is who you say he is, then we'd better get to a terminal."

"Cyrus!" she screamed, throwing her arms around me. "You're actually going to do it."

"All right," I said with forced patience. "Let's not get too excited. I'm about to break a vow I took for life. I don't see this as a cause for an all-out celebration."

"Sometimes," she said, "you gotta break the rules. Even Dad has been known to make exceptions."

"Yeah? Like what?"

"The flood, for one."

"What? That old story again?" I was skeptical. "What did he do, pull the drain plug early?"

"Not quite. The original plan called for no survivors. He was going to take Noah and his family to heaven."

"But that would have left nobody on earth," I commented, running my hand through my beard.

"Exactly," she said, letting her long hair fly in the wind. "He felt that he might have made a mistake when he put people on earth in the first place. The challenges to survive, take care of the world, and still prepare for an afterlife seemed too great. But he changed his mind at the last minute and told Noah to build the ark."

"Well," I said condescendingly. "It was a nice story you just told, but I'm still thinking about the prospects of breaking into Sigma's Top Secret disk. I'll try it, but it doesn't look good."

"Why can't you work from your Macintosh at home?" she asked, putting on some Ray-Bans as we turned into the sun.

"I can't access anything off site," I answered, following suit and throwing on my Wayfarers. "We're not modem-linked. It would make the Top Secret disk too vulnerable to the outside world. So I really haven't begun to find a way to check the file's security."

"You will. I know it," she said confidently, and felt my large bicep.

"You been reading my horoscope?" I asked, ruffling her hair a little.

"I don't do the future. Just the past." She bit my hand playfully as she pulled it from her hair.

"Oh yeah?" I said, putting my hand back on the steering wheel. "Well, what about Vinnie? You knew he was going to be on the road, or perhaps you planted him there."

"That was different. He needed you. I heard him wandering around that night, whimpering. You were his only hope."

"How did you know we were going to meet that night?"

"It happened the same night Euterpe disappeared," she began, resting her bare feet on the dash. Erato explained that she had been at a poetry reading when she got an emergency beep in her head. It was the answering service informing her of Euterpe's strange message. They always put family calls through first as instructed. When Erato asked if there were any other messages, and they said a call had come from the future.

Apparently, it happened every once in a while. Since time has no meaning or boundaries in eternity, muses can get future calls or past ones. The answering service usually screens them out, but this was a very strong signal. They thought it might be Euterpe again. It wasn't, but luckily they had traced her whereabouts to Sigma.

The second call was Vinnie. Erato didn't know why it came through, but when it did, she picked up his pain, realizing later that I was to cross paths with him the next night. All she could find out was that Vinnie was a dog and was going to lose an ear. She decided to name him after my favorite painter.

"So it wasn't me," she explained, sitting up and putting her feet back on the floor. "It was destiny that brought you together. It gave me a chance to help you start believing, or at least question your perceptions of the spirit world."

She reached over and played with the gearshift. "I knew that the spirit visitation in your childhood was your first encounter with ghosts. I had to build on that the only way I could, by using Vinnie and my powers of persuasion, which have been greatly diminished with my becoming human." She frowned. "In fact, the longer I stay here, the more my extrasensory perceptions fade. I don't think I could even repeat the nightclub trick again."

She turned and stared at me, taking off her sunglasses to emphasize her point. "That's why I'm counting on you to be far enough along in your belief in the spirit world to take it from here. I need your help now more than ever."

"I . . . I see," I said slowly, feeling the weight of responsibility squarely on my shoulders. "Well, anyway, let's get home and see if anyone's called about Vinnie. Then we'll swing by Sigma and see what we can do."

"Cyrus," she said, looking at me. "You don't have to say any more." She reached over and carefully removed my sunglasses, causing me to glance her way. "I can see it in your eyes," she said. "You do believe."

"Yeah," I sighed. "Or maybe I just want to."

"That's always been good enough for Dad, and it's good enough for me too." Looking concerned, she leaned over and placed her hands firmly but gently on my shoulder.

"You're going to be all right with this, aren't you? Look, I know you just wanted to live your life and be happy like everyone else, but you've forgotten something."

"What's that?" I asked, confused.

"There's something inside you that won't die. You've tried to hide it, but it didn't go away. It was your desire to be a part of something great someday, to do something that could make a difference. Believe me, saving my sister could make a big difference in the world."

When I didn't say anything, she elaborated, rubbing my neck slowly and softly.

"The power of poetry and song can't be measured, even by your world's powerful instruments. But take my word for it. They make the earth more than just a planet spinning in some small corner of the universe."

"But I'm nobody," I argued, staring ahead at the road. "Just a regular guy. People like me never make much of a difference."

"People like you"—she suddenly kissed me on the cheek— "have the power to change the world."

"But what if I fail? Then what?"

"There's no failure in trying," she said, mussing up my hair. "Only in giving up. Winning isn't everything. Trying your best is. You wouldn't pull out of a tough wave, would you?" she asked, moving her hand inside my shirt. "I've seen you. The bigger the wave, the harder you try to stay afloat. This isn't any different. This, Cyrus, is your time to perform."

She slowly rubbed my chest with her hand, letting the hairs flow between her fingers. "Look inside and tell me you haven't waited all of your life for this chance," she said softly, "this moment to take on the world. Look at the wave destiny has sent your way, and then tell me you're going to pull out and go home. Don't do it for me, Dad, *or* Euterpe; don't even do it for the world if you don't want to. Do it for yourself. Your time is now." She squeezed my chest, and felt my hard stomach.

I couldn't say a thing. She was absolutely right. She had done her homework this time. That feeling of being a part of something that could make a difference never got erased from my life's disk. There was only one thing to do.

I pulled over and stopped the car, then reached over and hugged her. She took her hand out of my shirt and hugged me back with both arms. She still felt alive with electricity, but under control, like a power station over a raging waterfall.

"Wish me luck," I finally said. "I've got a wave to catch."

"I'll do more than that," she said, smiling. "I'll be on the board with you. But remember, you have to get us to shore. I can only watch for rocks."

"Deal," I agreed, pulling back to look at her. "And maybe a kiss for the winner?"

"That's right." She frowned good-naturedly. "We never did finish what we started." She scooted over next to me and squeezed my thigh.

"Hey," I said, pretending to be serious, "I'm not *that* easy. Besides, there's a time and place for everything, and right now, we've got work to do. I don't want to get *too* distracted; I've got some ideas we can try on the terminal."

I pulled back on the road, adding, "And since we're on the subject of me, what do you see in me anyway? I mean, look at *you*. What man doesn't want the beautiful daughter of powerful parents, but I'm just an ordinary . . ."

"That's what I like about you," she cut in. "You don't overstate your abilities." She placed her hand on my shoulder and continued, saying she found it challenging to help people reach their artistic pinnacle. She saw in me someone of great potential. Apparently, I just needed an opportunity to show my stuff to the world. Muses were great at helping people reach their creative potential. It's one of the things they were born to do, but it had to be someone deserving.

"Anything else you look for?" I asked.

"You're fishing for compliments," she said in a sassy tone. "But if you must know, a nice guy with a big heart and good looks isn't exactly a turnoff for a girl."

"Stop it," I said, starting to blush.

"Well, you asked for it. Feel better now?"

"Yeah, guess I do."

"Don't let it go to your head," she warned, tapping my forehead. "We're going to need your noggin to get us out of this. . . . Besides, we probably won't have time for much of a relationship once this is over. So let's not get our hopes up."

"All I said was a kiss for the winner," I reminded her. "And you're the one who's been exploring my body."

"Yeah," she said. "Guess I got lost in the moment. Animal attraction is a trait I picked up when I became human. Comes with the territory." I decided not to respond to that one.

When we got home I left the engine running and ran upstairs, quickly checking the answering machine. No messages had been left.

I went back down to the car, but it was too late. The Mustang had finally coughed itself out in the street. I informed Erato that the time had come at last for a mandatory tune-up. She understood, waving exhaust fumes from her face.

I rolled out my junior league car oscilloscope while she played with Vinnie. I got the points and plugs installed, and the timing set. Something bothered me as the signal danced across the oscilloscope, but I couldn't quite put my finger on it. Deciding to drop it for the time being, I shut the hood and went in for lunch.

We sat down for soup and sandwiches about two o'clock, and just as I was cleaning up the phone rang. It was Juanita Vaya.

"Cyrus," she ordered, "meet me at my lab at work. I've got something I want you to hear."

20

Playback

We met Juanita in the main lobby, signing Erato in as a guest and getting her an Escort Required badge. Juanita explained on the way to her lab, wearing the standard white lab coat, a plain white blouse and blue slacks underneath. In short, the picture of scientific professionalism, especially with her hair pulled back in a tight bun.

Janet had agreed to let Juanita run some tests. She thought it over and realized she was being too paranoid about the file. Since Juanita was cleared for her own invention, Janet was going to let her access it and report back with the test results. Evidently, Janet was busy with other matters and couldn't be there.

Juanita had decided to give us a chance—to see if there was anything unusual on the backup tape. It was in the same digital format as videotape, so we would play it through a VCR. That way, if there was any audio or video message deposited on it, it would play on the TV monitor. But if there was nothing, that was it. We'd have to go to someone else to find Euterpe.

It actually sounded like a bonus, since I hadn't even considered the possibility of a visual image. Now we could both hear and see any message or clue. I looked at Erato, but didn't have to say anything. We both knew this was our big chance.

We went into Juanita's lab, which was neat, clean and filled with the usual line of high-tech equipment—though all we needed was a VCR and monitor.

Turning to Erato in private, I asked, "How are we going to hear or see Euterpe? She's coming from another dimension, right?"

"Well," she said, puzzled. "I didn't exactly think of that. We wouldn't be able to. But we can't be absolutely certain. After all, she was able to send a screen message."

"All right," I conceded, "let Dr. Vaya play it first. Then maybe we'll think of something."

Juanita popped the tape into the VCR and pushed the play button. All we got was a snowy, silent screen. Nothing moved or spoke in the snow for fifteen minutes. The only sound was the low hum of the player turning the tape, barely audible, even after I turned up the volume to full blast to see if we could possibly hear anything. We didn't.

Reaching over and hitting the eject button, I examined the tape, and, learning nothing, handed it to Juanita. She assured us that she had played the whole thing on a digital tape recorder before we came over to double-check for audio. But it all sounded the same.

"I wanted you to hear it for yourselves," she said, looking at us. "I'm sorry, but unless you can convince me there's anything else on the tape . . ."

I turned to Erato, and we had a little conference behind a bank of digital meters. "I can see this isn't going to work at all," I concluded, shaking my head.

"Now what?" she asked, dejected, and looking at the concrete floor.

"I have an idea that Euterpe probably knew we wouldn't be able to see or hear her on the tape," I assured Erato. "Maybe she left a screen message somewhere in the data."

"What have we got to lose?" Erato shrugged, glancing around the lab at nothing in particular. "We're stuck."

We walked back over and stood behind Juanita as she straightened some things on her workbench. She spun around slowly, waiting for our next move.

"Doctor Vaya," I began, turning to her with my hands out. "We realize that the tape doesn't contain any video or audio message, as far as we can tell. What if you dump the data to a computer and throw it up on a monitor?"

She crossed her arms and tightened her lips. "If I did that," she said carefully, "you'd be looking at the RAM chip test data, and that's strictly . . ."

I held Erato back with my hands on her shoulders. "Okay," I said, frustrated. "What if *you* look at it and tell us if you see anything that looks like a message of any kind?"

"Well . . ."

Erato spoke up. "Doctor Vaya, you're our only hope right now. The key to my sister's disappearance could still be on that tape. Won't you at least try?"

Juanita saw the desperation on our faces. She raised her hand and rested it on her chin, thinking about the situation.

"I suppose," she began, "that since I have to study the test commands to solve the bidirectional transfer problem, I could scan it for stray data.

"In fact," she added, showing sudden excitement, "that may be the reason the transfer isn't working."

"What do you mean?" I asked.

"*If*," she replied cautiously, "and this is a big *if*, there is extraneous data somewhere in the test command programming, it might interrupt the transfer of data."

"Doctor?" Erato said, prompting an explanation.

"Don't you see?" Juanita said excitedly. "If there was a message inserted somehow in the middle of the execution commands, it would most likely stop the whole transfer process."

"Doctor," Erato said, running her hands through her hair and exhaling. "If you see anything in the data, anything at all—"

"Certainly," Juanita answered with assurance. "I'll call you both in a few hours and let you know one way or the other." She stopped and went back to straightening her workbench. "But don't get your hopes up too much," she added carefully. "It could just be a programming error."

I almost asked if I could help in case it *was* a programming anomaly, but of course that would have been out of the question. So we went home and left her with the tape. On the way I turned to Erato.

"You realize that it's possible she won't find anything," I said soberly, changing lanes in traffic.

"Of course."

"And that we have no way of knowing if that tape is really the backup for the Euterpe file," I added, shutting off my turn signal. "Janet could just as easily have given Dr. Vaya a file that only contained previous test data. We just don't know."

"In that case, we've done about all we can do. If Janet wants to play hide the file, then we're out of luck."

"Still," I continued, changing to third gear, "if Janet is innocent . . ."

"I don't see how," she scoffed, rolling her eyes, still disappointed by the results in the lab.

"Well," I offered, "since this whole thing sounds insane, how about this for a wild idea. Maybe when Euterpe showed up to answer a call from Irving Berlin, she got in the path of some kind of digitizer and was converted to bytes and bits. Janet didn't realize it because *one*, Euterpe's invisible, and *two*, she can't be heard. Janet then discovered her RAM chip test data didn't work, but didn't know why."

"What about the screen message you picked up? Wouldn't Janet have gotten one too?"

"Maybe she wasn't looking at her monitor. It happens all the time. You can't watch every line of computer code roll by without getting bored. She probably went off to do something and didn't even notice." Turning onto Ocean Avenue, I headed toward Walnut Place. "I don't know. But I'd sure like to take a look around that classified lab."

Erato patted my leg. "Well, let's not get too far ahead of ourselves," she said, almost cheering up. "After Dr. Vaya calls, we'll make a decision of some sort."

"Okay," I agreed, scratching my beard. "Fair enough. . . . Hey," I said suddenly, trying to make the best of the situation. "We've got a couple of hours. Let's go out to dinner. I want to try out some of my new clothes. And I want to see what you look like in that dress." I pulled over and stopped in front of my apartment. When she didn't say anything I added, "Well, what will it be? McDonald's, or Dairy Queen?"

21

The Kiss of the Muse

"Very funny," Erato said to my choice of restaurants. "But if we're going anywhere, it's going to be something a little more sophisticated. I've had enough fast-food for now."

"Carrows Coffee Shop," I replied.

"Not quite. How about La Ventana?" she suggested, getting out of the car.

"La Ventana? You have to have a reservation for someplace that fancy."

Erato started walking toward the stairs. "Yeah, I know," she replied. "Ours is for eight o'clock."

"Are you sure you're not the muse of comedy?" I laughed, chasing after her. "When did you have time to make one?"

"When you were tuning up that bathtub on wheels," she replied, halfway up the stairs. "Now, get dressed. We'll hit the cocktail hour first. It'll be a great place to watch the sunset."

We took showers and got dressed. I put on the charcoal pin-striped suit she had bought me, along with my two-hundred-dollar shoes and hundred-dollar tie. She looked stunning in an elegant pale peach evening dress with matching shoes, the diamond watch, and a string of satiny pearls. I stared at her and she whistled at me.

"You, Cyrus Major, are one handsome devil."

"Don't mention that other guy's name, will you?" I answered, trying to be cute. "It makes me nervous."

Halfway there I pulled over, stopped, and killed the engine, staring at Erato and shaking my head. We both knew by the looks on our faces that we couldn't go through with it.

"You thinking what I am?" I asked, exhaling.

"You're right," she nodded, not really having to read my mind. "We can't do this, phone message or no phone message. I can't stop thinking about my sister. I'm already feeling guilty about the day we spent shopping. We've got to go back, and wait for the call in person. This is too important to leave to some answering machine. Besides, we may have to act fast if we get new input."

I agreed without a word and was all set for a silent drive home. All set, except that I had forgotten the most important thing about tuning my car. The battery had grown progressively weaker and I had ignored it. My mind had been glued to the engine analyzer and the signals on the scope. The condition of the battery had completely slipped my mind. Well, I guess you can figure out the rest.

I looked around and we were the only ones on Mountain Drive, miles from anywhere, and a thousand feet from the nearest cross street. "Sit here," I said to Erato, after the battery got too low even to turn the starter. "I'll get out and push. It's flat here, but there's a downhill section of road just ahead."

"Nonsense," she replied sharply, "I'll go find a house and call a tow truck."

"Nothing doing," I argued, grabbing the door handle. "I got us into this mess, and I have to get us out. I'm going to prove to you that you don't always have to buy your way out of every situation."

"Okay," she agreed reluctantly. "But that's a new suit, remember?"

"Yeah," I said, getting out. "How could I forget?"

I tossed my jacket in the backseat, loosened my tie, and began to push the car, telling Erato to pop the clutch when it got up to ten miles an hour. It didn't look all that hard. If I could get us past the flat spot we were on, the road went a little downhill.

I got behind and pushed. It went slowly at first, but soon the car got going pretty fast, and it didn't look like any help would be needed.

We swung around a corner and down a little grade, hitting the hill at a pretty good clip, but it was starting to level off again.

"All right!" I yelled. "Pop the clutch!"

She let it out so fast that I catapulted over the trunk and landed in the backseat, my legs dangling over the passenger's seat. By the time I got myself upright, the car had stopped. It wasn't running, and we were still on pretty flat ground. I got out and went over to the driver's side, reached in, and turned the key.

"I forgot," I said, almost out of breath, "to tell you . . . that the key must be on."

She started laughing, and I started laughing. She got out of the car and threw her arms around me. We were laughing so hard tears were in our eyes.

"Dead batteries," I said, wiping the tears away, "always make me cry."

"You know what?" she said, looking coyly up at me. "I've . . . I've never been kissed. It's not something you can practice with your sisters."

"You're not feeling . . . high-voltage, are you?" I asked nervously.

"Try me and see," she said with a sweet smile.

I leaned down and she lifted her head. We stood there for a long slow second, and then, standing in the street next to my dead car, I kissed her, feeling something stir deep inside me as my lips gently met hers.

A tingling sensation emanated from her lips and began to sweep slowly through my whole body. Waves of vibrant energy pulsated through every part of me until it felt as if I would lift off and fly.

The world began to fade away and my childhood encounter with an angel began to form before me. The vision was clearer and I was fully awake this time. The angel sat on my bed in long, white, flowing robes, wearing a hood. Her head was down so that I could only see her slim, strong hands. They were holding my hands down at my sides as I struggled to free myself and fly.

In the struggle I awoke and she let go of me, flying off and out of the room. But just before she went through the ceiling she turned and looked my way, tossing her hood back and showing her radiant smiling face.

Suddenly, I was standing by the car again, holding Erato. I pulled back, kissing her softly on the neck.

"It was you," I said, hugging her gently. "The angel on the bed."

"Special assignment," she said with a sigh. "A little boy's soul was trying to fly."

"But . . . why you? Why did *you* come?"

"Poetic words," she said, "are not the only things that make the soul fly. Sometimes poetry lies in the unspoken cry of the soul to be free. You wanted to fly, to escape a world that didn't understand you. That is the life of a poet. Cyrus, you may have suppressed it almost all of your life, but poets always have the same desire—to soar, to do something beyond just treading the earth for seventy years. They need to make a difference."

I couldn't say anything. She was pulling my secret life right out of my insides and showing it to me.

"And you know what else?" she asked serenely.

"What?" I was clinging to every word.

"We're standing in the street," she reminded me.

"I don't care," I said, leaning her against the car. "Not anymore."

"You will," she said, as the car started rolling away. "I left it in neutral."

I let her go and ran after the car, jumping over the door, and almost ruining all hope of ever having children when I hit the steering wheel. She took off her heels and ran after the car, tossing her shoes at it when she got close enough. One landed in the backseat. The other, naturally, hit me in the head. When she got to the trunk she began to push.

"What are you doing?" I asked over the backseat. "Get in."

"I didn't want you to think I was just a helpless damsel in distress," she said, puffing away.

"Jump in," I ordered, looking over my shoulder at her. "Or we'll both be in distress." I glanced down at the speedometer. We were going ten miles an hour. It was time to pop the clutch. I let it out just as Erato went airborne. She landed draped over the passenger's seat, her head buried in the cushion and her feet kicking the air, looking like one of "America's Funniest Home Videos." She got herself upright and I started the car, driving home without a stop.

"Next time," she said, as I parked at the curb, "call a tow truck, will you?"

When we got upstairs I noticed we both had all but ruined our clothes. Erato pretended to be angry about it.

"Look," I said when we went inside, "my dead battery wasn't all that bad. It got you kissed, didn't it?"

That made her angry for real, so she chased me around the couch for awhile. By the time she caught me I had ducked into the other room and flopped onto the bed.

"I didn't mean it," I confessed. "I *wanted* to kiss you."

"Well . . . ?" She smiled, landing on top of me, then leaned forward. Our lips met for a long, slow, wonderful second. Then, just as it was starting to get interesting, the phone rang.

22

Projections

"Cyrus," Juanita said into the receiver, "I'm sorry. I meant to get back to you sooner, but I got carried away."

"What have you found?" I asked nervously, gathering my wits.

"Nothing, I'm afraid," she apologized. "At least no message was stuck anywhere in the data. I did find the transfer problem though," she added excitedly. "A couple of lines of code were somehow reversed. The processing instructions just looped back endlessly, stranding the data. It was really quite simple. So simple I think Janet overlooked it. The transfer command structure . . ."

"Doctor," I interrupted. "It's classified, remember?"

"Of course," she agreed. "You won't tell Janet I . . ."

"I don't remember anything after the part where you didn't find an inserted message."

"Thanks, Cy. I owe you one."

"Don't worry, Doctor. We may need you yet, but for now, I'm going to call Janet and tell her everything myself. It's the only viable option I've got left."

"You're doing the right thing."

"Thanks for trying. Good-bye."

I hung up, picturing in my mind Euterpe stuck on Janet's original file, and that the backup was a phony. Oh, it contained test data all right, but not what we wanted—the voice or image of a muse. That made me think. If Erato's sister *was* somehow reduced to digital bits on a hard disk, was that like someone's being brain-dead?

I turned to Erato for more help in the matter, and she explained that her sister Urania had confirmed that since Euterpe was only a spirit, digitizing her just might be possible. Obviously, a three-dimensional human being with weight and substance could not survive digitizing. But spirits would have very small weight and space requirements.

Obviously, spirits were invisible to most of us. People who saw them were able to tune in to spirit activity through a little-used part of the brain. They were able to access portions of the brain reserved for ESP, psychic abilities, premonitions, and such that the rest of us could only dream of doing. They could, given these abilities, sense the presence of spirits.

"Hey," Erato said, sitting up on the bed. "Why don't we find a psychic and see if she can sense Euterpe's presence on the disk?"

"That's great," I sneered. "Let's just look in the phone book and pick one out."

"Why not?" she asked, undaunted. "It can't hurt. If we can get some professional backup for this, maybe we can convince Janet to give us access to the file. Except . . ."

"Except what?"

"You've got to be careful with this kind of thing," she warned, looking out the window at the stars. "Everyone who advertises is not necessarily an expert. It's a great field for charlatans and frauds."

"Then what do you suggest we do?" I asked, rubbing her back.

"Call Janet. See how she likes our idea."

"She'll think we're nuts." I pulled her on top of me. "Besides, why can't *you* tell if Euterpe's on the disk? She's your sister. Blood is thicker than data, isn't it?"

"Like I said"—she smiled and gave me a quick kiss on the nose—"I'm losing my powers. I don't think I could tell anymore."

"Why didn't Zeus know about this right away?" I asked. "How come he just found out? I thought gods knew everything."

"Like all bureaucracies," she replied, "it sometimes takes a while to get a message to the top." She opened my shirt slowly, like the doors to a hidden room. "If we're going to convince Janet, we'll need proof. So, either we get a qualified psychic, or . . ." She began to run her fingers over my chest. "*You* could give it a shot."

"All right, I'll call Janet," I said, suddenly slipping her dress down over her shoulders. She was wearing a black lace bra, and filling it out easily. "I'll call Janet," I added, holding my breath. "It's worth a try. But first . . ."

She reached over and handed me the phone off the nightstand. "But first," she repeated.

It was after one in the morning, but I rang Janet. Much to my surprise, she answered the phone herself.

"Look," I said, after exchanging hellos, "I know it's late, but this is an emergency. Does the original Euterpe file have anything to do with sound waves?"

There was a long silence, then, "I can't answer that. It's classified."

Suddenly, I couldn't hold back any longer. I just had to say something to get her attention, though it might cost me the file and my job.

"Janet, I know you're not going to believe this," I blurted. "But I have Euterpe's sister here."

"I'm afraid that's not possible," she answered flatly. "Euterpe is a file, not a person." Before I could explain, she added, "Cyrus. It's late. I'm sure she's a very nice girl. But be careful. She *could* be a spy."

"I know it sounds incredible but . . ."

"Look, did you ask yourself how she could possibly know about the file? Only you, me, Juanita, and Cooper even know of its existence. For all you know, this girl you're with could be part of some college prank. At least I hope that's all it is. Otherwise, I'm afraid I'd have no choice but to let you go."

"Didn't Dr. Vaya talk to you?" I asked impatiently.

"Yes, and I'm afraid you've even got her thinking about this so-called kidnapped sister theory of yours. Let me put it this way. You are a fine programmer, and we need your services, but I'm about to let you go if this continues any longer."

"I can prove she's telling the truth about her identity."

There was a long silence. Then a quick reply. "Come to think of it," Janet said, "I'd like to meet her, face-to-face. Bring her in tomorrow morning. We'll clear this whole thing up once and for all."

I said good-bye and hung up. Erato started in on me about saying I could prove her identity.

"Simple," I said, "We'll just pull the song routine with the CD player in Janet's office. That will get her attention, and get us a free ticket into the file."

"Cyrus, I've already told you more than once that I don't think I can read thoughts now."

"Well, have you got a better idea? Melt some more ice maybe?" When she didn't answer, I added, "Where's your confidence? You haven't forgotten your 'don't-pull-out-of-the-wave-early' speech, have you? At least the song trick is something we can try."

"I just hope this works," she replied, rolling her eyes.

"Look, I'm beat." I yawned. "Let's get some sleep and talk about this in the morning."

Reluctantly she agreed, since it was past one-thirty and we were exhausted. Both of us crashed like falling trees onto the bed and were gone. Even if I had wanted to get some fire burning between us, I was too tired to start the kindling. Besides, Vinnie had taken up permanent residence between us, dusting my face now and then with his long, black tail. It woke me up once, and I realized the *found dog* ad would appear in the morning paper. I secretly hoped they would lose it, or forget to run it.

I knew Erato would probably be gone soon, but keeping Vinnie would at least remind me of her, and that magical summer—the kind that happens only once in a lifetime. One of those summers that changes you forever, and from which your simple, crazy heart never recovers.

23

Psychic Powers

Since Erato didn't trust her mental powers a hundred-percent, we had to go with her alternate idea. Monday morning was spent making a telephone search for psychics, which was about the last thing I ever thought I'd be doing.

Over English muffins and peanut butter I phoned several "spiritual consultants" about our predicament, purposely not giving away too many details for fear of scaring them off. We just said Erato's sister was being held captive, and we wanted to verify her "presence" before going to the authorities. One psychic was out of town, three were not handling this kind of thing, and one said she'd give it a try.

Madame Perushka explained that she had fielded more bizarre requests, like uniting departed loved ones and even checking on the souls of dog and cat ghosts. I was beginning to wonder if she was too weird even for us, but Erato waved me off with a mouth full of muffin, and we agreed to meet her at some mobile home park in Channel Islands.

Now, mobile home parks aren't what they used to be. She lived in a one-hundred-thousand-dollar double-wide, complete with cactus garden and enclosed patio. She had the obligatory scarf on her head, long, pointy nose and nails, and flowing Gypsy gowns. So at least she looked the part.

Before we launched into the exact details of returning Erato's sister from computer prison, Madame P. insisted on reading our palms. For the rather modest price of fifty dollars she would tell the fortunes displayed on the lines of our hands, and verify Euterpe's presence at the location of our choosing. Even with our newfound wealth, a bargain was a nice thing to find, so we paid up and turned over our palms.

She read mine first and noted that I was "sensitive" to psychic phenomena, such as otherworld vibrations and the like. I quickly dismissed that as her standard come-on, and turned Erato over to her.

Madame Perushka took one look at Erato's palm and pulled back, astounded. "In fifty years I have never seen a palm like this," she said. "Yours is both old and young at the same time. You are a contradiction of nature. You have a very noble heritage, yet are down-to-earth and practical. You have come from far away, yet your home is only as far as the nearest shore. It is indeed strange. You must come back someday for a complete reading."

"Sure," Erato agreed with a sly smile. "Next time I'm in town."

"Now, what can I do for you two?" Madame Perushka asked, satisfied with Erato's answer. "Where is your sister, trapped in some prison or something? Maybe you should be contacting the American Civil Liberties Union, instead of an old Gypsy like me."

"Naw," I said, patting the back of her hand. "You're doing fine. We want you to come to work and take a reading. See if you can feel the presence of her sister."

She reached over and held Erato's hand. "Yes," she said without hesitation. "Your vibrations are so unusual. It should be easy to tell if your sister is nearby."

Once at work, I signed them in as guests and we marched off to the computer center, home to the mainframe and a couple of minicomputers for engineering work. All, of course, were networked together so they could exchange files in seconds. It was like every other computer center, filled with the steady hum of whirling disk drives and spinning tapes. It was a den of near-quiet electronic efficiency, vibrating with the energy of shared information.

Madame Perushka couldn't resist making a comment upon her arrival. "This is a canyon of great power. The knowledge here is extraordinary. Now, where do you want me to start?"

"Here," I said, pointing to a terminal. "As I log on and type the filename, I want you to put your hands on the CRT and see if you feel anything."

I sat down and called up the file, getting the usual message. *Your user profile is not cleared for this level of access. Please see the systems manager if you wish to enter.*

"Place your fingers on the name of the file," I requested, motioning with my head to the green CRT screen. "See if you can feel anything, anything at all. And please, don't lie to us. We paid the fifty dollars, we want the truth. If she's not here, let us know."

She very carefully placed her fingertips on the screen, closing her eyes in deep concentration. A full thirty seconds passed before she looked up soberly and said, "I can see that you want the truth. And the truth is that I don't feel a living presence."

"Thank you," I said, "for being honest." I looked at the door and nodded. "You can go now."

"No!" Erato said abruptly. "Take her over to the bank of hard disks. Let her put her hands on the drive."

"All right," I agreed. "It's worth a try."

I led her over to the waist-high cabinet. Inside, stacks of hard disks containing billions of bits of data whirled like the rings of Saturn.

Madame Perushka unashamedly placed her hands on the drive cabinet, knelt, and rested her head on the side of the unit. She sat there immobile for a long time, not giving away a thing. At last she lifted her head from the console and said, "You are rare. You have asked for honesty and you shall get it. I cannot feel life inside of this spinning world of data. I can only feel electricity and magnetism. That is all. I am sorry. I believe you are sincere. I just cannot feel a living presence."

I helped her up and thanked her for what I didn't expect, complete truth. On the way to the door she reached into her pocket and gave me back the fifty-dollar bill. "Here," she said with downcast eyes. "I cannot take your money. Sincerity has no price. . . . But you"—she looked me straight in the eyes—"have the power. When you are ready to use it, the information you seek shall be yours."

"Me?" I said sheepishly. "Surfers don't have spiritual powers, just water in their ears."

"Say what you will," she said, and then pointed to Erato. "But she has chosen you carefully. And she is the key to your power."

I gave her a questioning look, but decided to drop it before they ganged up on me. Then we took her home. On the way she said if there was anything else she could do, just call. She would be glad to help. I thought that was going to be the end of it, but Erato started in where Madame Perushka had left off.

"You realize, of course," she began, on the drive back to Sigma, "that she was right about your abilities."

"Ah, come on," I scoffed, slapping the steering wheel. "I'm about as psychic as a computer. I don't know anything about that kind of stuff. And I'm beginning to think I don't want to."

Erato wasn't impressed by my denial. She put her feet on the dash and leaned back, glancing casually at me. "All right, let's do a little nonvolatile memory check," she suggested. "Do you remember the Super Bowl three years ago? How you dreamed the winning team and the winning score?"

"Coincidence."

She reminded me about that car wreck I had visualized four years earlier—the overturned Volkswagen with the guy's arm sticking out of the window. "And your last girlfriend— you dreamed about your trip together to Mexico, and that a peasant woman with two starving kids would sell her a silver necklace."

"Déjà vu," I defended, barely remembering the last incident.

"Nice try," she said, her hand on my knee. "But you can't have déjà vu about the future. Those were premonitions. Foretelling of future events."

I thought about it long and hard. "My only regret," I said at last, "is that I didn't bet on the Super Bowl."

"Make fun of yourself if you want," she said seriously. "But you have the power. You just can't accept it. And you know why?" She reached up and turned the rearview mirror so that I could only see myself in it. "Ego. You don't want any of your old college friends, whom you don't even see anymore, to think you're some kind of Shirley MacLaine weirdo, do you?"

"Nonsense, I can handle it," I defended. "I can handle all of this spoon bending, past life regression, reincarnation, and soul transmigration stuff with the best of them." I fixed the rearview mirror.

"Good." She pulled on my shirtsleeve. "Now we're making progress. So, please listen. And listen good. My sister sent that message to you because she knew you were the only one who could save her. How can I get that through to you?" She pointed her finger at me. "That's right, you, Cyrus Major, named after the brightest star in the sky, have almost unlimited potential. You have things inside you that others only dream of having. And yet you waste your abilities." She began to play with the gearshift.

"You have the high-frequency receiver inside you that is given only to poets and madmen. You, and you alone, are Euterpe's hope. And yet you turn your back. You try the easy and the obvious. You try to have Janet release the file. When all you need to set my sister free is to be still and listen to the great ocean of lyrics floating in the atmosphere . . . as endlessly as a waterfall in a rain forest. And then write those words down."

"What are you saying?"

"I think reciting an original lyric poem will set her free." She threw up her hands in frustration, but she wasn't finished. "I didn't want to have to tell you this," she continued, looking out the windshield. "But I didn't think you were going to be such a blockhead. I would have thought that anyone with your brain wave activity would figure it out. But since you didn't and time is running out, I'm telling you now."

She reached over and grabbed me by the collar. "I can do very little. I am only a muse on temporary assignment; all I can do is assist. Only true humans can make a lasting difference in the world. She needs you. *We* need you. You have it within you to set her free—password or no password.

"So do me a favor; quit passing the buck, quit looking for somebody else to pick up the tab, and quit fooling around. This may sound stupid to you, but if Dad has to intervene, either the world suffers what you people call natural disasters, or he stops my sister from inspiring anyone else. Then lyric poetry, along with your best songs, will go south for the winter. Maybe for a thousand years; who knows? And who cares? Not you, I guess."

There was a long, awkward silence. Finally, while stopped at a red light, I had to say something. "I can see why Zeus doesn't interfere with your career," I admitted, glancing her way. "You're good. Real good . . . Yeah, I know that I've got some kind of power. It started when I was a kid. I could *feel* things, events coming that nobody else could. It scared me, and so I stopped listening to it, just shut it down. I was doing all right until you came along—until that message came up on the screen.

"Look," I added, pulling away from the stoplight and staring at her. "I've never even tried out whatever small powers might be in this head, and I don't even know what to do, but tell you what. I'll try. Promise . . . I'll see if I can make contact with her." She threw her arms around me, and we almost skidded off the road. "*Try*, I said," as I steadied the wheel. "That's all I can do. And if it doesn't work, back to the other way: science."

"Nothing doing," she beamed, hugging me hard. "Let's do them both in parallel. I don't care which way sets her free. I just want her back."

"Good," I said, putting my arm around her. "Because I'll need you to be there when I talk to Janet. It'll be a battle of the great persuaders. Don't worry; my money's on you."

"All right, but I'm going to need your help," she informed me. "And if we win," she added, looking at my torn upholstery, "we buy you a new car."

"Deal," I smiled, mussing up her hair.

"Your really love your sister, don't you?" I asked at last, turning into the driveway to Sigma.

"Poetry," she informed me, "is thicker than water."

Deciding to change the subject, I looked over at her, noticing an inner glow on her face. She seemed pleased with the way things were going, and I suppose she should have been. After all, she had finally gotten through to me, in more ways than one.

Suddenly I was thinking about what it would be like to spend my life with her, if only it were possible—what it would be like if we could be together after her life on earth was over.

In the short time since we met she had become more than someone out to save her sister, more than a summer fling. She had skillfully maneuvered her way inside my heart. She had become my inspiration. I wasn't the first person to fall in love with his inspiration, and not the first to try to make it last.

24

The Showdown

Once back at the plant Janet brought us right in. She sat behind her desk, wearing a gray pin-striped suit. This time she left her black pumps on. We sat in her leather chairs, sporting newly acquired polo shirts, walking shorts, and deck shoes, looking like something out of the Lands' End catalogue. We explained as best we could that Euterpe was not just a data file, but might hold information regarding the whereabouts of Erato's missing sister. Needless to say, Janet was skeptical. She wanted proof.

"We know that Dr. Vaya had a backup," I said delicately, pulling at my tight shirtsleeves. "But we think the original untouched file created last Wednesday night contains a clue to the location of Erato's sister."

"Cyrus, of all people you should know that a backup is an exact copy of the original," she reprimanded. "It hasn't been tampered with, if that's what you mean. So why on earth would you think there's information about missing persons on it?" Janet seemed genuinely puzzled. "What could that file possibly have to do with this woman's sister?"

"Her name's Euterpe," Erato said carefully.

"Yes, I know," Janet answered with disbelief, straightening a gold Sigma symbol on her lapel. "But you have to admit, this sounds like a pretty crazy coincidence. We've never employed anyone by that name, nor is she anyone I've ever known. It looks very suspicious that she has the same name as my test data file, which just happens to be named after a Greek muse."

I was prepared for this. "The coincidence is probably why it happened," I offered, leaning forward in my chair. "Why a message was left on your file. Her sister must have thought it would be the only place she could leave a clue to her whereabouts."

Janet had been sitting comfortably behind her desk, but now she got up and began to pace the carpet.

"But the file's Top Secret," she said over her shoulder. "Who was she working with here at Sigma who could access *that* file? There's really only me, Doctor Vaya, and Cooper." She whirled around and stared hard at Erato. "And why has your sister disappeared?"

"We believe," I said carefully, resting my hands on my knees, "that she was working with *you*."

"But that's impossible," Janet said, raising her voice and placing her hands on her hips. "How could she be working with me if I don't even know her?" She looked at me in bewilderment. "Cyrus, what's this all about?"

Then she stared at Erato. "If you're FBI," she said flatly, "I'll need identification, and a plausible explanation for this . . . this strange accusation."

"I'm not with the FBI or any other organization," Erato explained, waving her hands about. "I just want my sister back."

Janet stopped posturing, went back to her desk, and sat down. She picked up the nesting doll and began to fumble with it. "Then show me some proof," she ordered. "Some kind of sign. Anything to prove that your story's for real, and I'll let you see the file. Fair enough? Otherwise, *I* go to the FBI."

It was time to go for it. I knew that it wasn't going to be easy, but since I didn't figure Janet for the believing-in-ghosts-and-spirits type, I'd have to try to put it in terms she might accept. I took control of the conversation.

"We'd like to show you identification," I began, standing up. "And prove to you that she's FBI, and that Euterpe's the code name for an operative. That would be more plausible than what we're about to say."

Erato gave me a nod that said I had the floor. I asked Janet if she believed in extraterrestrials, and she conceded that it was at least possible. Then I pointed out that visitors could come here from another world. If that world wasn't visible or audible to us, we'd never know they were here unless one of them came in contact with some special equipment that receives signals from deep space—and her frequency pattern was disturbed and somehow digitized.

I told Janet that Erato had come from such an invisible world. She had been materialized in human form for one specific purpose—to find and retrieve her sister. The poetic screen message I had received was a distress signal.

I walked over and placed my hands squarely on the desk. "Erato is here to recapture the contents of that file," I went on, looking straight into Janet's eyes. "According to her culture, and ours, she has a moral right to take the remains back to her world."

There was a long, stiff silence, and then Janet finally broke it, leaning forward and meeting me almost head-to-head.

"*And*," she asked skeptically, "if she doesn't come back with the remains?"

Erato stood up and joined me at the desk, answering for herself. "My father is a very powerful lord in my world," she said as a warning. "He can destroy the earth anytime he wishes. We have been visiting here for thousands of years without detection. I don't want an interworld incident; I just want her back."

Turning to Janet, I asked, "Was any special equipment on that night in the lab that could have digitized a signal from deep space?"

"I'm sorry," Janet said gruffly, sitting back in her chair. "But as you know, that's classified."

"The backup," I said, pounding the desk, "did it contain absolutely all of the data you took that night? Or is some of it contained on another file that we don't know about?"

Janet leaned forward and stood up. "I'm sorry," she said, coolly shaking her head. "But that's classified. . . . Look, this whole story's just a little too wild for me. I don't get to the movies much."

I wasn't giving up. It looked like I had her on the ropes. I glanced at the jukebox.

"In Erato's world beings have telepathic powers," I said. "So we'll prove to you she's got error free ESP. No one on earth is a hundred-percent accurate with that stuff. But she isn't from this world. What do you say?"

Erato gave me a sour look, but I was confident after the nightclub incident, forgetting for the moment that Erato had said her powers were waning.

"Go on." I stood up straight and gestured toward the jukebox. "Pick a song from one of your CDs. But don't tell us the title. We'll tell *you* what it is. Better yet, just so the whole thing is fair, write it down on a sheet of your stationery, and put it in the top drawer of your desk. Erato will pick it from the playlist and push the button. If we're right, the file's ours."

"One song doesn't prove a thing," Janet said without batting an eye. "Let's see if you're really up to the challenge." She thought for a moment with her hand on her forehead. "Three," she said finally. "I write down three songs and put them in the floor safe. You play them—in the correct order. That's the deal."

Erato looked at me and shook her head. "Forget it," she grumbled. "I'm not putting my sister's freedom on the line for some stupid parlor trick."

"All right," Janet smirked, plopping down in her chair. "You had your chance at the easy way out. Let's make this really interesting." She spun her chair so that it faced the wall behind her, where a huge microchip blow-up hung almost floor to ceiling. Then she spun back again.

"New game," she said with a sly grin. "You pick the songs from over by the window, without seeing what's on the playlist ahead of time. Cyrus writes them down from the chair over on the other side of the room, with no verbal clues from you. If they match what I'm going to put in the safe, then the file's yours to scan."

"Great," I shrugged. "Not only does Erato have to read two minds, but she has to make them match up. Are you sure you don't want to make it more difficult?"

"It's certainly not fair," Erato frowned.

"Listen, sister," Janet said like one of those hardened prison matrons, her eyes boring into Erato. "I don't know who's paying you, or how high this espionage job goes. But if you can pull off this stunt, then I'm no match for you. You want the chip data. You've got one chance. But if you screw up, the FBI's going to be burning out an overhead bulb on you."

"If you're finished . . ." Erato broke in with a touch of sarcasm.

"Just one more thing," Janet declared. "If your little parlor trick doesn't work, Cyrus is gone. He'll never set foot on this property again. Let's just say I'm having a two-for-one special."

"Okay," Erato said with fire in her eyes. "You've got yourself a deal. You've pushed me too far. But if I win, Cyrus gets full system manager privileges."

"All right, but stop wasting time," Janet ordered, looking at the digital clock on the wall. "I've got a meeting in fifteen minutes."

Janet wrote down her selections and dropped them in the floor safe under the carpet by her desk. Erato walked over and stood by the window, her arms folded in defiance and firm resolve. I moved over and sat in a leather chair opposite the desk with a pencil and paper in my hand, ready to write, though I didn't know how all of this was going to work. Erato soon let me know. She stared intently at Janet. Then she turned and looked out the window.

"Cyrus," she said softly. "Close your eyes. Don't think. Don't even try to concentrate. I need your mind open, relaxed. Think of something you love. You're riding a wave. A beautiful girl is walking down the beach. Her hair is flowing over her shoulders and blowing gently in the breeze. She is coming toward you. You stop and get off your board, gliding slowly into her arms. She leans forward and whispers in your ear. 'If you love me,' she says, 'play these three songs for me. And then you are mine, and we will be one.' "

I was completely relaxed, falling into the vision Erato had painted for me. Suddenly, I grabbed the pencil and quickly wrote down three lines, not knowing what they were. Without opening my eyes, I folded the paper and put it in my pocket. The beautiful maiden in the vision began to kiss my neck, moving slowly down my chest until . . .

"Cyrus," Erato said gently, "you may open your eyes now."

Much to my dismay, the vision vanished, and I was back in the office. I placed my hands in my lap and remained seated.

Erato walked slowly over to the jukebox and quickly scanned the playlist. She punched three buttons. One of the CDs flipped to horizontal and plopped down on the turntable. A split second later Bette Midler began singing in a sweet faraway voice. "From a Distance" played beautifully all around us. Janet winced a little, but didn't say a word.

Erato was back at the window, gazing out to sea. When it ended it was replaced by Whitney Houston's "The Greatest Love of All."

The third disc began to spin as the laser beam read the grooves. But there was no sound. Not even static. Three minutes later, Janet spoke.

"Nice try," she said, almost laughing. "But that one's blank. I keep it as a scratch pad in case I want to make a new one. I always have a blank. You, sister, have picked an erasable CD. Sorry."

"No tears for me," Erato said coldly. "That piece of paper in Cyrus's pocket says 'The Sounds of Silence.' And that's what played."

"Sorry," Janet said, stroking the nesting doll. "But that's the title of a song by Simon and Garfunkel."

"Foul," I declared, bolting to my feet. "Erato wouldn't know that from what I wrote down. She gets another try."

Janet slipped out of her chair and walked over to the juke-box. She punched a button and the words began to pour forth in timeless golden tones.

"That," she said confidently, "is 'The Sounds of Silence.' . . . Time's up," she added, leaning back on the jukebox. "I've got a meeting to attend."

"Are we in or out?" I asked angrily, making a fist. "Do you want me to turn in my badge or what?"

"Not just yet," Janet said, thinking. "I have a few things to check on first. Then I'll let you know."

"When?" I asked, still perturbed.

"If the guard lets you in this afternoon," she smirked. "Then you'll know."

"Come on, Erato," I said, unclenching my fist and grabbing her hand. "Let's get out of here. If she's got one fair bone in her body, she'll realize it was an honest mistake."

None of us had any more to say. It was time to leave. When Erato and I got to the door, Janet had something to add.

"As a courtesy," she said, taunting us. "I'll let you know before I destroy the file. I wouldn't want you to go on hoping for nothing."

"Thanks," I added sarcastically. "Don't do us any favors."

"How did you do that?" I asked Erato, pulling the paper from my pocket. "Even David Copperfield would have been impressed."

"You don't completely believe in psychic powers, do you?" she asked, shaking her head. "I can see there's still some little part of you that wants to hold on to only what you can see, hear, and touch."

"Well," I admitted, "ESP is pretty nonscientific. But I'm getting closer to a hundred-percent acceptance by the minute," I added, holding her hand tighter. "You did look pretty good in my vision."

"Who said anything about the girl being me?" she said, raising her eyebrows and squeezing my hand hard.

"Whoops, sorry . . ."

"You realize," Erato continued, "that this proves your pow-ers are real. You were the one who picked the songs from

Janet's mind. When you wrote them down I was able to sense the titles from the vibes you were sending."

"You," I said, putting my arm around her, "are a very tricky lady."

"You," she replied, gently kissing my neck, "put out some powerful signals. Now, take me home so I can get some cash. I want to go shopping. I've only got six days left until I go poof, you know. Want anything from Sears?"

"Sears? I thought you were a rich girl?"

"I just thought you could use some tools."

"What I could use," I said with exaggeration, "is a crystal ball."

"You forget," she said. "That's what this thing on your shoulders is for. You've already proved it's in good working order. Nice job of thinking on your feet back there. Extraterrestrials and all that."

"Desperation does that to me sometimes," I admitted. "This time we got lucky. . . . Well, maybe not, but at least we tried."

"Yeah," she replied, looking deep into my eyes. "We sure did."

25

The Handshake

Before Erato's next shopping expedition, I talked her into lunch and a walk on the beach. So after dining on the exquisite cuisine of Burger King, we took Vinnie to the shore, this time down by the Biltmore.

Besides tearing into the surf and chasing birds, he brought back everything I threw. I found some pieces of driftwood washed up on the sand, and we took turns tossing them into the waves for Vinnie. After his swim I cleaned out his ear, dried him off, and put on a fresh bandage to keep out the dirt and sand.

On the way back from the beach I remembered that it was the day the ad would come out in the paper, and didn't like the way it felt. Vinnie had taken to me and Erato and we were certainly taken by him. His kind, gentle nature was evident by the way he set his head on your shoulder or lap to be petted. He never barked, except at the mailman and the trash collector, which was to be expected. It also meant his hearing was working well, since he always heard them long before they got to the apartment.

Later that afternoon, I dropped Vinnie and Erato at home and went to work. Erato decided to take the bus downtown and go shopping, but I made her promise not to get me a new car, saying the Mustang was fine for now. She finally agreed, but not without a fight. Before getting in the car to race off to work, I did something as a matter of course—I called Janet. There was no answer.

At the front lobby the new female guard didn't say a word, so I went over to my office. Cooper ignored me at first, though he was sure to have been briefed on everything. After everyone else had gone home, I couldn't stand the silence anymore. Walking into his office, I started in on him—to see if any information could be pried out of his tightly organized memory—but didn't learn a thing. Finally, getting nowhere, I gave up, and got ready to go back to my terminal.

"Actually," Cooper said on my way out, "I don't blame you for being upset. Janet tried to short you on the data with the incomplete backup. That was very untidy of her. It was worth a try, I guess—to see if you were really serious about the file, or were just seeing how far you could go before getting . . . terminated." He took a drink from the glass of water on his desk and set it down.

"I guess now she'll straighten all of that out," he said with a swallow. "But really, Cyrus. This latest scam. Did you honestly think she'd believe all that extraterrestrial nonsense? Frankly, I'm disappointed in you. Despite your looks and questionable pastimes, you are a good programmer."

Acting as if I didn't hear him, I asked, "Do you believe in anything beyond what you see and hear?" I pointed around his austerely decorated office. "Or do you think this world is it?"

"I think," he said, opening his arms and sweeping them around, "this is pretty much it."

"Well, that's a real shame." I frowned. "Because if this is all there is to life—hardware, software, and a little firmware—then God has no imagination. Even I could have set up a little intrigue, something to keep people guessing."

Cooper narrowed his eyes. "Go on. What's your point?"

"The point is that if all of the mysteries in the universe are solved, then where's the fun? Where's the wonder? The myth and the magic? I didn't believe much in that sort of thing. But lately I'm beginning to wonder. I think that whoever created this universe *has* got imagination, and much more than you or I. It's possible that he or she left many things hidden just out of reach, just beyond sight and sound, waiting for us to discover them like kids finding Easter eggs."

Knowing I might need a prop to stress my point, I had brought something from home for the occasion. I produced an egg from one of my pockets and proceeded with my show-and-tell.

"You ever see the look on a little kid's face when he finds a hidden egg?" I asked, pointing to the one in my hand. "The only look that can top that is the pleasure on the face of the parent who hid the egg."

"That's the most interesting thing you've ever told me," Cooper said to my surprise. "And I'll tell you something since this is probably your last week anyway. I don't hate you and I'm not trying to get you fired. All I've been trying to do these last several months is get you to grow up."

"Well, then, I guess we're even," I laughed, setting the egg on his desk. "All of my efforts have been to get you to loosen up. So, given your views of the here and now, you don't buy the extraterrestrial story at all?"

He shifted forward in his chair and planted his feet squarely on the carpet. "It's fun to speculate," he said. "But the real world comes down pretty hard on dreamers."

"Yeah," I nodded with a friendly grin, "I guess you're right." Somewhere, far off inside me, there was a sun rising on our relationship. Sure, he had indicated it wasn't all-out war between us many times, but we had never stopped glaring at each other long enough to realize what we both feared the most: he feared my reckless attitude about life, and I hated his guarded caution.

Suddenly, without thinking, I thrust my hand out for him to shake. "Here," I said. "we don't have to be friends, but we can at least be civil and courteous."

He looked at my hand, but didn't grab it. He slapped me on the back instead. "Your hand's dirty," he said, and walked away from his desk.

"Wait," I said. "I'll go wash it."

Suddenly, he spun around and came back, putting his hand out for a shake. "You're right," he smiled apologetically. "Your dirt's only skin-deep. Some people are filthy to the bone."

We were just in the middle of a long overdue handshake when my phone rang. I ran down the hallway and caught it on the fourth ring. It was Juanita. "Get Erato and be in my lab in an hour," she ordered. "I've got something to show you."

26

Euterpe Erased

I phoned home, but Erato wasn't there. I left her a message on the answering machine to call or take the bus and meet me at work. Not hearing from her an hour later, I hoofed it over to Juanita's private lab. Once there I explained that Erato had gone shopping and, hopefully, would be along soon.

Juanita explained that we might need her to identify a voice-print if we were able to isolate a message on the disk.

"Then I assume," I said, leaning against her workbench, "that you've found a way into the original untouched file, the one that contains *all* the data."

"Janet agreed to let us into the master file using her password," Juanita said, smiling as though she had won a small victory. "But just until midnight. Then she says she's taking the file back."

"Then she *was* lying about the backup," I concluded, "just as Cooper said. It wasn't the complete file."

"She only lied to protect her chip data," Juanita claimed, stuffing her hands into her lab coat. "But now she's giving you a chance to prove your wild theory."

"Then she believes?" I raised an eyebrow.

"Don't be silly," Juanita scoffed, suddenly rummaging through a pile of plastic tote boxes on her bench. "She flatly refused until I mentioned pursuing a search warrant. She wasn't really scared, as you can imagine, but she didn't want to give the police access to the contents of the file."

Juanita produced a circuit board–sized container from the bench top. "What I haven't told her is that I've solved the transfer problem."

I crossed my arms and stood between her and the workbench. "Doctor," I said, "if you don't mind my asking, why are you doing this? If you've solved the data transfer using the backup tape, you don't need the hard disk file. What interest could it possibly hold for you now?"

As Juanita began looking for a test fixture for her board, she explained.

During the most recent experiment, it had become obvious that Juanita hadn't been given the whole file, just the part that was giving Janet trouble. Therefore, Janet must have been trying to protect something else on the file.

Juanita stopped pacing and looked me squarely in the eye. "When I challenged her," she said, "Janet consented, then ordered me to clear this up once and for all. She said that Erato had proved herself today in the office."

"Did she tell you about . . . about Erato's real identity?"

Juanita got a funny look on her face. "You mean that Erato and her sister are visitors from another dimension? Naturally, if that were true, it would explain many things."

"Naturally," I repeated with a shrug, "you don't believe it. But if the soul can be stored temporarily in a human body, then why can't a spirit be stored in another medium? You can argue that the soul only resides in a *living* body, but it's the soul that gives the body life. If a spirit is capable of entering another medium such as a disk, perhaps it gives life just as the soul gives the body life."

Juanita sat down on the edge of her workbench, container still in hand. "I'm a scientist, Cyrus, not a theologian. But I must admit," she added, smiling wryly, "it is a very intriguing theory. Digitizing a sentient being in a sort of cryogenic state. It would be a quantum leap for science. Impossible as it sounds, if it could be done using today's technology, one can only imagine the possibilities." Her eyes lighted up. She got an intense look on her face, and set the container down on the bench.

"Then you think it could have happened to Euterpe?" I said at last. "I mean, it's theoretically possible that she was digitized."

"Highly unlikely," she said.

"But if she was, could we set her free again?"

"I seriously doubt it," she admitted, carefully opening the protective container and removing the RAM board. "But first things first. We transfer all the data from the hard disk to the monitor and see if anything unusual turns up." All the while Juanita had been reaching over to an adjacent workbench and searching through a pile of computer hardware.

"Well," she said at last, pulling a mounting fixture from the stack. "Here it is, right under my nose." She looked at me and smiled. "We've got work to do. Let's fire up the system."

She locked her test fixture into a setup on the bench and plugged the RAM board into it, then turned and walked over to her terminal, ten feet away. Next she logged into Euterpe and began to copy all one hundred megs to her RAM board. About halfway through the phone rang. It was Erato; she was in the lobby.

"Where have you been?" I asked into the receiver.

"I told you I was going shopping."

"Well, Ms. Responsibility," I scolded, "while you were cleaning out the mall, Dr. Vaya got us into the file. Don't move. I'll be right out."

When we got back to the lab, Juanita had finished copying the data to RAM, and it worked perfectly. Then she sent the data from RAM to a video monitor.

At first, the usual snow showered the screen while the white noise of near-silence filled the room for fifteen long, tense minutes. Just as we were about to give up, a faint, distant, blurry sound came out of the speaker, like a whisper from eternity. Somewhere in the snowy picture a vague shadow moved ever so slightly. We all got excited, but had to be very still to hear anything.

Juanita played it a number of times. She amplified and filtered it so we could make it out better. But the more she amplified the sound and tried to isolate the picture, the more broken-up the signal became—until at last we had to give up. We just couldn't see or hear anything clearly.

"Play it one more time," Erato ordered. "Something's not right. Whatever it is, it doesn't sound like her voice. And even if it does, I haven't *felt* anything. She's my sister; I would feel it if she was present. My powers may be limited to the human scope now, but I would know it if her voice was in the room. I'm sure of it."

Juanita played it one more time and Erato closed her eyes. After a couple of minutes she stomped her foot and said, "Stop, Doctor. Don't go on. This isn't working. If that *is* her voice, all we're doing is playing a recording of it. Her spirit is not in it. This is beginning to look like a hoax. We can't make out the voice, and that shadow could be anything."

"But her poem says she's shipwrecked on the banks," I reminded Erato. "It has to be the memory banks—what was on the disk. Because if it isn't, she could be anywhere."

"All I know is that I don't feel her presence," she complained, upset by the test results. "You're supposed to be the psychic—do you feel her anywhere around here?"

I thought for a moment. "No," I said, shaking my head. "I don't feel a darn thing. What do you think, Doctor?"

Juanita was somber, but direct. "I think Janet picked up some signal noise at the end of the data," she said, leaning back against her workbench. "I don't think we've got anything concrete, certainly not enough to prove anything."

"Then let's go home," Erato said, disappointed. "I'm sorry, Doctor. But it's no use. She's nowhere around here. For all practical purposes, she's either lost, or . . . she's terminated."

"But she's immortal," I protested with upturned palms. "You said so yourself. She *can't* be terminated."

"If she's in an unrecoverable state," Erato argued, "she might as well be."

"She's not dead," I finally said, almost angrily. "She's only lost. Look, I know she's around somewhere. I can feel *that* much. I just don't know where. But we'll find her. I promise." I touched her softly on the shoulder. "Come on, let's go. We'll figure something out.

"Thank you, Doctor," I said as we turned to leave. "If you think of anything—anything at all—we'll be willing to try it. We've got nothing to lose that we haven't lost already."

"Except lyrics," Erato said sarcastically, looking at me. "You can kiss Top 40 radio good-bye."

After we left the lab, Erato sat in my office and waited for me until my shift was out. Just before closing I checked the Euterpe file. It had completely disappeared—probably erased. I sat speechless, pale with shock. A minute later, with my eyes still glued to the empty space on the screen, I suddenly received a new mail message. When I typed in READ MAIL, the following appeared.

Save me from this world
Whose double dimensions
Defy my efforts to escape.
Make me whole again.

My world does not move
Until it starts to spin.
I am in your presence
And at your bidding,
But you know me not
Time is running out.
I am not dead,
Only inert.
Free me if you can,
Or live a life
Without singing

"It's Euterpe!" Erato shouted over my shoulder, hugging me hard. "She's alive and she's somewhere near, if we only knew where to look. Why can't she be more specific?"

"Because she didn't write that poem."

"What do you mean?"

"She didn't write it. And she didn't write the first one either," I surmised, holding her hands on my shoulders. "These are clues from her captor. This was written by Iberlin. Janet is keeping us on the string. For some reason she wants us to keep looking for Euterpe."

"But why would she do that?"

I spun around in my chair and looked up at her. "Have you forgotten what strange games humans like to play?" I asked, still holding her warm hands, now pulsating with power. "This is a riddle. We have to solve it in order to set Euterpe free. For some reason, perhaps only for her own amusement, Janet has engaged us in a battle of wits, including the noise planted at the end of the tape to keep us interested . . . But I, for one," I added, yawning, "am too tired to think about it any more tonight."

We went home and fell right to sleep, all three on the bed. I dreamed that Euterpe was trapped in a prison and calling for help. She was behind a wall, but I couldn't find the door. I looked and looked, but it was nowhere to be found. Later, at an ancient open-air marketplace, I bought a treasure chest. When I got home and opened it, there was another key inside. I ran to the locksmith and he told me it was the key to my heart.

Pulling up my shirt, there was a keyhole, right in the middle of my chest. I put the key in and turned. There, inside my heart, floated out the image of Euterpe. She was singing "The Sounds of Silence" by Simon and Garfunkel. And she was, at last, free.

I woke Erato and explained it to her. She said I was nuts and to go back to sleep. I rolled over, put my arms around Vinnie, and dozed off. The next morning Janet called. She wanted to see me right away—alone. Before I could say a word, she hung up.

27

The Trap

Since Janet wouldn't discuss a thing over the phone, I got dressed and went right in. Naturally, Erato wanted to go along, but Janet had told me to come alone. I suggested Erato go shopping or something. She informed me there was more to her life than shopping, and that she was planning to take Vinnie for a walk on the beach—a secluded one where with any luck, she wouldn't run into her dad. She went into the bedroom and opened the suitcase, saying she was planning a surprise.

"Look," I said from the doorway, making an emphatic gesture with my hands. "Don't go getting me anything."

Once I showed up in Janet's office, she didn't waste any time getting to the heart of the matter. She sat behind her desk, wearing a green silk pants suit and a string of pearls.

"You're wondering why I erased the file," she said matter-of-factly. "The simple truth is that Juanita just told me about the solution to the RAM transfer. So I don't need that file anymore. I made a new one, and renamed it, incorporating the changes to the test commands. Besides, Juanita said there wasn't anything unusual in the data other than some signal noise."

I sat in the same leather chair as before, saying the first thing that came into my head. "Erato's sister never was on the disk, was she?"

"Now you're finally being realistic. As I said before, the file was just test data, nothing more."

"Who created the Euterpe file, and why?"

She reached over and touched the stacking doll, but didn't answer.

"Well," I said, "it's either you, Cooper, or Dr. Vaya. Unless we've got a hacker, of course."

"We believe we have a spy," she said coolly, stroking the doll.

"I'm guessing that at first you thought it was me."

"We weren't sure if you were involved," Janet said calmly, folding her hands in her lap. She explained that someone had been trying to access the test-data file two weeks earlier. Cooper had reported attempted break-ins, always on his shift. So last Wednesday night she'd set up a little sting by planting a fake file for the 'guest.' When I didn't care to see the data after Juanita had solved the transfer problem, they knew I wasn't the hacker.

I was puzzled. "The only people who could have possibly known about the file are myself, Cooper, Dr. Vaya, and you."

"There's one other person," she said calmly, leaning forward. "Someone who should not have known anything. Unless, of course, she hacked-in."

"Erato? She's just looking for her sister, remember?"

"Yes, I know," she smiled. "And she certainly showed up at an opportune time—the very night the Euterpe file was created. What you didn't know was that Erato was at work in the classified computer lab." She got up and moved around to the front of her desk, bare feet and all.

"The poem and the file she created were her bait," she went on, crossing her slender legs. "She used them to set you up.

"We figured she was working with the security guard. He supplied her with the secret Iberlin account and password, which I planted in my desk. The next morning I discovered it had been broken into. We couldn't get him to talk, but there's no other way she could have got in and out without being spotted or setting off an alarm."

Straightening a hairpin, she told me that the guard must have picked up some information about the RAM chip from her office and passed it along to Erato. But he could never get enough to complete his task of stealing everything on the chip.

She hung her head for a second and then looked back up at me. "Of course, it's my own fault for leaving enough information lying around for him to sell. But he didn't have the test data—the key to how the nesting works. That was on the disk, except for the full backup in my safe. And for that he needed the DATANEST file. I planted a fake version on the Top Secret disk, which was accessed . . ." She looked me squarely in the eyes. "By the lovely Ms. Erato, I believe.

"Of course, I couldn't tell you. I thought you might be working with her."

"Why?"

"Three attempts were made between three and four in the afternoon, just after you got to work."

"I was probably in engineering, talking to one of the designers."

"We know, but there seemed to be enough time for you to stop at an unused terminal in one of the open labs and attempt a break-in. But that's all in the past now. You've been cleared."

Janet walked to the window. I was speechless, so I just let her continue with her fantastic story.

"Erato's most brilliant work, though," Janet continued with a sweeping gesture, "was yet to come. She quickly realized that the DATANEST file wasn't real, but a trap to catch a spy.

"Since she had made a complete folio on you, she knew that you were susceptible to new age beliefs." Janet looked at me, sunlight illuminating the side of her face. "She used that as a basis to launch her whole wonderfully clever story. Once she had established you as a believer, the rest was feasible.

"Still at the terminal, she had to think fast, but she was up to the task. Drawing on her knowledge of Greek mythology, she cast her clever scheme, renaming DATANEST Euterpe, giving it a new creation date, sending you the poem, and then logging off.

"She knew that you would be getting off soon, but also that your tenacity would keep you on the terminal long enough for her to leave and get herself to the bus bench out front."

She parted the drapes, looking out at nothing in particular. Turning from the window, she looked toward her lab. Juanita opened the door and stepped into the office. She was wearing a lab coat and a serious expression.

28

The Plan

Janet stood by her desk and pointed toward Juanita. "The reason we called you here is that we need your help to catch them."

"*Them*?" I asked, stretching my legs, but not getting up from the chair. "You think there's another partner besides the guard?"

"We ran a check on Ms. Erato," Juanita said gravely, hands in her lab coat. "I had her fingerprints from my lab mapped. Nothing. She has no arrest record. We believe Erato is her code name, and she's an operative for a man known only as Zeus."

"She wouldn't have registered fingerprints," I defended, putting my hands behind my head. "She's only been human for a couple of days."

"Cy," Janet said, ignoring my comment, "we think that the competition picked her *because* she had no record, and thus no fingerprints on file anywhere. That way she couldn't be traced."

"Then you've been playing me for a fool," I spat out.

"Not exactly," Juanita answered, leaning on the desk. "We need you, as Janet said, to help us bring her in."

"Why don't you just have her picked up?" I asked, exasperated.

Juanita sat on the edge of the desk. "We haven't got enough on her," she admitted. "We need to catch her in the act, or the FBI won't budge."

I leaned forward in the chair. "I suppose you think she's using me to get to the real file—the one I haven't even seen. I don't even know what it's called."

According to Janet, Erato figured she had the plans with the tape backup, and then with the master hard disk file. Naturally, Juanita's little experiment proved there was no alien entity on either one. But Erato knew that already, in Janet's view, and needed me more than ever to find the real test data.

"How can you be so sure of all this?" I asked, wrinkling my forehead.

"We can't," Janet said, going back to the window. "That's why we're proposing a . . . a test. We set up a phony RAM chip file and see if she takes the bait. If she's not after the plans, she won't care about the RAM file, just the so-called Euterpe file, which will be reinstated later today.

"The real plans will remain hidden somewhere on one of the disks, just as they are now. She'll never know where. And for security reasons, we can't tell you either."

"You mean the chip plans were never in the Top Secret files?" I asked, perturbed.

Janet revealed that the RAM file had been moved off the classified disk and hidden away in some inconspicuous spot, some boring file that nobody would access. Naturally, it was password-protected in case anyone stumbled onto it. Janet moved to the window and pulled the cord, slowly opening the drapes and letting sunlight pour in through the window.

"Forget it," I said. "This is a sting operation, and I want no part of it."

Juanita got up and went over to the jukebox, scanning the titles for a second. "If she is innocent," she began, not looking up, "this may be the only way to prove it."

"And if she *is* proved innocent," I asked, stretching my arms in front of me, "what about her sister?"

Janet was about to speak, but Juanita cut her off. "Then we will do whatever we can to get her back," she promised. "But frankly, from a scientific standpoint, I have to tell you . . ."

"Never mind," Janet said with a wave of her hand. "One thing at a time. If she does turn out to be the genuine article, you will have our full cooperation. And that goes for Cooper as well."

"Just how much does he know?" I asked, getting to my feet.

"Only what he has to," Janet said, slipping her hands into her pants pockets. "He doesn't know as much as you. And we're not going to tell him. We don't think he could handle it. He just thinks Erato is your girlfriend. We're leaving him out of the loop on this one."

"Good," I said, turning to leave. "That much I agree with." I stopped and pointed at Janet. "But before you set your trap, I want to know how you explain the songs she picked from the jukebox."

"Parlor trick," Janet waved off with her hand. "She never verified what *I* wrote down, just what *you* did."

"Yes, but she pressed the selection buttons based on what was written on my sheet of paper. I was sitting right here in that chair," I added, gesturing with my hand. "She couldn't have seen it from that distance. The window is fifteen feet away. How do you explain that?"

"We figure that she may have *some* limited psychic abilities," Janet admitted condescendingly. "Apparently she can read the contents of certain open minds, but more likely she saw the reflection of what you wrote in the window. It's like a mirror when the curtains are open."

I looked over at the window, and she was right. I could see a complete reflection of the office. "But still," I protested. "There's the distance factor."

"We've checked that," Juanita said, coming toward me from the jukebox. "Go over to the window. I'll sit in your chair and write down three songs."

I walked over to the window, studying the depth of reflection on its smooth surface. The image in the window was very clear. Looking at a certain angle, I could see what she had written on a piece of paper she had pulled from her lab coat. Somehow the refracted light even seemed to magnify the image, so that I was able to read all three of her titles.

"If you remember," Janet said, seated back behind her desk, "she had you close your eyes. So you couldn't see her reading the reflection on the glass."

"Still," I said to both of them, "she would have to have twenty-twenty vision."

"And a very quick mind," Janet added, placing her hands on her desk. "She knew that you were possibly psychic and might be able to guess what I wrote down. And you did," she admitted, "much to my own surprise. But she got fooled on the Simon and Garfunkel song. That's why she came up empty when it played."

I brought up the mental feats Erato had accomplished the night we went dancing, saying that she had picked songs before the band played them, and also from my drawing of the moon and the river on my napkin, which I never showed her in advance.

"So I suppose you think the nightclub incident was pre-arranged," I surmised, and proceeded to explain how Erato had picked a song over drinks.

"That would have been easy," Janet answered, leaning back in her chair. "She must have slipped a note to the waitress to give to the band when you weren't looking."

"And my second song, 'Moon River'?"

"What you wrote down must have reflected off the waitress's tray," Juanita explained, "or your glass. She could have read the reflection. Did Erato move the glasses out of the way so you could write down your song?"

"Yeah," I admitted, pushing my hands in my pockets. "Maybe she did. I really don't remember. It doesn't prove anything, but I'll go along just to show to you she doesn't want the RAM file. After that's been established, I want permission to search through every file in the system until we find a clue to where the real Euterpe is hidden."

Juanita spoke first. "But that's thousands of . . ."

"We can't give you that kind of access," Janet interrupted, "but we'll help you with the search. You have my word on it."

"Very well," Juanita said, almost snobbishly. "But for your sake I hope she is innocent. Otherwise, she's going to prison, I'm afraid."

"Thanks for the vote of confidence."

"Cy." Janet leaned forward in her chair. "We're counting on you."

"Yeah," I said ironically, standing by the window. "It's great to set your friends up to get busted. Gives you a real good feeling."

"There may not be much time," Janet said, ignoring my comment. "Zeus could pull her back at any time. So here's the plan."

I waited for them to explain the whole thing, saving my last jab until right before leaving. On the way out the door I turned and said, "One more thing, Doctor. Either she's a magician or she's a muse. But when you figure out the melting ice cube trick let me know . . . unless, of course, you think she's a human microwave." Then I turned and walked out.

I would have to go home and spring the plan on Erato, and see if she took the bait. And on that warm sunny day in paradise, that was about the last thing I wanted to do. I didn't believe what they had said about her, but I saw an opportunity. Putting their plan into effect could free Erato from suspicion once and for all, and then we'd have the file for sure.

29

Good-bye, Yellow Brick Road

I went to my cubicle, logged on, and checked for the Euterpe
file. It had been reformatted in a condensed mode, reduced to
ninety-six megabytes, and reinstated as planned. I checked on
the second file, E-Chip, which was the decoy for the RAM
chip blueprints. It was there too.

The stage was set. I was supposed to tell Erato that Euterpe
had needed to be reformatted, and was then reinstated, sharing
disk space with the E-Chip plans. Janet figured Erato would
access Euterpe first to throw me off. Then, after calling it up
on the computer screen and finding it empty of secret plans,
she would say that it didn't *feel* right, and ask to access the
E-Chip file. If she didn't, she would be cleared, which was
certain to be the case.

Janet and Juanita had tried very hard to win me over. I
hadn't cracked under the strain of their explanations, though
my mind had weakened a little. I wasn't even sure if I could
look at Erato without giving something away.

So I went home, but she wasn't there. She showed up half
an hour later, walking from the direction of the bus stop by my
apartment. She wasn't carrying any shopping bags, only her
purse. When she came through the front door she didn't give
me much of a chance to speak. She started in right away.

"What did Janet have to say?" she asked, plopping down on
the couch.

"The complete original file's been reinstated," I said coolly.

"Why now?" she asked, setting her purse on the coffee
table. "Why did they finally decide to come forth with everything?"

"I told them I was going to the FBI," I lied, leaning back
in my recliner. "That even if they hid the data somewhere, the
Feds would put a lock on the place and seize everything. That
would set them back long enough to let the competition catch

up. Then Janet's precious chip would be nothing special."

"And they believed you?"

"They couldn't chance it. They may not believe in you, but they're scientists. Neither one of them can make a move until you're disproved. Boy, they're sure going to be in for a big surprise when we prove you're for real—and that Euterpe is too."

She sat straight up on the couch, hardly able to contain her excitement. "I . . . I thought it was erased."

"No, just reformatted. That's how Dr. Vaya got the noise out."

She frowned. "Wait a minute. What do you mean, reformatted?"

I sat forward and planted my bare feet on the carpet, explaining that Janet had put it in the condensed mode, removing the empty spaces. Juanita said the spaces contained noise. The only difference was that it took up less disk space.

"I hope they haven't damaged it," she said anxiously.

Getting up, I walked over to the window, watching Vinnie come out of the bedroom and cuddle up to Erato. "It should be fine," I said stiffly, staring at her. "We do this all the time."

"Yeah, but not with this kind of data."

"It shouldn't make a difference," I defended, waving my arms. "It's all digital."

"When can Dr. Vaya meet us in the lab?" she asked, petting Vinnie.

"This afternoon . . . By the way, where have you been?" I turned around and faced her. Taking a deep breath, I challenged her. "You haven't been shopping. You don't have any bags."

She didn't answer at first, just scratched Vinnie's good ear. "I . . . I was just looking," she confessed at last.

Suddenly, seeing her sitting there in all innocence, I got cold feet. I moved over and sat on the coffee table.

"Look," I began. "They said you're a spy. They think you got in that night using the security guard, and that you're working for an operative who goes by the code name Zeus."

"Boy," she laughed. "And I thought *you* watched too many spy movies."

I hung my head, and then looked up at her. "I wasn't supposed to tell you any of this, but . . ."

She guessed the rest. "They want you to set me up," she surmised. "They think I'll go for the chip plans."

"Yeah, and I was going to do it. But just to show them you're for real." Beginning to flush, I added, "I . . . I'm sorry. It was all I could think of to get one last chance at finding Euterpe . . . but now I can't go through with it. Maybe . . . maybe you'd just better go . . . I don't know. I thought this would be easy. But I can't look at you knowing I could have jeopardized the whole thing."

"Don't be silly," she said, reaching over and taking my hand. "I'm not going. Not until I prove once and for all who I am. Let's go along with their plan. I certainly don't need the RAM chip file. I won't go anywhere near it. That way we can see what's on the complete, unedited Euterpe file."

Pulling my hand back, I told her that nothing was on the file we hadn't already seen or heard. When they filtered out the noise, they erased what we thought might be Euterpe's voice. Now the file only contained test data.

With doubts and disappointment starting to creep in, I leaned forward and grabbed her shoulders. "Your sister," I said gravely, "is gone. And nobody thinks you're from another dimension. I'm . . . I'm not even sure myself anymore. Maybe I just *wanted* to believe. I'll admit that you do have some extraordinary powers. But . . ." I motioned at her purse. "Look, you said you were going shopping, but you haven't brought anything home lately. That's not like you. What were you doing? And why all the secrecy?"

"It's a surprise, remember?"

I got up and put my hands on my hips. "Mirrors," I sighed. "They said you did it all with mirror images."

"Turn on the radio," Erato ordered. "I'll show you."

"No," I said, turning my back so I couldn't look at her. "No more parlor tricks . . . Look," I added, turning slowly around, and finally looking at her. "You're a nice girl and . . . I like you more than I've ever liked anyone, but right now I'm a little confused. Maybe you'd just better go. I've ruined everything, and there's nowhere else to look for your sister. So why not leave it alone and go back to your . . . *world* or wherever you came from. This is too complicated for me. Muses, spirits digitized on hard disks, Greek gods. This is starting to sound like some . . . crazy story. I can't deal with it anymore. I'm burned-out on the supernatural. Tell Zeus, or whoever he is, to bail her out. I have to get back to normal before someone has me committed."

Erato hadn't given up on me yet. "How about a sign?" she asked, undaunted. "What if I show you a sign?"

"You mean, like in the Bible?" I said sarcastically. "Parting the Red Sea or a burning bush? Maybe you could blow a trumpet and make the walls of this apartment fall down."

She shook her head. "Boy, they really got to you, didn't they? Look, give me until tonight. I'll think of something, even if I have to talk to Dad."

"I wouldn't do that if I were you. They think he's behind this whole thing. They'll pick you both up. . . . Just go, will you? Just please leave me alone." I stood up and walked to the window, staring out blankly. "I've got to sort this thing out."

"All right," she said, grabbing her purse. "If that's the way you want it. But I'll be back, and it won't be for fun and games."

I turned around and stared at her. "Erato, this is *serious* . . . Wait, I've got an idea. Let me talk to Zeus. I want to hear what he has to say. Why he needs the chip so badly. Maybe we can work something out."

"What do you mean?" she asked, slinging her purse over her shoulder.

Having suddenly lost all faith in her, I guessed Zeus was a competitor of Janet's. "Could he use a washed-up former hacker at his company?" I asked. "I've been embarrassed so badly at Sigma, I'm ready to call it quits." I pointed my finger at her. "No espionage, though. I won't steal secrets."

Undaunted, she bent over and petted Vinnie. "He doesn't talk to mortals," she said quietly.

"Okay," I said, gesturing toward the ceiling. "I'll play your game. But why would he talk to you? You're as human as I am, maybe more so."

She stood up and gave me a sincere look. "No, Cyrus. I'm not. I just look like one. You forget I only borrowed this body and my time's almost up. I've only got until Saturday night at the most. After I talk to Dad, he may pull me back on the spot."

I walked away, stopping to stare out the kitchen window at the mountains. Looking over my shoulder I said, "This is probably it, then. . . . Well," I added, dejectedly, "it's been fun." She stepped slowly toward the door. "Hey," I said, turning halfway in the window. "What about your stuff?"

"You keep it," she said, not looking back. "I won't need any of it where I'm going. But don't toss it for a couple of days. If I can get absolute proof, I'll be coming back."

"Might as well," I agreed. "I sure can't wear any of those dresses; they're way too small."

She opened the door and reached down to pet Vinnie, who had come over from the couch. Then she stood up and walked out. I went over and held the door open, watching her go down the steps.

"Hey, Angel," I blurted out. "I'm going to miss you."

"Naw, you won't," she said, not turning around. "First good wave comes along and you'll forget all about me."

"Forgive maybe, but not forget."

She turned at the bottom of the stairs. I couldn't let go of her. She was the only woman I had ever really cared for, the only one who moved me inside. But under the circumstances, there was no choice. I stared long and hard at her, wanting to remember her forever.

"Bye, Surf Rat," she beamed, looking up at me. "If you ever need me, try writing a poem sometime. I'll tell them to make sure and put the call through. And remember, I only show up for the best. You may not know it, but there's a poet in there somewhere."

"Naw, pure computer," I answered, wiping mist out of my eyes. "All machine. Hearts are for poets. I've got a CPU . . . Go on," I added. "Get outta here. . . . Hey, one more thing."

She stopped in her tracks, now at the curb. She glowed in the afternoon sun as if a light from heaven had come to take her home. "Okay," she said. "Shoot."

"Any regrets?"

"I never got to make love."

"Anything else?"

"Pizza. I never got to try pizza. One thing's for sure, though, it's safer than making love."

"Is that all?"

"Well, now that you mention it. I can see why humans fall for each other. It makes life worth living." When I didn't say anything, she added, "Cy, I . . . I was starting to . . . well, anyway . . . Bye. It's been real."

After she disappeared down the block I suddenly realized that the suitcase full of money was still in the closet. I ran downstairs toward the bus stop, but when I got there, the bus was pulling away. Walking back dejectedly, I had a long talk with Vinnie, explaining to him that I didn't want her to go, but I didn't want her to get caught either, just in case she wasn't for real. We took a long walk on the beach, and I kept looking for that old man in the wet suit, but no such luck. I realized again that the newspaper ad had come out the previous day, but couldn't bear to look at it. I might lose two things I cared about in the same day. It didn't feel very good.

I went to work and moped around, informing Janet by phone that Erato got jumpy and didn't take the bait. She had split, and wouldn't be back. "Unless she can prove she's really an extraterrestrial," I had said, laughing. Janet laughed too, but differently, and thanked me for smoking Erato out of her hole. I didn't like her saying that about the woman I loved. But what did it matter? Janet informed me that she was going to leave the files intact for a few days just in case Erato circled back and tried to break in. I said I doubted it, but you never know. Stranger things have happened.

After a routine night I drove home, foolishly looking at the empty bus bench as I passed by, and noticing dark clouds forming overhead. Not unusual in other parts of the world, but it never rained in July in southern California.

30

Fire and Rain

Once at home I went upstairs and turned on the TV, hoping to get a late report on the weather, but my set only got the one local channel. A rerun of *Footloose* was playing, so I turned it off.

I hadn't bothered to put the top up on the Mustang, although the clouds were rapidly growing thick and dark. The wind was blowing fiercely, pushing giant gray cloud puffs inland so fast that it looked like one of those time-lapse photography documentaries on some nature program.

Still, I didn't go down and put the top up. After all, the morning surf report had said nothing about any storms screaming across the Pacific. Heck, it barely rained in the winter some years, and summer storms were all but nonexistent, especially coming in unannounced.

Turning on the radio to my favorite pop station, I waited for a news bulletin, but no dice. So I listened to some sounds and almost forgot about the weather. But then it started to bother me—so many clouds coming to town without an advance media campaign. I stepped out on the balcony, which overlooked the street and had a pretty good view of the mountains over the treetops. Crowding in with my bicycle, two surfboards, and some miscellaneous car parts, I sat in a lawn chair.

With pop vocals providing background music, I watched the low-flying clouds slam up against the four-thousand-foot mountains like a pileup on the LA freeway. Then, suddenly, the thick, heavy sky gave way, slashed open in several places by tremendous bolts of lightning. The clouds crashed together, sending me back a little in my lawn chair. Rain began to spill from the sky like a spring waterfall in a high mountain pass, drenching the streets below.

I became engrossed in nature's show, watching intently as brilliant flashes of white light shot jagged electric swords at the earth. Dozens of lightning strikes lit up the dark sky like some massive night assault illumined by flares.

By the time I got my wits back and made it to my car, there was water on the seats and floor. Luckily, I had parked under the huge elm tree out in the parkway, so not that much rain had yet hit the car.

I hurriedly put the top up, just missing the lower branches of the tree. A lightning bolt hit the lawn across the street and I ducked onto the car seat. Getting up, I looked over. No damage, but a big, jagged black mark was burned into the lawn.

I finally got the top latched and the windows up, then dashed for the stairs. Something made me look back. When I did, the passenger's side window was still down a couple of inches from the top. I turned to run for the car.

Suddenly a powerful shaft of burning white light hit one of the branches of the elm tree, breaking it off with a loud crack. It fell in the street with a fiery crash, just missing the trunk of my car, and shooting flames from the bare stump. The rain doused the fire as a column of white smoke took to the sky.

Another lightning bolt came right behind it, making a direct hit on the trunk of my car, scattering hot light everywhere, like a welder's arc hitting metal. Then a piece of it hit me in the chest like molten shrapnel, knocking me flat on the front lawn. My body shook with muscle spasms. Sparks flew off my chest as electricity buzzed through me like touching a couple of power lines together. Then the feeling was gone, and I was out. I don't know how long I lay there, but it must have been hours. When I finally came to, my body had been drenched by the rain.

Slowly sitting up, I checked that all my arms, legs, and other vital parts were still intact. My Hawaiian shirt had been on fire, but the rain had doused it. I took it off and tossed it on the lawn. Other than losing a few chest hairs, I seemed okay. But I was buzzing like a transformer on a telephone pole.

Almost delirious, I got up and staggered toward the street, instead of running for the apartment as any sane person would have done. For some confused reason, I wanted to check the Mustang for damage.

When I got there it looked almost normal, except for the singed top and the spot where the lightning bolt had hit the trunk. The paint had bubbled away in a large jagged area. It gave the rough impression of a foot-high zigzag that resembled a crude letter Z.

Suddenly the lightning, thunder, and rain stopped as quickly as they had started. The clouds lifted themselves over the mountains and moved on. It became so quiet that I could hear the radio upstairs. A newscaster was saying: "Local scientists and meteorologists are still sorting out what has just happened. Apparently, a massive but highly localized cloud system just off the coast appeared out of nowhere and rapidly moved onshore. This sudden storm is so unusual that there is literally no data on this type of weather phenomenon. We will have more later as information becomes available . . ."

"Shoot," I said, starting to recover my senses and staring at the trunk. "It *was* him. Mr. Z. How could I have been so stupid?"

Gathering myself, I staggered upstairs and sat on the couch. Vinnie came out from under the bed, and we comforted each other for a long time. We sat glued to the radio, waiting for an update on events.

That lightning bolt was my sign, whether I wanted one or not. I was wrong to doubt Erato, and now she was gone, perhaps forever. I had missed any further chance to help save Euterpe.

All my life I had managed by hiding behind a smart mouth—protecting my vulnerability with clever remarks as my shield. I was scared to death of revealing my soft inner self to anyone, until Erato showed up. I was ready to tell her everything, but had chickened out, losing my courage when doubt rushed in to replace it. But now that she was gone, I was beginning to fill up with something more powerful than doubt—regret.

I had told her to leave because I didn't have the guts to trust her. Opportunity had knocked, but I sent it away. Now I wanted to run after it, but didn't know where to look. All I knew was that it had stolen my heart on the way out the door.

What did it matter if we could only be together a couple of weeks? I'd always have our days together the same way Bogie and Bergman would always have Paris, and it would have been worth it. Sure, I'd still have our few shared moments together to remember, but it hadn't ended right. Too much had been left unsaid. I wanted to tell her that she had saved me from loneliness. But she was gone, and I wanted her back.

As I got up and shut off the TV, a knock at the door startled me. My nerves were still a little jangled from the lightning strike, and my body tingled all over.

"Mr. Major?" a generic looking CHP officer asked when I opened the door.

"Huh?"

He gave me a funny look, but went on. "Cyrus Major?" he asked, flipping a notebook.

"Uh . . . yeah. What can I do for you?"

"Do you know someone in her early twenties, blond hair, five feet eight, about one hundred and . . ."

"Erato," I said, worried. "Has she been hurt?"

His expression never changed. "Could you identify her? She's out in the patrol car."

I bolted past him and down the stairs. She was sitting in the backseat, but it wasn't until her drenched hair and smile filled my eyes that I knew she was okay. We didn't speak. She jumped out of the backseat and into my arms. We hugged hard for a long time.

"Then I take it you two know each other?" the officer said behind us, holstering his notebook.

"Never saw her before in my life," I said with her head on my shoulder. "But I always take in strays."

"Thanks," Erato said to me, "for the ego boost."

"I . . . I thought you were a goner," I said, holding her at arms' length. "Shoot, I thought *I* was a goner. I got struck by lightning. Look, tell your Dad I didn't mean it about the dirty old man crack will you? I don't think I can survive another lightning bolt attack. I'm still buzzing."

The officer shook his head and said his good-byes. We started up the stairs. "Where have you been?" I asked, not letting go of her. "I was worried sick about you."

"Before or after the lightning?" She gently kissed my neck.

"Well, okay. But don't disappear again without leaving me a lightning rod, will you? I almost got killed."

When we got to the top of the stairs, she petted a very excited Vinnie. Looking at her, I got an idea. "Hey, you know that part about making love?" I asked. "Maybe we'd better do something about it while I'm still in one piece. Unless, of course, you'd rather have pizza."

"Boy, what's gotten into you?" she grinned, taking off her wet leather jacket. "You'd think you were glad to see me or something."

"Never mind," I answered, starting to turn red. "I was just kidding."

"Yeah," she replied, tossing her jacket on the back of a kitchen chair. "I thought so. But I don't think we can get a pizza at three in the morning."

"Look," I said, ignoring her comment. "I need a hot shower, so if you'll just excuse me . . ."

"Sure. Mind if I join you?" she asked coyly, pulling her wet T-shirt over her head.

"What kind of question is that?" I asked, staring at her upper body.

"Just thought I'd better take you up on this before you cool off," she winked, and peeled off her Levi's. "There is, however, one condition."

"I knew it," I said, not taking my eyes off her. "What?"

"No more doubts," she insisted, unbuttoning my Levi's.

"No more doubts?" I asked, stepping out of my pants. "The tree at the curb just got a massive trimming. My car's got a custom paint job and fringe around the edges. I'm still buzzing from being struck by lightning, and you think I have doubts?"

"You forgot something," she grinned. "Looked in the mirror lately?"

I went into the bathroom and stared in the mirror, hardly believing my eyes. My beard had been all but burned off. Fortunately my chin was undamaged. But there was something else. The hairs on my chest had been burned off in a crude letter Z, like one of those razor haircut jobs. I made a fist and raised it to the ceiling.

"Look," I said. "I don't mind the custom chest hair job, but if you didn't like my beard, why didn't you just say so? I can take a hint."

Erato took one look at my bare chin and said, "Anyone with a strong chin should show it off. Now, let's take that shower, shall we?"

"Well, I don't know," I said with fake seriousness. "Will you still respect me in the morning?"

"I'll make you a deal," she replied, raising an eyebrow, then running her hand through my new custom chest haircut. "I'll respect *you* if you believe in *me*."

"Deal. And another thing. I thought lightning bolts never struck twice in the same place."

"Depends on who's pitching them."

We shook hands on our agreement, got undressed the rest of the way, and stepped into the shower. After hugging and kissing and soaping each other down I said, "If lightning strikes me now, at least I'll die with a smile on my face."

"Not yet," she said, biting my neck. "But you're about to."

31

Creation

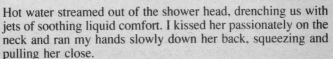

Hot water streamed out of the shower head, drenching us with jets of soothing liquid comfort. I kissed her passionately on the neck and ran my hands slowly down her back, squeezing and pulling her close.

She was rubbing against my stomach and running her hands all over my body. Our lips met as I gently pushed her back against the shower tiles. Streams of water pelted my back as she held me in a firm embrace, her fingernails digging gently into my shoulders. I was too amped to worry about her voltage, having enough of my own.

I closed my eyes and was gone, almost unconscious, as passion poured over me. Our bodies moved as one. I was swept away by an all-consuming feeling of free-falling, and then by the sensation of a raging ocean pulling me under and drowning me, as I wanted to be drowned. I was in a place inside myself that vibrated with the deep, joyous rhythm of an endless song of life, reverberating in sensual ecstasy— life's gift of making a new spirit out of the delirious union of two souls. It was electric. And from that moment on, I was never again afraid to touch her.

The feeling rose until it reached a crescendo, and then we collapsed into each other's arms, barely able to stand, but I held her there, not wanting to let go. Finally, we melted softly into each other's arms.

"Erato," I said, looking deep into her eyes. "I . . . I think . . ."

She placed her hand over my mouth. "I know," she said softly. "But there's nothing we can do. We're worlds apart. And I think we're wasting—"

This time I put my hand over *her* mouth. "No, we're not," I said. "We're not wasting anything. It doesn't matter how long we have together. We have this moment. We'll always have—"

"*Water*," she said, taking my hand off her mouth. "We're wasting water."

We dried off and went to bed, unable to keep our hands off each other. Soon, we were loving each other again—more slowly this time, with a passion that built gradually like a great moving wave and ended like a sunset, quiet and glowing.

"Still want that pizza?" I asked, finally breaking the silence.

"Right now," she said, cuddling me, "I've got all I want. Do you know what happens when someone in heaven volunteers to become human?"

"No, what?"

"She gets promoted. Being human helps her development. It has something to do with understanding and compassion. You know, the walk-a-mile-in-my-shoes stuff."

"Does this mean you won't be a muse anymore, after this whole thing is over?"

"Who knows? That's for Dad to decide. But if we don't get my sister free soon, my name is mud."

"Hey, your dad's a scary guy," I frowned, plopping back on my pillow. "Has he been watching 'Zorro' reruns or something?"

"What's that supposed to mean?"

"He customized the paint job on my car. One of his thunderbolts drew a Z on my trunk, not to mention this." I pointed to my chest. "He isn't much for penmanship, but I got the message."

"Hmmm. Do you want me to ask him to try it again?" she asked, half-serious. "Maybe he can do a cleaner job of it next time."

"No thanks. I got the message. What did you say to him, anyway?"

"Nothing."

"Nothing?"

"I didn't see him," she replied, rolling on top of me. "But I think we'd better go to the beach tomorrow. This is his way of telling me it's time for a talk."

"One heck of a paging system you've got there."

She kissed me long and slow, then pulled back. Rolling off me, she threw her head onto the pillow and stared up at the ceiling. "We've got a big day tomorrow, but I'm not doing anything until I talk to Dad."

I rolled onto my side and stroked her hair, then looked out the window at the moon spreading its pale light across the sky. "Can I ask you a question about your dad?" I asked.

"Depends. Like what?"

"Does he really know everything?"

She looked at me. "Naw, he doesn't keep track of all the details. But he can know whatever he wants to in an instant."

"What about individual lives? I mean, what people do."

"Only if he's interested. Why?"

"Well, if he doesn't know already, do you have to tell him about . . . us? I mean . . ." I stroked her cheek softly. "The most recent part?"

"Why not?" she asked, confused.

"What if he doesn't like me? What if a mortal isn't good enough for his daughter? What if you're . . . pregnant?"

"Then I would have a baby," she said right off, blowing a hair from her face. "I've always wanted one, but it wasn't possible until now, of course."

"Would you have it in heaven or here?"

"Human babies aren't born in heaven," she reminded me. "That's what earth is for."

"What would that make our son? He'd only be half-human."

"Our daughter? A poet, of course. That's what *I* want."

"Erato," I said, smiling at her. "You've been thinking about this."

"My clock is ticking," she stated. "I'm going to be pulled back pretty soon. Unless, of course, I'm having a baby. Then maybe my parents would let me stay."

"You're a sneaky, conniving, scheming, wonderful genius! Quick," I said, diving under the covers, "we've got work to do. Babies to make.

"Now, let's see if we can get one started. . . . But first, I want to know something. Are you just using me to experience motherhood?" I joked.

"I came here with two objectives," she answered seriously. "To get my sister back and experience as much of life as possible in what short time I have. I didn't plan on . . ." She looked me in the eyes and then hugged me. "I didn't plan on falling for you."

"You mean . . ."

"What I mean is that I came here to help my sister and advance my career a little by being human. I . . . I was trying to make it strictly business and not mix it with pleasure, but was failing miserably. The look on your face when I left tonight made me want to run back upstairs and tell you it didn't matter if we set Euterpe free. Dad would do it anyway, even if we failed—and the world would just have to suffer the consequences. But I had to go, to let you send me away, hoping that you'd take me back when you came to your senses and realized we were meant to be together, if even for just the blink of an eye. After the sky lighted up I knew Dad was up to something and I got worried about you, so I flagged down this policeman and . . ."

"I never should have let you go," I admitted. "But I was confused. I'm not anymore. I want us to be together, always. Talk to your dad. Tell him we did the best we could to find your sister, but we need his help now. And tell him I want to be with you no matter what. We've got to find a way to be together. Tell him . . . tell him we want a baby if you have to. We've got to get through to him."

"Then you want . . ."

I reached over and put my arms around her. "Yes," I said without hesitation. "I want to marry you, have babies *and* a life with you. No matter how long it lasts. Tell your dad his lightning bolts didn't scare me off. Tell him I won't give you up. Tell him . . . tell him I *can't*."

We held each other for a long time, not making love, just wanting to be close. And then, in the early morning hours of that long, incredible night, we slept.

32

Zeus at the Beach

The next morning, after breakfast, all three of us piled into the Mustang and took off for the beach. Erato said that's where her dad would be if we needed to find him.

The good news was that the car started right up and ran fine, despite the singed roof and custom paint job on the trunk. It wasn't even too wet inside, considering the storm. We sat on towels and zipped off down the road.

One thing was peculiar, though. I couldn't get any pop vocals on the radio. The only stations that came in were playing all instrumentals, or had talk shows. At least one station should have had a vocalist.

"Uh oh," Erato said, spinning the dial. "This may be a sign."

"A sign?" I said, staring at the road. "What do you call last night?"

"Last night was nothing compared to a thousand years of instrumentals and talk radio. Even opera buffs will be upset."

"But how would he do that?" I asked, frowning at her.

"Amnesia. Nobody remembers how to write song lyrics anymore or something like that. Thus, no singing."

"Wait a minute," I said, adjusting the rearview mirror. "Your dad's been watching that movie *Footloose* or something."

"Pardon?"

"Dancing was not allowed in that movie," I informed her. "Now, no singing."

We passed a car with a vocal on the radio. "Wait," she said, grabbing my arm. "So far it's localized. It's only affecting your radio. Probably just the lightning." She shut off the radio with a shrug and sat back in her seat.

Pulling up to a stoplight, I noticed the guy next to us had a funny expression on his face. His radio had gone suddenly from vocal to instrumental. Looking confused, he spun the dial—but couldn't find a station that had any vocals. He pulled out a CD and stuck it in the player. The music to "Like a Virgin" came out of the speakers, but no singing Madonna. Judging from the confusion on his face, her voice must have been erased.

So that was how Zeus would do it. All recorded singing would be erased. The human voice would be left a silent instrument—past, present, and future.

The guy in the other car ejected the CD and just for laughs began singing the national anthem, but halfway through he forgot the words.

"See," I said, nodding his way. "It's starting to happen."

"Nonsense. Lots of people forget the words to that song."

"Oh, yeah? Well, sing a song. Any song," I demanded, pulling away as the light turned green.

She thought for a moment, and drawing a blank said, "I can't think of anything right now."

"Not even 'Happy Birthday'?"

"How *does* that go anyway?" she asked, thinking to herself. "Let's see, it's right here on the tip of my tongue."

"Look, we've got to see him right away," I said, desperately. "A lot of people are not going to like this. Not to mention record companies. Heck, even bad singing is better than no singing."

"No, that's where you're wrong," she corrected me, brushing her hair with her hands. "The human voice is a beautiful instrument, but silence is better than bad singing. Take it from me."

She directed me to pull into the beach parking lot adjacent to the university. It was the same place I had dropped her off that first night. I was starting to think maybe seeing her dad wasn't such a great idea after all. Who knew what Zeus would say or do? But knowing how handy he was with electricity, I suppressed my fears and shut up about it.

"Turn left," she ordered. "And go down to the far end of the parking lot, past the pier and restaurant. I want to go to the place by the cliffs where I was staying on the beach. That's where I came into the world, and that's where he'll be."

"Okay," I said, spinning the wheel counterclockwise. "But we'll have to wade across the inlet through waist-deep water.

You do realize that's where all the nude bathers hang out."

"Exactly," she answered straight-faced. "You don't think I came into the world with clothes on, do you? Nobody else does."

"But what about all that money?"

Erato explained that her mom had planted a cache of rare pearls in a conch shell for her on the beach. She traded a couple of them for some clothes with a sunbathing biker chick, hocked what remained at a pawnshop and went shopping for the rest of her outfit, then met me at the bus stop later that same night.

She looked down at her chest. "As you can see, I liked the Harley T-shirt, so I kept it. Figured it would make me look more down-to-earth."

We parked, got out of the car, waded fifty yards across the inlet, and came up on the shore. A narrow strip of sand threaded its way between the cliffs and ocean, winding around corners and coves all the way to Santa Isabella's wide, flat tourist beaches. This long secluded strip of sand was perfect for sun worshipers to get that allover tan, and could also be used to spend a few nights on the beach if you were discreet and watched for high tides.

We had walked about a half mile down the white sand when Erato stopped suddenly. It wasn't the nudists up ahead that got her attention. A hundred yards down the beach a silver-haired senior citizen sat in a lawn chair, sporting one of those screaming Day-Glo yellow wet suits and some Wayfarers. A multicolored surfboard dripped beside him as he looked out to sea.

"It's *him*," Erato confirmed. "You'd better stay here. I've got to go it alone."

"Good luck," I said, grabbing a stick for Vinnie to chase. "Remember," I added, suddenly getting cold feet. "I'm just a friend."

She hugged me and said, "No you're not. I won't lie. If he asks, I'll tell him the truth."

"Of course," I agreed. "I'm being stupid. Tell him we're in . . . you know."

"The word, Cyrus Major," she said, walking away, "is *love*. Look it up. It's in the dictionary next to *love affair*. It happens to people sometimes."

"Yeah, guess you're right," I said sheepishly. "Love happens." I thought for a moment and asked, "Hey, do you think your old man could spring for a new paint job on the Mustang?"

"Don't be silly," she said from twenty yards away. "Acts of God are not covered."

"Never mind," I shrugged. "It was just a thought. I think"— I looked down the beach—"someone's waiting for you."

She walked slowly toward her dad, her Harley T-shirt barely covering her pink bikini. Trying not to look, I picked up a stick and tossed it into the waves. Vinnie charged out after it, breaking through the surf and swimming as only a water dog can. He grabbed it in his teeth and raced back, dropping it at my feet and shaking saltwater all over me. We did this over and over. Meanwhile, Erato had reached her dad.

They talked for a long time. Zeus never got out of the chair. He just sat there looking out to sea, listening and talking occasionally between sips of what looked like a bottle of sparkling water.

Erato put her hands on her head, then patted her stomach and pointed my way. Vinnie was just scrambling out of the water, and he mistook this as a sign to come. He bolted down the beach toward them, stick and all. I almost ran after him, but stopped after a couple of steps, deciding he was excited, wet, and on his own.

When he got there Zeus stood up, took the stick out of Vinnie's mouth, and tossed it into the ocean. Vinnie tore after it and brought it back, shaking himself on both of them. Much to my great amazement, Zeus got down and actually wrestled Vinnie for the stick. Now I had seen everything.

After awhile they both grew tired, and Zeus fell back in the sand. Vinnie came over and licked his face, and Zeus sat up laughing. Erato reached over and hugged her dad, and he hugged her back as any father would. Then she ran excitedly back. When she and Vinnie got to me she was beaming.

"He says I can stay," she smiled. "At least until we free Euterpe." She patted her stomach. "Maybe longer . . . There's just one thing."

"Uh oh. I knew it. What is it?"

"He said he won't interfere again on one condition."

"What is it?" I asked impatiently.

"He wants to ride a Harley."

"What?"

Looking up at me she said, "He read my T-shirt."

"Oh no," I laughed, reading the words on her chest. *God Rides a Harley.* "Well, that's not so bad. What if you would have been wearing a heavy metal T-shirt? He might have made us take him to an ear-busting concert. Let him ride," I said, shrugging my shoulders. "What do we care?"

She sat down in the sand. "No, I'm afraid you don't understand. He wants us to get him one, by sunrise tomorrow."

"Well, so what?" I said, looking down at her. "You're loaded. Let's go buy one."

"*Was* loaded."

"What do you mean?" I asked, confused.

"When you were at work I gave all the money to charity."

"You did *what*?"

"That was going to be my surprise," she mumbled, not looking up. "I got tired of your giving me the poor-little-rich-girl treatment. I wanted us to be able to make it on our own, without my parents' help." She lifted her head and finished her confession. "So I emptied out the suitcase and gave it all to the homeless shelter."

"You did *what*?"

"Look, we can probably still get the money back. I can say it was a mistake." She gave me a sympathetic look. "Cy, if you could've seen the looks on their faces . . ."

"No," I said, looking out to sea. "You're right. It's my fault for making fun of you. Some people may be homeless, but it's their planet too. Besides, it was your money." I turned back and stared at her. "So now what? He expects us to steal one?"

"Dad doesn't condone theft," she answered, getting to her feet. "He wants us to borrow one. He only wants to ride for a little while. Then he says we can return it."

"Why doesn't he just go poof and create one?"

"Not his style, I'm afraid. He doesn't want to interfere with the laws of nature unless it's an emergency. He doesn't like breaking his own rules."

"And I suppose if we don't *borrow* this Harley, he'll intervene." I was still upset.

"Yes," she replied, hugging me. "And it won't be all that great. Euterpe could be taken out of this world for a thousand years, maybe more."

"I . . . I don't get this," I said, frustrated.

"Don't you see?" she said, looking up at me. "Human beings got Euterpe into this mess, and now they have to get her out."

"Well," I said, getting perturbed. "What about Vinnie? Couldn't he at least give him back his ear flap? Or would that mess up some grand design?"

"Vinnie's a lucky dog," she said, smiling and looking down at him. "Dad sealed up his ear. I was wrong about the salt-water. The salt was okay, but the moisture was causing an inner ear infection." She got a guilty look on her face and added, "I guess I blew it. . . . But Dad took one look and fixed him up." She petted Vinnie, who had shed his bandage.

I knelt and inspected Vinnie's ear. Not only were the stitches gone, but the wound had completely healed over. The flap was still missing, but it looked as though he had been born that way. Hair had even grown over the skin where the stitches had been.

"Dad stepped in," Erato went on, "saying it was an emergency. And that's not all," she added. "He's got big plans for Vinnie."

"What sort of plans?"

"The secret kind," she replied, poking my ribs. "Now, let's get going. We've got a motorcycle to borrow."

"Hmmm, I see. Does he have a particular color in mind?"

"Naw," she shrugged. "He likes them all."

33

The Storyteller

We got back to the car and dried off. Flipping on the radio confirmed that songs with lyrics had returned.

I began to see the difficulty we were going to have finding an unminded motorcycle. Harleys are rare treasures to their owners, who sometimes put all of their life savings and most of their soul into purchasing their dream machines. The bikes were more than modes of transportation, more than lean mean street machines; they were works of art. Somehow, you just couldn't say, "Hey, mind if I take the pride and joy of your life for a spin on the beach?"

On the way home I made a suggestion. "Maybe I can buy

one on trial and return it the next day. We could tell them I
made an honest mistake."

"I don't think so," Erato said, shaking her head. "Besides,
then it would be used."

"Yeah, you're right," I agreed, coming to my senses. "That
was a bad idea. Well, what's *your* suggestion, just walk up
and ask some guy that looks like Hulk Hogan if we can take
his scooter to the beach?"

"We've only got one chance," she said, resting her feet on
the dash. "We'll have to wait until you get off work. Then
we'll go out looking."

"Right," I said sarcastically. "And I suppose we're going to
find one with the keys in the ignition. Unless you're a hot-wire
expert."

"Don't be ridiculous," she said confidently. "If you want to
catch fish, you go to the water."

"Uh oh, I don't like the sound of this." I looked at her
T-shirt. "And I suppose we're going to use you for bait?"

"Unless you think *you* can get picked up in this shirt."

"What do *you* know about beer bars?" I asked, glancing at
her profile.

"I got a call once from some poet trying one of those
real-life experience things," she informed me, moving her
seat back a little. "Didn't work out though. In the middle of
writing his poem, he got hit over the head with a pool cue."

"Great," I scoffed, turning onto Walnut Place. "I can hardly wait."

At work later that day I tried to ignore Cooper. It wasn't
easy. He was surprised and elated about my clean-shaven face,
coming into my cubicle to celebrate the event.

"Hey," he beamed, hands on his lapels. "There's hope for
you yet. That girlfriend of yours make you shave it off?"

"Nope," I answered, not looking up. "Her dad did."

"Her dad? . . . Wait," he said, cupping his ears. "Is that
wedding bells I hear in the distance?"

"Could be," I said with a smile, then looked up at him from
my chair. "Hey, Coop. Why didn't you ever get married?"

"Look at me," he said, wrinkling his forehead. "I'm a tedious,
difficult, boring, perfection-driven yuppie. Women lost interest
when most of us went to jail in the eighties for stock market
fraud. Nobody wants a pain in the neck like me around."

"Well, would you look at that," I said, getting a thought.
"We're more alike than you think. I'm at one end of the

spectrum, and you're at the other. You think any woman in her right mind wants a surf slob that refuses to grow up?"

"Sure," he said, surprising me. "This is California, remember?"

"*Woman*," I said, spinning around in my chair, "not teeny-bopper. I just got lucky with the one I've got. She doesn't know any better. She's new to the West Coast."

"You'll never believe this," he said, looking me straight in the eyes. "But I wanted to be a lifeguard once. Thought it would be a good way to impress the girls in high school. Couldn't swim, though. Held me back a little. I was too embarrassed to even take swimming lessons."

"I don't know anymore what impresses girls." I confessed, leaning back in my chair. "Or women for that matter."

"You seem to be doing pretty well with the one you've got," he observed, leaning on the corner of my desk. "I hear she's a stunner."

He sat down in my guest chair next to the desk. "Now, what does your girlfriend want with the file anyway?"

"It's not the file she wants," I said, arranging papers on my desk. "It's her sister."

"How's that?" he asked in disbelief.

"Her sister's from another world," I said, not looking up from the desk. "Erato thinks someone trapped her on the hard disk. But it doesn't look like it now. We tried the data, all we could get was a lot of snow and a faint garbled voice track."

"Look," he said with a wave. "I'm sorry I asked. I thought you were going to level with me. But now you're playing me for a fool. Cyrus, wake up and join the real world."

"Yeah, you're right," I apologized, realizing I had gone too far, then made something up he might understand to see if I could solicit his help. I got up and looked over the top of my cubicle. Not seeing or hearing anyone, I went on, "She doesn't want the RAM chip plans," I explained, and then told him the story about Euterpe working on a Top Secret assignment inside Sigma before her strange disappearance, and that we believed the real Euterpe file contained information that would lead us to her. I added that Juanita and Janet were working together to hide the file.

"Thanks Cyrus," he said when I had finished, a little stunned and frozen to his chair. "I appreciate your telling me the truth. I . . . if I see anything . . ."

"Well, I've got to get to work," I said, rolling my chair up to my desk. "Remember, we never had this conversation. . . . And another thing, have a nice night."

"Thanks," he said, looking a little pale. "You too." He got up like someone who had just been told he had terminal cancer and left without another word.

I wasn't sure Cooper could be trusted to search for the file, but I had to do *something*. Maybe coming right out and hinting for his help would locate Euterpe. Then again, it might make things worse. That was a chance I had to take, but not the only one. If everything went according to plan, later that night some unlucky bike owner would be cursing his lost Harley.

34

Biker Bar

Before closing up for the night, I checked both files. Neither had been erased, meaning that Juanita and Janet were still awaiting Erato's return. Sure, Cooper could have gone to them, but he had my story to think about. If he believed me, maybe he would look for the real file on one of the system disks. There were thousands of personal files—much too big a job for one person working at it part-time. Soliciting Cooper's help was at least a place to start. Meanwhile, we had a Harley to round up.

On the way home I saw my star peeking just barely above the horizon, looking as if it were getting dimmer and sinking at the same time.

When I got there Erato was ready to go. We took Vinnie along for protection in case we had to make a run for it.

Erato was dressed to kill: the black Harley T-shirt, matching leather jacket and boots, tight blue jeans, and too much makeup, including stop sign–red lipstick. I was to be her kid brother from the surf. I was pretty big in the muscle department from paddling out for waves, but surfers don't scare bikers much, especially ones with gear chains in their pockets for fighting.

There weren't many biker bars in Channel Islands, but we found one on the rough side of town. It had the necessary string of cycles leaning on their kickstands out front. The name, Hog Heaven, just about said it all.

We left Vinnie guarding the car, and strolled slowly past the row of chopped Harleys, checking for keys left in ignitions. Needless to say, we didn't have any luck.

Truck-driving tunes greeted us at the door, and once inside we got the full flavor of the place. It was a genuine beer bar all right, with neon signs of Miller, Coors, and Bud blinking to the beat.

The place sported a couple of well-worn pool tables, a wooden floor flaked with sawdust, and a clientele that looked like they could take their bikes apart blindfolded, put them back together, and not have any parts left over. The crowning glory was a velvet painting over the bar of a buxom nude riding a Harley.

Erato wasted no time. She sauntered over to the bar amid stares and ordered us a couple of bottles of Coors. All twenty or so Hog lovers stared us down, including a bleached blond with an enormous chest and matching rear end sticking out of short ragged cutoffs.

Some linebacker-sized bruiser moved in quickly, standing next to us as we sat at the bar. He wore greasy jeans, biker boots, and a dirty, sleeveless Harley T-shirt.

"Welcome to California," he said to my Hawaiian shirt. "Now go home."

"Name's Erato," my date said without flinching. "This here's my brother, Cy. He's a local."

"So I see," the bruiser smirked. "My friends call me Chainsaw. Anybody gives you crap, sweetheart, you let me know. We don't like strangers much, but anybody with a Hog is welcome."

"Guess we'd better drink up then," Erato said to me. "And get out."

"What the hell for?" Chainsaw asked, puzzled. "You just got here. Besides, I like what you do to a T-shirt."

"Had a Hog, lumberjack," Erato said smugly. "Some jerk stole it. Came here lookin' for him."

"What's his name?" Chainsaw inquired, concerned. "We don't take kindly to thieves." He turned and looked around the place. "If he's here, point him out. I'll give him a handlebar necklace to wear home."

Erato looked to me for help with the story. "We're not saying he's here," I chimed in, sitting on the bar stool next to her. "But there's a black Harley out there with flames on the tank that looks real familiar."

"Hell," Chainsaw spat out. "There must be a thousand choppers around with flames on the gas tank."

"That's why I can't prove it until I get a look at the serial number," I replied. "If it hasn't been filed off."

"Hey, Hammerhead!" Chainsaw bellowed across the room. "Somebody's got a question about your Hog."

A six feet seven, three-hundred-pounder got up and staggered over. "What's the problem?" he belted out, staring at me. "Surf Crap here botherin' you, lady?"

"Naw," Erato said coolly. "How long you had that Hog?"

"Six years." He glared at me. "Why, you want to wrestle me for it?"

"Nope," I replied, sipping a bottle of Coors. "Just looking for a thief."

"What?" he said, doubling up his fist. "You want to eat that bottle? Or just pick it out of your nose?"

Chainsaw cut in, raising his arm between us. "The lady got her Hog stolen," he explained. "Seems it looks like yours. Just a case of mistaken identity, I reckon."

Hammerhead was still mad, and kept after me. "We don't like surf slime in here. So . . ."

"Cy," Erato said with a nod towards me. "Head on home." She looked at the bikers. "If there's any fighting, it's gonna be over me. Not him."

"Yeah, guess you're right," Hammerhead said with a glance at me. "He ain't worth bloodying a fist over."

"You sure?" I asked, looking at Hammerhead's sweaty forehead.

"Cy, buzz on home," Erato ordered. "I'll catch a ride. Lumberjack here says he'll give me a lift. Unless his old lady won't let him."

"I live alone, Hog lady," he said, a little angry. "And the name's Chainsaw. . . . Yeah, beat it, punk," he added, out of the side of his mouth. "I'll give your sis a lift right to her door—on my open-air, two-wheeled limo."

I reluctantly agreed, but Erato and I talked about it first, standing by the saloon's front doors. She said, "Let's not fight. I've already had that experience, and I didn't like it much."

Walking out slowly, I didn't want to let Erato go it alone. But she pulled me aside and reminded me of our plan. I was to follow them to his place. She'd get him drunk so he'd pass out and we'd borrow the bike for a couple of hours. We'd have it back by the time he slept it off. I just hoped it would work.

When I got to the car, I heard Hammerhead shout, "Hey Chainsaw. I'll arm wrestle ya for the chick."

"You'll arm wrestle a fistful of knuckles, pea brain," Chainsaw answered. "Now go back to your table. Your beer's calling you."

I waited down the street with Vinnie, and about a half-hour later they came out. Chainsaw had his arm around her. They got on his chopper and headed off down the road, stopping once at an all-night liquor store to get a twelve-pack of beer.

Afterward, I followed them through the dark side of town. Vinnie became real uneasy, as if he didn't like the neighborhood. He began to pace nervously back and forth on the seat, whining up a storm. He got so riled up that I had to pull over and stop. Luckily, the cycle had just pulled into a driveway, so I parked under a nearby tree to wait.

Chainsaw's house was a run-down shack with a bunch of half-demolished cars on the lawn and a pickup in the driveway. Transmissions, rear ends, and engines were rusting all over the place. It looked like a junkyard without a fence or a guard dog.

An hour later my nerves had had enough. Getting out of the car, I told Vinnie to stay put, and proceeded on foot. It didn't seem to be much of a problem for him, since he was already on the floor in the front seat, curled up and hiding.

When I got to the front door, it was open. Inside, Chainsaw was lying face down on the couch. Erato was underneath him. Luckily they both still had their clothes on. Besides a decorating job that looked and smelled of early dump, there were twelve empty beer bottles strewn about.

Coming through the door slowly, I heard heavy breathing. Erato whispered loudly to me. "Hey, help me get this redwood off me. I can't budge him."

I went over and picked him up, enough so she could scoot out from underneath. "You okay?" I asked, concerned.

"Yeah, just got pinned when he fell on me."

She grabbed the keys out of his pocket and we dashed out the door. She put a key in the Hog's ignition, popped

the kickstand and began to roll the bike out of the driveway.

"You ever ridden one of these?" I asked, helping her push
it.

"No, but I watched him do it," she confirmed with a nod.
"I think I've got it figured out. . . . Where's the car?"

"Down the block. Vinnie got scared and hid on the floor.
Let's get out of here."

By then we had maneuvered the chopper to the end of the
driveway. She got on, put in the clutch, and rolled down the
street. About halfway down the block she kick started it. It
blasted awake, still a little warm from being ridden. I ran back
to the car, got in, and started it up.

"You can get up now, Vinnie," I said as he lay on the
floor, still shaking and whining. "We're going to the beach."
Vinnie liked the sound of that word, and crawled up on the
seat. "Shoot," I said, petting him. "That was almost too easy."
And it was.

By the time we rolled past the place, Chainsaw was coming
down the drive, waving a buzzing saw in one hand and a
pistol in the other. "Hey!" he yelled as the Harley disappeared down the block. "Come back here or you're dead
meat!"

Then it got worse. He recognized me as we drove past, even
with my lights off. Vinnie was smarter than I. He ducked down
as we passed by, right before Chainsaw emptied the gun into
the side of my car. Luckily the windows were down, because
a couple of bullets whizzed by where glass would have been.
One of them would have given me a shave if I hadn't already
been given one the night before. Three more bullets made nice
buttonholes in my passenger's door.

Chainsaw was in the street, throwing the buzzing saw at me,
but it fell short. Well, almost. It bounced off the trunk, leaving
a nasty gash.

I flashed on the headlights and put my foot to the floor.

Chainsaw ran back to the house. By the time I turned the
corner, the pickup truck was pulling out of his driveway. He
stopped and grabbed the saw lying in the middle of the street,
tossed it in the truck bed, and came after us, engine racing and
tires squealing.

I followed Erato and we lost him at the freeway on-ramp.
We faked like we were going toward LA, got off at the next
ramp, and turned around. I saw the pickup zoom past on the

freeway overhead, and it wasn't slowing down.

Pretty soon I was behind Erato as planned, cruising down the coastal frontage road and heading straight for the Channel Islands pier. Chainsaw must have taken the bait and figured we were from LA stealing Hogs, because I never saw his headlights behind us all the way to the pier.

As we pulled into the parking lot I had only one thought. I just hoped Zeus appreciated our efforts.

35

God Rides a Harley

Zeus was out on the pier. We could see his profile under one of the overhead lights. He was standing up against the rail with a fishing pole and a line in the water, wearing old Levi's, a lumberjack shirt and work boots.

Technically, the beach closed at sunset, but Erato drove the bike around the gate and into the parking lot. I parked the car alongside the road, then walked in with Vinnie. Erato rode right out on the wooden pier and up to her dad, who greeted her with a pretty big smile. The beach patrol was not around, so we had the place to ourselves.

I watched from below the pier while Erato got off and Zeus got on the motorcycle. Erato climbed on the back, and off they went.

They took a spin to the end of the pier, which was several hundred feet, and headed back for the parking lot. Soon they were buzzing all the way down to the far end of the parking lot and back, picking up pretty good speed and dodging the bumps. When they whizzed back past the pier, Zeus was laughing and Erato was holding on tight.

The next thing I knew Zeus had taken the little wooden boardwalk that led halfway to the water—at least it did last time I was there—but now extended all the way to the surf.

Before they got to the waves he turned and revved it up a few times. Then he did a wheelie and took off down the firm wet sand along the surf line, headlight leading the way. They must have been going fifty miles an hour by the time they got to the end of the beach, which was about a half mile away.

Suddenly he decelerated, braked and turned around, then came racing back. They zoomed by me and jammed on down the beach, shifting gears, spinning out, and having a heck of a time.

This went on for about half an hour, and then he spun it around and took the boardwalk back up to the parking lot. He got off and Erato took over. Zeus went back to fishing on the pier. He passed me on the way, smiling but never saying a word. I was scared to death, and didn't move an inch. He casually glanced at me as he walked by.

In his eyes vibrated the power to create and destroy worlds. His glance pierced right through me. It looked all-knowing, full of understanding and compassion. He stuck his hands up as if to give me a high five, but I was so overwhelmed and bewildered, I just froze.

As he passed by he patted me on the back, and my whole body vibrated with warm, glowing electricity, making my nerves tingle from head to toe. Afterward, I couldn't fully recall his face. All I remember was that it was very distinguished and fatherly. And to my great relief didn't look like Charleton Heston, George Burns, or even John Houseman.

I stood there for so long that time evaporated. The next thing I remember was the first hint of light coming up over the eastern horizon.

Erato pulled up next to me and was beaming. I looked around. Zeus was gone—fishing pole and all. "Where . . . have I been?" I asked in a daze. "It's almost sunup. And where's your dad?"

"You've been standing like that for an hour," Erato finally said. "Dad does that to people. He's gone now. You sure missed a good light show."

"Light show?" I repeated, still half-conscious.

"Yeah," she laughed, revving up the bike. "He took off into the sky like the space shuttle. Lighted up the whole world for miles."

"Yeah," I said, shaking off a case of the space outs. "Guess I was out of it."

"Get on," she said, nodding. "We have to get this bike back to its owner."

"Back to its owner?" I stared at the bike. "Look at it. We have to get the sand out of the wheels first. It's filthy."

"Yeah, I suppose you're right," she shrugged. "Is there a self-service car wash around here?"

"No time for that," I remarked. "The sun's coming up." I looked over by the Seaside Cafe next to the pier. "Hey, there's a garden hose behind the restaurant," I said. "We'll use that—wait a minute. Listen to me. Do you think if we get caught, Chainsaw's going to be happy that we washed his bike after we stole it?"

"*Borrowed*," she corrected me, shutting off the bike and headlight. "We just borrowed it. And if we wash it off, maybe he won't kill us."

"I doubt it. But let's do it anyway. Can't hurt."

We rolled the bike behind the cafe and hosed it down, planning to let it air dry on the way back. "You realize," I said, washing the spokes, "that your dad just might get us killed."

"I thought you *wanted* to go to heaven when you died," she smiled.

"I do. But not *yet*. Besides, we still have to free your sister." I looked at her, standing beside me. "Yeah, what *did* he say about that?"

"He said we were on our own. He wouldn't interfere—at least for the next few days. He gave us until midnight Saturday. Then he steps in. Lightning bolts and all."

"I don't understand your dad," I said, shaking my head. "Why can't he just get her back without making a big fuss?"

"I wouldn't be too critical if I were you."

"Why not?" I asked, turning off the hose and setting it down. "I'm sure a little criticism won't hurt him."

"No, but it might make *you* look bad," she informed me, winding up the hose. "I saw him touch you. He doesn't do that very often. Once maybe every thousand years. When he does that, it means you're in for a big promotion."

"You mean," I asked, with a worried expression, "angel status?" She nodded. "Oh, great," I sighed. "I told you I don't want to die yet. Doesn't that count for something?"

"He won't take you before your scheduled departure date," she explained, wrapping her arms around me from behind. "To tell you the truth, I think he set up this whole thing so you could do something for him and he could reward you."

"What for? He doesn't need me."

"You'd be surprised," she said, hugging me. "Besides, he wants the father of his grandchild to have a good job."

I broke loose and spun around, getting pretty excited. "What?" I yelled. "You mean you're . . . Isn't it too early to tell? It's only been a couple of days."

"Dad told me," she smiled. "He knew I wanted to be a mother *and* have a career. He made it so." Her eyes grew big. "We're expecting."

I threw my arms around her and hugged her hard. "I can't believe it," I said, shocked. "*Me*, a father. I always wanted to be a father. Are we supposed to get married or something? How much longer do I have as a human? Can I say good-bye to my parents? Can I erase my files?"

"Hold it," she ordered, pushing me away at arm's length. "One thing at a time. First of all, Dad says that in his eyes we already *are* married; we can have a ceremony later. He didn't tell me the rest. Said he wants to surprise me. We don't know yet if I'm going to stay on earth to have the baby, or if you're coming back with me. But we'll know soon enough."

"Saturday night at the latest," I said, thinking about her departure date. I didn't know whether to laugh or cry. So I kissed her hair. "Look, we've only known each other a couple of days. Doesn't somebody have to ask the other person if they want to get hitched? I may be old-fashioned, but whatever happened to the one-knee proposal?"

Erato pulled away and got down on one knee, taking my hand in hers. "Hey," she said, suppressing a grin. "Do you want to get married or do you want to get struck by lightning again?"

"Well," I laughed. "Since you put it that way."

She squeezed my hand hard. "*Cyrus, you* were the one who was about to use the *L* word, remember?"

"I . . . I know," I answered, getting cold feet. "But it's so sudden. I . . . I just haven't gotten used to the idea. Besides, how can you be pregnant?"

She was disappointed. "Don't tell me you've forgotten the other night?" she asked, perturbed.

I looked straight down at her. "I, young woman, will never forget the other night. Yeah, I do feel the *L* word coming on, but . . . I just need a little more time."

"No sweat," she said, standing up. "You've got until Saturday night. Heck, today's only Wednesday. Well, Thursday morning actually. Take your time. I don't want you to feel pressured."

"Thanks," I smirked. "I appreciate that. Answer one more question, before I make up my mind. What kind of job has your dad got for an ex-hacker surf bum?"

"Something about writing programs to automate our muse request lines or something," she said, shaking her head. "And don't worry about taking care of our daughter. We can alternate."

"Did your dad tell you it was going to be a girl?"

"No, just wishful thinking."

"Good," I replied, starting to get on the Harley. "Then we can share day-care responsibilities with our *son.* . . . Hey, do they have waves up there?"

"They have whatever you can imagine," she said, climbing on the back.

Suddenly, Vinnie came charging out of the surf, raced up next to us and shook off, getting everyone wet. Then he broke into a barking fit. Someone big was coming our way. When he got within fifty yards Vinnie cowered and got behind me. He started whimpering.

"Uh oh," I said, getting off the bike. "I may become an angel any second now. I recognize the power tool in that guy's hand. That's Chainsaw."

36

Chainsaw at the Beach

Before we could do anything, Chainsaw was on top of us. "Appreciate you washin' my Hog," he said with a smirk. "But next time you plan on stealin' somebody's bike, you might consider askin' permission. Mr. Teeth here," he said, nodding at the chainsaw in his hand. "Don't take too kindly to borrowin' without leavin' a note."

He reached over and pulled on the cord, but it didn't fire up. He did it a few more times, but it never sprang to life. I almost felt better. He tossed it aside with a laugh. "Guess I won't be needin' Mr. Teeth to give you a haircut, Surf Punk. I'll just pull them out one at a time."

"Wait!" Erato said, desperately. "There's an explanation for this. We just borrowed your bike for my dad. He's old, and never got a chance to ride one. He wanted to ride just once before—"

"Don't see any senior citizens around here, lady. The way I got it figured, you were plannin' on makin' off with my bike. I got no beef with you, sweetheart. I know your boyfriend here talked you into it. But you'd best be gettin' out of the way, unless you aim to be goin' with me. Cause by the time I get through makin' chiropractic adjustments on Clamshell here, it's goin' to take two ambulances to get him to the hospital."

He moved toward the bike. Erato and I scattered in different directions. He came after me. I started backpedaling in a circle, trying to think of a way out of this without getting a huge hospital bill, when I tripped over Vinnie and sprawled out on my back. Erato went for the garden hose while Vinnie stood his ground and growled fiercely.

"Better get that mutt outta here!" Chainsaw yelled. "Before I tear off his other ear."

Vinnie didn't stop growling and snarling. Chainsaw made a swift move and got him by the scruff of the neck. He held Vinnie up and looked him coldly in the eye. Chainsaw suddenly looked surprised. He seemed to be staring into Vinnie's open mouth. "Hubcap!" Chainsaw yelled. "Where the hell you been, boy?"

Without saying another word, he walked toward his truck, some fifty yards away, holding a squirming and kicking Vinnie by the neck.

I got up and went after him, "Hey, I thought your beef was with me?" I yelled, pointing a finger at my chest. "That's my dog you're running away with. You come back with him right now, or I'll . . ."

"You sure talk funny for a guy who just stole somebody's wheels," he said over his shoulder. "Besides, this here's *my* dog."

"Prove it."

He whirled around, holding Vinnie out with his jaw open and shoved him in my face. "You see that missin' molar back there? I got the tooth that fills the hole right here." He pulled a chain around his neck and out came a large tooth with a hole drilled in it—attached to the chain.

"That," he said proudly, holding it out, "is Hubcap here's tooth. It's my good luck charm. Now, if you want to fight about it, we can go to the police station right now. Otherwise, you best beat it. Cause after I get him chained up in the back of my pickup, I'm comin' after my bike and anythin' else that's in the way."

"Look," I pleaded, thrusting my hands out. "I took him in after he lost his ear. You shouldn't have let him wander around loose. He almost got killed. Tell you what, I'm willing to forget this whole thing if you let me have the dog."

Chainsaw laughed real loud. He turned and tossed Vinnie in the back of the truck. Then he chained him up next to the spot he had reserved for the Harley. Smiling at me he said, "Much obliged for carin' for my dog, but I'll be takin' him back now."

"But—"

"But nothin'. This is your lucky day. I'm goin' to reward you for showin' up with Hubcap here. I'm not goin' to bash in your skull. Now, unless you want your face smeared all over the front page of the mornin' paper, you'd better take your girlfriend and beat it before I get in a not-so-charitable mood."

"You son of a—" Erato put her hand on my mouth from behind.

"Much obliged," she said. "We'll be going now."

I tried to argue, but only a bunch of muffled sounds came out. I suppose it was for the best. Going after him would only have landed me in more trouble.

"Cyrus," Erato said, leading me away. "Let him go. Vinnie's not yours. You'll only make matters worse."

"Yeah, but that guy's going to abuse him," I argued, wrestling free. "I know it. Look, Vinnie's so scared he didn't even put up much of a fight. That guy beats him. I know he does. We've got to do something."

"Great," she said, dragging me away again. "I suppose you want to file a complaint with the SPCA or something."

"Well, why not?"

"Don't be stupid. You've got no proof of anything. Look, we stole his bike. They'll probably think we stole his dog too."

"Well," I said reluctantly, stopping in my tracks. "Then let me go . . . I just want to say good-bye; that's all."

"All right," she agreed, letting loose, "but anything funny happens, and everything could be ruined. We still have time to save Euterpe, you know."

"Your dad knew Chainsaw was following us," I said, gritting my teeth. "Why didn't he do something?"

"He did. He let us get away. Don't you see that?"

"Yeah, but what about Vinnie?"

"*Hubcap* is in Dad's care now," she said, pointing at the truck. "He used him to free us. Now he owes him. Anybody that gets used by Dad for any reason, even a dog, gets rewarded."

"Okay," I said, starting to calm down a little. "If you say so. But I still have to say good-bye."

I ran over to Vinnie while Chainsaw was inspecting his bike. Reaching over the side of the pickup, I hugged Vinnie long and hard. He licked me and whined a little.

"Don't worry, boy," I said. "I'm coming back for you. "This guy probably doesn't read the lost and found ads, so he doesn't know who I am. I'll come back for you when it's safe. Promise."

Just as Chainsaw started yelling at me, I broke away, grabbed Erato's hand, and left, looking at poor Vinnie tied up in the back of the truck. Once at the car, I turned to Erato. "I can't believe we steal a bike from a guy and Vinnie turns out to be his dog. I just can't believe it."

"*Borrow*," she said, trying to calm me down. "We borrowed the bike—and his name's Hubcap."

"Fine," I said sarcastically. "But what I really want to know is Euterpe's whereabouts." I started the car. "Did Zeus give you any hints?"

She hit me on the arm. "No, but let's go check your terminal," she grinned. "I've got an idea."

"I think I'd better go alone," I answered. "I told everyone that you skipped town. And I'd better go *now*, while I still have a job. Besides, maybe Cooper's found the file. I think I've got him looking."

"How did you manage that?"

"I'll tell you on the way home," I said, pulling away. "And you can tell me your idea."

37

The Assignment

Once at work, I was to put Erato's plan into action, logging on and looking for a clue to where her sister might be filed. Erato said I should look for personal song files, suggesting that we might have overlooked the obvious. I turned to her as we pulled up to my apartment.

"Of *course*," I said, hitting my head with my hand. "Janet herself gave it away. If you want to hide a tree, try the forest. All along we've been thinking it had to be some one-hundred-meg file. That was the decoy. Your sister could be supercondensed. You said yourself she didn't need much working memory. She could access files from your mother. Isn't that what you do when you need background and storage? After all, your mom *is* the goddess of memory."

"Exactly," Erato agreed, smiling. "We don't store everything in our heads. Thousands of years of data is just too much to keep track of all the time. Besides, the older you get, the more volatile your short-term memory becomes, so we solve that problem by uplinking to Mom. She has unlimited data banks available for us to use. When we need something loaded into our consciousness, we just close our eyes, concentrate, and a program downloads the files. It works perfectly."

I shut off the car. A question came to mind. "Why haven't you used it to get the info on where your sister's stored?" I asked.

"There's a problem," she frowned. "As a human, I have all my own storage, and am not allowed to access heaven's data files. Besides, Dad said Mom wasn't to interfere."

"Can't you mentally hack-in?"

"That's funny, coming from you," she laughed, slapping the dashboard.

Leaving Erato at home, I went off to work and the guard let me in without a hitch, though it was only nine in the morning. I told Cooper I had some programming to catch up on and it worked. He left me alone. I didn't ask if he had looked for the

Euterpe file, not wanting to push my luck so soon. Besides, if it turned up somewhere on an unclassified disk, I might not need him.

I logged on and looked around for an hour, scanning for clues to lyric related stuff. There were three sub-directories with song titles, belonging to three different accounts. One was called Mike's Music. I looked in it. No surprises here. Just a bunch of files with song titles that Mike Faranwhite liked. Inside each file were merely the lyrics to a pop song. Big deal.

The next one I found, Top 40, was just that. Jack Tupanoff's ongoing chart of current pop tunes. An old hobby of his. He liked to guess what songs were on the charts, and in what order. This was a fun file, and not the one we needed.

The third file, Lana's Lyrics, had promise, but turned out to be encoded lyrics from some frustrated secretary's poorly written songs. The code was simple, and I broke it in less than a minute. I closed it up, thoroughly stumped.

"Now what?" I said to myself, scratching my head.

Calling Erato at home, I explained my findings.

"There's another file that's even more obvious," Erato said over the phone. "Actually, two files. The new Euterpe file, and the RAM chip file."

"Let's try Euterpe," I said, wondering a little about Erato's motive. I logged on using the Iberlin account, and the simple password "muse" that Janet had given me for accessing it. It contained the original poem, only an expanded version. A new verse had been added, and looked like this:

> *I am not always where I appear*
> *Yet I am always very near*
> *A song in your heart*
> *Caresses me*
> *Soft words of love*
> *Will set me free*

I read it to Erato over the phone, and without hesitation she said, "Try the other file."

"Of *course*," I said into the receiver, getting an inspiration. "Janet hides the real Euterpe on the RAM file, knowing that if anyone tries to access it, it will look like a security violation. But if it *is* your sister, how will we know unless we access it? And maybe we won't know even then."

"We'll know," Erato promised. "How big is it?"

"It's only a megabyte."

"Cy, this is probably our last chance. If you can access it, we can transfer it to floppy, and find a way to free her later."

"Okay," I agreed, and took a deep breath. "Here goes nothing." I typed in the filename, and got right in. When Janet had given me the Iberlin account, she had given me everything associated with it. I began to scan the file. Page after page of integrated circuit drawings and specifications followed.

"Either this is the RAM file," I said, receiver stuck between my shoulder and ear, "or the phony plans to see if we'd bite. We did. Now we're done for."

"Copy it to floppy anyway," Erato ordered almost gruffly. "If it's for real, we can use it to bargain for my sister's release."

Without saying anything I switched to the PC on my desk and logged on. I threw a floppy in the slot on my drive and downloaded the file, then ejected the disk.

"Got it," I said. Afterward, I logged off and drove home, thinking never to question Erato again—but halfway there an idea surfaced. I wanted to test myself one last time, just to prove there never *was* anything to worry about. It would be my chance to gloat a little about my new found faith in her.

I got home and ran upstairs. "This," I said, holding it up. "Is my proof. They said you would try to access the file. And they were right. What do you have to say in your defense," I added, half-mockingly.

"Cyrus," she said, throwing up her hands. "I thought we went through this already. Remember the lightning bolts and all that? The only value that file has for me is to bargain for my sister's release. How can you doubt that?"

"I'm sorry," I said, starting to turn red. "I just wanted to show myself how stupid it was not to trust you a hundred-percent; that's all. I guess it wasn't such a good idea. But I knew you'd come through. Look, it was a dumb trick. I'll never pull anything like that again. I made a mistake."

"Well, your little joke wasn't funny. You disappoint me, Cyrus Major. You don't believe in anything but your own survival. After all we've been through, you still don't believe me. You're a real son of a . . ." She marched to the kitchen.

"Wait!" I yelled. "Where are you going?"

When she came back with a meat cleaver, I said, "All right, if you want the disk *that* bad, you can have it. You know I could take that knife away from you, but I don't want anybody to get hurt, especially our . . . baby. I still care about us, believe it or not, and I was going to accept your proposal of marriage. Well, maybe now that's impossible. But when he's born, I want to see him, okay? Or did you make up the part about being pregnant just to get the RAM file?"

"She," Erato said seriously. "When *she's* born."

I held out the disk, and she took it from my hand. She set it up vertically on the cheap gold shag carpet, piling up threads around it so that it stayed put, though quite precariously. She raised the meat cleaver with both arms and came down hard, splitting the disk roughly in half.

"There," she said. "That good enough for you?"

I couldn't say a word. Instead, I got up and went over to her. She stood up and hugged me, meat cleaver and all.

"We'll find a way to get her back . . ." I promised, holding her against me.

"There are some things I have to tell you," she said, pulling away slightly.

"What? Tell me . . . Anything. I don't care what. I deserve whatever you're going to say."

"You're going to need that knife sharpened, for one thing."

"Okay, I figured that much."

"Your carpet needs shampooing in a bad way."

"All right," I agreed, looking down. "I can see that."

"And . . ." she hesitated.

"Go on. I can take it." I lifted my head and waited, expecting the worst.

"You're going to have to write a poem."

"*What*?" I couldn't believe it. The worst had come true.

Erato assured me we'd never find the file Euterpe was on in time to free her, especially since we'd accessed the off-limits chip file and copied it. Janet was onto us for sure now. If Euterpe was on one of the mainframe hard disks, the only way to get her out was for me to write a poem, just as her screen message said. It was her poem to me.

"I, uh, don't know," I stammered, still holding her. "I don't think I can do it. I've never *had* to write one before, except in school." Stepping back and holding her at arm's length, I pointed at myself. "This guy writes code," I informed her. "Not iambic pentameter. It won't work. I'm no good at it."

"How do you know that?" she complained. "You just haven't

tried in a while. Besides, it's our only chance now. You have to do it . . . tonight. Tomorrow may be too late. We may be locked out of the system forever."

"Can't I just write a program?" I asked, half-seriously.

"Look, it doesn't have to be polished. It only has to be personal. If you write a poem about something you really care about, it *will* be perfect." She moved in for a hug.

"I don't know," I said, embracing her. "What will I write about?"

"Write about something you care about, something you love: the ocean, Vinnie." She stopped and kissed my neck. "Our baby. It doesn't matter. If it's true, Euterpe will be set free."

Turning her around slowly, so that I was behind her, I carefully placed my hands on her stomach, still flat as a cliff face. "Okay," I said at last. "It looks like you leave me no choice. I'll try, but no laughing. . . . Hey, I've got an idea. Why can't *you* do it? You know more about this than I do."

She spun around and looked up into my eyes. "Only a human being can write poetry," she said sincerely. "I'm just on loan. It has to be *you*. To write a poem powerful enough to free her is going to take someone who has laughed, loved, cried, and lived for years, not just a couple of days. It takes the sweet suffering of life to make a poem."

"But, listen to you," I argued. "You have as much feeling as any human I've ever met, a lot more than some."

She pulled away from me and sat on the couch. "I didn't want to bring this up," she said, getting even more serious. "But my dad said *you* had to write it, or Euterpe won't be freed. And if she's not freed, you can't marry me."

"Great! I'm glad there's no pressure on me." I made a grand gesture. "Imagine the headlines in the *Heavenly Herald*: Rookie Poet Strikes Out! World without Lyrics. Child Muse Homeless. Film at Eleven."

"When you stop feeling sorry for yourself," she commented, lying back on the couch, "go to the computer and try. Complaining doesn't do any good."

Without answering I walked over to the window and looked out at the elm tree with the fallen branch.

"Are you going to be okay with this?" she asked. "Are you at least going to try?"

"Yeah, in a minute," I said wistfully. "But not at the Macintosh."

"Why not?"

"Programmers think at computers," I answered, looking at the mountains. "Poets stare out windows."

She got up, came over, and hugged me from behind. "I believe in you," she began. "I know you can do it. Look, somewhere out there is your star, the brightest one in the sky. If it were night, we could still see it. But it's out there, just the same. Use your psychic powers if you have to. Close your eyes and imagine a scene, feelings, and words."

"I haven't written anything in years," I confessed. "I'm afraid."

"Of what?"

"Expressing my feelings." I opened my arms wide. "Exposing myself."

"This is the nineties," she reminded me. "It's okay to be yourself." She bit my ear. "Men even wear earrings now. It's okay to be sensitive."

"If you don't mind," I said, turning around to face her, "I'll just write the poem, thank you. I'm not quite ready for the Pirates of the Carribean look yet. Hey . . . does the future of the world really depend on this?"

"Who knows? But *our* future does."

"Do you want to spend it here, or in heaven?" I asked, kissing her hair.

She poked me in the ribs. "I want to spend it with you, silly. But . . ."

"But what?"

"The dirty, gold shag carpet goes."

"Glad you like it," I said, smiling. "Hey, wait. That gives me an idea."

"About remodeling?"

"No, for a poem."

"A poem?" she asked with a mixture of hope and confusion.

"Out of my way," I ordered, running for the Macintosh in the corner of my bedroom. "It's input time."

"You got an idea for a poem from this crappy carpet?"

"Stop complaining," I said, running through the bedroom doorway. "When the muse strikes, the poet writes."

"Hey, did you mean it about marriage and all that?" she asked from the other room.

"*Hey*, sometimes that's what two and a half people do when there's love involved."

"You're getting closer," she beamed, now in the doorway. "You almost said the *L* word in a direct sentence."

"Be quiet, will you," I protested, flipping on the Macintosh. "You're breaking my concentration."

"That's okay," she said, ignoring me. "I love you too."

"I'd *love* to talk," I answered, hitting the return key, "but I'm writing a poem right now. If you'll leave your name and number after the tone, I'll get back to you as soon as I return to planet Earth. Beep."

38

Inspiration Point

I tried about as hard as anyone could to come up with a poem, first constructing one about Vinnie since I was starting to miss him. I won't even repeat some of the lousy verse. Then there was something about the sea and surfing, but it came out pretty tacky. Finally, I got started on my feelings for Erato, but I just couldn't put them into words. Who said I was a poet anyway?

An hour went by, and in one last foolish attempt, I constructed a poem that looked more like lines of code for a program than something from the heart. Finally, in total desperation, I walked to the bedroom doorway. Erato looked up from the morning paper as she sat on the couch.

"It's no use," I confessed. "I can't do it. Poets are born, not created out of necessity."

"Let me see what you've got so far."

"Are you kidding?" I protested, rolling my eyes. "What I've got could fill a shot glass—except it won't get anybody high. It'll probably just make them sick."

"Did you do what I told you?" she asked, scolding me. "Did you try to write simply and from the heart?"

"Yeah, but it looks more like something that came out of my stomach after dinner."

She got up and followed me into the bedroom. I hid my head in my hands while she sat on the bed and stared at the verses on the screen. She read them all carefully, without saying a word.

Then she turned to me and said, "I . . . I see what you mean. When was the last time you wrote about your feelings?"

"I thought so," I said, disgusted. "I may not recognize good poetry, but I can smell a dead fish when it's lying around. Any other ideas?"

"I think," she said, putting her arms around me, "it's time for me to inspire you. That's what I do best, you know."

She reached up and gave me a long sensuous kiss. I was tired, but not too tired to get turned-on. "And just what does this have to do with love poetry?" I asked, pulling away a little.

"You figure it out," she winked. "But I'll give you a hint. Surfing is like poetry in motion to you. Well, I know another *S* word that poets think is poetry in motion."

"Are we talking love here, or are we talking—"

"What we're talking about," she said, nibbling on my ear, "is getting you in a relaxed state of mind so that you can catch some poem floating by, or perhaps one will bubble up out of your heart."

She pushed me down on the bed and scooted on top of me. Slowly, softly, she began to kiss my forehead and face until I almost became unconscious with passion. I felt myself floating away on a cloud of deep sensuality, completely lost in her. She began to kiss me all over, and then we made love for the longest time. I fell asleep with her on top of me. It was heaven.

Somewhere in my sleep I began to dream. I was with Erato and we were shopping at the music store. I was pushing a little blue-eyed blond in a shopping cart. Looking into her face, I saw Erato and myself. In a voice as sweet as birdsong she looked up and said, "Daddy." She pointed to a CD on the rack—Simon and Garfunkel. It had the words "The Sounds of Silence" written on it.

Picking it up, I went to the checkout stand. The clerk put it across the bar code reader and rang it up. I paid for it and carried my little angel to the car—a brand new, bright red Ferrari. Vinnie was waiting for us in the backseat, only he had grown his ear back. That was when I realized it must be a dream, and started to wake up. Grabbing the little girl, I hugged her hard, trying to hold onto the vision of her, but it was too late, my eyes were open.

"She's beautiful," I said, turning to Erato, who still looked asleep. "Just like her mother. Just like the woman I . . . I love." I reached over and kissed her.

"I know," she whispered, not opening her eyes. "She will be special. She's the daughter of a muse and a poet."

I lay back down and went to sleep, trying to bring back the dream. Just before I drifted off again, I bolted upright in bed. "Wait!" I said. "I've got it."

"The *poem*," Erato beamed, sitting up. "I knew you could do it. I just knew it."

"No, not the poem. The *solution*."

"To what?"

"To the poem in the Euterpe file. It came to me in my sleep. Don't you remember? It said that her world was one of double dimensions. Round and flat, I figure, like a disk. But we had it all wrong. She's not on a computer disk."

"I don't get it," she said, making a face.

"Look, it's too simple," I answered, exhaling. "Just because she's digitized doesn't mean she's on a hard disk. That's where Janet wants us to waste our time looking. A digitized voice track can also be put on CD.

"It's perfect," I laughed, flinging up my arms. "When Janet picked that as the third song she picked the real thing, and I guessed it. The Sounds of Silence is not an empty disc at all. Your sister's on that CD."

"You didn't guess it," Erato said with excitement, jumping out of bed. "How many times do I have to tell you? You're psychic."

"Yeah, maybe so. Maybe I am. How about that?"

"In Janet's office we couldn't hear anything but silence," Erato surmised, "because her voice would be too soft. Her whispers from the other side could not be heard sufficiently unless we further amplified them."

"That's correct," I agreed, grabbing Erato and pinning her to the bed. "And if my hunch is right, hearing her voice will set her free. Once her voice is set free in the audible sound range, it will cause her to manifest. It will bring her to life the way speaking a poem brings *it* to life. I'm sure of it."

"Then all we need is that disc," Erato said, not struggling beneath me. "And an amplifier. It would have worked before if only we had the CD, instead of that phony computer file."

"Yeah," I said, kissing her quickly and letting her go. "I don't know for sure if it will work, but I know she's on that CD. Get dressed. We're going to the office."

"Maybe we should wait until after Janet goes home," Erato suggested. "She's not just going to hand it over."

"Yeah, you're right," I agreed, getting up and pacing the floor. "What time is it?"

"Just after three."

"Okay," I nodded, thinking on my feet. "Then in a couple of hours I'll drop you off at the bus bench. She'll never check there. I'll come out and get you as soon as everyone's gone home. That'll probably be six o'clock at the latest."

"We still have lots of time," she said in a sensual voice, lying down demurely on the bed. "Let me inspire you some more."

"Naw," I said, not really serious. "I don't want to get overinspired."

"Tell me about our daughter," she requested, changing the subject and propping up on her elbows. "Tell me all about her."

"It was only a dream."

"Dreams can come true, you know," she said, wistfully. "Did you ever think we'd be together?"

"You've got me there," I admitted, still excited about my new plan, I looked at her lying on the bed. "Hey, I just thought of something. Is there . . . you know . . . lovemaking in heaven?"

"Not like here," she winked. "Not like in this bed, anyway."

"If your dad takes you up after we free Euterpe," I surmised, climbing on top of her, "then we may be running out of time together. I think I'd better reconsider. Inspire me."

"No," she said seriously, lying back on the pillow. "I think it's your turn to inspire me."

39

Shooting the Gap

I dropped Erato at the bus stop in front of Sigma and parked the car. When I got to the front desk, the security guard wouldn't let me in. She said I was instructed to turn in my badge, so I got on the phone in the lobby and called Janet. Much to my great surprise, she took my call.

"Cyrus," she said sharply, "I'm sorry. You remember the

arrangement. No one was supposed to access the chip file. I'm assuming that Erato put you up to it."

"Yes, but that was only because her sister wasn't on the Euterpe file. The whole thing was a setup," I said angrily. "If you wanted me fired, why didn't you just do it on the spot?"

"Since you're being so frank," she answered coldly, "I'll tell you. I had to be sure Erato was our spy. She proved it when she had you access the chip file. I *told* you the chip file only contained phony schematics and blueprints. Didn't you believe me?"

I defended my position. "Look," I said, squeezing the receiver. "Erato wants nothing to do with your chip plans, or the fake ones."

"I wish I could believe you," she answered, almost distantly. "But I have a record of your downloading the RAM file to your PC. That means you've got a copy in your possession, unless she talked you out of it already. Even though you don't have the real plans, it's still stealing, and proves my point about her. I want the file back, or I'm going to the FBI."

"We destroyed it."

"I thought you might say that. So just to be sure, I'm having Erato picked up."

I whirled and looked out the window. Erato wasn't sitting on the bus bench. Without saying good-bye, I slammed down the receiver and raced out the door. The guard went after me, but by the time she drew her gun, I was already the hundred yards to the bus bench and past it. Erato was nowhere in sight.

I cut across the lawn to the parking lot. The guard drew her weapon and aimed, yelling for me to stop. I'll never know if she had orders to shoot, because just then she was knocked flat and her gun went flying.

A seventy-five-pound black Lab with one ear bounded over her back and came straight for me, catching up by the time I got to the car. He jumped over the passenger's door onto the front seat.

"Vinnie!" I yelled. "Where the heck did *you* come from? Never mind. Let's get out of here."

But he had other ideas, and began licking me on the face like a kid licking his last ice-cream cone.

"If you don't stop that," I said, fighting him off, "we're not gonna make it out of here."

I started the car and backed out of my parking spot, looking around furtively for Erato, but she was nowhere in sight. The guard was just getting up when I raced out of the lot.

Vinnie stopped licking me long enough to growl fiercely at the guard, who had found her gun and aimed it at the rear of my car as I turned onto the boulevard.

"Go ahead," I said to Vinnie as we raced away. "Growl at her good. She isn't about to shoot anyone over some missing floppy disk."

Just then I heard the gun go off behind me, and a bullet hit the rear bumper. "Geez, how come everyone's using this old tin can for target practice?" I said, nervously. "You'd think I was a wanted criminal or something."

Turning the corner, I blasted toward the university. Three plain white sedans pulled into the parking lot. A bunch of clean-shaven guys in sunglasses and dark suits got out and ran toward the guard. As I barreled down the road, they were pulling into the street and heading my way. There was still no sign of Erato.

I had to think fast. Going home would surely get me picked up. I'd either have to lose them in Island View, the community adjacent to the university that was home to miles of off-campus housing, or cut through the school and figure out a place to hide until some strategy could be pieced together.

Then I hit upon a plan. Turning right and then making a quick left, my car was on a sneak path to my proposed destination. By the time the white sedans caught up to me, I was in Island View, weaving my way through streets of apartment complexes. The cars split up, one following directly behind me, the second circling around to the left to block my escape, the third taking a straight shot for the far entrance to the campus by the Channel Islands pier. That maneuver was designed to keep me from cutting through the school and sneaking onto the freeway. They had me wedged in, but that's exactly what I wanted.

The gray suiters were probably from some FBI office, and wouldn't know the local terrain. It reminded me of some LA surfers getting on each side of me on some big wave, trying to force me to wipe out. But we had a saying for that: Don't mess with the locals. In the water I knew just where the rocks and shallow water were, and used that knowledge to my advantage to foul a few attempts by out-of-towners trying to make me take a dive. Having also spent a lot of time on the streets around the university, I knew where the dead ends were, and where to turn.

Hauling along the street by the cliffs, I suddenly made a hard left, sending the sedan behind me flying into a barricade that marked a dead end. The car flipped clean over the metal posts, landing back on its wheels.

"Tailgaters," I said to Vinnie, "are such unsafe drivers."

In my rearview mirror I could see the men get out of the car. They were pretty shaken up, and in no condition to follow. As I looked back at the road, the second car appeared off my right bumper—just where I wanted him. He was tooling down the road like an inexperienced surfer crowding me on a big wave. I passed him and made a sharp right, clipping the corner of his front fender and spinning the hapless sedan around, giving the passengers inside an unpleasant surprise.

"Watch where you're going!" I yelled, shaking my fist. "I have the right-of-way here."

By time they got the sedan straightened out and pointed in the right direction, I headed down another street, one that dead-ended at the edge of the school. Memory told me there was just enough room between the concrete barricades and a large pine tree to squeeze through, unless someone had parked his car in the way. But this was mid-July, and school was out. The coast should be clear.

The sedan behind me must have radioed his buddy, because suddenly there were two cloned sedans in hot pursuit, fifty yards behind and taking up the whole road. Dodging a few parked cars, I pushed down farther on the accelerator. The car was flying. Soon the moment of truth came. I pulled into the clear past the last parked car and there it was—the opening.

When I was a freshman and under twenty-one, I had used this opening to keep from getting busted while leaving a beer bash. It was sort of the back way through the school, and most of the party animals knew it as a way to escape when the cops came. I was hoping to use it one last time.

The trick was not to brake the last few yards, but to accelerate off the driveway and over the small hill between the tree and the barricades, like shooting the pier on a fast wave. The speed would propel the car though the opening provided you had the right angle. Most people would automatically hit the brakes, and that only caused the car to slide in the dirt. More than a few had left their bumpers and doors imprinted in that huge pine at the end of the road. The tree always won the contact sports.

If you survived that, another adventure on a dirt road with gopher holes and ruts awaited you—not to mention being dangerously close to the thirty-foot cliffs over the Pacific.

The whole journey got elevated to some sort of rite of passage for many of us. Disaster awaited those who failed. Needless to say, a lot of cars and egos were wrecked out there, though miraculously, no one was ever seriously injured.

"For your safety," I said to Vinnie, grabbing the collar I had given him, "please keep body parts inside the car at all times."

Shooting straight for the gap, I slammed the gas pedal to the floor. The Mustang was doing fifty by the time it hit the opening. It was do-or-die time.

We shot the gap and vaulted onto the dirt road without flipping over, slowing to forty and then thirty by the time I looked in the rearview mirror.

The first sedan crashed miserably into the pine and spun to a stop. The second was doomed, slamming headlong into the side of the first in an ear- and metal-crushing concert.

As both cars disappeared in the distance, people were slowly getting out and shaking their heads. My car was practically useless now. Every law enforcement officer in town would soon be looking for a bullet riddled '65 'Stang with a boy and his dog aboard. It was time to put phase two of my getaway plan into action.

The car had slowed to ten, so putting my foot on the gas kept it at twenty as I circled the campus, my outside wheels perched precariously on the dirt path along the cliffs. Three feet to my right and thirty feet below, waves crashed on the rocks. The car was going slowly enough that I wouldn't get too broken up when I jumped out before reaching the edge.

But I had made a serious miscalculation. There might be people below on the beach. I stopped at the edge, got out, and looked down. Much to my good fortune, there were only a couple of surfers left that day. "You might want to move!" I yelled. "This beach is about to become a parking lot!

"Wait a minute," I said to Vinnie. "What's the matter with me? Littering the beach is a five-hundred-dollar fine. . . . Come on," I added, backing away from the cliff. "Let's go put it in student parking. At least that's a ticket I can afford."

Knowing the east entrance might be covered with gray suiters, I parked the car under a tree in one of the more obscure student lots and hoofed it down to the beach. Luckily, no one saw me, and no G-men had arrived yet, as far as I could tell.

I could only think of one place to go. The Channel Islands pier was only a quarter mile down the beach, and beyond it, the water-crossing to the nudie beach.

"Come on," I said to Vinnie. "Let's hide out at the birthday suit beach. Anybody wearing more than a Hawaiian shirt and jeans will be easy to spot."

Vinnie and I went down the stairs and hit the sand. There would be only a few hours, at the most, before they searched the secluded bare-all beach, but it was several miles long, and there were plenty of places to sneak up the cliffs and make it back to town—unless they got out the coast guard helicopters. That was a chance I'd have to take. But the beach figured to be my only chance to find Erato if she was still free.

We started walking.

40

Shadow on the Sun

I couldn't find Erato anywhere around the pier, and knew that sticking around would only get me picked up by the police or some government agency. So Vinnie and I walked on down toward the nudie beach. No one suspicious was around, so we found the beach access and took the three-hundred-stair steps up the side of the cliff to a field between housing developments. The area was known as the Mesa, and marked the dividing line between Channel Islands and Santa Isabella, where the well-to-do took over the land from the working class.

I planned to lie low in that grassy field until sunset, and then figure it out from there. Not being able to go home contributed to my decision. Turning myself in would probably mean the end of Euterpe, so I had to find a way to get back to Sigma without being caught.

I hid in the tall, dry grass and tried to dream up every possible scenario that might work and think of anyone who could help. There was Cooper. Maybe, but it was a very dangerous long shot. He knew everything by now, and I could get set up for a sting pretty easily by contacting him.

That left the highly unlikely choice of a complete stranger, or, oddly enough, Chainsaw. It wasn't as crazy as it sounded. I did have his dog. Luring Chainsaw out using Vinnie as bait was a possibility. If I could draw him into a plot that would bring him angry and armed to the lobby of Sigma, it might create enough confusion for me to slip around back and break into Janet's office long enough to steal the disc.

Sitting on the edge of the world that day, I decided I'd have to jeopardize Vinnie's freedom once again—maybe his life.

Standing up, I looked at the mountains, then played with Vinnie. "If this doesn't work," I said, "and I lose you, I'll never forgive myself. . . . Come on," I said, roughing up his ear. "We've got work to do."

I started across the field. Knowing that this could be my last look at paradise, I turned one last time to the ocean. A small sea gull raced across the face of the setting sun. For a moment he was silhouetted against the burning fireball, a black shadow of fluttering wings struggling against the ocean wind. The sun blinded me for a second, and when my vision returned the bird was gone. The sun sank slowly into the sea, leaving in its wake a brilliant array of orange, pink, and red light, pulsating away from it like a heart sending out liquid life.

In that moment it became clear. There was someone else involved, behind the whole thing, and it wasn't Zeus. It was so simple that I should have thought of it before, but it was too scary. I'd ask Erato if it was true, if she ever showed up again.

I started walking toward the rough side of town. It would take a couple of hours, but I wanted to be on Chainsaw's door that night to deliver a message to him—one he wouldn't like.

Just before leaving, I pulled a folded blank piece of paper from my pants pocket, and one of those small, scorecard pencils left over from my last eighteen holes of lousy golf. But now it had a higher calling. I scribbled some lines that had flashed across my mind like a plane pulling a banner. It wasn't much, but it was a start.

41

Going After Chainsaw

Quickly deciding it would take too long to walk to the other side of town, I launched another plan instead. Luckily, I still had my Ray-Bans, since they were an integral part of the plan. Vinnie was the cause of having to improvise a little.

I took off my belt, hooked it to Vinnie's collar, put on the sunglasses, and waited at the nearest bus stop. I had no idea if they would believe my act of being visually impaired, and accept Vinnie as my guide dog. But since I only had a couple of bucks in my wallet, not nearly enough for a cab, it was worth a try.

Fifteen minutes later the city bus came. I don't think the driver believed my story about being vandalized, losing Vinnie's harness, and having some skinheads break my white cane and run off, but he just couldn't chance it. If I was telling the truth, the city would be in big trouble for harassing the handicapped, so he let us on the bus.

My plan included leaving a note on Chainsaw's door, hoping he wasn't outside working on a truck or something. Getting off the bus at the corner nearest my destination, I thanked the driver profusely, then continued on foot.

As I approached, I didn't see anyone in the yard, so I tied a nervous Vinnie to a tree with my belt and sneaked carefully toward the front door. Just as I was wedging a note between the door and the jamb, there was a familiar voice over my shoulder.

"I wouldn't do that if I were you," Erato said matter-of-factly.

"Well, why not?" I protested. "Somebody's got to do something." I turned around and threw my arms around her. We hugged hard for a couple of seconds. It felt good to hold her again. Standing back, I looked at her and said, "And where have *you* been? I was worried sick."

"I had to split when the Feds showed up," she replied, running her hands through her hair. "I figured you'd turn up here sooner or later, especially when Vinnie ran past me in front of Sigma."

"Well, I don't know how he got away and found me," I shrugged. "But I need him to draw Chainsaw out to run interference while I break into Janet's office."

She gave me a concerned stare. "You mean while *we* break into her office. But you've got it all wrong, we don't need Chainsaw. He's too dangerous. Now come away from the door," she ordered, turning to walk away. "And bring the note. I've got a plan, and it's better than yours."

"Yeah? Well, you haven't heard mine yet."

"Take my word for it."

"Okay then, Ms. Muse, what is this grand idea of yours?"

She didn't say a word, just kept walking away. When she reached the sidewalk, she looked over her shoulder and said, "We use the computer."

That got my attention. I grabbed the note and hustled over to her. She continued walking, back toward the business district.

"Okay, I said, letting Vinnie go, "I'll bite. But I want some answers first."

"All right," she said, stopping to wait for me. "You've got a deal, depending on the questions, of course." She bent over to pet an excited Vinnie.

"I figured something out," I said with raised eyebrows. "Since your dad never comes to earth unless it's absolutely necessary, something big is up. Somebody important is after your sister. Otherwise, your dad would just snap his fingers and bring her back. I think it's the devil himself. What do you think of that?"

Erato stood up and started walking. "You're right," she said over her shoulder. "It's Lucifer."

"I *thought* so. Who is he posing as," I joked. "Cooper?"

"Nope. We just came from Mr. Big's local headquarters for his operation."

Catching up, I grabbed her shoulder. She stopped. "You mean," I said. "Chainsaw is . . . Are you sure?"

"No," she said shaking her head. "*He's* not Lucifer, if that's what you mean. Just one of Luc's flunkies."

"Like what? The Secretary of Torture?"

"Very funny, Cyrus. Look, this is serious."

"But he *can't* be," I protested, throwing up my hands. "He's just some biker."

"What did you expect," she laughed. "Horns and a tail? He

knew we needed a Harley, so he made himself available."

"Hold it. Wait a darn minute. If what you're telling me is true, then you almost . . . almost slept with someone who works for—"

"We all make mistakes," she shrugged. "Besides, it was a chance I had to take. I wouldn't get too excited. He's probably not even the President of Vice. He's probably just a hit man. Luc wants the disc all right, but he usually doesn't show up in person."

"Yeah, well, you said *that* about your dad," I argued, hands on my hips. "Erato, think about it. What a coup it would be for one of Lucifer's operatives to say he slept with the daughter of Zeus. It would humiliate your dad."

"Dad doesn't humiliate easily," she informed me, then explained that the real coup would be to have his daughter imprisoned on a compact disc in Luc's possession. Chainsaw was working on someone inside Sigma to get the disc. He probably would have had it already, but Erato didn't know what the insider wanted in return. So far, he was holding out. All Erato claimed to know was what the devil wanted from Chainsaw: the disc—and someone's soul. His price was always the same. He granted a wish and got a soul.

"Naturally," I said coolly. "He already has Chainsaw's."

"Not yet, but he's working on it."

"Sounds like the plot of *Damn Yankees*," I said, smiling nervously.

"Sort of," she agreed. "But this time Luc's after something bigger: the soul of a muse. With that in his possession, Dad might get mad enough to pull all of the muses out of this world. Who knows? Life could even degenerate into savagery in a few decades if there was no inspired artistic expression. Of course, Luc would like that. Sort of like *Lord of the Flies*."

"Or lord of the *files*," I said, trying to lighten up the situation.

"Actually, Dad's an old softy," she commented, trying to convince me. "I think he's only bluffing. He wouldn't actually do it, if you ask me."

"Yeah, well, this is the same guy that brought us the great flood, remember?"

"Look," she said, touching my shoulder. "I'm sorry I withheld information. I just didn't want to worry you about the big *D* getting involved."

"Mr. Flames," I said, wrinkling my forehead. "Yeah, it's pretty scary all right.

"Who's the insider?" I asked, cooling off and kissing her neck.

"I'm not sure yet."

I pulled back and gave her a disbelieving look. "Well, the insider has to be one of the major players," I surmised. "The way I see it—either Janet, Juanita, or Cooper."

"I concur," she answered smartly. "But the main thing is to get possession of the disc."

"Okay," I nodded. "But if we can't use Chainsaw, what's this plan about the computer?"

She kissed me long and slow, then pulled away. "You hack-in from a terminal," she informed me.

"What good will that do?" I frowned. "And exactly how do we get back inside Sigma? That's why I needed Chainsaw. My note told him to meet me and Vinnie there. He was going to create a distraction so I could bust into Janet's office."

"Don't worry." She smiled coyly. "*I'll* create the distraction."

"Well," I acknowledged, looking at her profile. "You've got me there."

Vinnie stood on his hind legs and came between us, wanting some affection. "Hacking-in does two things," Erato said, petting Vinnie. "It makes them think you're still looking for the real Euterpe somewhere on a system hard disk, and it makes them think you're at a terminal inside Sigma."

"I *will* be."

"True, you'll write a program that automatically keeps trying passwords. They'll trace the terminal ID, and come after you. But you won't be there."

"Okay, where will I be?"

"Going out the back door, while I sneak past the guard and into Janet's office."

"Brilliant, but will it work?"

"That's what I'm betting," she smiled. "But when they discover no one at the terminal, they'll get wise and check everywhere—especially Janet's office." She knelt and began to wrestle Vinnie. He growled happily, loving the attention. After a minute, she stopped and went on. "I'm hoping the break-in attempt will make them think you're somewhere else long enough to get the CD."

"This somewhere else, where is it?"

"The classified computer lab . . ." She studied my blank expression and added, "Just take my word for it."

I told Erato I thought Janet was the contact. She'd been acting like she didn't *want* us to have the Euterpe or the RAM chip file, yet she must have left the screen clues, using the Iberlin account. At first I couldn't figure out her game, but now it was clear. She must be Chainsaw's contact and as such was trying to keep Erato on the hook. Janet wanted to capture her *and* Euterpe—present them to Lucifer as a two-for-one special. That was why she was holding back the disc from Chainsaw.

"I know it sounds crazy," I continued, feeling my bare chin. "But I don't know what's crazy and what isn't anymore. All I'm saying is that if they are after you, then we'd better be more careful." I helped her up and patted her stomach. "Especially with precious cargo on board. Come on, I've got just about enough cash for us to catch the bus, but I doubt that anyone else is going to fall for the blind bit I used to get over here."

"Well, you can try it if you like," she shrugged. "But I say we take a cab."

"With what?"

She opened her bulging purse, but didn't show me inside. "I've got money."

"How?"

"Dad bailed me out."

"*Ah ha,*" I said, exaggerating my voice. "I thought the rich girl supported by her father was out. Image problem, remember?"

"It *was* out," she said defensively. "I . . . *we* needed help."

"How much did he give you?"

"A hundred and fifty."

"That should do it." I nodded approvingly. "Besides, I'm getting hungry. You *did* say a hundred and fifty dollars?"

"Thousand," she grinned sheepishly. "One hundred fifty thousand. It was buried in the sand. I picked it up on my way over here."

I shook my head. "Rich girls . . . Hey, wait a minute. I don't hack anymore, remember?"

"No, and you won't now—a program will. Besides, it's just a diversion."

"Hey, wait a minute," I said, having a thought. "Just how do you propose we get into the classified computer lab?"

"Leave that to me."

"But won't *any* available terminal do?" I asked, confused.

"Don't you want to see what Janet was working on?"

"Of course!" I yelled, hitting my head. "What an idiot. That lab holds the key to everything. That's where Euterpe was captured. Why didn't I think of it before?"

She put her arms around me and said, "You did, but you forgot. That's one of the reasons I'm here. To fill in the blanks so you can solve this whole mystery."

"We," I said. "So *we* can solve it . . . *together*. Erato, you're a genius! How did you say you were getting us into the computer lab?"

"I didn't, but here's my plan."

42

Tennyson

As we walked toward town, Erato explained her plan. Then she turned to me and said, "Cy, we need to talk. I want to see what kind of life we can plan."

"Assuming," I added, "that your dad lets us stay together."

"Well, he'd better," she insisted. "He practically promised."

"Yeah, maybe. But he didn't say for how long, right?"

"True," she replied, raising her eyebrows. "But if we have some sort of plan, I can present it to him before it's too late."

"Wait," I said. "Did your dad sanction our marriage or not?"

"Sure, we just don't know the details yet," she explained. "Let's just use getting married on earth as a working assumption, for the sake of argument."

"All right," I began, stopping to pet Vinnie as he stood on his hind legs. "Guess I just want what everyone else wants: a good job; a family; a safe, clean world to live in. You know, the regular stuff. Doesn't sound very original, does it?"

"Originality isn't important to me," she said, rubbing my back. "Sincerity is, even when disguised as humor. I think you're really sincere deep inside. You just hide it sometimes.

Ever thought about writing verse for a living?"

"There you go again," I protested.

"No, really. I mean, after all of this is over. Think about it. Look inside that head. Forget the fact that you don't have much experience, and that it's not macho. What do you really think?"

"Writing poetry doesn't pay many bills," I said, staring at the sidewalk. "Writing programs does."

"Forget about making a living for a moment," she said, waving her hands. "I've got lots of loot, and access to as much as we will ever need. So, assuming money's no object, what does it say in your heart?"

"Okay, so you've found me out; I confess that much," I admitted, grabbing her hands. Her fingers slipped between mine. Warm vibrations pulsated gently through them, like an electric massage. "I've always admired the great poets: Byron, Shelley, Keats, Emily Dickinson, Dylan Thomas—or Bob Dylan, for that matter. But who can compete with those giants?"

"Who has to?" she frowned, biting my fingers gently. "The point is to find your own voice, based on your experiences and point of view. The words come from *your* spirit." She pulled away and sat on a nearby fire hydrant. "Don't you remember sitting on your bed as a child and reading nursery rhymes," she went on, "and how much fun it was making up your own?"

"Yeah, but—"

"Just think about it," she interrupted. "That's all I'm asking. Now, let's get some food and call a cab."

We got going again and reached the east side business district. The sun had gone down, and the boulevard bustled with lights and the sounds of horns honking, mufflers humming, and brakes squeaking.

Erato called a cab from a pay phone outside a Wendy's fast-food. While waiting for it to arrive, we ate burgers and fries, drank Cokes, and sat outside watching traffic flow by like a river of headlights on one side and taillights on the other.

We wolfed down the food, including two burgers for Vinnie and finished our talk. Erato picked up the philosophy lesson where she had left off. "The great tragedies in life are not being yourself and hiding your feelings," she informed me. "Writing poetry is simply finding words to attach to feelings, ones that lead you to discover yourself—your whole self. You may think you're a left brain person, but I know you have both sides working."

"I admit I'm embarrassed a little by my feelings," I agreed, watching the stars come out overhead. "But who isn't?"

"This is the nineties," she said with her arm around me. "It's okay to be human. We talked about this already, remember?"

"No," I replied. "You talked about this." I laughed a little, and she caught me in a confessional mood, telling her how I used to climb up on the roof of my parents' house with an astronomy book and pretend to be studying the sky. But inside the book I cut out a space big enough to hold another book. It was an old trick, but it worked. I always took a book of poems.

When I got older and tried it at school, some of the guys saw it was a book of poetry. The humiliation was so great that I went home and threw all of my poetry books away. I had never opened another one since. The whole incident reminded me of one of my favorite poems by Tennyson. I'd never forgotten it.

> *Once in a golden hour*
> *I cast to earth a seed.*
> *Up there came a flower,*
> *The people said, a weed.*

"Poetry is a magical thing," I said after a long silence. "Unfortunately, too many guys think it's only words for the weak." I turned and looked her straight in the eyes. "But you know all of this already, don't you?"

She mussed up my hair. "Yes, but I wanted you to bring it up," she said. "I wanted you to rediscover yourself. You're twenty-three now, Cyrus. You don't need peer approval anymore. Strong *and* sensitive—that's what women like these days. It's an unbeatable combination."

"And that's what you want?"

"I want you to be yourself"—she pointed to my temples—"both brain halves. I want a complete person. Not a fake macho man."

I thought for a moment. "It's weird, though . . ."

"What?"

"I . . . I like programming as much as I liked poetry."

"Well, there is a certain beauty in well-written code," she agreed. "I've seen your programming. It's eloquent, almost poetic."

"My right brain coming out, I suppose," I said, exhaling. "You know, the other day I really *did* try. I wanted to write a real poem. I wanted to slash away the rust and get to the shiny part of the sword. But I kept thinking of a program. I guess the terminal is mightier than the sword."

"Did your very first program run? Your very first lines of code," she said, squeezing my arm. "Did the program execute perfectly?"

"Of course not. I had to debug it."

"Then debug your poem—the one in your head. Keep asking yourself if it says what you really want it to, what you really feel."

"Is there another way?" I asked, still too scared to show her the poem I had started at the cliffs. "Putting what you feel into words is so hard."

She leaned over and whispered in my ear, "I'll tell you a trade secret. Give in to your feelings and the words will come automatically. It's easier that way, but it takes more courage. Feelings can be tough to face. But you might try it."

"I might have to," I agreed, glancing down at the paper in my shirt pocket, "if your plan doesn't work. Wait a minute. Is that why you picked me to free Euterpe—because I'm a suppressed poet?"

"That, and availability. Your being in the right place at the right time helped."

"Thanks, I needed that vote of confidence."

"Hey, don't feel too depressed," she said, laying her head on my shoulder. "I've given you some options."

"You're a real modern woman."

"Got that from Dad," she answered, snuggling up. "He always gives people options. But sooner or later, he shows everyone the truth. Of course, contemplating the truth in heaven is better than in Antarctica. It's hard to concentrate when you're shivering."

"Is that why people choose the devil? They'd rather burn than freeze?"

She got a serious look on her face. "People are desperate sometimes. And make funny choices. But Dad takes that into consideration."

"If we blow this," I said, looking at the stars overhead, "could you get me a down parka? I want to be warm when I contemplate the truth."

43

Erato's Plan

It took a little talking, and a halfhearted attempt to make Vinnie look like my guide dog, but when the cabbie arrived, he let Vinnie come too. Of course, Erato's fifty-dollar bill didn't hurt our chances. She was forced to flash it when the cabbie refused to let my guide dog ride with us. Needless to say, the cabbie had a change of heart in a hurry.

Erato's plan was actually quite simple. Sometimes, that's what works best. Once we got to Sigma she would walk into the lobby. We were sure the guard would be on alert in case either of us showed up. Erato's appearance should produce enough excitement to get the guard to chase her out of the building. I would hide in the bushes and sneak past when everyone came out.

The ingenious part of the plan was that Erato had acquired the former guard's name and address. She had charmed someone at the protection agency to get the information. Then she had taken the city bus to his house when the FBI pulled up at Sigma, stopping at the beach to pick up the buried treasure her dad had left.

The guard was angry about being fired. Janet claimed he entered a secure area without her permission the night I sent him to the classified computer lab. He was mad enough to give Erato the cipher lock combination to the lab. The only question that remained was whether the combination had been changed. It was worth a try, but I'd have to get there fast, before the guard got back to her post and caught me busting in on closed circuit TV.

Other than that possibility, I saw one other problem: getting out with the CD. Waiting for the bus wasn't going to get us a very quick getaway, and neither was running down the boulevard. Since Erato had a lot of cash, we had the cabbie take us to the airport so we could rent a car, forgetting that there was probably an APB out on both of us.

He dropped us off and we headed for the car rental complex. Unfortunately, as we neared the building, we saw a lot of suspicious-looking men in suits hanging around. They could have been waiting to see if we'd try to catch a flight or rent a car to get out of town. So the three of us left quickly and quietly on foot, heading for the beach.

As luck would have it, Channel Islands pier and the university were only a half mile from the airport. We were touching the sand in no time. From the beach we would have to hike past Cal U. and circle back to Sigma, which was only another two miles. Or we could could call a cab from a pay phone on campus if we didn't want to hoof it. When we got to the bottom of the stairs leading up to the campus, we stopped to rest. I had an idea.

Erato gave me a frustrated look. "Now what? Call another cab?"

"Naw, no time for that." I pointed up the cliff in the direction of the student parking lot. "We'll take the Mustang. I'll bet it's still where I left it," I added, optimistically. "Unless it's been impounded."

"According to the radio report I heard on the bus," she told me, "a tall, blond, wavy-haired, blue-eyed fugitive is believed to be driving it, and was last seen heading toward LA."

"Fugitive? How rude," I frowned. "Didn't they mention the Hawaiian shirt?" After she shook her head, I said, "I'm hurt."

"You're crazy," she observed, shaking her head. "How can you joke at a time like this?"

"How can I not? This is sheer lunacy. Wait'll they catch us. The media will love our story. Donahue, Oprah, Geraldo. Our social schedule will be booked months in advance. After we get out of jail, that is."

"If you're through making celebrity plans," she said, looking up at the moon and back, "can we get going?"

"Just a minute," I said, holding up my index finger. "This time it's my turn to make the plans."

I made Erato and Vinnie wait at the bottom of the stairs while I sneaked over to the student parking lot where the Mustang had been left. It was a heck of a long shot, but it was worth a look. After all, who would have thought I'd be stupid enough to stash my car at the university and escape on foot, when the freeway was only a mile down the road? The answer quickly became clear: *no one.*

There, still sitting in the same place, under a tree between two other junkers, was my Mustang. No one was around. I got in and drove to the parking lot at the top of the stairs. I left it running, got out, and ran down the steps. They were gone. My heart began to pound. Racing around the cliff, I just about ran over them.

"Erato!" I said, catching my breath. "I thought we agreed you wouldn't disappear like that again."

"I saw headlights on the cliff," she replied defensively. "How was I supposed to know it was you?"

"Never mind," I said with a wave. "Let's get going. I've got the Mustang."

We ran up the stairs, piled in, put it in gear, and headed off toward Sigma.

"Hey," I declared, pulling out of the lot. "We've still got a minute or two until we get to Sigma; tell me about *your* plans for the future."

"Very funny."

"No, look," I said, getting serious. "I told you my embarrassingly simple dreams. Now tell me yours—before I never see you again."

"What do you mean? You going somewhere?"

"No, but *you* might be," I said cautiously. "I figure if we free your sister, you're going to be called back to the front office by your dad. I'm not stupid enough to think for one minute that he's going to let you marry a mortal, let alone a surfer-turned-programmer."

"But—"

"And if we don't free her," I interrupted, turning onto Ocean Avenue, "I'll be doing time at the South Pole or being used as a lightning rod."

"Dad wouldn't do that," she said stiffly.

"Yeah," I said, slapping the steering wheel. "And lightning doesn't strike twice in the same place, either."

"You just have an incredible sense of timing," she answered smugly.

"Yeah, tell me about it."

"Okay," she agreed, "I'll make you a deal." Glancing behind us and seeing nothing following the car, she continued, "We get out of this safely tonight, CD or no CD, and I'll tell all."

"All?"

"Well, almost all."

"Deal. We'd better go around the long way and park across the field from Sigma," I suggested. "Otherwise, we could get spotted."

"You are full of so many good ideas," she answered, a little sarcastically. "You'd think someone with a mind like yours could write poetry."

I didn't answer, just went straight through the next traffic light and headed out of the university. A minute later Erato looked at me and asked, "How much time will you need to set up the break-in program?"

"Five minutes," I said, pulling into off-campus housing. "That should do it."

"I just hope it's enough," she sighed.

"So do I," I replied, glancing her way. "I want to know what's in your head before you split. Kind of a funny part of my personality, wanting to know my lovers before they leave me."

"Cyrus," she said suddenly. "I'm not leaving you. I don't care what Dad says. I'll fight for us—all three of us," she added, patting her stomach.

"All four of us," I said, petting Vinnie's head on my shoulder. "They gotta let dogs into heaven, or I'm not going. I'll bet they don't even have leash laws."

"That's true," she admitted. "But that's all you're getting out of me. . . . We're here," she said, looking up. "And I've said too much already. Park this thing. We've got a disc to borrow."

"Borrow," I repeated. "*Stealing* is more like it."

"Thieves," she informed me in a fake snooty voice, "don't get into heaven right away. We, my dear, are taking back what is rightfully ours. They can have the disc. We just want the contents. That's not stealing; it's retrieving stolen data."

I didn't argue, just pulled into the parking lot nearest the back of Sigma and shut off the engine. The moment of reckoning had arrived. The data-retrieval mission was fully operational. The only thing between us and the disc was a field of pampas grass, a seven-foot fence, the light emanating from the lobby out front, some closed circuit cameras, and burglar alarms. At least, that's all we could see from the parking lot. Anything else would be dealt with as encountered.

44

The Break-in

Once out of the car, we wove our way through clumps of pampas grass as big as haystacks, carefully avoiding the razor-sharp edges of their long blades. Most of them were over our heads, so we didn't have to crouch to avoid being seen. I instructed Vinnie to keep a low profile and to avoid barking. Hopefully, he would get the idea. After all, Labs were considered pretty smart in the dog kingdom, being used as drug sniffers, handicapped helpers, and, of course, as excellent guide dogs for the visually impaired.

It was possible that a trap was set for us, and that the Feds and cops were well-hidden. But we didn't see anything unusual. Vinnie's hearing was working fine, and he didn't detect any strange noises. That was our signal to put the rest of our plan into action.

As usual, a couple of company cars and vans were parked in the back lot, but otherwise, the coast was clear. With any luck we could get in and out before anyone suspected anything, but I would have to stay out of sight of the surveillance cameras mounted on the roof at the corners of the buildings. That would be accomplished by waiting near the fence until Erato's upcoming appearance in the lobby, when she could draw the guard outside.

After that, I would sneak around the main building and enter the lobby from the other direction, while Erato and Vinnie kept the guard busy. Hopefully, the distraction would last long enough for me to race through the lobby to the classified computer lab. It was only five hundred feet from the front desk, so I might be able to make it before the guard got back to her post. Once in the lab, I would write and run my program, then dash for any emergency exit, knowing I would be seen by the hall cameras. That should bring the guard my way.

Erato would enter through the lobby while the guard chased me down the hallways and out an emergency exit at the back of the building. Erato would break into Janet's office, steal the CD, go out the back door to the lab, and meet me at the fence. That is, if everything went according to plan. It was time to get started.

We emerged through the last clump of pampas grass and headed for the property line. A modest seven-foot fence separated Sigma from student housing and the rest of the world. It sported a few complimentary strands of widely spaced barbed wire. The design wasn't intended to keep out real intruders, since anyone serious about entry could easily put their hands between the barbs and climb over. But it did give the impression that you were on private property.

We threw Vinnie over first, figuring Erato might need him for added protection in case things got rough. We weren't thinking too well, though, because he almost got his steel choke chain caught on one of the barbs. But he made it, and so did we with some effort. Once over, Erato and Vinnie strolled the two hundred yards or so to the back of Sigma. They progressed along the walkway to the front edge of the main building, knowing they were on camera. Erato made it look like a routine visit by someone's significant other.

They got to the front of the building and marched around the corner. I hid between a large bush and the back fence, anxiously waiting to make my move.

A long, tense minute followed. I almost came out of hiding, but suddenly Erato and Vinnie came flying around the corner of the building, the guard in hot pursuit. Her gun was holstered, but she was waving a nightstick and yelling. She was young, strong, and agile, but no match for a Labrador.

When Erato stepped onto the big side lawn, she unleashed Vinnie. He immediately started barking. I could see him out of the corner of my eye, protecting Erato by standing his ground.

The guard pulled her gun and tried to draw a bead on Vinnie, but he sensed her aggression, and didn't like being harassed. He dashed back and forth so fast that the guard couldn't get a shot off. Erato backed away across the lawn toward the street, yelling for Vinnie to come.

Having seen enough, I slipped out of the bush and bolted around the back of the building, listening to Vinnie's barking and the guard's yelling. She still had her back turned when I came around the corner, dashed into Sigma and past the desk. Racing down the hall, I could still hear Erato calling to Vinnie.

He stopped barking. Thankfully, no shots had been fired. The next thing I heard was the guard in the lobby, calling for a backup. We hadn't thought of that. It could shorten our time considerably.

Never breaking stride, I was at the door to the computer lab in less than twenty seconds, punching in the combination, not caring if the guard saw me on camera, and hoping Erato could get past the front desk.

Much to my relief, the door popped open on the first try. Once inside, I closed it and flipped on the light switch. Suddenly I was in another world. The lab seemed to have little to do with computers. Instead, it was filled to overflowing with fancy electronic equipment. Yet it was arranged in a very organized manner. I quickly scanned the room, searching for a terminal.

To my left, a bank of state of the art frequency analyzers, power generators, and god-knows-what filled one complete wall, floor to ceiling. It looked like something out of the new "Star Trek" engineering department. A rainbow of lights played tag all over the wall, chasing each other around the equipment. I almost expected Geordi La Forge to emerge wearing that air filter over his eyes and announce some imminent engineering catastrophe.

The far end of the room was fitted with a small wooden stage like an old playhouse, complete with purple velvet curtains. They were opened and displayed only a blank dark wall behind the empty stage. There were even two rows of theater seats near the door, and what looked like a sound studio glassed-in on my right, opposite the bank of fancy equipment. It sported several video monitors arranged in a large vertical square along the back wall. Behind the theater seats a fifteen-foot-high full-blown telescope was bolted to the floor, glaring at the ceiling, as if waiting for it to open so it could explore the heavens.

Several microphones hung at various intervals from a scaffold erected above the stage. Thirty feet overhead the ceiling formed a giant dome, sealed shut at the top.

Finally, in the center of the sixty-foot-square room sat a piece of equipment that was positioned where a movie camera would have been. But it didn't look like one—at least not exactly. It looked like the kind of television camera on wheels that you see in a studio, but attached to the front of the lens was a three-foot steel shaft and a complex arrangement of sighting and alignment devices bolted down in various places. The barrel was about rifle diameter, complete with a small opening at the bullet end, pointed toward center stage. On the side of this inexplicable piece of high-tech machinery, a single word was stenciled neatly in two-inch letters—MUSE.

It was overwhelming. This room had to hold all of the clues to the entire incident, and must have cost a fortune to build. But I didn't have time to figure it out.

I found a single terminal inside the glassed-in sound room. It was hooked in series to a number of tape recorders, but I had a hunch it was connected to the mainframe as well.

Firing up the terminal, I was greeted with good news. The system was up, and my account was still active. No one had bothered to expel me.

Once on the screen it was a simple matter of starting my little program. It was almost too easy. In seconds, I was into the swing of things, executing a program that tried to break into the Top Secret disk. I set it up to keep knocking on the door, trying passwords, going down every word in the electronic dictionary. I was hoping that by the time they discovered where it was coming from, Erato would be breaking into Janet's office and stealing the CD.

"Okay," I said aloud. "All set. This should keep them busy for a while."

It was time to go. I shut the door behind me and raced toward the far side of the building, opposite Janet's office, heading straight for an emergency exit. By the time my feet hit the last long hallway to freedom, the guard had taken the bait. She came flying around the corner, ten yards behind me, gun drawn, yelling the usual stop-or-I'll-shoot stuff. Judging by the tone of her voice, she was enjoying this, but so was I, knowing Erato must be in Janet's office.

Twenty feet from the emergency exit I put on the brakes, ducking down as my tennis shoes grabbed the floor tiles. It wasn't a perfect move, but I managed to keep my balance and slide down on one knee, like squatting on a surfboard on a fast ride.

Sure enough, the guard broke over me like a wave, tumbling toward the emergency exit. I got up and ran for the exit, grabbing the crossbar and flinging open the door. The guard rolled through to the parking lot, gun and all. The alarm screamed in my ears.

Watching the door close automatically behind her, I suddenly had a change of plans, and bolted for Janet's office, knowing the guard would circle the building and come in the lobby again.

That should leave me enough time to get to Erato. I raced off down the hall to the added sound of bullets riddling the metal emergency door behind me.

"Don't mess with the locals!" I couldn't help yelling over my shoulder, and disappeared down the hallway. Thirty seconds later I was at Janet's door, which Erato had knocked open using a fire ax she had pulled from the wall. It was still in her hand as I raced through the office door.

Vinnie barked once before Erato muzzled him with her hand. He couldn't see me in the dark, but I whispered loudly for him to be quiet, and he shut up immediately. Then he jumped up and almost licked me to death.

"Okay," Erato said as my feet hit the carpet. "Let's get the CD and get out of here." ·

"Wait, not so fast," I answered, grabbing her arm, and catching my breath. "I've got an idea. Let's set up the amp while the CD's still in the jukebox and play it now, before we're discovered."

She shook her head. "No, Cy. That wasn't the plan. Let's just grab it and get out of here."

"Listen," I argued, still breathing hard. "The guard called for a backup. They may be in the parking lot already, waiting for us to leave. If we get caught with the CD on the way out, we're goners." I stopped and pointed to Janet's lab. "But if we find the right equipment behind that door, we can set her free without leaving Janet's office. All we need is a microphone to pick up what's playing on the disc, and an amplifier to make it audible. Come on."

She thought for a moment. "Well . . . all right," she said impatiently, hands on her temples. "But let's get a move on."

The lab was locked, but I kicked it open, which surprised me. Once inside, we noticed plenty of high-tech stuff all right, even a CD recorder and player that erased. Janet could make her own CDs that way.

We didn't have to say much; we knew what we wanted. I grabbed a high-sensitivity microphone and a suitcase-size amp with a built-in speaker, and we went back into Janet's office. I set up the microphone next to the jukebox speaker and plugged it into the amp. If anything was on that disc, we'd make it audible or die trying.

Looking for a 110-volt outlet to plug the sound system into, I noticed one under Janet's desk. Climbing under and plugging in the amp, I saw a red light blinking underneath the desk. That meant there was a security light blinking in the lobby. Even if we hadn't been picked up in the hallway on video, the light meant the guard was surely running toward us, probably with some backup.

"Quick," I said, getting up and banging my head on the desk, "Grab the disc. I'm sure she's on her way. We've got to get out of here."

Erato made a move for the jukebox. Loud whispers in the hall and the sounds of rifles being cocked filled the air. Vinnie woofed real loud.

"Forget it!" I said to Erato in a whisper. "It's too late. They're at the door."

She went for the jukebox anyway, so I tackled her. We both went to the floor. The door was rattling. We got up, and I dragged her forcibly by the arm toward Janet's lab, planning to escape through the back door. Vinnie began to bark big-time. I yelled at him as we stepped into the lab, but he sat frozen by the front office door, bellowing at the intruders in the hall.

We had barely entered the lab when the office door began to fill with bullets, splintering the expensive wood. That got Vinnie moving. He headed for the lab to join us.

"Too bad," I said nervously, slamming the door between the office and the lab. "Honduran mahogany is getting hard to find these days."

Erato gave me a weird look, and we ran for the back exit, purposely knocking lab equipment on the floor to block the path, and hoping the welcome wagon wasn't waiting for us outside the back door.

I opened it. Luckily, the coast was clear. But I was sure there were more eager defenders of justice running around the building toward us, most likely with guns drawn.

Just then the door between the office and lab burst open, sending splinters flying. The guard and some guys in suits piled into the lab, guns drawn and pointed everywhere. Vinnie stopped to bark. As we stepped through into the parking lot, I yelled for him to come. He made a dash for us, jumping equipment as he went.

He blasted through the back door to the accompaniment of bullets ricocheting off oscilloscopes and power supplies. I slammed it shut behind him. Then we took off for the back fence.

The support officers were coming around the building, guns waving, ready to make short work of us. Vinnie barked out a steady stream of warnings, but the pursuers slowed for only a second, and took up the chase again. That second was long enough for us to cut a sharp angle to the fence, making the police readjust their firing positions. If we could make it over without getting our bodies filled with extra holes, we would be gone, losing ourselves easily in the pampas grass.

The nearest of them was still a hundred yards behind us when we hit the chain link, but we had a new problem. We'd have to toss Vinnie over again, and risk getting him caught on the barbs he had barely missed the last time. I bent down to remove his choker.

Erato looked at me and Vinnie, and then over her shoulder at the enemy. She turned toward them and raised her hands, as if to give herself up so we could escape. I looked back along the fence and saw a company car parked parallel to it not twenty yards away. In the haste and confusion, I hadn't noticed it before, but now it was clear. It was our chance at escape.

The men slowed when Erato raised her hands. A commanding voice behind them yelled, "Hold your fire!" At least someone would rather have us alive. I recognized the voice as Janet came jogging up alongside the cops.

Without saying a word, I grabbed Erato's sleeve and dragged her back before she could surrender. She got the idea and we broke for the fence. Uniformed police and three-piece suiters held their fire as we climbed onto the roof of the parked car. Erato was up and over in a flash. I grabbed for Vinnie but he turned and barked, avoiding my grip. Not having time to argue, I leaped for the fence and bounded over. The cops closed in, still nervously holding their fire. I yelled at Vinnie to jump the fence.

Vinnie saw we were on the other side and suddenly jumped from the roof of the car. His paws caught the top of the chain link between the barbs, and he was able to wiggle over. But on the way down, his collar caught on the barbed wire, and he was hanging there—choking.

One of the men raised his rifle and aimed. I stretched my arms out, but couldn't quite grab Vinnie's collar. He was squirming and starting to whine pretty loudly, wiggling for his life. His fur had bunched up and blocked the choker from passing over his head. The chain held him fast and tight, cutting off his wind and leaving him dangling helplessly from the fence.

Just before the cop pulled the trigger Janet yelled, "Cease fire! There is not going to be any bloodshed on my account!"

Seeing my opportunity, I reached up and got hold of whatever I could, grabbing his body in one arm and yanking the chain over his head with the other. Luckily, it slipped over his missing ear flap, clearing his head completely. As I pulled the choker off the barb, he came down with a thud and rolled to his feet. We dashed for the tall clumps of grass, the choker in my hand.

"Cyrus!" Janet yelled. "It's no use. Give yourself up! It's only a matter of time now. This is a small town. You can't hide out much longer. Make it easy on yourself. Turn yourself in. It doesn't matter anymore. The plans are safe. You can . . ."

We were out of range, zigging our way through the field toward the car. By the time anyone got over the fence after us, it was too late. We were starting the car and leaving. We were both surprised when a volley of bullets hit the back of the car as we pulled away. Luckily no one got hurt, but someone had overruled Janet.

"For crying out loud!" I yelled. "What does everyone think this is? Bonnie and Clyde? I'll never get all these holes patched up."

I gunned the engine and pulled away. A few more shots were fired, but nothing found its mark, except for the one that shattered the rearview mirror.

We were long gone before anyone got near us, but the disappointment was too much to bear, too much to talk about; so we joked about other things instead, and tried to forget— at least for the moment.

"Any ideas on accommodations?" I finally asked, a little tired and nervous.

"A motel, I guess, but not in this town."

"Motel? I don't go to motels with strange women," I remarked, trying to ease the tension. "Especially ones I don't know very well."

"Oh, I get it," Erato said, shaking her head. "You want my *dreams, desires*, and *life history* stuff now."

"Hey, you promised."

"Yeah, guess I did. But this is a bad time for it, don't you think?" She leaned over and flipped on the radio. It still worked, and was halfway through "Burning Down the House" by the Talking Heads. "Could we just find a place to sleep?"

"Sure," I agreed, looking around and seeing no followers. "Naturally, home is out, and they'll be checking the motels, but I know a place on Mountain Drive. Overlooks the whole city."

"Why not?" she laughed, resting her feet on the dash. "I hear a lot of girls sleep with men in cars."

"I wouldn't call it *sleeping*," I said. "But it'll be just you, me, and the stars." I looked in the backseat. "And Vinnie, of course."

"You're not planning on using that on me, are you?" she asked, looking at the choker in my hand. It was her way of saying she was loosening up.

Vinnie whined and I patted him. Pulling over, I checked his neck, then fastened the choker on him. "Hey, old boy," I remarked. "How about that? Losing that ear might have just saved your life. I don't think I could have slipped the chain off if that ear flap was still there. It probably would have caught your flap. Funny world we live in. Looks like your neck's going to be okay. It's not bleeding."

"Yeah," Erato said, carefully touching my neck. "But yours is. You must have scraped it on that pampas grass back there." She pulled a Kleenex from the glove box and dabbed my neck. The bleeding stopped.

"Nice try," I quipped, "But I think you're probably a vampire."

"Not really," she said, leaning closer toward me. "But the neck is a good place to start biting. Tell me. Is this place really . . . private?"

"It's a little turnout behind a big rock," I said proudly. "Nobody'll be there. It can't be seen from the road."

"Good. Then we can leave the top down. I've always wanted to make love under the stars."

"With your dad watching?"

"He's got better things to do."

"So I noticed," I replied, rubbing my clean-shaven chin.

I got back on the street and headed for Mountain Drive. Once there the road began its slow, winding climb up the side of the hill, and we started our ascent to the stars.

"Now," I said, "about that talk on dreams and desires."

"Desires first," she said right off, grabbing my leg. "Followed by talk. Dreams are better afterward."

"No argument there. Your star or mine?"

"Yours," she said, smiling. "It's brighter."

"Yeah, and I'm about to turn up the candlepower."

45

The Dreams of a Muse

On the way up the mountain I explained the contents of the computer lab as much as I could. We both agreed it held the key to Euterpe's digitized existence, but without the CD, it didn't seem to matter much. We had come so close, yet she was still a dimension away. We'd have to dream up another rescue plan. At the moment, though, we were fresh out of ideas.

I pulled over at Lookout Rock and parked the car. Stars flickered overhead and city lights blinked below, while sparks flew in the backseat of the Mustang. Vinnie sat on the front seat, standing guard in case anyone got ideas about sneaking up and stealing my magnificent driving machine. I was glad we were off the street and had a big boulder between us an the road behind.

Afterward, we cuddled for a long while. Finally, when I couldn't stand it any longer, I stated my case to Erato.

"Okay," I began, "now it's your turn. I want to know what you really want out of life, *human* life, and why you picked me to fall for—besides accessibility to your sister."

Erato sat up, put her feet over the passenger's seat, and looked at the moon, tucked in for the night by a blanket of a million stars. She told me that it started out as a dream to feel what humans feel. She had been harboring such desires for hundreds of years, curious about what her clients were experiencing when they wrote poetry. She wanted to really feel it. Then, finally, the opportunity came. She could work on freeing her sister and experience human life at the same time.

She brought her gaze down from the stars and looked at me. "But then you happened along. I didn't pick you—no consciously, anyway. My heart did, and you can't tell your heart who to pick. But I would've picked you anyway," she added, sensing my disappointment. "I'm happy being here with you. What could be more important than happiness?"

"I can't think of a thing," I said, sitting up and kissing her forehead. "Except maybe freeing your sister. But after she's free, I want you to ask your dad if you can stay here. I want to spend my life with you—here on planet Earth."

"But . . ." She hesitated, staring at the stars. "There's my career as a muse. If my sisters can't cover for me while I'm out being human, then . . . he'll take me back to the other side. . . . Well, there's still hope," she said, turning toward me. "Maybe he'll make you a spirit so we can be together."

I took a deep breath and put my arm over her shoulder, slipping her fingers between mine. "I don't know if I'm ready to give up being human yet," I said with a sigh. "Heck, I'm only twenty-three. Sure, we could have the baby in your world, and I would help raise it. I could even write programs to streamline your schedule." I stopped and kissed her cheek. "But going to heaven sounds an awful lot like being dead. How about I live here with you and the baby, then we go off to heaven afterward. That sounds more normal to me."

"Being married to a career muse is not what you'd call normal," she informed me. "But I'll ask Dad if I can stay. We still don't know who's going to do my work if I live here. My desk will be piled up as it is when I get back."

"Well, if your sisters are too busy to cover for you, can't your dad get someone else?"

"How?" she asked, squeezing my hand. "Place an ad in the job section of the *Heavenly Herald*?"

"You've got eight sisters," I reminded her. "And you said yourself things were slow for you right now. If I promise to write a program to screen out crank calls and phonies, one of your sisters could take your place—at least until you get back. What's sixty or so years to a muse anyway?"

"If we could work out this career thing without Dad's getting involved, I think it might be doable."

"How about asking for maternity leave, then?" I asked. "Many employers are getting on board with it these days. Then, a few months after the baby is born, you can go back to work if you want. I'll . . . I'll even go with you, if that's what you want."

Vinnie was feeling neglected, so he climbed over the seat and lay on my lap. I turned sideways in the backseat and put my legs over Erato's, petting Vinnie at the same time.

"Baby leave," Erato said, thinking about it. "I might be able to handle that." She turned and looked me square in the eyes. "You'd really give up your life on earth for me?"

"And the baby if I have to," I replied forcefully. "When we get to heaven, though, I still want a programming position."

"You love me," she said, smiling.

"Look, when you disappeared the other night I realized that I might lose you," I said seriously. "I might still lose you, but love doesn't happen along every day. I want to be with you. Your world *or* mine. Call me corny, but just take me with you. That's all I ask."

"Cyrus!" she beamed, her eyes growing big. "Listen to you. You *do* love me. It'll be just like the movies. Just you and me, and baby makes three."

"Babies."

"Babies? How many do you want?"

"One of each," I said right off.

"What if we have two girls?"

"Then we'll try for three."

"Nothing doing," she said, petting Vinnie on my lap. "The days of big families are over. Two's the limit. No matter what."

"Deal," I said holding out my hand, and we shook on it. "Then it's settled."

"At least between us," she replied, resting her head on the back of the seat. "I still have to convince Dad. He can be old-fashioned about some things."

"Like what?"

"Life and death," she joked. "That sort of thing."

"Look, I know what you're getting at," I objected, raising my voice. "I'm not a god or a god-in-training or anything like that. I'm not even an angel. But darn it, I love you. There, I said it. And that should be good enough. Besides, I'm a decent programmer, and you're pregnant."

"There *is* still one thing you can do that might convince him," she said, watching a shooting star.

"Yeah, I *know*. Write a poem. Don't think I haven't tried." I patted my shirt pocket. "But I don't know. It's hard. I don't think I can pull it off."

"Try again," she whispered. "I don't want to give him any reason to refuse. If we at least have something to show him"—she pointed to her stomach—"besides this, he might rule in our favor. Of course, there's always the lightning bolt wedding. Sort of like a shotgun wedding, only . . ."

"All right, I get the idea," I said, waving my hand. "I'll try again."

"Have you got anything so far?" she asked, carefully.

"Not much."

"Let me see it."

"Wait a minute," I frowned. "Am I the first?"

"Don't be ridiculous," she defended, half-mad. "Of course you're the first. Don't you remember, I was a virgin?"

"No, not that," I answered, turning red. "Is this the first time you've fallen in love? You must have visited many men in your profession, in the spirit of course."

"Well, you weren't exactly *the* first," she admitted, squeezing my legs on her lap. She explained how she had fallen in love a couple of times with great poets. But they were drunks and drug addicts. Erato wasn't into tragic sufferers too much. Watching them stagger to bed turned her off.

"Okay, I can accept that," I nodded. "Here's my poem, then." I reached into my shirt pocket and pulled it out. "So far, anyway." I unfolded it and handed it to her. "But remember, it's not finished yet."

She took it carefully in both hands and said, "Mind if I read it aloud? That's what brings poetry to life."

I looked around, and seeing no one but Vinnie, who sneaked up and licked my nose, nodded my approval. "Might as well. I don't think anyone will hear you laugh way out here."

"Whatever I do," she insisted, staring at the page. "I won't laugh." She held it up in the moonlight and read aloud.

She came to me like a wave
Of passion and beauty
Reaching easily inside
And spinning me down
An endless tunnel of joy

She caressed me softly
Her arms spilling over me
Like cool soothing liquid
Drowning me in sweetness and love

I fell helplessly into her embrace
Never wanting it to end
Then the wave reached
The shore

And rushed raging and reckless
Crashing over me

I was lying
On hard wet sand
She was gone
And I was empty
And alone

I looked up
Blinded by love

"Cyrus," she gasped. "It's . . . it's beautiful. Tragic, but beautiful."

"Like I said, it's not finished," I answered, a little flushed with embarrassment. "The ending could go either way, if you get my drift. I can't finish it until I know our fate."

"Well, I'm working on that part, remember?" She leaned over and threw her arms around me and Vinnie for a big hug. "Soon as I see Dad again," she beamed, "I'll plead our case. But do me a favor; finish it the way you want it to end. Sometimes, you can make your own destiny."

"Yeah, sometimes," I said, kissing her forehead between Vinnie licks.

"So what's your rescue plan now that they're onto us?" she asked.

"Go to sleep. I'll tell you in the morning."

"Why not now?" she asked impatiently.

"You'll never believe it," I said, shaking my head.

"Try me," she insisted.

"I will, in the morning. Good night."

"Okay," she agreed, raising an eyebrow. "But it better be good."

"It's better than good," I said in an exaggerated voice. "It's unbelievable. Good night."

"How am I supposed to sleep now?" She rolled her eyes. "Wondering about your unbelievable plan?"

"Trust me. It will work. If it doesn't, we're both dead. That's all."

"Oh, great. Thanks for making it easy, Cyrus."

"Good night, and pleasant dreams. . . . Come on, Vinnie," I added. "We've got some sleeping to do."

46

Convertible Sunrise

The yellow sun came pouring into the convertible pretty early. As soon as it popped up over the mountains, it was spotlighting us. Vinnie and I were sprawled out in the front seat, while Erato snoozed in the back. I had to hang my feet over the passenger's door to get comfortable, but slept pretty well considering the accommodations.

I woke sleeping beauty and explained my plan for the day. The agenda included leaving the car where it was parked, since it was an easy target now and might get spotted. We would hike down the mountain to a pay phone and get chauffeured by taxi to the International House of Pancakes, where we would eat breakfast, saving a pancake or two for a hungry dog. Then we would check in across the street at the Turnpike Lodge, if they had a vacancy and would let us in before noon. It would make a good base of operations—halfway between Sigma and downtown Santa Isabella. We would get showered and take Vinnie to the vet, where he would be boarded for the time being. It was too dangerous to take him all over town with that conspicuous missing ear.

To throw them off further, we would buy some tourist clothes at this little shop at Seamen's Wharf. They were looking for a ratty surfer with a worn-out Hawaiian shirt and torn jeans, not a well-groomed out-of-town type. Erato would wear something touristy as well. Then I would be ready to spring my main plan, not telling Erato until the last moment to savor the surprise.

Everything went pretty much as planned. We got some pancakes, a room, and cleaned up, which included a bout with a water-loving Labrador who wanted in the shower. It was a little crowded with the three of us. Somehow we managed to get Vinnie bathed, but he kept shaking water on us all the time. Then we took a taxi to the vet's, explaining to the driver that Vinnie needed some shots.

We dropped him off and I said a reluctant good-bye, telling Vinnie we'd be back in a couple of days at the most. I hoped that the Feds or Chainsaw weren't already checking all vets and animal shelters in the area for leads.

We got back in the cab and headed for the pier. By midmorning we were in full tourist gear: matching khaki walking shorts, expensive designer safari shirts with brightly colored macaws front and back, new Wayfarers and Rockport walking shoes, Olympus camera, and guidebooks. In short, we looked like Ken and Barbie go to the beach. We ate fish and chips at some tourist place on the pier, and then it was time to spring the rest of my plan. Sitting on a bench outside the Fish Ahoy restaurant, I was ready to launch my assault.

"Let's get to a pay phone," I said at last, downing a Diet Mountain Dew and finishing my chips. "We have a call to make."

"Okay, you've kept your plan a secret long enough," Erato informed me, chewing on her last chip. "But I need to know what's going on. We're in this together, in case you hadn't noticed. Now, who are you calling?"

"Cooper."

"Cooper?" she repeated with a big frown. "Isn't that a little dangerous? He could be working with the enemy."

"We'll have to chance it," I said, shaking my head. "He's the only one I've got left on the inside. I've given up all hope of convincing Janet and Dr. Vaya. But there's still a chance for Cooper—if he's not too involved already. Of course, he could be Chainsaw's contact for the CD."

"Yeah, what about that possibility?"

"Then we're ruined," I said with a shrug. "But he's our last chance. Unless you've got a better idea."

"And if you're wrong?"

"We start packing for the South Pole," I joked, looking out to sea. "If Cooper *is* involved, we're finished already. But if he's not, it's the only way we're going to get the CD."

"All right," she said reluctantly. "Go ahead. But remember, we've only got until midnight tomorrow."

Getting up from our bench and leaving the scraps for sea gulls, we found a pay phone nearby and I called Cooper's work number, not knowing if he'd answer, or if the line was bugged. He picked it up on the fourth ring.

"Systems. Cooper here."

"Coop, it's me, Cyrus. I need your help."

There was a long silence. Then: "I suggest you turn yourself in to the authorities," he said flatly. "Attempted file theft is a felony now. Maybe if you give yourself up, they'll go easy on you."

"Look, I don't care about the RAM chip plans," I stated. "And I can prove it."

"How?"

"Get me the CD in Janet's office," I ordered, glancing around. Not seeing anyone suspicious, I went on. "The one marked Sounds of Silence. Not the Simon and Garfunkel. The other one."

"Why should I?" he asked, suspiciously.

"It's the only way I can prove my innocence."

"Okay, suppose you're telling the truth. How will what's on the CD prove your innocence?"

"Because what I'm about to tell you is too impossible to be anything but the truth." I looked at Erato. "And if what I say isn't on the level, I'll turn myself in."

"What makes you think I'm not having this call traced right now?" he asked matter-of-factly. "And some government agents aren't on their way to pick you up?"

"Because you're a rational, intelligent human being," I said with sincerity. "And I *thought* we were almost on the verge of friendship, or at least mutual respect. Look, obviously the RAM chip plans aren't on the CD. You can play it yourself, but all you'll get is silence. It's an encoded message."

"Of what?"

I held my breath, then realized I'd have to try the truth. I told him that it was a voice track of Erato's sister, the muse of lyric poetry. That Janet was experimenting with voice pattern capture, and somehow Euterpe got digitized and transferred to CD.

"I thought you said I was a rational, intelligent person. How am I supposed to take this—this—impossible story? It must be a cover for something else. Otherwise, the FBI wouldn't have been involved. There must be some secret message on the compact disc. I'm sorry, but I just can't give it away."

"I'll prove it."

After a long hollow silence, Cooper answered. "I'm listening."

"Get me the disc," I ordered. "I'll supply the CD player, but you need to pick up a high-sensitivity microphone from Janet's lab—and an amp. We need to amplify the voice to the audible range. That should free Euterpe."

"You're serious, aren't you?"

"Of course!" I yelled. "Who would make up something like this? It's too crazy to be anything but the truth."

"Maybe," came his icy reply. I was starting to lose him as a player in my plan. My jaw dropped in disappointment.

Erato tapped me on the shoulder, so I put my hand over the receiver. "Tell him I've got a message for him," she said like a line from a Godfather movie. "From his brother." I looked at her funny. "Just tell him," she insisted, pushing my shoulder.

I told him and a long stiff silence followed. Finally, in a defensive voice, he said, "I can't do anything until Janet goes home. Meet me at the bus stop out front at six o'clock."

"What about the Feds?"

"They've moved on," he said confidently. "Said they've got bigger fish to fry. More important things to do than chase some ex-employee looking for hacker's revenge."

"You sure?"

"You'll have to trust me on this one," he said, like we were friends again. "I trusted you. Now it's your turn to trust me."

Erato was whispering Chainsaw's name to me, trying to tell me something about him.

"Okay, you got a deal," I said into the phone. "Hey, one more thing. Ever heard of some guy called Chainsaw?"

A long silence and then, "He's my brother."

"*What*?" I yelled.

"You heard me. Be here at six."

He hung up the phone and I turned to Erato. "We have some talking to do," I said, glaring at her.

"Yeah," she agreed, casually tossing back her hair. "You might say that."

47

Cooper's Story

I hung up the phone and looked sternly at Erato. "You've been holding something back," I said. "I thought we were in this together."

"I didn't know if we'd have to use Cooper," she explained, defensively. "I didn't want to play all of my aces at once. Besides, Dad told me to hold my cards close to my chest. He wanted to see if you could figure it out yourself."

"What else are you keeping from me?" I asked, searching for secrets in her eyes.

She threw up her hands. "That's it," she said. "I'm all out."

"You sure?" I frowned, watching sea gulls dive for fish.

"Promise." She took her hand and started to make a gesture. "Cross my heart and hope to—"

"That's fine," I said, grabbing her hand before she crossed herself. "But what if I hadn't figured out that we needed Cooper?"

"But you did," she said, holding my hand. "So now we wait—until six, anyway."

"That's right," I agreed, suddenly embracing her. "We take a long walk on the breakwater and you tell me all about Chainsaw and Cooper."

"Hey, no problem," she said, pulling back and straightening her hair. "The harbor's beautiful in the afternoon. All those boats bobbing up and down, the waves crashing on the rocks . . ."

"My confidence crashing on the—"

"Cy, I'm sorry," she said, holding my head in her hands. "You don't know how badly I wanted to tell you, but Dad said it was better if I didn't. Be a sport. We can free my sister now if Cooper does *his* part."

On foot we headed for the breakwater, which was only a quarter mile from the pier, taking the sidewalk to the harbor. The breakwater curved around to protect the docked boats.

The walkway was wedged behind a waist-high concrete wall that separated us from the crashing waves below. The tide was going out, but every once in a while a big wave would hit the rocks and drive up and over the wall, sending a sheet of water skyward without much warning. Between dodging these last powerful waves, I organized my line of questioning.

"How does Chainsaw fit into all of this?" I asked, my arm around her waist. "Now that I've found out he's Cooper's brother, I want the truth . . . all of it."

She took a deep breath and began, telling me they were both born in that run-down shack on the other side of town. Their parents had met in a biker bar and were always drunk. Their mother died in a motorcycle accident on the way to pick up Cooper from the library. The old man blamed young Cooper, saying if it wasn't for his son's stupid studying their mother never would have got on the bike after four beers.

After that things got worse at home. Old man Cooper began beating the boys. For years they both endured the beatings in silence. Until one day Cooper finally had enough and left home at sixteen. He never went back.

He moved to Texas and worked his way through college, finally securing a degree and a job in computer science. He was very good and did very well, but was laid off during a recessionary cutback. He couldn't find another job that he liked, and was out of work for a year.

The systems manager position came up at Sigma and he took it. Needless to say, he didn't tell his father and brother he was back in town. But eventually, they both found out.

One night the old man showed up drunk on Cooper's doorstep, cursing and yelling at his son for deserting him and Chainsaw. He got out of control and began to beat Cooper, bringing him coughing to his knees.

Finally, Cooper realized he wasn't young and small any more, and he got up and fought back, striking his dad a strong blow to the face. He had been saving up that fist for so long that it was powered by years of anger. The blow struck the old man so hard that it sent him sailing backward down the steps.

He died of a fractured skull when his head hit the pavement below. No charges were filed. Five neighbors testified it was self-defense, but Chainsaw never forgave him. Much as Chainsaw had hated the beatings, he still loved his dad.

Chainsaw got pretty far down on his luck after that, living not much better than a sewer rat. Then one night in a daze of drug highs, he met a man who promised him heaven on earth. Wealth, drugs, booze, and women were all his for the asking. All he needed to do was hand over a single compact disc. Nothing more. It was too good to pass up.

Chainsaw approached his brother, saying he was off drugs and it was time to talk. Cooper wouldn't talk to him at first, but Chainsaw persisted. Cooper finally agreed to meet him in the lobby of Sigma—tonight. What he didn't know was that Chainsaw only wanted to get into Janet's office and steal the CD.

Erato stepped back as a late wave crashed over the walkway, spraying us a little with saltwater.

"Now," she sighed, "comes the strange part."

"The strange part?"

"The man," she went on, ignoring me, "was no ordinary industrial spy, but an agent of Luc himself. Chainsaw doesn't know he's in danger of losing his soul. But once we set Euterpe free, Luc will lose interest immediately, and drop Chainsaw like last year's calendar."

"This is even wilder than I thought. He's about to turn your sister over to the devil."

"Don't worry," she said, pulling on my collar. "We've got an appointment with Cooper before Chainsaw does. First come, first served, as they say down here."

"I hope you're right." I looked at my watch. "But we'll find out soon enough—in about an hour and a half."

A policeman came walking down the breakwater toward us. He was checking us out pretty closely, so I decided something had to be done to throw him off. When he got a few feet away I took the camera from around my neck.

"Say," I asked, looking straight at him. "Could you take a picture of us? We want to remember this beautiful city."

"Sure," he said, surprised. "Stand over there by the seawall."

We gathered by the wall and put our arms around each other. Just as he snapped the shot a wave came over the top and drenched us. We all had a good laugh and I thanked him, then made it to a phone and called a cab. It was time to go. On the way over to Sigma I asked Erato to tell me the extent of Janet's and Juanita's involvement. Were they innocent, or what? Was Euterpe's capture an accident? The result of some experiment gone awry?

"I would," she said with a blank expression. "If I knew. There are some things Dad won't tell even me. This is one of them."

"Did your Dad tell you how this whole thing was going to turn out?"

"Nope, didn't want to spoil it," she grinned. "No one on earth's allowed to know the future. It would make for an unfair advantage. Sort of like insider trading, or something like that." She looked at me. "Except for certain psychics."

"Well," I said, watching for plain white sedans out the window. "Right now, we're about to do a little insider trading. I just hope our insider is willing to swap the disc for our story."

I looked at her stomach, still flat as ever. "Are you absolutely sure about this ... this family we're making?"

"That is one of the few things in the future I am sure of just now."

The cab pulled up to the front of Sigma. After it left we walked over and sat on the bus bench as ordered. I could see the cabbie looking in the rearview mirror and shaking his head. I can only imagine what he thought after overhearing our conversation, not to mention seeing us take a cab to the bus stop.

48

Playing the Disc

At precisely six o'clock Friday night Cooper walked out to the bus bench. A whole contingent of FBI or police could be waiting to pounce on us, but Cooper didn't have that kind of look in his eye. He looked like he had been caught with his hand in someone's floppy disk file, and as Erato predicted relieved about it.

We told him everything that we knew about him and he said all of Erato's information was accurate, but he wasn't quite ready to hand over the compact disc on our word alone. We would have to prove the contents of the CD were "out of this world" as claimed.

Cooper went inside and got the guard to check on something in one of the outlying buildings, then sneaked us in through the lobby. He led us to Juanita's lab, where we could easily access the equipment to perform our simple test run.

"You have to admit," Cooper said, opening the door to the lab, "your story is not believable by itself. But if what you say is true, proof should be easy. Just play the CD."

"It might not be quite *that* easy," I said, rolling my eyes. "But let's hope it is. We don't need any more trouble."

Much to our good fortune Juanita had left the setup as before, when we had tried playing a message from VHS tape, complete with an oscilloscope, meters, and computer hookups. I remembered a few things she had done and modified the system to feed from the CD to an amplifier and speaker, then deposit the digital signals on a blank tape. I wanted a backup just in case we couldn't free Euterpe. We could save it for later.

Erato quickly checked the setup and made a few adjustments. I trusted her, knowing she had an excellent memory.

"Now," I said at last, "all we need's a CD."

Cooper produced the CD from out of his suit coat pocket and showed us the label. Handwritten in Janet's pen were the words: "Sounds of Silence—blank disc."

"Forget that blank disc stuff," I said with a wave. "It's just a cover."

Cooper nodded and put the CD in the player, then pushed the play button.

"Well, here goes," Erato said with a sigh.

A long tense near-silence followed. The air was filled only by the powerful electric hum of the amplifier. After about five minutes Cooper said, "I don't think there's anything on it. This is a blank. Maybe we should just—"

"Wait," I said impatiently. "Let it play. This could just be long leader."

After fifteen more long, empty minutes Cooper said, "Well, are you satisfied?"

I looked at Erato and then at my oscilloscope and meters. No signal, no needles jumping. I was brokenhearted.

"Darn it!" I shouted, pacing the floor. "I know she's on that disc. Let's see if anything's on the other side."

Cooper went over and started to open the CD player. Suddenly, the needles jumped on my meters and a faint signal flashed quickly on the scope.

"Hold it!" Erato yelled. "We've got something here."

Cooper stepped back and said with disbelief. "Well, I don't hear—"

"Shhhh!" I shouted, stopping near an overhead speaker. "I hear something. Listen."

Somewhere hidden deep inside the sound of power vibrating through the amp and out of the speaker just above me, a faint, distant voice was talking. Whispering really, but not distinctly enough to be understood.

"That's her!" Erato shouted, standing next to me. "I recognize the pitch of her voice."

We let it play for five minutes, and then the voice stopped. We played it again, trying to make out words. A few syllables were semidistinct, but we had to strain pretty hard to hear them. We tried cranking up the power a couple of times, but the amp drowned out the words like storm waves crushing the voice of someone lost at sea.

Then we went the other way, diminishing the power, but when we turned down the amp, the voice faded away to nothing.

"I'm afraid this is the best we can do," I said, disappointed. "We'll have to make the most of it."

Erato began to scribble down some of the sounds that seemed to make words.

Why. . . . . . called. . . . here . . . is. . . . not. . . . sake . . . poetry. . . . must leave now. . . . No . . . breaking up shipwrecked . . . banks . . . terrible ocean . . . Save . . .

We filled in the blanks as best we could.

Why have you called me here? This is not for the sake of poetry. I must leave now. No! I'm breaking up! This is the shipwrecked daughter of Zeus. Calling from inside the banks. Save me from the terrible ocean. Save me from.

"This last part," I said, staring at the paper in Erato's hand. "is from the first message left on my screen. But then it ends abruptly. That means Euterpe *did* write the first verse, the one that illuminated my screen. Someone else wrote the other verses, and left them later for me to find. Possibly to get us to come here." I looked at Cooper. "Is this a trap," I asked seriously, "to capture Erato as well?"

"No," he said emphatically, his eyes getting big behind his glasses. "I swear it. I've told no one of this."

"All right, I'll accept that," I said, patting him on the shoulder, and seeing the surprise on his face.

The flip side was blank. "Either she's been transferred to someplace else," I said finally. "Or she's . . ."

"Cyrus," Erato said, handing me the CD. "Touch this. I want you to hold the disc in your hands. See if you can feel anything. Anything at all. See if she's still on the compact disc."

I took it in both hands and held it for a long time, closing my eyes and pressing it to my heart. After a while I began to perspire and grow faint. Erato grabbed my shoulder. With a couple of drops of water leaking out of the corners of my eyes, I opened them and looked up.

"She's gone," I said. "She's not on the disc anymore. Thanks, Coop," I added, wiping my face with my hand. "You did all you could. You can do whatever you want with the disc. We don't need it now."

"I . . . I believe you," Cooper said, hanging his head. "I believe you're sincere. Under the circumstances, I'm going to put the CD back in Janet's office where I found it."

"Well," Erato said dejectedly, turning to Cooper, "thanks for everything. At least we know she's not on the CD."

"What will you do now?" Cooper wanted to know.

"Keep looking," Erato said, glancing at me. "She's bound to turn up somewhere."

"Maybe I could get Janet to help you look for her," Cooper said in all innocence.

"No . . . no, that's all right," I said, my hand on his shoulder. "We'll manage somehow. Tell Janet she can have the disc *and* the job. I've caused enough trouble around here for one summer."

Nobody said anything. Erato and Cooper went for the door while I shut down the equipment. Just before walking out I popped the microcassette from the player and tossed it in my pocket.

"I'd like to keep this," I said to Cooper. "To remember her by."

"Of course," he said. "I don't see what harm it can do now. . . . We'd better sneak you out of here, though. You're still off-limits by being on company property."

We said good-bye. Cooper opened an alarmed back door, which brought the guard running. By the time she got there, we were out of the front lobby and on our way to the bus stop. Erato looked in my pocket before we got to the street. "Were you able to erase the CD?" she asked hopefully.

I shook my head. "Nope," I said. "I'm afraid now there are a master *and* a backup. At least I *hope* there are only the two."

She reached in and took it out of my pocket. "Wow, this feels warm," she said, holding it in both hands. "Very warm . . . almost tingling."

I winked. "You might say it has a certain feel to it. Lyrics, after all, give music some of the feeling."

"And muses," she said, smiling, "give lyrics *their* feeling. You figured out yet how we're going to free her?"

"Nope," I answered, looking down the block for the bus. "But I'm working on it. Can you get me files on Dr. Vaya and Janet?"

"I'll try," she said. "I might still have a back door into the big database in the sky. My mother insisted Dad leave a connection open so she would be able to contact me in case of emergency. I'll try it tonight."

"Sure has to beat the lightning bolt method," I observed. "But you know what? That lightning bolt did more than I thought. It sort of energized me somehow." I rubbed my chest. "I feel like I have some kind of power in here somewhere. If I can tap into it, maybe we can free your sister."

She put the tape in her purse for safekeeping and placed her hands on my chest. "No fooling," she agreed, her eyes getting big. "I think you've got enough electrical energy in you to power a radio station. You harness that, and we'll bust her out for sure. Got any ideas?"

"Nope. But I sure miss Vinnie. Let's stop by the vet's and get him."

"All right. But on one condition."

"What's that?" I asked, cautiously.

"We stop by the airport."

"Why, you flying somewhere?"

"No," she said, rubbing my chest. "I want to rent a car."

"Yeah, good idea," I agreed. "This cab business can get expensive. But as long as we're at the stop, let's take the bus."

"I was thinking about Vinnie," she informed me. "If we rent a car, we won't have to fight with cabbies anymore."

The bus came and we got on. Just as it pulled away, two black-and-white police units turned into the parking lot, lights flashing and sirens blasting.

"Hope we get to the airport before they stop the bus," Erato whispered as we sat down.

"We will," I said, getting up and stepping toward the exit. Erato followed quickly behind as I explained to the driver we had changed our minds—and keep the change. We darted off the bus and ran to the field behind Sigma, ducking down just as the cop cars whizzed by and stopped the bus. We walked the long way through Island View and the university until we got to the airport.

Unfortunately, there were some black-and-white units out front, so we ducked out of sight and sneaked on down the road, trying to figure out how to get some wheels. When we got to the corner of Ocean Avenue and Airport Drive, I looked up and smiled.

A six-foot plastic hand sat squarely on the roof of the corner building, palm side out, outlined in deep red neon. A brand-new white Cadillac convertible was parked behind, alongside a chopped Harley. It was time to ask a favor.

Once inside, Madame Perushka said that she had been waiting for us, and what took us so long? After hearing our story, Madame P. insisted we take the Caddy for as long as we needed it. She would be fine with the Harley. Besides, we'd need the car to pick up Vinnie. We piled in and were off.

49

The Arrest

Erato closed her eyes to rest and we headed for the vet's. Vinnie was raring to go. He jumped all over us, nearly licking both Erato and me to death. I paid the bill and asked for a bandage, even though Vinnie didn't need one. The vet's helper gave me a look, but I didn't explain. Then we were on our way, but not before the Doc Sutapu came flying out to the car, ranting and raving about how Vinnie's injury had been fixed, and didn't look like it had ever been stitched. We didn't have time to discuss it. I just turned to Erato on the way out and said, "What's the matter with this guy? You'd think he'd never seen a miracle before."

The bandage was in my hand when I climbed into the car.

Erato gave me a weird look. "I've got plans for this," I said, stuffing it in the glove box.

"Think that tape will be safe in your purse?" I asked, changing the subject. "Janet probably knows about our visit to Sigma by now. I'm sure she doesn't want a copy of the CD contents floating around loose."

"I don't think Janet's involved with how my sister got digitized," Erato said, sitting back against the red leather seat.

"What makes you think that?" I asked, starting the car. "You dream about it while you were out?"

"I wasn't catching Zs," she informed me, a little perturbed. "I was accessing the database on Janet. I found nothing on her but a very strong desire to protect the RAM chip file. That seems to be her only concern. She doesn't believe my sister has been kidnapped. She's strictly an engineer. She doesn't believe in the supernatural."

"I don't blame her," I smirked, putting it in gear. "It's nothing but trouble."

She gave me a look and said, "You don't mean that."

"Are you absolutely sure she's not involved with the digital image of your sister?" I asked with a frown, pulling away from the curb.

"I can't be one-hundred-percent certain," she shrugged. "There was noise on the line during the data transmission. I think Luc was trying to jam the signal. But I didn't receive anything that might implicate her." She petted Vinnie's head as he rested it on her shoulder from the backseat. "I know this much: she's not Iberlin."

"If you're right," I answered, "that only leaves Dr. Vaya. She *would* have the brains, ability, and equipment to digitize Euterpe. But what's her motive? Can you access her file?"

"Not yet. I used up a lot of energy during the last transmission trying to override the noise. I won't be able to get any more information until I recharge. That means a good night's sleep. I'm not a machine, you know."

I looked at her profile. "No, that's for sure. . . . Look, I hate to ask a dumb question, but I'm only human, okay?"

"Humans are always playing dumb. Ask away."

"How does info get into someone's file?"

I pulled onto Ocean Avenue and headed for the Turnpike Lodge. Erato informed me that at one time everyone had their own personal caretaker, and note taker. Humans called them guardian angels. But there got to be too many people on earth because of the population explosion, and not enough spirits in heaven. The baby boom didn't help any. Eventually, heaven began to get programmers, and they designed some software that automatically records actions performed by individuals— and logs them into each person's database. The latest software package released, Version 5.2, had worked out most of the bugs, like attributing not just actions, but intentions.

Unfortunately, feelings had yet to be programmed into the software, she told me. How a person feels about her actions is very important to the total picture. Ironically, only the human mind has a memory system that can attach the correct feelings to actions and subsequent memories.

"Unbelievable," I remarked, shaking my head in disbelief, and stopping at a red light. "Programming in heaven. Some guys get all the good jobs."

"I have a secret to tell you," she whispered, "about when you leave this world."

"What is it?" I frowned, expecting the worst.

"I can't say it outright. But think of this: what kind of person has strong feelings, and can articulate them?"

"A poet, of course."

"And what kind of person could write a program that incorporates the subtlety of feelings into the actions associated with them?"

"A programmer," I said, my eyes growing wide.

"Now, here's the equation," she stated. "Suppose I want to be with you for a long time, say forever, plus or minus a few hundred years or so."

"Thanks," I said, rolling my eyes.

"And I want you to have a good job," Erato continued, undaunted, "in this world *and* the next. So you develop your natural abilities as a poet and you're a shoo-in for the feelings program job."

"Is that a guarantee?" I asked. The light turned green and I pulled away.

"You know better than that," she scolded. "But think how it will look on your résumé."

"Oh, I get it," I said, raising my voice. "He who dies with the best résumé wins. Hey, I thought the eighties were over."

"Stop being so critical," she complained. "You want the job or not?"

I leaned over and kissed her on the cheek, but not before Vinnie licked my face. "You're darn right I do," I beamed. "It's nice to have something to look forward to besides playing a harp on some cloud. Thinking about that bores the heck out of me."

After a long silence she asked, "Why do you suppose the CD experiment didn't work?"

"If I knew that I'd be back in the lab," I said as we crossed over the freeway. "But there's got to be something missing somewhere. I just haven't figured it out yet. She *is* on the disc, and the tape. We just have to get her freed up . . . Hey," I said, slowing down as I passed a couple of police cars at a doughnut shop. "Hand me the tape. We've got to be more careful from now on."

"What are you going to—"

"Just hand me the tape," I demanded. "Those guys are checking us out."

"Especially since you just ran that stop sign," she informed me.

"Oh, great!" I yelled, looking at the back of the stop sign in the rearview mirror. "Now you'd really better hand me the tape."

As she reached into her purse, both of the black-and-whites were filling up quickly with officers. One of the units said K-9 on the side. This was going to be close. I pulled over and stopped, grabbed the bandage from the glove box, wrapped it around Vinnie's head, and stuffed the tape between the layers of the bandage.

"There," I said, sitting up. "At least now Euterpe has half a chance."

Sure enough, they came with tires screeching and sirens blaring. I didn't try to outrun them, not in a borrowed Cadillac. I looked at Erato. We both had the same thought. It was time to turn ourselves in. I shut off the engine.

"Vinnie," I instructed him, "I know you understand me. Meet us at home. I don't want you to stay and fight. Home, Vinnie. Go home. When I give the word. Got it?"

"You really think that's going to work?" Erato said, wrinkling her forehead.

"How do I know?" I shrugged. "But it's worth a shot."

At first, I thought we'd be lucky and get off with just a ticket, but when they forced me to hand over my driver's license, it was all over. They had found their fugitive. Cops quickly surrounded us, pointing loaded pistols our way.

The K-9 unit brought out a good-sized German shepherd. They ordered us out of the car with hands up. We did so about as slowly as possible, so we wouldn't look like we were going to pull anything. Vinnie got out and growled at the shepherd.

"You'd better control your dog!" one of the officers yelled. "Or I'll have to put him down!"

"Vinnie!" I shouted. "Home! Home, boy!"

The officer restraining the German shepherd unleashed his dog, and he darted toward Vinnie. I'll never know whether Vinnie was scared or following orders, but he took off like a shot in the direction of home. He made a beeline for the freeway, the shepherd right on his tail.

The officers never fired a round. All of us were watching the dogs dashing across the field and down the hill to the freeway. There was a six-foot fence in between, but this time with no barbed wire. Vinnie was up and over it in a hurry. The shepherd was halfway over when his trainer blew a dog whistle. He jumped down and trotted back.

The cops didn't think my trick was particularly funny, but I explained that we were just trying to avoid damage to a police dog, telling them Vinnie had lost an ear fighting a pit bull. That's why the bandage—but the bull had lost his life.

Out on the freeway the high-pitched squeal of tires braking pierced the air. Then, two more sets of screeching tires.

They didn't exactly thank me for sending Vinnie home. Instead, they booked us in the county jail and impounded the car—breaking and entering, stealing secret files, running a stop sign, and all that. A thorough strip search, a traffic ticket, and twenty four hours later, we were free to go. Janet had dropped the charges. But it was six o'clock Saturday night, and we only had until midnight. The police called Madame P., and she confirmed our right to use the Caddy.

"Great," I said to Erato, climbing into the car. "What's Janet up to? Maybe she's trying to make a deal. Something like dropping the charges if we give up on Euterpe."

"I don't think so." Erato assured me, getting in the passenger's side. "I did some thinking in there. Looks to me like Dr. Vaya is our problem."

"Great! You finally accessed—"

"Who said anything about accessing," she defended. "Ever heard of deductive reasoning?"

"You can explain it to me on the way home. *Home*," I repeated, starting the car. "Hey, at least now we *can* go home. I just hope Vinnie's okay."

Erato was too tired to explain about Juanita on the way home. She dozed off instead. The arrest was too much of an ordeal, I figured. So I didn't press her for answers about deductive reasoning, or anything else for that matter.

When we got upstairs the place had been ransacked and Vinnie was still missing. The light on the answering machine was blinking. It was Janet.

50

Star Wars

Janet's message said she was at work and needed to talk to me as soon as possible. She was sorry about the arrest, but it was the only way to get hold of us. After dropping the charges, she couldn't get to the jail before we split. She was too busy assessing the damage to her lab.

Needing a little time to think, we straightened the place up first, instead of calling her back right away.

"Whoever was here was looking for the tape," I said to Erato. "And meant business. Maybe it's a good thing I stuffed it in Vinnie's bandage. Otherwise, the cops would have had it for sure. Speaking of Vinnie, we'd better take a ride on the freeway. See if there's a black mess in the middle of the road."

"Cyrus!" Erato shouted. "Don't say that."

"You did hear the tires screech," I said sarcastically. "Didn't you?"

"Sure, but I didn't hear a thud."

"Now look who's being morbid. But before we go check the freeway, I need to talk to Mrs. Okana. She must have heard someone rearranging the furniture up here. Maybe she saw something."

We went downstairs and caught her at home. She met us at the front door and said she did hear a lot of banging around overhead, but she thought maybe we were romancing or something and didn't want to disturb us. I asked her if she saw anybody come or go and she said no. But just when we turned to walk away she changed her mind.

"Wait a minute," she said, brushing silver hair from her forehead. "I did hear something. A loud muffler out front."

"Like a motorcycle, maybe?" Erato asked, hands on her hips.

"Yes." She nodded. "I couldn't place it at first, but now that you mention it, it sounded like a large motorcycle. And it was pulling away in a hurry."

"Thanks," I said, turning to leave. "You've been a big help."

We got in the Caddy and headed for the freeway. Erato turned to me and asked, "How do you suppose Chainsaw knew about the tape? Did he beat it out of his brother?"

"If my guess is correct," I replied, turning towards the on-ramp. "I don't think he knows. He's still looking for the compact disc. My place was a good place to start—unless he got to Janet first."

"Are you going to call her back?" Erato asked, concerned.

"Yes, right after we see if Vinnie's lying on the freeway somewhere."

When we got to the spot where he would have been I slowed down. Seeing two sets of fresh skid marks, one on each side of the low center wall, I pulled over and stopped.

"Well," Erato said, getting out and looking around. "I don't see him anywhere."

"No," I agreed, standing beside her. "And more important, there aren't any blood puddles. I don't see any drips anywhere either. He might still be okay."

"Where do you suppose he is?" she asked over the noise of speeding traffic.

"First, we'll stop by the animal shelter," I replied. "We'll call Janet from there." I looked at my watch. "Wait, it's seven-thirty. They're bound to be closed. I've got a better idea. Let's go by Dr. Vaya's. See if we can get the truth out of her."

We got back in the car and drove over to her house. Her mother answered the door. She was small, pale, gray-haired, and almost hysterical. Juanita was out, but that wasn't the problem. Some big biker had forced his way past her, torn the place up pretty good, and left. She was getting ready to call the police when we showed up.

She turned and motioned with her hand. "Look at this place. It's a nightmare. I kept asking what he wanted but he told me to shut up unless I wanted a free trip to the emergency ward. My husband's deaf, and was upstairs asleep. The brute scattered Juanita's CDs all over the place. . . . If you'll excuse me, I'm calling the police now."

"Come on," I said to Erato. "We're going to Sigma. Janet's message said to call her at work. We're going there before Chainsaw shows up with his favorite weapon and forces his way past the guard."

Back in the car I asked Erato if she could make an emergency access to Juanita's personal file in the sky, and she told me she was too upset to try again, and that her powers were fading too fast to try it anymore. She had tried it at the jail, and couldn't even get an open line. She was clearly frustrated.

Once we got to Sigma, I rang up Janet from the lobby.

"Cyrus," she said with relief. "Thank God you're here. Don't move. I'll be right down."

Five minutes later she was in the lobby, this time wearing a lab coat over her blue velvet pants suit and matching high heels. She started talking on the way to her office.

"Someone broke into my lab," she said angrily. "He sawed off the lock and came through the back door. He made a mess of the place just after I got cleaned up from the other night."

"Did he get into your office?" I asked, walking swiftly beside her down the hallway.

"No, the guard called the police for a backup, and when they arrived, whoever it was sped off on a motorcycle." She stopped and placed her hand firmly on my arm, then looked at us both. "Look, about the other night . . . I realized you were only after the voice track file . . . and . . ."

"Forget it," I said, dismissing her apology. "Then you don't know about Chainsaw?"

"Who?"

"Cooper's brother," Erato explained. "He's also after the CD, only for all the wrong reasons. He's dealing with the . . ." She inhaled. "Let's just say he's working for the competition, and leave it at that."

Janet jammed her hands into her lab coat pockets. "Why does he want the voice track?" she asked, puzzled. "I thought someone was after the RAM chip plans. I thought *you* were, until Cooper told me about borrowing the blank CD. He said you only wanted to get a voice freed up from the disc. Look, you know I was only protecting the RAM chip plans. I thought—"

"You don't have to explain anything," I said, motioning for us to get walking again. We continued down the hall and I added, "Your file's clean. At least you're on our side now."

I told Janet that I thought Juanita was Iberlin, and that she had created the fake Euterpe file on the mainframe hard disk only as a diversion. She knew someone would come looking for the real Euterpe and wasn't finished experimenting with her yet.

Janet just kept walking, leading us to her office. I went on with my theory, saying that Juanita had humored us by pretending to help free Erato's sister, knowing the real Euterpe was on the compact disc in Janet's office. Juanita knew because she had created *that* CD in the classified computer lab.

"She's not Iberlin," Janet answered. "We still don't know who the hacker is. But Juanita never told me Euterpe was"— she looked at the ceiling and back—"a live spirit," she said with disbelief. "I thought she was just a signal from space."

Janet explained that one of Juanita's experiments involved sending and receiving signals in deep space. She had all kinds of elaborate equipment in the classified lab. The roof would open up like a planetarium so she could process signals from deep space. She even had lasers in there for military research.

We had reached the lobby to her office. As we marched by her secretary, Janet told her we were not to be disturbed by anyone except Juanita.

Stepping through her office door, Janet went on, saying that when she called the FBI, they weren't much interested in the RAM chip plans, but the military stuff really turned them on. Juanita was part of an inner circle of scientists working on top secret Star Wars research.

Once in the office, we preferred to stand, while Janet sat on the edge of her desk and flipped off her shoes. "She asked to hide the space data on my blank disc," Janet said. "She didn't want the signal to be tampered with until she finished her experiment."

"Okay, listen," I said, gesturing. "This is very important. What kind of experiment was she conducting the night Euterpe appeared on the computer? Was it Star Wars or something else?"

"I've told you all I know," Janet shrugged. "Except that she did say it involved lasers and bar codes. I figure she was using bar codes to transfer classified data on her research to the Pentagon."

"Bar codes?" I said, astonished. "Well, I'll be a son of a . . ."

"Look," Janet said, crossing her arms and glaring at Erato. "I'm an engineer, not a Trekkie. But if your sister's on CD, then I'll need proof."

"I know it sounds wild," I said, my eyes getting big. "But Star Wars sounded wild ten years ago."

"Storing extraterrestrials with 'spirit bodies' on CD is pretty futuristic stuff," Janet said, "But if it was possible, imagine what it would be worth. I'm not saying any of this *is* possible, but— Wait." Janet looked at Erato. "How did *you* get . . . humanized?"

"Sorry," Erato apologized, a little embarrassed. "That's classified, I'm afraid. Besides, it wouldn't be the same. I wasn't in digital format. Do you still have the disc?"

Looking inside the jukebox, Janet said, "Yes, I can see the disc with the label I wrote. As for the contents, well . . ."

"Then we've only got one choice," I stated. "We've got to contact Dr. Vaya and trick her into coming to the lab. We have to get her to recreate Euterpe." I looked at my watch: Ten forty-five. "And we've only got an hour and a quarter to do it. Otherwise . . . Is there a lightning rod on this building?"

"What?"

"Never mind," I said with a wave. "We've got to figure out a message that will get her here."

"So," Erato said, standing next to Janet, "I don't suppose there's any bar code research still on the hard disk, is there?"

"Sure," she answered. "Tucked away in . . . oh, I get it. We take possession of her research, and the CD. We tell Juanita that she doesn't get them back until she frees Euterpe."

I looked at Janet. "You can page her. She's got a beeper, right?"

"Sure," Janet agreed. "As long as she's within a fifteen-mile radius."

"If she's in town," I replied. "That ought to get her to come in a hurry." I walked toward the door, Erato in tow, then stopped and said over my shoulder, "Oh, and Janet, contact Cooper and get him down here. Someone has to reinstate my computer privileges."

"You can use mine," she replied casually.

"Does this mean I get my old job back?"

"You never lost it," she said, a smile in her tone. "I never terminated you. I'm a sucker for an underdog. I've never been one, you know."

"Until now," I said, turning around and looking at her. "If Dr. Vaya shines us on, we're in deep frozen yogurt. . . . We'll have some time after you page her," I added, still looking at Janet. "Tell her the bar code research goes on the national electronic bulletin board at eleven o'clock unless she shows up."

"It *what*?" she asked, astonished.

"You want her down here, don't you?"

"Yes, but . . ."

"Yes, but *nothing*," I stated. "We need to get her attention. We're the underdogs, remember? Speaking of underdogs," I said to myself, "I hope Vinnie's okay. Look, is anyone hungry? I'm starved. There's a convenience store on the corner. Now, who wants what at the minimarket?"

"Cyrus," Erato scolded me. "how can you eat at a time like this?"

"Hunger knows no danger," I remarked. "Besides, they have a bar code reader. Maybe it'll give me some ideas." I marched toward the door.

"Hold on," Erato said. "I'll go with you."

"Why?" I asked, stopping in my tracks. "You think maybe your sister's on a soda bottle?"

"How can you joke at a time like this?"

"You have to stay here to make sure Janet gets the right wording on the pager message," I said, and nodded toward the office. Janet gave me an incredulous look from across the room. "Besides," I added. "Who's joking?"

On my way out the door I turned to Janet. "Hey, what made you change your mind about us? At what point did we start sounding less crazy and more credible?"

"Well," she admitted with a shrug. "The whole thing still sounds crazy. But when Cooper said you didn't want the chip plans, I had to ask myself why a programmer and someone who goes by the name of a Greek muse would persist in trying to hear the contents of a CD in my office? Either they're imposters, lunatics, or genuine."

Janet said she knew we weren't imposters because the FBI found nothing that could connect us to the competition or any spy network. That was when she dropped the idea of Erato's being after Star Wars research or her chip. That only left the real Euterpe file.

"So, how did you decide we weren't lunatics?" I asked, still standing in the doorway.

"I haven't decided," she laughed. "My scientific curiosity wants to let you prove your story once and for all. Then, either we say good-bye to an extraterrestrial or two, or you say hello to the nuthouse."

"Thanks," I said sarcastically, "for the vote of confidence. . . . One more thing. I want to make sure Dr. Vaya shows up. Be sure it says something in your message about trashing the classified computer lab in an hour if she doesn't show."

I turned and walked out.

51

Stolen Moments

As I watched the clerk drag my tuna sandwich and Diet Dr. Pepper bottle across the bar code reader, I tried to form an idea of what Juanita was up to in her lab.

"What happens when you don't align the bar code exactly with the reader?" I asked minimarket clerk.

The young woman pushed a strand of long, black hair from her dark brown eyes, somewhat amused by my question.

"Well," she said shyly, "on the old machine you had to drag stuff across again until the reader picked up the code. But newer ones like this wrap around the object, find the bar code, and enter the item and price. . . . At least that's what my boss said."

"And it works every time?"

"Almost. Once in a while you still have to ring something up manually, but not as often as before."

"Thanks," I said, storing the information in my brain somewhere. "You've been a big help."

I paid up and took my dinner back to Sigma. When I got to the lab, there had been a major breakthrough. Cooper had shown up, and so had Juanita. She must have already been in the plant, and I had a good idea where.

"I see, Doctor," I said, chomping on my tuna sandwich, "that you got our message. I'm sure Janet informed you of our need?"

"That's why I'm here," she said somberly. "To assure you I have no knowledge of the whereabouts of the CD. I turned it over to Janet and that's the last I've seen of it."

"Maybe," I said, taking a swig of Diet Dr. Pepper. "But whoever ransacked your house seems to think you still have a copy somewhere."

"I am aware," she said, pacing in her lab coat, "that Mr. Cooper's brother, who calls himself Chainsaw or something, is searching for Euterpe. He seems to think it's on some disc somewhere, I'm told."

"You mean this disc?" Janet said, pulling it out of her brief-case. "Look, Juanita, I've already explained that no one's after the bar code research. But whatever or whoever is on this disc wants to come off. Either that, or Cyrus has my permission to take the classified computer lab apart until we get answers. . . . You've been holding back, Doctor," she added forcefully. "Let's have the truth about the contents of this disc."

"I don't know what you're talking about," Juanita answered stiffly, leaning against her workbench. "We tried to get the so-called 'spirit' off the hard disk. Evidently, you can't just digitize an extraterrestrial like some song. We tried that"—she looked at me—"remember? Be reasonable, everyone. That's black magic. I'm a scientist, not a wizard. Besides, even if something 'living' is on that CD, *I* can't free it."

"Yes you can," I said, setting my sandwich and drink down on a corner of her bench. "We know about your experiments with bar codes and space signals. My guess is that you've found a way to digitize objects, at least those in spirit format, and all you have to do is reverse the process. I don't know how you did it, but if you don't get Euterpe back to her world in"—I looked at my watch—"one hour, we'll confiscate the bar code research, and destroy the computer lab, one circuit at a time."

"Well," she said, jamming her hands into the lab coat pockets, "if you destroy the lab, it will be a grave mistake. I see you leave me no choice but to . . ."

Just then her voice was drowned out by the intercom over-head, blasting the message: "Ms. Stewart. There's a black dog in the lobby with a bandage over his head. He refuses to leave, and I don't want to have to call the pound. Please advise."

"Vinnie!" I shouted, and ran to grab the phone on the wall. I picked it up and dialed the lobby. "Don't move!" I yelled into the receiver. "I'll be right there." I looked around. "Don't anyone leave."

When I got to the lobby Vinnie jumped up and started licking me wildly. After a few moments I realized the guard had a frozen look on her face, and it wasn't from a heart attack. She motioned with her eyes at a spot below the counter, but by the time I got the idea, it was too late. Chainsaw stood up, sticking a gun in the guard's back.

"Good evenin', Cyrus," he sneered. "Nice night for a stroll to the lab. First, though, our friend here wants a guided tour of the janitor's closet."

He pushed his pistol farther into the guard's back and his captive obeyed, producing the keys that Chainsaw used to lock her in the closet around the corner. Then Chainsaw turned the gun on me.

"I ain't real happy these days," he frowned, waving the gun. "Stealin' my dog for the second time got me riled. But I'll tell you what. Let's take a little walk and you show me this so called E-terpe disc. Then I just might trade you for the mutt. Then again, I just might have to shoot the both of you. March, and no funny stuff. Bloodstains are tough to get out of the carpet."

I put my hands up and walked toward the lab, knowing he would probably pull the trigger if I led him to the wrong place.

"Tell me," I said, walking down the hall and looking at Vinnie. "Did he show up at your place?"

"Are you kiddin'?" he laughed. "This mutt's an idiot, even for a Lab. I found him layin' on your front porch. Figured I'd need him for bait. Figured right, I guess. Now, where's this la-bor-a-tory."

We turned the corner and walked into the lab, taking everyone by surprise.

"Well, well," Chainsaw smiled. "Looks like I hit the California Lottery..." He glanced at Cooper. "And if it ain't Mr. Success, the father killer. Well, nothin' can bring Dad back, but I reckon what's on that little disc should just about even us up on the finance scale."

"Enough said," I blurted. "Janet, give him the disc. That's what he came for."

"But—"

"Forget it," I interrupted. "If he shoots us, Euterpe will never be free. Our only chance is to hand over the disc."

"Now you're talkin' smart." Chainsaw said, motioning for me to stand over by the others. Then he stood between our little group and the door to keep everyone in his line of sight.

When Janet didn't budge, Erato said, "Cyrus is right. If we're dead, my sister's dead. Turn over the disc."

Cooper stepped forward. "Go ahead, little brother. Kill us all. But you'll have to shoot me first. If you've got the guts. At least I had the guts to get away from Dad. I begged you to come, but you chickened out. So go ahead. Shoot your own flesh and blood, Mr. Save-the-family."

The look on Chainsaw's face softened. "You think I stayed 'cause I liked the beatings? Somebody had to stay and take care of Dad. He sure couldn't take care of himself. . . . He never forgave himself for letting you run out. But I guess you repaid him."

"I didn't mean to kill him," Cooper said at last. "It was an accident."

Chainsaw's face hardened. He cocked the pistol and pointed it at Cooper's face. "Yeah, and so's this."

Erato grabbed the disc out of Janet's hand and stuck it in front of Chainsaw's face. "Here," she said. "There doesn't need to be any killing. Now, take this and get out. Stealing is one thing, but you don't want murder on your hands—especially your brother's."

Chainsaw hesitated and looked around, chewing on her words. Then he took the disc, stuffed it in his motorcycle jacket, and stepped backward toward the door, slowly waving his pistol as he went. He backed through and closed the door. Then we heard him run down the hall.

Juanita looked at me and then at Erato. "I hope you know what you're doing," she said dejectedly. "That was probably the last chance to—"

"Oh, I don't know," I said smugly. "Come here, Vinnie."

When he came over I patted his head. "The last time we ran the experiment with Cooper we made a tape backup," I announced, "just in case."

"Very clever," Juanita admitted. "I just hope you've got the right signals there. For your sake."

"We'll find out," I said, unwrapping Vinnie's bandage. "As soon as we play this . . ." I had the bandage off, but no tape. I looked through the bandage again. Nothing there.

"Shoot!" I shouted. "It's not here. It must have fallen out somewhere. It could be anywhere. . . . Quick," I yelled, jumping to my feet, "we've got a thief to catch."

I ran and slammed full-shoulder against the door. It gave a mighty crack and popped open. It wasn't locked. I ran down the hall, rubbing my shoulder. Everyone else was right behind me. When we got to the lobby, Chainsaw was just getting on his Harley.

"To the car!" I yelled. "He's getting away."

As we ran to the Cadillac and piled in, I said, "With that noisy muffler and single taillight, we should be able to track him pretty easily."

"Don't forget," Erato said, sitting next to me with Vinnie on her lap, "he's got a gun and he's liable to use it."

"Yeah, well, your dad's got bigger firearms and he *will* use them in"—I looked at my watch—"in exactly 45 minutes."

Juanita and Janet were not yet in the car, so I turned to them. "You two stay here and set up the experiment. We'll be right back with the disc," I shrugged, "or we'll be dead."

Juanita started to say something when I yelled, "Set it up in three dimensions! Just like you created it on the MUSE machine."

"Three dimensions?" Erato and Cooper said together.

"That's right," I answered, spinning the tires and drawing a bead on the single taillight ahead. "That disc is not a CD, and it's not a video disc. Euterpe isn't just a voice, or even a two-dimensional image. She had a third dimension. She's a holograph."

"This time," Erato said, "*you've* got some explaining to do."

"Yeah," I said, putting the throttle to the floor. "You might say that."

52

The Chase

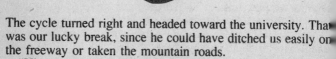

The cycle turned right and headed toward the university. That was our lucky break, since he could have ditched us easily on the freeway or taken the mountain roads.

"His contact must be at the beach," I said, pressing down harder on the gas pedal. "We'll never catch him. I just hope we can keep his taillight in sight until he pulls over."

"Just drive," Erato ordered, Vinnie still on her lap. "And what's this about a holograph?"

I explained that the new bar code readers wrap around objects. They project a holographic image that picks up the encoded message inscribed on the article. That was when it hit me that Juanita wasn't really working on bar codes. It was her way of disguising the fact that she was working on the next generation of holographs—three-dimensional moving images that could be digitized on a compact disc and reproduced in the round, so to speak.

"But they have that now at Disneyland," Cooper argued from the back seat.

"True," I conceded. "But I'm not talking about 3-D glasses, or seeing a projected image in the dark using mirrors. I'm talking about broad daylight, out in the open, in any setting . . . Dr. Vaya must have been working late in the lab the night I got the first message, testing her invention, when Euterpe accidentally showed up."

The cycle turned into the back road of the university. Keeping the taillight in view, I followed as closely as possible, but he seemed to be getting farther away.

I went on with my theory, saying that somehow Euterpe's vibrations must have been interfered with so that she got stored on CD, and had been there as a hologram ever since.

The cycle made a sharp left a hundred yards ahead. I took the Caddy wide, but it was moving too fast and bounced off the curb. Vinnie got knocked into the backseat, but Cooper held onto him while I steadied the car, going on with my story.

Evidently, someone made a fake file and placed it on the Top Secret disk, knowing I wasn't cleared for that level of security and couldn't access it. But why? And if Iberlin wasn't Juanita or Janet, then who was it?

I looked at Erato. She shrugged, Cooper did the same.

Meanwhile, I surmised, Juanita hadn't got her holograph machine working perfectly. So she stored the CD in the jukebox until she could figure out how to generate a three-dimensional moving image.

"That way!" Erato pointed, as the cycle went down the hill toward the beach. "What makes you think Dr. Vaya can free my sister now?"

"I have a secret weapon," I said coolly.

"What is it?" Cooper asked, still holding Vinnie and getting licked pretty good.

"If I tell you," I announced, "then it's not a secret and

besides, talking about it might jinx the experiment."

"Okay," Erato replied, hitting my arm. "Save your secret weapon. But first, you'd better catch Chainsaw, or it's all over."

"Look!" I said, pointing up ahead. "He's bypassing the turnoff. Darn, he's going on the freeway. And just when we were gaining on him."

Chainsaw could have outrun us easily on the freeway with that big Harley, but he made a mental error. In order to discourage us from following, he pulled out his gun and fired at us. Two shots hit the grill, and four missed badly. He must have been raised on old westerns, because he actually threw the empty gun at the car. It bounced harmlessly off the bumper, but he went abruptly off the road.

His bike found some gravel on the shoulder and began to swerve out of control. When he hit some ice plant, it grabbed hold of the wheels; he slowed down in a hurry. The bike hit a clump of pampas grass and he went flying over the top, landing on his back and rolling over several times before coming to a stop. The Harley just stuck in the ice plant, lying on its side.

We slowed to a stop and pulled over. Vinnie was out of the car first and made a dash for Chainsaw, grabbing the sleeve of his leather jacket and growling ferociously.

Chainsaw got up, but he couldn't shake Vinnie off his sleeve. He reached in with his free hand and pulled the CD out of his jacket pocket. Holding it in his fingers, he looked down the freeway. A police car and motorcycle suddenly approached from the other direction, so Chainsaw threw it down the freeway as far as he could into the oncoming headlights.

"Fetch, boy!" he yelled, laughing as Vinnie let go of his sleeve and darted after the flying disc, acting purely on instinct.

We stood in shocked silence as the disc rose high, cutting through the air like a micro-Frisbee. As it reached its highest point, it stopped for a second, spinning against a sudden offshore breeze that came sweeping off the mountains. Usually the wind blew constantly onshore, but once in a while, especially in the summer, the hot Santa Ana winds blew out to sea.

The disc sparkled in the moonlight of that clear, starry night, sending light beams flying off its smooth surface in all directions, like fireworks bursting on the Fourth. Then it slowly turned until its highest edge was into the wind and stopped spinning in place, like some alien spaceship awaiting its orders. Then, suddenly, it began to dive for the Earth. It picked up speed and spun faster as it raced toward the concrete fift feet below, a hundred yards from the oncoming headlights.

The flight of the disc had given Vinnie enough time to catch up, and when he saw it zooming over his head in the other direction, he bolted after it. The CD, Vinnie, and the cops all raced down the freeway toward the beach, getting closer together every second.

As the disc accelerated for the concrete, the cops finally saw Vinnie and slammed on their brakes. The cycle slid off the side of the road and the cruiser slid into the bare center divider, kicking up dust as it screeched to a stop.

The fate of the world spun on that disc, just as surely as the earth spins on its axis. The only thing that stood between the disc and the concrete was a one-eared black dog and the wind. Vinnie was still five yards behind by the time the disc was ten feet from oblivion, racing toward the earth at an incredible speed.

I nearly closed my eyes when the disc got five feet from the pavement, not wanting to see it crash. But just before it dived into the concrete, it caught a slight, onshore wind, an almost imperceptible zephyr blowing a cool gentle protest in the face of the hot mountain wind. Unbelievably, it was enough to turn the edge of the disc up so that it just cleared the pavement. It sailed only inches above the ground, Vinnie in hot pursuit. Slowly, it began a gradual, steady rise, one foot at a time.

Vinnie saw his opening and made his move. From six feet away he jumped. Suddenly he was five feet off the ground and opening his mouth, not twenty feet from where we stood.

He stretched out full-length and his mouth came down gently on the disc. He seemed to glide along forever, graceful and free, but at last he landed, disc in mouth, all fours on the dirt in the center divider. He pranced forth like it had been just another day at the beach, and came right up to me. He wouldn't give it up, so I decided we'd have to take him back with the disc in his mouth.

Nobody was paying any attention to Chainsaw, and before anyone realized what was going on, he had the Harley upright and was speeding off. The motorcycle cop took up the chase, but Chainsaw was pulling away.

I looked at my watch. "We've got twenty minutes to get to the lab and play the disc," I said.

"Providing," Cooper added, "there aren't any teeth marks in it."

"Labs," I defended, "have soft mouths. It may be wet, but it's not damaged."

I explained to the officer that we needed to get back to

the lab immediately or the disc would begin releasing deadly toxins into the atmosphere. He just glared at me. He looked at Cooper in his three-piece suit and asked, "Is this the truth?"

Cooper straightened his lapels. "Absolutely," he said. "We've got less than twenty minutes. Then the biggest toxic mess since the War in the Gulf begins. What's on the disc is so powerful that once released it begins killing all plant and animal life in a hundred-mile radius. It's carried on the wind and nothing can stop it."

"But don't worry," Erato assured the cop. "It's inert in its natural state. It's only activated by moisture."

The officer took a hard look at the wet disc in Vinnie's mouth. "In the patrol car, quick," he ordered. "We've got a deadline to meet!"

I looked at Cooper, Vinnie, and Erato. I was proud of all of them. But we were running out of time fast. There was no opportunity for a big speech. So I petted Vinnie, winked at Erato, and said to Cooper as we ran to the patrol car, "Coop, you're a heck of a . . ." I grabbed his lapel. "Heck of a friend."

As we pulled away, the officer said, "Nice speeches, all of you. But we had orders to get you back to the plant by a quarter to twelve."

"That's okay," I said to Cooper, slapping him on the knee. "It's the thought that counts."

I didn't say anything more to Cooper. I was too darn proud of him to say a word. I just petted Vinnie and patted my Hawaiian shirt pocket, the one that contained my secret weapon. But from that day forward, I never again made fun of anyone in a three-piece suit.

53

Euterpe Unlimited

Once back at the plant Juanita quickly verified my assumption about her work, and made some corrections. On the way to the classified computer lab, she filled in the missing pieces.

Before the whole incident started, Janet had recorded

videotape of a filmed stage play—the life of Irving Berlin. Juanita made a copy on a videodisc CD, and was using it to generate a 3-D image using the MUSE machine. The name is an acronym for Micro Universal Signal Encoder, or in layman's terms, a holograph machine. We turned a corner and she went on.

The MUSE had been aimed at an open space center stage. As the image of Irving Berlin came on the monitors in the adjacent sound room, Euterpe suddenly appeared on stage, made visible by MUSE laser when she accidentally walked in front of it. It disrupted her frequencies so much that she began to break up into digital pulses. The result was that Euterpe got stored on CD as a hologram, erasing the image of Irving Berlin in the process.

We were at the door to the classified computer lab. Juanita explained that her efforts to lead us astray were meant to protect her research from hackers, and buy time, so she could study the image of Euterpe. She explained that after digitizing the muse, she left to get something from her private lab. When she returned, someone had played the Irving Berlin tape, and the terminal showed a file created—Euterpe, along with a screen message about the shipwrecked daughter of Zeus.

"I know it was wrong," she apologized. "But it was my only chance to experiment with a live image. I'm sorry to say that . . . that I haven't perfected it." She glanced down at Vinnie, the CD still in his mouth.

"What's wrong?" Janet asked, standing behind us.

Juanita opened the door to the classified computer lab, and we went inside. She explained that she had tried to free Euterpe a couple of times, and actually had projected a 3-D image in the lab, but couldn't get it to "come alive"—to break free. It was still stuck on the disc.

"I was going to come to you with all of this," she confessed. "But the scientist in me took over and wouldn't let me do it. Not until I had a solution."

She flipped on the overhead light and continued. "I realize this doesn't excuse my actions, but I hope it explains them. I . . ."

"Doctor," I interrupted, looking at my watch, "there's not much time. We only have until midnight—nine minutes—and then Euterpe's dad pulls the plug on all of this."

Juanita got a wide-eyed look on her face. She stared at Erato, and almost turning pale said, "You . . . you're not an extraterrestrial at all, are you? You really are . . ."

"Yes," Erato confirmed. "And so is my sister. But we've no time for theological discussion. Can you get the machine working by midnight?"

Juanita looked at me. "I . . . I'm having problems with the software."

"*What*?" I shouted, throwing up my hands. "Why didn't you call me in? I can't believe this. You have a software glitch and you tell me *now*? What in the—"

"Cyrus!" Erato yelled, grabbing my arm. "Be quiet and listen. What's the problem, Doctor?"

Juanita began walking over toward a stack of computer printouts. We followed in tow. "Something in the subroutine-processing command," she said, rubbing her forehead. "The MUSE will store and replicate images, but not at full power. If Euterpe's set free, we'll need much more power than I can generate now. I've got a bigger generator on order, but it's three weeks away."

"Set it up," I demanded, staring at the three-foot high stack of printouts. "I'll look at the software. Now, show me the problem."

She mumbled a few words to Janet, who began moving things quickly around the lab. Then Juanita pulled one of the printout stacks to the top and said, "It's localized to the power circuit. I'm afraid with my current capabilities, it's the best I can do without damaging the equipment—unless you can think of a way around the main power circuit."

"Doctor," I said, sifting through the printouts, "you realize that troubleshooting these things can take days, even weeks."

"Just look at it," Erato ordered over my shoulder. "It's worth a shot."

I raced through the code, but couldn't see a thing that could be improved. The job was just too big, and it was five minutes to twelve. Then, miraculously, a single line of code stared up at me. It didn't look right.

"What's this?" I asked.

"That's where I fixed the RAM transfer problem," Juanita answered over my shoulder. "I'm using Janet's new chip. I needed a lot of memory in a small space."

"Doctor, this may fix the transfer," I said, almost mad, "but it's costing you power." I pointed at the printout. "Look at this. By clearing the way for data transfer, you've limited the power circuit commands."

"I had to do that until my new generator gets here," she

defended. "I'm afraid it's the best we can do, under the circumstances."

Erato and Janet were back. The setup was complete. "Let's
bypass it," I recommended. "Route to full power."

"That could blow the generator," Juanita said nervously.

"It's our only chance to get the power we need," I reminded
her.

She stood up from leaning over my shoulder and turned
around. Looking at Erato she said, "This could blow the whole
lab sky-high. But Cyrus is right. It's our only chance now."

"Do it," Erato ordered. Janet and I nodded in agreement.
Ten seconds later I was at the terminal, typing in the override
commands, while Juanita fired up the system. When I finished,
we had three minutes left.

The lab was the same as before, except that while we had
been chasing Chainsaw, Janet had arranged a chamber of
seven-foot mirrors in a tight hexagonal pattern center stage.
She had another mirror positioned at an angle atop the setup
so we could watch. Juanita had helped check the power and
communication lines.

"It will take a minute to warm up the system and balance
the circuits," Juanita said. "Then all I have to do is throw the
switches on the MUSE."

The experiment included playing the image of Euterpe on
the monitors in the next room, at the same time running the
signal through the MUSE, and then shooting its laser through a
space where the mirrors lined up. This would make her appear
3-D. The mirrors were Janet's idea. They would enhance the
image's intensity by reflecting and recirculating the energy as
the laser beam ricocheted off their shiny surfaces.

"Doctor," Erato interrupted. "All I want to know is, will I
get my sister back?"

"That," she answered frankly, "is what we're about to find
out."

Looking at my watch, I said, "We've got two minutes. Let's
do it."

"All right," Juanita said. "Here goes."

She threw some switches on the far wall, and the TV monitors inside the glassed-in room sprang to life. The image of
Euterpe suddenly appeared on all of them, just as she had been
captured. She was as lovely as Erato, but with long, red hair
and freckles. She was dressed in one of those flowing Greek
gowns, repeating the confused message we had heard before.

Next, Juanita fired up the MUSE and shot a white laser beam into the hexagon onstage through a narrow opening between two mirrors. The whole canyon filled with streaming laser beams, crossing and colliding at incredible speed. A small, glowing cloud of white light began to form in center, blocking out the image of Euterpe.

Slowly the cloud of light grew, collecting light beams and assembling them into a vague form. The entire canyon pulsated with white light. Juanita quickly passed out goggles with smoked-glass lenses to protect our eyes. It helped a lot, but there was only a minute left until midnight.

The cloud grew until it began to overflow the mirrors. Laser beams shot out of the tiny space between them like liquid sparklers. *T* minus forty-five seconds.

Suddenly there was a tremendous explosion that rocked the mirrors, like a star going supernova. The TV monitors had blown in rapid succession, sending fragments into the glass wall between us. It cracked, but held. Everyone stepped back.

"We're past the point of no return!" Juanita yelled. She looked at her gauges. "So far, the circuits are holding, but they're heating up fast."

The cloud of white light slowly faded out, dashing our hopes. I hung my head and put my arm around Erato. We had done our best, but now it was over. It had all been for nothing. Euterpe was gone. And only God knew where. We turned to walk away.

Then a great flash of deep purple light filled the room, changing to blue, and running through all the colors of the rainbow until it became white again. We turned around. Juanita hadn't given up. The laser continued to bombard the mirrors. *T* minus twenty seconds. A thin column of white smoke began to pour slowly out of a vent on the MUSE.

"We're overloading the circuits," she said gravely. "I'm going to have to shut it—"

"Wait!" I yelled, a strange sensation coming over me. "I feel something. She's here. I know it."

Then, out of the very center of the canyon, a figure began to form out of pure white light beams—faintly at first, but growing brighter. The beams collected into the stunning image of a beautiful young woman with long flowing hair and full-length gown.

Erato grabbed me. "It's—it's her!" she gasped. "It's Euterpe."

The figure was absorbing all of the laser beams so that h

entire form was filled with liquid light, glowing with radiant beauty. She began to rise slowly from center stage like the birth of Venus, her hands outstretched and lasers shooting from her fingertips. They ricocheted wildly off the walls, making the whole room alive with energy and light beams. Then, inexplicably, the figure stopped rising. Smoke poured out of the MUSE.

With nothing more to lose, Juanita turned up the power to maximum. But it did nothing. "She's stuck!" She yelled over the roaning generator. "I need more power, but the laser's at full saturation. I'm maxed out, I'm afraid. She's not going to—"

"How long can you hold power?" I asked above the roar of generators, crackling like a high-voltage line in a rainstorm.

"Thirty seconds more at the most. "Then we're gone. These circuits are not going to take the load much longer."

The hands on the clock became one at the number twelve. We were on borrowed time now.

"Hold it!" Erato yelled, staring at me. "Plug *me* into the circuit. I may have enough energy to—"

"Nothing doing!" I shouted. "The power's too great. You'll e electrocuted."

There was still one last chance. I grabbed Erato to keep her om running for her sister and pulled my secret weapon from y shirt pocket. I unfolded it and began to recite the rest of e poem—the way I wanted it to end.

> *Looking up I saw her soul*
> *Ascending the magic stairs.*
> *Borrowed angel freed from earth*
> *Taking to the heavens*
>
> *She smiled with luminous eyes*
> *And said*
> *That she would never leave me.*
> *She would be mine*
> *Every time*
> *I cast off upon a wave*
>
> *And as she rose*
> *Above the clouds*
> *My heart flew off beside her.*
> *"Please, keep it for me,"*

> *I said,*
> *"Until you come again.*
> *I will live without it*
> *Waiting for your return."*

Slowly, as the circuits of the imager strained beyond their limits, Euterpe absorbed all of the light and rose, floating free above the mirrors. Juanita shut down the MUSE. We didn't need it anymore. As it continued to smolder, she pushed a button and rolled back the roof. When Euterpe got there, she stopped for a second and blew me a kiss. A ball of light fired from her lips, almost knocking me down. I was dazed, but still on my feet.

Euterpe was smiling as she went up toward the heavens. We walked over and stood in the opening, watching as she ascended through some clouds that had just been ushered in by a cool ocean breeze. The wind, it seemed, had gone back to blowing in its old familiar direction. Then, beyond her in the sky, appeared the image of a great rocky mountain, complete with a giant, ancient stone structure sitting powerfully on a hill, mighty columns of marble supporting it.

Euterpe opened her arms wide, spreading blinding laser everywhere. She shot beams at Janet, Juanita, and Cooper. Each of them became immobilized, standing as if in a trance while their bodies slowly began to fill with white light. A minute later they were frozen in place, glowing like the light figures in *Cocoon*—luminous, beautiful, and completely absorbed in light.

Suddenly a single powerful bolt of lightning shot out of the clouds and hit the lawn outside. No one else could move, but Erato, Vinnie, and I ran out and saw what looked to be a jagged signature for the last letter of the alphabet burned into the lawn in ten-foot strokes.

"Your old man still needs to work on his penmanship," said to Erato.

She took the paper from my hands and held it up to read by moonlight. "It's blank," she said in disbelief.

"Yeah," I said. "I couldn't think of a thing to write."

"Figures," she chuckled. "Poetry isn't on paper anyway. It in the heart. . . . Let's go home."

"Your world or mine?"

"The one we're in right now will do nicely," she smiled.

"How long do we have?"

"Like everyone else," she said, hugging me, "not long enough. But this is probably our last night together. What do you want to do?"

"How about dancing?"

"Sure, if you like. Whatever you want. It's gentlemen's night."

"In that case," I answered, my arms around her, "a walk on the beach and a late movie's enough for me. I've even got popcorn. Heck, after that kiss your sister threw me, I think I could pop it in my hands. I feel electric."

"Yeah," she said, elbowing me. "When I get back I'm going to talk to her about moving in on my territory."

Back in the lab, Juanita was just coming out of it. It took her a while to speak, but with great difficulty, she swore she only had two copies of the data. One on digital tape, which she cut up in front of us. That only left the disc, which had been erased during the experiment, and the missing tape from Vinnie's bandage. That could be almost anywhere. Janet and Cooper were still out of it—vibrating, immobile bodies of light. So, deciding to let them cool down, Erato, Vinnie, and I left.

The police had brought the Caddy to Sigma, so we drove it home. On the way I turned to Erato. "Okay then," I said. "We now that Euterpe herself left the first message, but who left the other two? The ones that give clues to her whereabouts? Surely it wasn't . . ."

Erato tried to look confused, but it wasn't working. She was starting to smile slightly out of the corner of her mouth. Finally she couldn't hold out any longer.

"I . . . it wasn't me," she said, placing her hand on her chest.

"Well," I conjectured. "It had to be someone who could access the computer system without leaving a footprint. Wait a minute. You talked to the guard who was on duty that night—who did he say was in the lab?"

"Oh, just some old guy in a lumberjack shirt and jeans. Seems he had a badge with the name I. Berlin on it. It was on the guard's list that night, but not on the master list the next day. That's why he was fired."

I looked up at the sky, talking to Erato as I stared at the stars. "I thought you said he didn't like to interfere?"

"Only when he wants to," she reminded me. "He must have thought you needed a little help finding my sister."

Once at home, we watched a late movie, popped some corn,

and went off to bed holding each other. I finally shut my eyes at four-thirty. At five, with the first hint of light outside my window, I felt suddenly cold and alone. When I opened my eyes, she was gone.

54

Taking Vinnie Home

Getting up, I ran from room to room, which didn't take all that long in a one-bedroom apartment. When I dashed into the kitchen, there she was, making coffee.

"I couldn't sleep," she said, tightening the sash on her silk bathrobe.

"Don't scare me like that," I said, exhaling, my heart pounding in my chest. "I thought you were gone forever."

"Well, might as well get up," she sighed. "This is probably our last day together."

"Don't say that. I'll go with you if I have to . . ." She gave me a blank look so I added, "The programming job, remember?"

"They have to review your résumé first," she informed me, sitting at the kitchen table. "You know how these things go . . . but we have something to do today, before I leave."

"What?"

"Return Vinnie."

"Are you kidding?" I asked, upset. "I wouldn't give him back to that guy for anything. In fact, I'm about to call the police and tell them where he lives, unless somebody already beat me to it. He deserves to be—"

"Cyrus," she cut in, sipping coffee. "Vinnie's not ours. We have to return him to his rightful owner, even if we don' want to."

"Forget it," I said, and began pacing the floor.

"Hear me out," she requested, setting her coffee down. "I have an idea. You can probably get him back by turnin Chainsaw in, but that would be pretty unethical."

"Unethical?" I protested, hands on my hips. "What do ethic have to do with it?"

"You remember the eighties," she answered, unperturbed. "Well, the *greed* decade is over. Selfish motives are passé. Now it's the *we* decade. We're all on this planet together, remember?"

"Some of us longer than others," I mumbled, rolling my eyes. "Look, what's right is to turn that maniac in."

"Is that what you want?"

"No . . ." I pointed at Vinnie, curled up on the couch. "I want to keep him."

"Then go tell Chainsaw that you won't give him up without a fight," she suggested, running her hands through her hair.

"I still ought to turn him in."

"What has Chainsaw really done?" she asked, looking into her coffee cup. "Stolen a disc with something on it he really didn't understand? Locked a guard in the closet and frightened some people? Blamed his brother for his dad's death? Well, now that disc is useless and he's probably more scared than all the rest of us put together." She looked up sharply. "He was dealing with the devil; and as for blaming his brother goes, Chainsaw just can't face the truth—that he joined his own father in a life of debauchery. . . . Let him go," she added with a wave. "Living with his actions is enough punishment."

"Nice speech," I said, looking out the window at the mountains. "But I get the feeling you're not telling me everything. Is there some other reason, some 'cosmic' reason to let him off the hook?"

"Yes. Dad said to let him go."

"Well," I said, throwing up my arms. "Why didn't you just say so? Might makes right. Father knows best and all that."

"Cyrus, you may not believe it, but Dad does know what he's doing."

"Yeah, right." I turned in the window and glanced at her. "I don't think anybody said that after the San Francisco earthquake in '89. But I'll tell you what. I'm sure Chainsaw would exchange Vinnie for his freedom."

She placed her hands carefully around her coffee cup. "Meaning what?" she asked.

"Meaning I won't turn him in. If I keep Vinnie now, we can avoid the confrontational approach."

She got up and poured me a cup of coffee. Standing by the sink, she stated, "Dad said something else."

"Great!" I shouted sarcastically, sitting at the table. "What?"

"He said we had to go see Chainsaw."

"When did he say that?"

"There was a message on my screen—when I closed my eyes and accessed Janet's file on the big computer in the sky. And by the way, he offered his congratulations in advance for freeing my sister."

"Can you prove that?"

"No, I don't have a network connected to a printer on earth." She walked over and handed me the cup of coffee. "Imagine what problems that would create. But never mind. Get dressed. We have a biker to see."

I didn't want to go at all, but I figured if worst came to worst, I could drive off with Vinnie and still call the cops. Chainsaw ought to get something for stealing, and scaring everyone half to death.

When we got there he was under his truck. I felt like kicking him between the Levi's, but I noticed his Harley was gone. Maybe somebody had paid him a visit already. We left Vinnie in the car and parked in the street. He hunkered down on the floor in the front seat.

"Hey, Chainsaw," I said, looking down at his feet. "Come up for air. I've got a deal for you."

He slid out from under the truck with a large, greasy crescent wrench in his hand. He had a mean look on his face. I was about to pick up a two-by-four when he surprised me and broke into a slight smile.

"Well, if it ain't Surf . . . Rat. What can I do for you?"

"It's about Vinnie," I stated flatly. "I want to keep him."

"Well, I don't know what for," he laughed. "He's a worthless mutt as far as I'm concerned. Go ahead if you want. Call the cops if you want. I don't give a—"

"Enough said," I announced. "Come on," I said to Erato. "Let's get out of here before I change my mind about calling the police."

"Hey," he said, friendly-like and holding out his greasy palm. "No hard feelin's." He noticed me looking at his hand, so he reached down and picked up a clean shop rag and some hand cleaner to wipe it off. When he did, a brand new gold chain fell out of his dirty T-shirt. Attached to it was a cross and some Harley wings. Both looked solid gold. I stared at him for a long time, but didn't reach for his hand.

"Aw, come on, Cy," Erato said, slapping me on the back. "It isn't like *you* never did anything wrong. Remember the class schedule at Cal U.?"

I didn't budge, just looked around at nothing in particular. "Where's the bike?" I asked, playing for time.

"You ain't gonna believe this," he grinned. "Some old guy in a wet suit came by this mornin' and offered me fifty grand for it. So I said what the hey, there's a sucker born every minute, and took the cash."

"Is that for real?" I asked, looking at Erato, but she just looked away, a slight smile on her face.

"Sure is," Chainsaw said, cleaning his hands. "He told me the deal was that I had to forgive my brother, or at least forget about it. Seems he knew all about me. Said I just hated myself and was tryin' to take it out on Max. Said we all make mistakes." He finished wiping his hands with the rag and tossed it on the ground.

"*Max*," I repeated. "I forgot he had a first name."

"Told him I'd think about the forgivin' and forgettin' stuff," Chainsaw went on. "For fifty grand I'd definitely give it a try, anyway. He was a funny old guy. Even made me throw Vinnie in on the deal. Told me you'd be along to claim him."

I still couldn't bear to shake his hand. Instead, I reached out and gave him a quick hard slap on the palm.

"Hafta do, I guess," he said. "Can't say as I blame you none. I can be a real jerk sometimes."

"Yeah," Erato said, looking at me. "All of us can sometimes."

I turned and walked away, a little mad at myself. Here I was all prepared to hate this guy forever, and he goes and reforms on me. "Did you see that gold cross?" I said to Erato, opening the car door. "Talk about playing it up big. And I thought your dad didn't speak to mortals."

"He doesn't normally, unless it's important. But in an odd way Chainsaw helped free Euterpe."

"How do you figure that?" I asked in disbelief, getting in the Caddy.

"If he hadn't stolen the disc," she explained, standing beside the car, "you might never have had enough time to come up with the holograph idea, and Juanita sure wasn't going to volunteer her new invention on her own. She's pure scientist."

"Wait a minute," I protested, slapping the steering wheel. "I would have figured it out."

"Did you have it figured out back at the lab before we chased after Chainsaw?" Erato climbed in the passenger's side and stared at me, waiting for an answer.

"No, I guess not."

"So when did the idea first hit you?"

"Oddly enough, when I saw the Harley's taillight pull out of the parking lot," I admitted, Vinnie now licking my face. "It reminded me of the bar code reader back at the convenience store. And then I thought, if it wraps around it has to be projecting in three dimensions."

"So, without Chainsaw . . ."

"Well, I *might* have gotten it," I answered, pushing Vinnie onto Erato's lap.

Suddenly, Chainsaw was at the car, leaning over and looking at Vinnie. "Mind if I say good-bye to Hubcap?" he asked.

"If he doesn't bite you," I answered.

"Oh, he ain't the kind to hold hard feelin's." He reached in, and Vinnie shied away at first. Then he sat up straight on Erato's lap, letting himself be petted, even licking the hand cleaner off Chainsaw's fingers.

"Mutt always did like hand cleaner," he said, shaking his head. "Bye, Hubbie. These folks will care for you now. And a lot better than I ever did. Sorry about the ear. . . . Well, see you in dog heaven."

"What happened that night on the freeway?" I asked, no angry anymore. "When he lost his ear."

"Don't know exactly," Chainsaw shrugged. "But I got theory."

"You got theories?"

"Cyrus," Erato ordered. "Shut up and let him finish."

"I was at the beach," he began, standing up straight. "Two weeks ago Thursday. It was pretty late and I had this girl with me."

"Just cut to the chase, will you?" I requested. "Spare us the details of your love life."

"Well, drivin' home I was payin' more attention to her than to Hubcap in the truck bed," Chainsaw explained. "He must have fallen out. By the time I noticed and retraced my steps he was gone. After that I was out of town on a bike run. But when I got back . . . well, I guess you know the rest."

"And you think he fell out of the back of the pickup and lost his ear on the pavement?" I asked.

"Either that, or he jumped out to chase a hubcap."

"Why do you say that?" I asked, wrinkling my forehead.

"That's how he got his name," Chainsaw answered, then explained how he used to toss hubcaps and Vinnie'd chase them, bring them back, too. The tooth that got knocked out was from a hubcab tossed too hard straight at him.

Chainsaw tucked his cross back under his shirt and went on with his story. "One day he was ridin' in the back of the truck and the car next to me throws a hub," he continued, crossing his massive arms. "Next thing you know Hubbie's out of the truck and chasin' the cap. Almost got himself killed bringin' it back."

"There was a hubcap sitting on the side of the road," I said, "the night I met Vinnie. It had blood on it, too. He must have got hit chasing it down."

We drove off and went to the beach, played all day in the surf, and had a heck of a good time, despite Vinnie's rolling in some dead seals and stinking up the Caddy in the process. But all through the day I couldn't help thinking about losing Erato. Surely, though, her dad would have mercy on us after all we had been through, especially since we had fallen for each other and were expecting our first child.

Dinner out didn't help, and I tried to drown out the growing pain of impending separation with lots of beer. Erato couldn't eat or drink, so she became the designated driver on the trip home. Even Vinnie looked sad, feeling our mounting uneasiness. At three o'clock in the morning I closed my eyes from sheer exhaustion and slept an uneasy, dreamless sleep. When I awoke my arms were wrapped around Vinnie and the sun was up.

Erato wasn't in the bed next to me or anywhere in the apartment. This time she was finally gone, and I was alone, except for a CD she had left in the mailbox.

As soon as I pulled it from its brown paper bag, I knew exactly what it was. The label had one thing written on it loud and clear, in darn good penmanship: the song title "When Will I See You Again?"

55

Fond Farewell

Knowing that I'd need some help with the disc, I rang up
Juanita. "Can you meet me in the lab in an hour?" I asked.
"I really need your help."

"Sure, but—"

"Can you get the holograph imager working?"

"I . . . I'm not sure. It sustained substantial damage to its
circuits the other night. What's this for?"

"I have a CD I want you to play." There was silence on the
other end. "Look, Erato's gone and she left me this disc. I've
got to see what's on it. You're my only chance."

"Okay," she agreed at last. "I'll meet you there in forty-five
minutes."

"Thank you, Doctor, I . . ."

"Forget it. I owe you one. I'll see you there. Good-bye."

Grabbing my keys, I drove much too fast to Sigma, and
waited in the lobby, fearing the worst: that Erato had left
the disc as a sort of holographic Dear John letter. The pain
of missing her was just starting to set in when Juanita showed
up. I handed her the disc and we went to the lab.

After looking over everything and assessing the damage, she
declared, "The equipment has been stretched beyond its limits.
I'm afraid it may be overstressed. The power generator may
not be able to put out enough wattage to repeat the experiment that set Euterpe free. Not too mention the damage to
the MUSE."

I looked around the lab, which looked pretty much like the
night we freed Euterpe, except that the broken TV monitor
had been removed and the mess cleaned up. Unfortunately, the
MUSE machine was completely cooked. I stared at it dejectedly.

"Look, I said hopefully, it won't be necessary to overload the
system. We just need enough power to view the holograph."

"Well," Juanita said, patting the side of the MUSE, "I'm
afraid this one's out of it. But I have a prototype in the back

I used to develop it. It can't handle a lot of amps, but—"

"Fair enough," I nodded.

"Give me a hand with some of this equipment," she said. "We'll have to use the backup emergency generator—and even then, we can't be sure my old imager will still work. I haven't used it in a year." She looked at my face. "But we'll try. What have we got to lose?"

"Nothing we haven't lost already."

We rolled her prototype out of a storage room and dusted it off, then parked it next to the MUSE, plugged it in, and got everything hooked up to the backup generator. She put the CD in the player. Just before she flipped the switches we moved the mirrors out of the way.

"We won't need the mirrors," she informed me. "We don't want to excite the image, just view it. . . . And before I forget, I am sorry about holding on to Euterpe, but it was my big chance at understanding three-dimensional image capture. I don't know what to say but . . ."

"I forgive you, Doctor," I said, plopping down in one of the theater seats. "I tried to keep a muse myself. But who doesn't want to hold on to his inspiration? Looks like neither of us succeeded. As much as it hurts me to say this, Erato must be shared with the world. A muse can't be tied down and limited as we are. She must be free. I've made my sacrifice, and now I'll just have to live with it. Let's get started."

Juanita threw the switches on the imager. I heaved a sigh of relief as it shot a laser beam center stage. Slowly, a vague image began to take shape, then took on a female form. In a moment I could make out her unmistakable features. I knew she had gone over to the other side because she was wearing a flowing white gown, like an ancient Greek goddess. But it was her, and more lovely than ever.

"It seems to be working fine," Juanita said proudly, patting the prototype on the side. "It'll do fine as long as we keep it at low power."

"Cyrus," Erato began, "I'm leaving you this message because . . ." I pushed the hold button on the imager and she stopped midsentence.

"Would you mind, Doctor?" I asked. "I'd like to be alone with my . . ."

"Sure," she said, putting her hand gently on my shoulder. "When it's done just push the stop button. Or replay it if you like. I'll be out in the lobby."

She left and I went back to the beginning.

"Cyrus, I'm leaving you this message because I am no longer a human. By the time you get this I will have returned to my world. This is not completely of my own choosing, but my work up here isn't finished yet. I have asked Dad to let you visit, and he says he'll think about it. He *is* happy you freed Euterpe. He said it could not have happened without your poem. It was your poem that provided the extra surge of power she needed to be set free—not to mention reprogramming the software. He will take that into consideration when you are assigned a job up here after your time on earth has ended.

"I wanted to say good-bye in person, but perhaps it's better this way. I don't know if I could have let go of you if I was still on earth." She patted her flat stomach.

"Yes, I am still pregnant, and little Elysha is coming along fine. She will be beautiful, I know. She will have your blue eyes and blond hair. And Mom says my sense of duty. She is bound to have the heart of a poet, and I have vowed to find a way to let you see her.

"I will never forget my stay on earth, and I will never forget you and our time together. I am here now, but my heart is with you. Any time you want me just say my name, or better yet, write a poem, and I'll be there by your side. You may keep this disc and play it until we are together again. Whenever you do, I will be in the room.

"I learned some things about being human. Despite all of the pain and fears and failures, there are things a spirit can only learn by being human, especially the part about feelings. I still want to learn to stand up on a surfboard—and experience motherhood.

"Well, it looks like the last one's going to happen in heaven, unless I can get clearance for a visit to earth. It doesn't look too promising at the moment with all of the work piled up on my desk.

"I told Dad about my proposal to have you write feelings programs to record human experiences and he said he liked the idea, but he hasn't yet decided when to break in a new version of the software. He says it would take a major installation, and not just a patch-in job.

"I have to go now. But I want you to know that being human is a special gift set aside only for the best of souls, so make the most of it. But don't go taking the whole thing too seriously. Take time for laughter. For in laughter, the soul is smiling.

"Please remember that I miss you, and love you—and that someday, someway, we'll be together again. Hey, doesn't that sound like the lyrics from a pop song?

"Well, bye for now, and remember—yours is still the brightest star in the sky. And oh, Dad says he's working on his penmanship, and thanks for the critique."

Her image faded away, and my heart went with it. I played it two more times, then shut everything down and went to the lobby.

Juanita, seeing my crushed spirit, put her arm around me. "We'll all miss her," she said. "But you much more than any of us."

"Do you have the keys to Janet's office?" I asked. "I have a CD I want to put in the jukebox."

"Sure," she said sympathetically. "Come on. You can tell me about it if you want."

I couldn't say a word all the way there. Once inside, I put the CD in a back slot in the jukebox.

"Doctor," I said, turning to her, "if you want this for research, you can borrow it any time you like. But you have to promise not to erase it."

"You have my word," she smiled, and crossed her heart.

"Swear on a stack of RAM chips?"

"Pull out the CD," she said half-seriously. "I'll swear on it if you like."

"Thanks," I said, smiling. "I believe you."

"That disc," she commented, looking at it in the slot, "may just give me the clues I've been looking for to make three-dimensional free-moving holographs. Think of the possibilities."

"You have to promise one more thing," I requested, staring out the window.

"Anything. Anything at all."

"You won't let the holograph research fall into the wrong hands—the Stars Wars hands. They've got enough electronic toys to keep them busy for a while."

"If I get a patent," she explained, standing behind me, "it's good for seventeen years."

"That's fair enough," I chuckled, turning to face her. "But we both know that in a few years your patent will be obsolete."

"Sure—but by then, who knows what I'll be working on," she said excitedly, thrusting her hands into her lab coat pockets. "Travel to the spirit world, maybe."

"Would you work on something like that?" I asked hopefully.

"Only in the name of science, you understand."

"Of course," I nodded. "But keep your head down. This building might take some lightning strikes. We've had a few storms lately."

"Yes," she agreed, turning to leave. "Strange weather for southern California in July, wouldn't you say?"

We closed the office and said our good-byes in the parking lot. As I watched Juanita pull away, the dam of feelings broke inside me, and wave after wave of tears flowed down my face. When they finally stopped I went by a liquor store and got a bottle of rum, some Coke, and got rip-roaring drunk.

After the sun went down I was a half bottle gone and too drunk to drive. So I got Vinnie, stuck the quart in one hand, the dog leash in the other, and headed for the beach.

I was just about blind with liquor and rage, and somehow stumbled down the bike path toward the Channel Islands pier, fielding insults from night cyclists.

Staggering out on the pier, I walked to the very end, Vinnie leading the way. I was mad at Zeus, and had something to say.

56

Yelling at God

Vinnie curled up at my feet as the stars spun overhead. "Well, Old Boy," I began, staring at the heavens. "Thanks for the show of confidence. And for trusting me to spend my life with your daughter. I realize I'm only mortal, an average programmer, and a lousy sentimental poet. But I guess that's not good enough for you. What's the matter? Not quite up to the standards you laid down for a son-in-law? Well, excuse me for being human, but it was your idea to make us mere mortals, or have you forgotten?

"Look, don't blame me for falling in love with a goddess. Have you looked at her lately? She's all grown-up.

"And as for me, a lowly part of the human race, if I'm not mistaken, somewhere in that book of yours it says something about being created in your image—or are humans one of your big mistakes, like thorns on roses, or disease-carrying mosquitoes?

"If you ask me, I say it's kind of rotten to be overprotective of your daughter. What's the matter? Afraid she'll become too human to make it to heaven if she shares a life with me? I suppose you're embarrassed that your daughter is having the baby of a lowly earthling—someone from the other side of the tracks.

"Well, if that's the way you feel about it, then go ahead. Strike me down. Throw one of your lightning bolts. Be my guest. Take the easy way out. Then you won't have to deal with me anymore. But remember, you created men and women to live on this earth. If the human race isn't good enough for you, then it's your fault, not mine."

I leaned over the railing of the pier, still staring up at the stars. "Oh, and one more thing. That promotion. You know, the one to angel status? Well, I'm ready for it now. I want to be with Erato. So if you strike me down, put us together. It's the least you can do for her and our baby.

"Look, Erato has never had a life of her own. It's been nothing but duty and career since day one. And I think you're cheating her. A good parent would want her to have the life she wanted. I'm not much, but I love her more than anything else in the world. I want to be a father and husband, and if you keep us apart, our baby will never know her real father.

"I'm not totally selfish. You can have her back in fifty or sixty years. What's that to you? Not much. But to me it may be all I've got.

"Look, people aren't so helpless and dumb. We built Hoover Dam, the pyramids, and that motorcycle you wanted to ride so badly. And we invented the surfboard, don't forget. . . . Oh, never mind. That's all I've got to say. Later, *Dude*."

Suddenly, my feet went out from under me and I was over the railing, headed for the water. I hit the surf twenty feet below and blacked out. I woke up lying in my bedroom. Vinnie was licking my face. Janet stood beside the bed, extra casual and wet in torn Levi's, bulky sweater, and much to my surprise, high-tech tennies.

"What happened?" I asked. "What the—"

"You must have fallen off the end of the pier," she answered. "Someone left a message on my terminal to meet you there tonight. It was signed simply with the letter *Z*. She explained that she was parking on the street when she heard my yelling, and Vinnie's barking. He was in the water, yelping up a storm, and I was beside him, facedown. Between barks he was pulling me by the collar to shore, but it was going pretty slowly. Luckily she got to me before I drowned. But after I started breathing, I passed out. She brought me home.

"How did you get me upstairs?"

"It wasn't easy. But Mrs. Okana and I managed somehow. You've been mumbling about Erato for hours. Cyrus, I'm sorry she was taken from you. But . . . you knew what would happen when Euterpe was free."

"Yeah, but it doesn't hurt any less."

She turned and looked out the window at the rising sun.

"At least you had someone who cared for you," she remarked. "Which is more than many of us can say. . . . Look at me," she said over her shoulder. "I'm married to my company. I was ready to do anything to protect some stupid invention that will be obsolete in a few years.

"Maybe life's too short for that. Maybe that's what this whole thing has been about—to remind some of us that there's more to life than profit and loss, win and lose. There's so much more: music, singing, poetry, and yes, even surfing. And lots of other things. Things I'm missing out on."

"Does this mean you're selling the company?"

"No," she laughed. "It just means I stop working eighty-hour weeks. I'll need a new operations manager to run things from now on. Henkins called this morning. He's not coming back. Something about permanent stress leave or something. The new manager only has to work forty hours a week if he wants to, maybe fifty, tops. What do you think?"

"Stress leave?" I repeated, wrinkling my forehead. "Great. Well, anyway, the promotion should make Dr. Vaya very happy."

"She's a scientist, not an administrator," Janet said, coming over and sitting on the edge of the bed. "I need her for research."

"Cooper will be fulfilled."

"Nope. Too stuffy."

"Wait a minute," I protested, putting my arms behind my head. "You're not looking at *me* for this position. That's ridiculous. Besides, I'm not through sulking." I reached down and pulled the covers over my head.

"Exactly. If I make you operations manager, then you won't have time to brood, mope, or sulk," she said, pulling the covers down so my face was exposed. "In short, you won't have time to feel sorry for yourself."

"Yeah, but what about surfing?" I argued. "I'm starting to go through withdrawal already."

"I'm not asking you to grow up right away," she said, half-joking. "I'm just asking you to run the company; that's all. So I can take it easier. I'll still be CEO. You can surf before and after work—and on weekends. You can even wear a Hawaiian shirt if you want. This *is* California, after all."

"This isn't a sympathy offer, is it?" I asked, sitting up and resting on my elbows.

"I don't have time for that," she said forcefully. "I'm just looking at the best person for the job. Juanita and Cooper are too single-minded. I need someone relaxed, more versatile. Somebody with compassion and insight."

"I'll think about it," I said seriously. "But what about my replacement?"

"You can pick her yourself," she smiled. "Some fresh kid out of college will do nicely. . . . Preferably someone with hacking experience," she joked.

"Suppose I take the job," I said with a half-smile. "What do I need to know about running a company?"

"Nothing I can't teach you," she said, getting up and pacing the room, then explained that I could take courses in management at the university. She'd be with me every step of the way. According to her, I was the only one with enough brains and creativity she could trust to run the place.

"Besides," she added, "think what it could do for your chances of winning Zeus over. Think of your résumé. You want the job, it's yours." She stopped pacing and looked at me. "Or I can hire a stranger from the outside, something I don't want to do."

She continued, "You'll be great. I'm sure of it. A year of training, more if necessary, and you're all set. You already know how to manage information. Now I'll show you how to manage a company. You've got the most important ingredients already: intelligence, imagination, and you're not a quitter. You proved that last night. Taking on Zeus was a heady idea. It could have got you killed . . .

"Listen to me," she laughed. "I never used to believe in myths and now I'm talking about Greek gods as if they were real. Well, what happened in the lab went a long way toward convincing me that there's more to life than meets the scientific eye."

"Unfortunately," I shrugged, "taking on Zeus *didn't* get me killed. But let me ask you a question that's more down to earth.

If I take the job, do I get a company car?"

"Of course."

"Full system manager privileges this time," I demanded, pointing at her. "And I mean *full*."

"Comes with the job."

"Use of the jukebox?"

"Jukebox?" she exclaimed. "You're moving into my office. I'm building another one onto the lab for myself."

"How can I turn this down?" I shrugged.

"You can say no," she replied, hands on her hips. "But think of the future. You've got to grow up sometime. This is a good beginning, wouldn't you say?"

"When do I start?"

"Take all the time you want," she said, making a sweeping motion with her hands. "Relax. Vacation. Visit your parents if you like. Just be ready to start at eight in the morning."

"Thanks."

"Don't mention it."

She picked up her briefcase and headed for the door. She was still a little wet. Just before leaving the room she turned and said, "You have a management class at the university that starts Thursday from ten to eleven. Don't miss it."

"Thanks again. What if I had turned it down?"

"No problem. I would have sent Cooper."

As she left, I got a good look at those high-tech tennies. "Hey," I said, before she stepped out the door. "Did something happen at the pier tonight that I don't know about?"

"Like what?" she answered suspiciously, turning towards me.

"Like something unusual. You've changed a lot since the last time I saw you."

"All right," she admitted. "I wasn't supposed to say anything, but I had trouble getting you to shore. Then some old guy in a wet suit came swimming up from the bottom of the ocean. He even had one of those tridents in his hand. He . . ." She hesitated, not wanting to tell me. "Look," she said finally. "It sounds crazy coming from me, but he stood up and the waves stopped breaking. The water began to recede until I was standing on sand, halfway to the end of the pier. He helped me put you in my car and walked back to the ocean. Then with a wave of his trident, the water came in again, and he swam off.

"Cyrus," she added, very seriously, "these things are not supposed to happen. It got me thinking, that's all I can say."

Without another word, she turned and walked out.

57

The New Dress Code

Just for shock value I wore my new suit to work the next morning. As expected, it blew everyone out of the water, especially Cooper. He was a little disappointed about not getting the management job, but he played it for laughs, donning a Hawaiian shirt after lunch and shedding his suit coat. So here's a guy with horn-rims, bright yellow flowered shirt, and suit pants. I called him into my temporary office and good-naturedly informed him that he had anticipated the new company dress code perfectly. He just laughed and put out his hand.

"No hard feelings, Surf . . . I mean boss."

"Boss-in-training," I reminded him, shaking his hand from behind my oak desk. "Look, I've already put you in for a raise. And . . . this is the good part. I'm letting you pick the second shift support person. You can go as square as you like."

"Hey," he smiled. "You taught me a lesson. This is California. Too much suit and tie stuff spoils the fun, and that's what we're here for, isn't it?"

"Coop, you been drinking screen cleaner?"

"No, just thinking," he said with his hands in his pockets. "I can't say I'll stay here and work under you forever. But in the meantime, I'll make the best of it."

"Fair enough. Now, get back to work," I winked. "And get me a printout on the RAM chip file."

"Hey, you're taking to this job pretty well."

"Like a fish to water."

The next few months were quite busy. I spent a great deal of time standing around in suits and Hawaiian shirts, directing such things as redecorating my office. A real surfboard got mounted on one wall, complete with giant, painted breaking waves. A glass case full of seashells occupied another, and a saltwater aquarium gurgled by the door. If I couldn't bring myself to the surf, I could bring the surf to my office.

I attended some beginning classes toward my MBA and got lots of help from Janet on how to run the business. It was a little tough at first, especially the accounting stuff, but I got pretty good at it after about six months of mentoring, and Janet seemed pretty happy.

As expected, Cooper resigned three months into my apprenticeship, and I wished him luck on his new system manager job back east. He said it was as much getting away from his brother as anything. Apparently he wasn't quite ready to make up with someone who sported permanently greasy fingernails and had beer bottles under his bed. On his way out he left a new motorcycle helmet on Chainsaw's porch.

Chainsaw got a job working as a motorcycle mechanic at the Harley shop, and was doing well with a new bike and helmet. He even came by to visit Vinnie a couple of times, and rode him to the beach on the back of that Harley. Vinnie's ear stayed healed up, but he will always be minus a flap on the one side.

The new RAM chip was a big success as soon as it hit the market last month. Orders are pouring in. Juanita's moved on to holograph research using the CD in the jukebox for a database. She hasn't got anything working yet, but tells me it won't be more than a couple of months before she has holographs dancing around the lab. The hacker who had been trying to get the RAM chip plans before Euterpe arrived stopped, and was never caught. The guard got his job back with a raise.

Janet began to relax more, as she had promised, and seemed to enjoy handing the company over to me piece by piece. She even took a two-week vacation in Hawaii and didn't take a laptop with her. She only phoned me twice. I was proud of her for that.

As for me, it had been almost nine months since Erato left, and even though I'd been very busy, I missed her terribly and wondered what our daughter would look like. She left me a pile of cash and some specific instructions as to its use, which I followed almost implicitly. I bought a bunch of suits and other nice clothes as instructed, but no one said I couldn't wear the new company uniform to work most of the time.

Erato had a whole truckload of furniture delivered to my new condo. Yes, she made me put a down payment on one with some of the money, and with what I was making as operations manager, I even qualified for the loan.

I still surfed on weekends—sometimes even after work—and it kept me in touch with nature and my past. In general I was in pretty good shape, except for that awful hole in my life.

I returned the Cadillac and started driving a company car. The Mustang never turned up. No big deal, but I loved that car. It could have been a classic with a little—no, a lot of work.

I played the holograph once a month, and walked away with wet eyes and cheeks. But thankfully, no other copies of the Euterpe file surfaced. And the microcassette tape, well, it never did show up.

I even fantasized that Luc had gotten hold of it and had threatened Zeus to hand over Euterpe or he would duplicate her, or worse, he wanted my daughter. But these were only some of my wilder ideas, and it's doubtful that anything like that would ever happen. In fact, I had just about given up on myth and magic. That is, until one night, for old times' sake, I decided to take the bus, waiting on the very bench that changed my life. I'd had a premonition the night before about seeing Erato once again, and she was driving some exotic sports car, of all things.

Every night for nearly nine months I looked foolishly at the bench on my way home from work, trying to make Erato materialize. Needless to say, it never worked. Evidently, neither had my yelling-at-Zeus plan that night on the pier. He just pushed a little wind under my feet and over the rail I went, or maybe I lost my balance because of the booze. It didn't matter much. I was still alive, and with Janet's help decided to make the best of it.

On the night I decided to take the bus home I had been working late, and strolled out and sat on the bench with one of those Walkman radios, still being a sucker for Top 40 tunes.

Waiting alone on the bench under the streetlight, I studied the one and only picture of Erato and me together. It brought her back. We were wet, happy, and standing on the breakwater. It was almost too painful to remember, but I couldn't let go of her for anything.

Suddenly, the darn radio stopped working, and it just had new batteries installed, so I banged it on my knee a few times. But to no avail.

Then, oddly enough, the thing came on, but I couldn't get anything but the instrumental side of Bette Midler's "Wind Beneath My Wings." I laughed it off, but there weren't songs with lyrics on any stations. Thinking about the missing cassette tape, I began to worry.

A minute later a set of headlights approached, slowed down, and stopped. I turned ghost-white. There, in elegant detail, was a brand new, bright red Ferrari with two surfboards strapped on top. The driver looked familiar.

58

Return of the Muse

The car glowed brilliantly. The gleaming new paint reflected under the streetlamp as if the car was under a spotlight. But none of it compared to the luminous shining smile on the beautiful face of the love of my life.

"Kind of dangerous to be out this late," Erato said, suppressing a grin. "Even in this town."

I was as frozen as a fish in ice, stunned and overtaken by the moment. Not believing it at first, I figured it was an apparition brought on by fatigue and desire. Slowly, carefully, my mind absorbed the input—and she was still there, in all her radiant glory. It *was* her. It had to be. Who else with her looks would be wearing an extra large Harley T-Shirt?

"Well, don't just sit there," she beamed. "Get over here and drive."

"Erato," I said, running for the car. "This is an F40. Do you realize this is a four-hundred-thousand-dollar racing machine?"

"Four and a quarter," she said nonchalantly. "But who's counting? Dad thought you needed some new wheels."

"Wheels," I repeated, still staring at the car. "This baby will do two hundred miles an hour," I gasped. "How in the . . ."

"Well," she said, patting her stomach. "*This* baby is due any minute. We're about to become parents."

"We *what*?" I yelled, looking down at her bulging stomach.

"Don't you remember?"

I leaned over the driver's door, hugging her hard. "Remember? It's all I've thought about for the past nine months."

"That's funny," she said, staring at her stomach. "Me too. We're having it tonight, in case you're wondering. The labor pains have already started."

"Labor pains!" I yelled. "Move over. We've got to get you to the hospital. Is it . . . you know, coming out yet?"

"Not yet. But it's getting ready," she assured me. "Now, help me around to the other side." I helped her out and slowly we moved around to the passenger's seat. "Now, don't kill us getting there," she added. "It's only three miles to the hospital. We'll make it if you drive sanely."

"But how did you get here? What's going on?"

"Dad made up his mind," she said matter-of-factly. "Your résumé finally came across his desk."

"Geez. Talk about bureaucratic red tape." I looked around the car, then put it in gear and sped away, but not too fast.

"Don't complain about the red tape," she said, holding her bulging stomach. "It would have been longer, but I moved your résumé to the top of the stack."

"God does paperwork?"

"Comes with the job," she explained. "CEO of the universe and all that."

As I tooled down the boulevard, I asked, "So, my résumé convinced him it was all right for us to be together?"

"That put you over the top," she said, looking at me. "But what really moved him was your speech."

"Speech?" I repeated, staring at her lovely pregnant profile.

"That night on the pier, when you almost drowned."

"Oh, that." I laughed, shifting gears. "I was trying to get him to strike me dead. I figured it was my only chance to be with you."

"He liked that," she said, amused. "And the way you expressed your feelings. He likes people who stand up for what they believe in."

"I stood up, all right," I said, rolling my eyes. "Right before I fell over the railing. Wait a minute—how long have we got together?"

She threw up her hands. "Don't know for sure," she said. "He decided to let nature take its course. No special dispensation."

"Fair enough." I looked around the car at the new red leather seats. "Guess you know about the condo."

She touched my arm. It felt good. She was electric. "Cy," she said with a giggle. "There's something under your seat."

Without saying a word, I reached under and pulled out the old glove box lid to the Mustang. There, in jagged detail, were my initials carved into the underside. I gave Erato a funny glance and handed it to her. "What's this for?" I asked, puzzled. "And where's the rest of my old car?"

"Dad thought you might ask that," she said, setting the glove box lid on her lap. "Well, he had the car compacted, but as you can see, he kept the glove box. He left the initials you carved in it to point out that your handwriting isn't so hot either."

"Heck of a guy," I said, "when he finally gets around to making a decision. But never mind all that." I stared at her. "I'm just happy you're here. Who's taking your place?"

"Euterpe. She's all caught up. Says she'll cover me for awhile."

"A while?" I protested, slapping the steering wheel. "Wait, if your dad liked my résumé, when does he want me to start?"

"Oh, sixty, maybe seventy years," she grinned. "Tomorrow maybe. Who knows? We're on earth now. Nobody ever knows how long they've got. That's why we have to—*oh!*—make the best of it."

"What was that?"

"She's kicking. That's all."

Pulling up to a stoplight, I stared at her stomach. "Is she coming out?" I asked, anxiously.

"Just drive."

She reached over and played the radio. Naturally, songs with lyrics were back again. We listened to "Two Tickets to Paradise" and then we were at the hospital.

While I parked the car, she gave them the details in the emergency room. She didn't have insurance or ID but a purse overflowing with hundred-dollar bills got us admitted, especially when she said we'd pay cash, and pointed to the Ferrari in the driveway. I got a quick class in birth coaching from the delivery room nurse and went out for some coffee.

Of all things, there was a minister in the waiting room. I didn't think anything of it at first, and then, on my way back to the birthing room, a light went on in my head.

"Wait here," I said to Erato for some stupid reason. "I'll be right back."

I returned fifteen minutes later with the minister in tow. The contractions were only a minute apart by then, so we had to hurry.

"Honey," I said, standing by the bed with the minister. "This man is a reverend. He says he'll marry us."

"Marry us! I'm having a—*oh!*—a baby."

"You want to get married, right?" I asked, nodding. "Well

why wait? He said we can fill out the paperwork later."

"You're crazy."

"I know," I said. "That's one of my strong points, remember? What do you say?"

"I do," she said like a marriage vow. "But we'd better hurry up. You're going to be a father pretty soon now."

The minister was dazed, but held a short ceremony, considering the circumstances, and we took our vows. He scribbled something on the back of a hospital brochure, and the delivery nurse signed as a witness. There wasn't a dry eye in the house.

After the final "I do's," I leaned over and kissed the bride. It was time for her to push. Forty-five minutes later out came the most beautiful angel on earth.

The doctor came in at the last minute to assist, and little Elysha Ann was born. She was seven pounds even, with blond hair and blue eyes. Naturally, we think she's going to be something special. She has such a glow about her. But then again, all parents think that.

A funny thing happened when we went home two days later. I stopped to pick up Erato's first pizza, and noticed that storm clouds had formed overhead. Then, just as we were getting in the car to head home, the clouds cracked open and a bolt of lightning struck—out over the ocean. I guess Zeus was tired of my handwriting critiques.

There was a huge crash of thunder, but it was odd. It didn't sound like regular clouds crashing together. It sounded like the powerful roar of a big motorcycle, and it was followed by peals of laughter. Then it was gone, yielding to a soft, gentle rain.

I don't know yet how everything will turn out, but Elysha and Erato have changed my life forever. I'm even writing a book of poetry in my "spare" time, of all things.

Naturally, I'm not yet ready to take that big promotion in the sky. I want to see how Elysha's life turns out, and ours. But one thing I do know. Inside each one of us lives the heart of a poet, and sometimes, if your star is burning especially bright and your heart is open and true, the muse will whisper in your ear, and feelings will begin to flow from deep inside. You can capture them if your mind is quick, and with the power of understanding, turn them like the wave of a wand into words. They don't have to be grand. They just have to be yours.

And when that happens, the music of poetry plays softly on your soul, and magic reigns supreme in the world.

Since moving to California at the age of five, David Lee Jones has never lived more than ten miles from the Pacific Ocean. He grew up spending summers on the beaches of southern California, and now lives within walking distance of the beach in Santa Barbara, California, with his wife, their daughter, and their water-loving, black Labrador retriever. His first novel, *Unicorn Highway*, is available from Avon Books; *Zeus & Co.* is his second novel.